"I'VE ... HELVOR SAID SUDDENLY, EYES YET FOCUSED ON THE DISTANT SHORE OF HIS DELUSIONS.

Ottemar moved closer. "What are they?" he asked in a hoarse whisper.

"Dark, dark," gasped Helvor. "I see their eyes, their hateful eyes, no eyes of men! Dark armor, spawn of night! And the bloated ones, the grasping flesh-eaters—a thousand of the maggot vermin. But see these others! These black-helmed killers. What are these, with their curved steel?"

Ottemar glanced back at Wargallow. "Steel? The Ferr-Bolgan do not carry blades—"

As he did so, Helvor erupted, flinging himself forward against the ropes. One hand snapped free of its thongs, but before he could fasten his nails in Ottemar's flesh, Ascanar thrust the torch at him. Helvor cowered back at once, spitting like a wolf.

"There are chains on our ships," said Wargallow from the shadows. "We'll take him from this place."

"AN INTRICATE, EXCITING TALE . . . SMOOTHLY AND SUPERBLY WRITTEN"
Robert Adams,
author of *The Horseclans* series

Other Avon Books in
THE OMARAN SAGA
by Adrian Cole

BOOK ONE
A PLACE AMONG THE FALLEN

BOOK TWO
THRONE OF FOOLS

BOOK THREE
THE KING OF LIGHT AND SHADOWS

ADRIAN COLE

BOOK FOUR OF THE OMARAN SAGA

THE GODS IN ANGER

AVON BOOKS ◢◣ NEW YORK

AVON BOOKS
A division of
The Hearst Corporation
105 Madison Avenue
New York, New York 10016

Copyright © 1988 by Adrian Cole
Cover art by Kevin Johnson
Published by arrangement with the author
Library of Congress Catalog Card Number: 90-93411
ISBN: 0-380-75842-3

First Avon Books Printing: March 1991

Printed in the U.S.A.

RA   10 9 8 7 6 5 4 3 2 1

Contents

Map of Omara   vii
Map of the Lands of the West   viii

PART ONE THE CHOSEN

1	Tannacrag	3
2	A Conversation with the Empress	18
3	A Private Council	31
4	Two More Conversations	45
5	On the Night Tide	60

PART TWO THE FORERUNNERS

6	Einnis Amrodin	77
7	The Woodweavers	90
8	Landfall	103
9	The Angarbreed	117
10	Grimander	130

PART THREE THE DEEPWALKS

11	Death at Sea	149
12	Spawn of the Deep	162
13	Sea Watch	176
14	The Ravensring	190
15	The Horn Moot	206

PART FOUR STARKFELL EDGE

16 Rannovic's March   223
17 Gloomreach   238
18 The Feasting Dark   252
19 Sheercastle   266
20 The Shadowflight   280

PART FIVE IN ANGER

21 Abyss   297
22 The War Bringers   311
23 The Chaos Gate   324
24 Holocaust   337
25 Aftermath   349

EPILOGUE   364

Author's Note   371

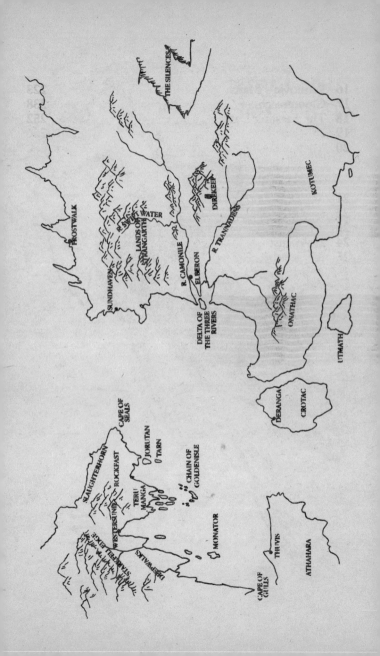

The Lands
of the West

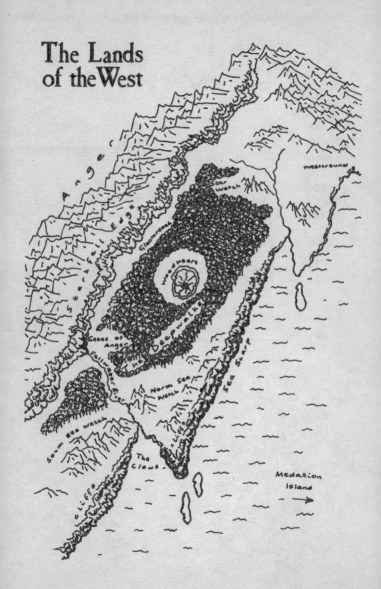

Those who seek power should consider this, that Omara understands very well its paradoxical nature.

If Omara should bestow power upon her life forms, this power gathers its own momentum in such a way that it detaches itself from its source: it becomes independent, self-indulgent, even destructive to that which gave it birth. Thus Omara's will to survive is not always best served by her children.

Power can take many forms; it can be expressed as love or as madness.

Love can be corrupted by power, and the power which love bestows can itself lead to madness: some would say, divine madness.

attributed to Einnis Amrodin

PART ONE

THE
CHOSEN

1
Tannacrag

ASCANAR HEARD the piercing scream in his mind. He had been trained to ignore such things, but there was a quality in the scream that could not be closed out, a wildness that spoke of unique fear, of terror beyond the bounds of any known pain. Though the madman was locked away in a rock cell of the island and his screams could not be heard here, still they remained fixed in the ears of those who had heard them. The exiled Administrator was not disturbed by the mental echoes; he felt no sympathy, no compassion for the wretch who suf-fered. Yet the implications intrigued him and had done since the creature had been discovered and brought here. Fortunate that he had fetched up on the rocks of this place, the bleak island of exile to the last few surviving Administrators of Eukor Epta's days of control. Ascanar almost smiled. No, the scream was not to be ignored at all, for it was a sound of hope to those who had been shut away from Medallion and the Empire.

The Administrator's thoughts were broken by a tapping at his door. He admitted his colleague, Dennor, an older man, whose expression suggested that his distress was not under control. Ascanar waved him to a bench: there were no lux-uries here on Tannacrag. Everything spoke of austerity, of coldness. The banished Administrators, those few who had survived the Inundation of Medallion that had preceded the crowning of Ottemar Remoon, had been allowed to bring little else with them but their wits. Tannacrag had previously

3

been uninhabited, a sterile rock squeezed between larger islands that skirted the south west of Medallion, rearing up
precipitously, difficult to approach by sea and even more difficult to scale. No more than a few miles long and one across,
it had a poor soil and little shelter. Ascanar, now the spokesman for his once powerful faction, had complained bitterly
but in vain about such a banishment, saying that it was little
better than execution.

"You can have the latter if you prefer," Simon Wargallow
had told him in a private audience after Eukor Epta's defeat.
At that time the Deliverer had made no secret of the fact that
he would have been happy to put every last Administrator to
the sword. Ottemar was more lenient, and Otarus, the Law
Giver, was relieved at the less barbaric decision.

The fact remained that Ascanar and his people were now
herded on this rock like sheep. They had no women, Wargallow had insisted on that much. All they had been given
was time, and when that ran out, their line would end. Those
of the Blood who had survived the brief war could never hope
to reform into a unit of any power. Their defeat had seemed
humiliating and final.

Until the arrival of the madman.

"They're here," said Dennor, his chest heaving with effort. He had once been quite a sturdy man, but Tannacrag
had given him a chill that worked havoc in his lungs. He
wheezed, coughing perpetually, his eyes dulled. His spirit,
Ascanar could see, was almost broken. Even his hope looked
beyond restoration. Too many of his fellows had become like
this.

Ascanar had not sat down. He nodded, standing above his
visitor and placing a hand on his shoulder. Dennor was puzzled. Such familiarity from the former Oligarch of Eukor
Epta was uncharacteristic: Ascanar was usually indifferent
and as aloof as his master had been. But the touch was cold.
Ascanar looked thoughtful for a moment. Somehow his sharp
features did not seem to have been affected by the grim sojourn on this rock; his eyes were as penetrating and clear as
they had ever been. How he maintained his strength, his dignity, was beyond the older man. It must be something unique

to the higher orders of the Administrators. There were younger men here who had the same stubbornness of will.

"Who is with them?" asked Ascanar. He left Dennor's side and gazed out at the gray afternoon. It obscured the stark fangs of rock beyond the sill, but could not muffle the perpetual snarl of the sea.

"The Emperor himself has come."

Ascanar's teeth flashed. It was almost a smile. "He could not resist." Then the rumors were not unfounded! Even Tannacrag had ears, though they had to strain to catch the whisperings of Empire. But the Remoon was not without his weaknesses. That much was true, it seemed.

"He is well protected," said Dennor. "If we dared to attack him—"

Ascanar made a dismissive gesture with his bony hand, but his impatience softened. "Attack? You think I am tempted to attack him here? And what would we use? Rocks? There isn't a sword on the island."

Dennor bowed his head apologetically.

Ascanar spoke less harshly. "There are other ways to bring a dog to its knees. They may take longer, but time is one weapon we do have." He turned back to Dennor, suddenly brisk. "Is the madman secured? Is every passage to him sealed?"

"Be assured, sire," Dennor nodded vigorously.

"Are there any Stonedelvers with the Emperor? I know they hate the sea, but they were the ones to cut this prison from the bare rock of the island. It seems they'll do much for the Emperor, including crossing the sea if he asks it."

"No, sire. There are none. Nor of the smaller ones, those of the earth."

Ascanar frowned at the thought of the Earthwrought. The Remoon had taken Eukor Epta by complete surprise when he had brought together so many strange allies. It still seemed amazing that he had done such a thing.

"Earthwrought," Ascanar murmured. "Then if there are none of them, the madman will not be discovered prematurely, and taken from us. Where is the Emperor now?"

"Barely landed. About to mount the outer stair. He has a

score of more of his guardsmen with him. And, I think, Ota-rus.''

Ascanar nodded. "The Law Giver? That's not unexpected. He keeps close counsel with the Emperor.''

"There's one other, sire," went on Dennor, his voice dropping, as if he feared he might be overheard. Ascanar noticed immediately and his eyes narrowed.

"Well?"

"I did not see his face—"

"You saw enough to form a conclusion?"

Dennor nodded. "The Deliverer.''

Consternation vied with fury in Ascanar's expression, but for only a moment. "Wargallow?" Surely the man was in the east. "He has kept his return here a secret. Are you sure it was him?''

"Perhaps it's my fear of the man, sire. Yet something in the way this man walked, his closeness to Ottemar—"

"You did well to voice your suspicions. If it is Wargallow, our task tonight may be far more difficult." Ascanar straightened. "But we are committed.''

THE CROSSING had been difficult. Reaching any of these for-saken rocks had always been a treacherous business, and even the fishermen of Medallion were wary of them. But, Ottemar Remoon mused as he stepped ashore, it was the reason why Tannacrag had been selected as the place to imprison the supporters of his former enemy, Eukor Epta. Any man sent to such an inhospitable place would rot, or lose his mind. Ottemar looked up at the steps that had been wretched out of the cliff by his loyal Stonedelvers. It had not been a task they had enjoyed, for the stone was not easy to work, and the sea seemed to mock their every effort with scorn, but they had understood the reasoning behind the task and had labored with a good will. Aumlac, their ruler, was as faithful a ser-vant to the Emperor as any man. The work done here was far from beautiful, but it served its purpose.

On the stair, Ottemar looked down at the churning waters as they flung themselves endlessly at Tannacrag's walls, cut-ting into them, working at them with a tireless energy that would never be stilled. Frowning, he turned away, as if the vision put unwelcome thoughts in his head. He gave his arm to the man beside him, Otarus, who had pulled his thick cloak tightly about him as protection from the gusting wind. Behind them, silent and seemingly unmoved, the shadow that was Wargallow followed.

The doors to the crude fortress of Tannacrag were iron bound, proof against the hostile weather. Torches blazed beside them, the wind tearing at them and pulling from them long tails of bright yellow. In the glow, a number of pale faces studied the climbers. The last of Ascanar's people waited, their eyes as cold as the sea, their minds closed. But this would be no trap. It would be, Ottemar was convinced, no more than a plea for mercy, a less grueling way of life. He had not discussed it in detail with Wargallow. Indeed, the Deliverer had been almost permanently busy since his return, a month ago, from the east. He had, nevertheless, insisted on coming on this short voyage to the home of the exiles, as though he feared the Emperor's disposition to be lenient.

"If you consider this meeting so important that you yourself must attend it," Wargallow had said, "then perhaps you'd better take me with you."

Ottemar had simply shrugged, though inwardly he had wished that the meeting could have happened while Wargallow was away. He had told Wargallow as little as possible: that he had received a message from Tannacrag, a missive signed by Ascanar, requesting an audience. He would have bluntly refused, but something had happened which could not be ignored. The Administrators had found a broken craft on the outer rocks of the island, and among the wreckage there were a number of dead seamen, and one who was alive. There was a madness in him, but among his wild cries and screams, there were some intelligible sentences. He had come from the far west. So much had Ottemar revealed to Otarus and Wargallow. He had burned the missive before speaking to either of them, and thus they had not seen the final sentence written in the precise hand of Ascanar. Yet those words burned brightly still in Ottemar's mind.

He was one of Rannovic's men.

The doors to Tannacrag's fortress were opened and the Emperor's party entered, the guardsmen forming an easy line on either side of him. They looked to be relaxed, unwary, but they had been chosen for their skill. Only a reckless or desperate force would have attempted to abduct or kill Ottemar. Wargallow understood Ascanar better; it would not happen here.

There was a hall, a drab place in comparison to the opulent halls of the rebuilt city of Medallion, and its walls were bare, not one tapestry nor statue adorning them. For windows it had narrow openings high up, each fixed with a grille. Though there was a log fire blazing comfortably in a wide hearth, there were no carpets, no rugs, and the tables were of dark wood, the chairs little better than benches. Ottemar scowled at them as he walked through them to meet his host. Tannacrag was far more of a prison than he had realized. Perhaps Wargallow would approve, but the Emperor wondered if it were wise to treat Ascanar and his people with such pointed derision.

Ascanar waited alone near the fire. He wore a single robe of coarse material which contrasted with the woven pelts of the Emperor and his retinue. He held himself well, a tall man, with the sharp features of his race, his dark hair swept back from a high forehead, his brows pencil-thin but marked. Whatever he had suffered here on Tannacrag, it did not show at the moment. He had a look of power about him, a spirit that would not be easily broken. And he had a coolness, something that seemed to set him aside from fear, and it lent him an air almost of contempt. He stepped forward and gave a polite bow of his head.

"I am honored, sire." There was no warmth in his voice; it might have been fashioned by the elements of the island about him.

Ottemar gestured to his guardsmen and at once they withdrew to the extremities of the hall, though mindful of their charge.

"I would offer you wine," said Ascanar, with a hint of a smile, "but you will appreciate that the vine does not prosper on Tannacrag."

Wargallow had let his hood fall and Ascanar was thankful that he had been warned that it might be the Deliverer who was coming. Had he not known, he may well have shown enough brief surprise for Wargallow to notice. He missed nothing, and as his eyes met those of Ascanar, the latter studied him briefly. Dressed in a dark cloak, the Deliverer hid both hands within it. Ascanar had seen that terrible right hand only once, in the Hall of the Hundred when Wargallow had first arrived on Medallion. It was a frightful instrument, that killing steel, reputed to move with blinding speed, and capable of despatching death quickly. The face of the Deliverer was calm, unmoved, and Ascanar reflected that he had never seen a man so completely in control of himself before, save possibly his own former master, Eukor Epta. But even he had fallen to the steel of the easterner.

Otarus, on the other hand, looked tired, hurt by the cold of the island. He wore numerous thick pelts and furs, and his white beard spilled over them in a silent cataract. He was an old man now, his face lined and weary, but in his eyes there yet burned the spirit that had rallied his own supporters in the difficult days before the Inundation. Ascanar nodded to him in deference: he had been a worthy opponent and one not to be taken lightly, even now.

The Emperor, like his predecessors, remained an enigma. He was still a relatively young man, though already the stress of controlling the Empire was beginning to show in his face, that and something else. Ascanar thought he already had the measure of this. And Ottemar must know it, too, else he would not have come.

"And you'll appreciate that we did not come here to drink with you," said Wargallow.

Ascanar switched his gaze back to the Deliverer, but kept his face as blank as he could. He expected no mercy from Wargallow. And with him, there was no lever. Was there a weakness in him? Something that could be gripped and used to manipulate him? Ascanar doubted it. Control of Wargallow would have to be achieved in other ways. Could he ever be used against the Emperor? Again, it would take a lifetime to achieve it.

"Your missive spoke of a survivor," said Ottemar.

How much of the note had the others seen? wondered Ascanar. But he suspected Ottemar had not shown it to them: it had been too direct in its conclusion.

"Yes," nodded the former Oligarch. He gestured to the seats, and Ottemar and Otarus sat at once. Wargallow preferred to go to the fire, though he did not take his arms from his cloak.

Ascanar sat with the Emperor. "Although you provide us with supplies and enough food to live, some of the younger men here like to amuse themselves by scaling the rocks and hunting gulls' eggs, or sometimes fishing. Tannacrag does not offer a wide range of diversions—"

"Which is why it was chosen," said Wargallow to the fire. He had no time for Ascanar's sarcasm.

"On such an expedition," went on the latter, "a boat was discovered. It was a curiously crude vessel, having been constructed, it seemed, in haste. And it looked as if it had been made from a larger craft that had been in some way damaged. It had come to grief on the western rocks of the island, and those who had been reckless enough to sail in it had either drowned or been pulped on the rocks. The sea here has a particularly spiteful nature, which is why I discourage my people from thoughts of crossing it."

"Have any tried?" said Otarus.

Ascanar smiled, though he was being patient. "In their minds, they all have. Otherwise, no."

"But one of the men in this wrecked boat did live," said Ottemar, leaning forward. "Is he still alive?"

Ascanar looked into the Emperor's eyes for a long time. It was impossible to miss the need there, the hunger. Ascanar leaned back, aware that Wargallow was looking down at him. "Yes. The man is alive."

"Where is he?" said Ottemar, his hands working at each other for warmth.

"Here on Tannacrag," said Ascanar calmly. "Quite safe."

Wargallow listened, wondering why it was that Ottemar should show so much interest in this shipwrecked sailor. He was of great importance to the Emperor, but Wargallow's gentle questioning had yet to discover why. The sailor had come from the west, but there was more to it than that.

Otarus coughed. "You must know that you cannot hide him from us."

Ascanar shrugged. "For a while I could. Your Stonedelvers would dig him out, no matter how deep we buried him. But, of course, you want him alive.''

"You mean you'd have killed him before we could find him,'' said Wargallow. This was the language he understood.

Ascanar gave a very brief nod. "I have nothing, not even my freedom. All I have is this madman from the sea.''

"What condition is he in?" said Ottemar.

"To be frank, he will not live for very long. He eats, but unless he is closely watched, he tears at himself, or tries to throttle himself. Then there are calmer periods. Sometimes he is quite lucid—''

"How lucid?" said Ottemar, too quickly.

"He talks of his voyages, though they sound as if they are voyages of the mind—''

"Voyages in the western seas?" prompted Otarus.

"It is why I assumed he would be important to you.''

"And why,'' added Wargallow, "you assumed you could use him.''

Ascanar again nodded. "Tannacrag is a prison. You chose it well. I want to be able to leave it and to take my remaining people with me. We know that we have lost Medallion. But there are lands in the far south, beyond the city of Thuvis in Athahara, where we could go. We have accepted our loss. In the south we would hardly be a threat to the Empire. Is that such a high price?"

Ottemar again answered quickly. "Perhaps not.''

"The madman,'' went on Ascanar, looking directly at the Emperor, "has spoken of many things, most of which mean nothing to me. Much of it will, I am sure, mean nothing to you. But he has spoken of Anakhizer, and of how he is preparing for war.''

"We know of such things,'' said Wargallow calmly.

"He has spoken of the Deepwalks, the forests that cover the shores of the west. From which no man has returned.'' Ascanar turned round to meet Wargallow's gaze. "Until now.''

"You attach significance to that?" said the Deliverer, with a look of mild surprise. Ascanar knew it to be feigned: he understood such guises perfectly.

He smiled. "Only because the madman seems to have been

into the forest. His party found a way into it, and some of them returned."

"Without their sanity," said Wargallow. "Which could suggest that any man who follows them would be a fool. Your information would seem to be a little flawed in value."

Ascanar was not at all put out by Wargallow's dismissal. "Others of the party did not return, and one might suppose they suffered the same fate that befell their predecessors."

"Has the madman spoken of them?" said Ottemar, tensing.

"The rest of the party? Vaguely."

"And are they dead?"

Something in Ottemar's voice warned Wargallow that the truth of the matter was close to the surface. What had he missed? Men had tried to penetrate the western continent before. Why should this expedition be so important? But then, bright as a beacon, the answer came to him. How could he have forgotten!

"Who led this party?" he asked, looking not at Ascanar, but at Ottemar.

"I repeat," said the Emperor, ignoring the demanding eyes. "Are they all dead?"

"Not if the survivor is to be believed," said Ascanar.

"Who led the party?" said Wargallow again, but he knew. Ottemar's anxiety proclaimed it.

"Someone of value to us?" said Otarus, puzzled by the sudden tension.

Ottemar got to his feet. *"Are they alive?"* he breathed.

Ascanar shrugged. "The madman hints that a group of them survived the foray into the Deepwalks but they have been taken—"

"Taken?" repeated Ottemar, his face suddenly haggard. "By whom? Anakhizer?"

"Possibly. The forest, perhaps. But you must put these questions to the seaman yourself."

Ottemar looked across at Wargallow, and Otarus could see that there was an understanding between them he did not share. He had become used to this. "Who led the party?" the old man said into the sudden silence. "Do you know?"

"A former pirate," said Ascanar. "A man who once had

a high price on his head, but who now rules the Hammavars, and who has made good their rift with the House of Trullhoon.''

''Rannovic!'' gasped Otarus, his brow wrinkling. ''But why should he sail to the *west!* Who knows better than Rannovic how dangerous those lands are?''

Wargallow watched Ottemar, knowing who the former pirate had taken with him on his voyage, knowing also that Rannovic would not have made the voyage had he not been beguiled into doing so. But this was no place to bring it into the open, not before Ascanar. Unless he knew the rest. Could he? He was sure of his strength in this bartering, sure that he had enough to win his freedom.

''You say the Deepwalks have claimed Rannovic and his party,'' said Wargallow. ''But that they are alive.''

''The madman has said as much,'' said Ascanar.

''By now they may be dead,'' said Wargallow. ''It would have taken weeks for the ship to have reached Tannacrag from the west. And even if we sent a fleet to look for Rannovic, how would we find him?''

''Ask Helvor, as he names himself. I did not bring you here to waste your time.'' There was a steel edge to Ascanar's voice now. ''He knows the way into the forest. Your friends may yet be alive.'' He directed this last to Ottemar, who flinched. There was no mistaking Ascanar's understanding of the Emperor's fears.

Wargallow returned to the fire. He knew precisely how strong a grip on the situation Ascanar had. Rannovic was not the prize, although he had become a worthy ally to Ottemar and alone would have been worth trying to save. But Rannovic, like Ottemar, had a weakness, and it may yet undo both of them. Sisipher, Brannog's daughter. Wargallow heard many rumors and tales: he was too discerning a ruler to ignore such things. In Medallion's streets he had heard of how Rannovic had tried to seduce Sisipher when she had first been captured by the Hammavars, and of how, in spite of her rude dismissal of him, he had yet kept a place in his heart for her. Wargallow also knew that Ottemar loved the girl. He had made a fool of himself over her once, but she had forgiven him that. Although she had come to love him in return, she had not let their duty to the Empire stand aside for them. She had left Medallion shortly before Ottemar's child had been born, and she had easily persuaded Rannovic to take her in his own warship. And they had blundered into the west! To the Deepwalks. What had they hoped to achieve there!

And now Ottemar, who was yet obsessed by the girl, would want to pursue her, Wargallow felt certain. He had a beautiful wife, the superb Empress Tennebriel, who had given him a strong son and heir: he had the Empire, its numerous allies, its great strength against the coming darkness; he had the support and loyalty of a dozen nations. Yet still he would seek his happiness elsewhere. Did he, perhaps, possess the legendary Remoon madness, the curse of his ancestors? Whatever his feelings, Ascanar had found them out and knew the entire history of them. He had calculated precisely how eager Ottemar would be to search for Sisipher.

The former Oligarch said blandly, "Shall I take you to my guest?"

Ottemar was looking at Wargallow's back. "Rannovic is one of our most faithful allies. If he is alive, we have to search for him. If we do not the entire Trullhoon House will be up in arms. You know well enough that my mother, Ludhana, was a Trullhoon—"

Wargallow swung round. "I understand your history well enough, yes! And I agree that Rannovic and his party should not be abandoned. But this is an expensive way to pay for it. To free Ascanar and his followers."

"Would you weigh that against our allies?" snapped Ottemar. "And if it gives us a way in to the west, Simon, a path to the forest and beyond—"

Otarus shook his head. "Sire, surely this is a matter for the Hall—"

"No!" said Ottemar and the word struck the walls and rang back. "I am the Emperor, not a puppet. The matter is decided. Ascanar, you will have your freedom. A ship will be prepared for you, manned by my navy. You'll be taken south, around Athahara and put ashore in safety." He took from his neck a chain and seal and held it out to the former Oligarch. "Here's my word on it. Witness this," he called to Otarus, loud enough so that the guardsmen would also hear.

Otarus gasped; this made the decision irreversible.

Ascanar bowed slightly. He took the proferred seal and held it in his hands for a moment, then returned it to the Emperor. "So be it."

Ottemar swung away from his companions and paced back into the hall.

Otarus rose, going to Wargallow. "This must be done as vowed," he whispered to the Deliverer. "We must uphold his promise. It is the law."

Wargallow nodded patiently. "Yes, yes, Otarus. In spite of what you may have heard about me, I am not without scruples."

"I suppose Ascanar can be no threat to Goldenisle now."

"I agree. But I do not like to see the Emperor being so precipitate. He should not rule by passion alone. I agree that Ascanar's people should be released, as my own enemies in the east were. But such decisions should not be made by one man. What else will Ottemar insist on, eh?"

Otarus nodded solemnly. "He should consult the Council on such matters."

Wargallow gently guided the old Law Giver by the arm, and they followed Ascanar and the Emperor, the guardsmen falling into step behind them. Wargallow concealed his amusement at Otarus' anxiety, and at his own hypocrisy: he had ruled the Deliverers as a dictator since Grenndak's fall.

Ascanar led them through a number of corridors and came to stairs that led upwards and not down into the heart of the fortress as expected. A number of doors had to be unlocked on the way, for Ascanar had been very precise in his preparations. Had Wargallow or anyone else attempted to find a way to the hiding place of the madman, they would have arrived far too late to prevent his death. And Ascanar belonged to a breed of men who would have sacrificed themselves rather than allow their enemies the pleasure of taking their prisoner without due payment.

The place where the madman was kept opened as a ledge over the sea. The wind howled beyond it, and the surf grayed as it pounded the cliffs below. Those who guarded the mad-

man were relieved when Ascanar came to them, knowing by
the presence of the Emperor that their unpleasant vigil would
soon be over.

Helvor was bound to a rock, although it was evident from
the condition of his ropes that he had chafed at them so often
he had frayed them and they had been re-tied more than once.
Ascanar went as near to him as he dared and held aloft a
torch. By its shivering light Helvor's face looked wild, his
eyes wide and staring. His hair was long and filthy, his beard
a dishevelled bush. Thick strands of saliva hung from his
chin, and his mouth sagged as if the jaw had been broken.

"Is this how you found him?" said Ottemar, appalled by
the spectacle.

"He grows worse," said Ascanar, himself unmoved.
"From time to time he is calmer, and speaks for minutes at
a time in a reasonable way, though much of what he says is
strange."

As if in response, Helvor jerked. "I've seen them," he
said suddenly, eyes yet focused on the distant shore of his
delusions. He seemed transfixed, as though he could envisage
again what he had once seen.

Ottemar moved closer. "What are they?" he said in a
hoarse whisper.

"Dark, dark," gasped Helvor. "I see their eyes, their
hateful eyes, no eyes of men! Dark armour, spawn of night!
And the bloated ones, the grasping flesh-eaters—"

"Ferr-Bolgan!" murmured Ottemar.

"Oh, yes! A thousand of the maggot vermin. But see these
others! These black-helmed killers. What are these, with their
curved steel?"

Ottemar glanced back at Wargallow. "Steel? The Ferr-
Bolgan do not carry blades—"

"And who is beyond them!" cried Helvor. "Ah, we saw
its kind when we lost Teru Manga. Herder! See him gloat as
the curved blades rip!"

"The Children of the Mound, in the west, just as we
feared," Ottemar nodded, turning again to Wargallow. As
he did so, Helvor erupted, flinging himself forward against
the ropes. One hand snapped free of its thongs, but before he
could fasten his nails in Ottemar's flesh, Ascanar thrust the

torch at him. Helvor cowered back at once, spitting like a wolf.

"There are chains on our ships," said Wargallow from the shadows. "We'll take him from this place."

"And my ship?" Ascanar asked of Ottemar.

"In two days it will be here. Be prepared to leave."

Ascanar bowed. Everything was already prepared. He had known Ottemar would not be able to resist the bait. So the girl was as precious to him as the stories told.

Wargallow had already left the chamber. Otarus and the Emperor followed him. "How will you interrogate the creature, sire?" Otarus asked softly.

Ottemar's face was drawn. "I will leave that to Wargallow."

Behind them there was a piercing shriek, and in it a sound of utter despair. Otarus watched the Emperor go down. The mantle of Empire sat heavily on these men, Otarus mused. It hardened them, as fire tempered steel. But in these days there was no other way, it seemed. It was the time of steel. Wearily he descended, and the stairs seemed to him then to reach down into an endless dark.

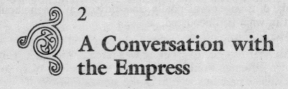

2
A Conversation with the Empress

TENNEBRIEL STUDIED the calm waters of the Inner Sea from the balcony. The day was cloudless, sunlight sparkling on the water, shaping the distant Heights of Malador clearly. Directly below the Empress the streets were being rebuilt even now, more than a year after the Inundation and Ottemar's coming to power. The Stonedelvers and their smaller companions, the Earthwrought, had done a remarkable job restoring the city, reshaping it and raising it from its own rubble, making of it a more splendid city than it had previously been, and the gardens flourished anew, their foliage and plants blossoming in spectacular fashion. To an outsider, it was as though the city had never known destruction. Tennebriel knew little of what it had been like before her marriage to Ottemar, as she had been a virtual prisoner on Tower Island, one of Eukor Epta's strongholds in the Inner Sea, but all those islands had collapsed, and the sea now was clear of them, save for one or two isolated rocks inhabited by bird colonies. Yes, the Stonedelvers were a strange race, and their skill with stone was almost magical, for they seemed to be able to shape it as a potter shaped clay, and they were able to move quickly below the earth as if they were wraiths within it. And more than that, they were intensely loyal to the throne. It was true that Ottemar had given them back their ancestral home, Malador, but it was not mere gratitude that made them the faithful servants they were. Tennebriel had heard much of how her husband had journeyed to the north where they

18

had once been in exile beyond Teru Manga, and of how he had brought them out of the grip of their enemies. But she had been able to glean little of that history from Ottemar, who spoke of it only occasionally, and did not say much about his part in what had occurred.

The Empress turned from the view, stretching as lithely as a cat, her hair cascading around her like silk, shimmering in the morning light. On the balcony with her was a cradle, and the child in it slept. She glanced at him, smiling to herself. How quickly his first three months had fled. She resisted the urge to lift him up and cradle him; it was always a joy to do so. Her love for the child was intense.

She thought of her husband and of her unusual relationship with him. There had been times when she had thought she must flee her life here and take her chance in the outside world, of which she heard only whispers, and other times when she wondered if she should find a way of destroying the Emperor. But as the first few months of her marriage passed, she began to realize that she could never hate Ottemar. She had never loved him, thinking that love had been burned out of her by the murder of Cromalech, who had been her lover. The child had taught her that she had been wrong to think that. Ottemar himself had never professed to love her. He had explained this very soon after their marriage, politely, a little nervously, telling her that he did not wish to cause her distress or make her life unpleasant in any way. She smiled when she thought of the day when he had tried anxiously to explain that they must one day have an heir, a child that would make the fusion of the three royal Houses absolute. It had taken him hours to come to the point, and clearly he had dreaded her reaction.

She had known then that what he asked was not unreasonable, even though she felt no desire for him. A little pity, perhaps, but that was no reason to share his bed. But the matter of an heir could not be ignored. She had suggested that they have an heir as soon as they could, making it quite clear as well that she wanted a child out of duty and that alone. Ottemar had not been stung or bruised by her reply. For him it was a matter of duty also.

That day, when they agreed on the child, marked the beginning of a new understanding. They spoke to each other after that of private things, sharing secrets that they would not have shared with any other. For the first time Ottemar spoke of the girl he loved, Sisipher, and of some of the times they had spent together before he had become Emperor. His passion for her, Tennebriel knew at once, was fierce. How well he hid it from those around him! And in turn, she gave him the truth of her own past, and of how she had been Cromalech's lover. Ottemar had been moved to tears by her description of his death, perhaps because he had thought of his own lost love, forbidden to him now, and they had wept gently together. It was then that they had made love for the first time, and although they did so again during the weeks that followed, Tennebriel felt sure that the child had been conceived that first time, out of grief, out of their tears for the past.

Tennebriel's respect for her husband was great. As soon as he knew that she was with child, he ceased coming to her and made no more demands on her. Their friendship grew, and in each other they had found someone to whom they could divulge things they would share with no one else. Ottemar also spoke of affairs of state, which he seemed to find increasingly tedious, and Tennebriel agreed that royal protocol exhausted her more than anything. But she had the child and worshipped it. Ottemar never interfered, though he loved his son, anxious to do whatever he was required to, guided by Tennebriel. He made life as pleasant and as interesting as he could for her, and almost everyone in the city assumed them to be an excellent match.

Life would have been acceptable, but for the rumors that crept ever in from outside the islands of the Chain. The smell of war hovered over the western horizon. Ambassadors arrived constantly, and Ottemar spoke to old friends from the east, where much was happening. Wargallow, his most faithful envoy, was recently returned from there, bearing some secret that Ottemar would not disclose. It was to do with power, for the impending war with Anakhizer was to be over power. Such things were not beyond the Empress and she dearly longed to know more, but she had to find out about these things indirectly.

From the shadows of her rooms, a figure emerged, and Tennebriel grinned as she saw who it was. It was the beautiful eastern girl, Dennovia, who had been brought by Wargallow and his party from the lands of legend beyond the eastern sea some weeks previously. Apparently it had been Wargallow himself who had suggested that this stunning girl, herself no more than a few months younger than the Empress, be given to her as a Companion. At first Tennebriel argued with her husband that she would rather choose her own Companions, but when she heard about Dennovia's background she became intrigued and had agreed to the post being made official.

Dennovia was about to kneel, but Tennebriel snorted. "There's nobody here, Dennovia. Don't bother with that now."

Dennovia smiled, brushing back her own dark hair, and went to look at the child. "And how is little Solimar? He has your looks."

"Do you think so?" replied the taller girl, pleased.

Dennovia was always relaxed when she knew they were alone. She had been amazed by the city when she had been brought here under the protection of Simon Wargallow and King Brannog, and for some time she had expected to be either married off to some noble, or secreted away in the palace where she could not make a nuisance of herself. She had even wondered if one day she might be killed, having once been the mistress of Mourndark, Wargallow's enemy. But it was true that she had saved Wargallow's life beyond the eastern continent. Perhaps this was his way of repaying her for that. She had met the Emperor, a strange man, who looked to Dennovia to have more on his mind than others would have thought, and she wondered if it had been Ottemar who had suggested she become a Companion to his wife. Whoever it had been, the decision had thrilled Dennovia, and as it turned out, greatly pleased Tennebriel, for the Empress had lived a closeted life and knew very little about the outside world. Although Dennovia had been here little more than a month, she had already provided the Empress with endless tales and anecdotes. Not only that, but Dennovia's exploits, her hinted affairs with a number of palace officials, which

had begun almost the day she had arrived, were a source of
endless fascination to the Empress, who would listen avidly
while Dennovia whispered her stories of intrigue. There had
been times when the Empress would have spoken of her own
dead lover, but she had refrained. She wanted nothing to
make her or her son vulnerable in any way.

"And what is happening out in the wicked city today?"
Tennebriel smiled.

Dennovia took a deep breath, smoothing down her short
dress with her hands, conscious of her beauty. She considered
Tennebriel to be quite the most beautiful woman she had ever
seen, though the girl did not use her beauty to its best advantage. But Dennovia knew also that she had her own
beauty, which she had honed like a tool, using it with such
expert skill that she suspected very few men in the Empire
could ignore it if she used it on them. Men spoke of power,
but Dennovia knew there was power in her beauty.

"I have heard," Dennovia began, and was at once cut
short by the laughter of the Empress. "My lady?"

" 'You have heard,' " repeated Tennebriel. "You always
say it as though you had been hiding behind a door and caught
something, whereas I'm sure you must have drawn it from
the unsuspecting lips of one of your lovers."

Dennovia giggled. "Well, to be honest, I did spend much
of the night with Fornoldur, one of Ottemar's guardsmen."

"Not while he was on duty, I trust?"

"Now, you know that discretion is my watchword—"

Tennebriel laughed again, enjoying herself. How Dennovia
had the nerve to carry through some of her exploits she could
not imagine. Did Wargallow know what the girl was up to in
the palace?

"Anyway," Dennovia went on, "I was with Fornoldur.
Did you know that your husband had received a message
from the Administrators?"

"The exiles?"

"Yes, on Tannacrag. Ascanar sent a message, asking for
your husband to visit him. In person."

"Ottemar would never go to such a place. He would have
sent one of the court."

"You would have thought so," said Dennovia softly. "But

some of Fornoldur's fellows in the guard were summoned the
other night. They went the next day to Tannacrag. And Ottemar was with them. So was Otarus. And of course, Wargallow.''

Tennebriel shook her head. "He's scarcely back from the
east and already he's busier than the rest of the court put
together. He and his other Deliverer—''

"Coldrieve? Yes, I've not been able to find out what it is
they have been working on. War plans, no doubt. Be thankful
they are allies; Wargallow is very powerful.''

"I sometimes wonder if he is more powerful than the Emperor.''

Dennovia caught the edge to the comment. "Possibly, in
some ways. But they serve each other, I know that. Wargallow's loyalty to the Empire is built on a strange fanaticism.
He sees the Empire as the salvation of Omara. There is no
danger of him using his power against your husband.''

"Well, you know these things better than I,'' nodded Tennebriel, though her fears remained. She had not known Dennovia long enough to be absolutely certain of her. If what
she said about the Deliverer was true, he was indeed a cham-
pion to be admired, as were all Ottemar's unusual allies.

"I am a stranger,'' said Dennovia. "I have no right to
demand your trust. But I can promise that your husband is
well served. In all things now there is one real enemy.''

"The evil in the west? Anakhizer?''

"Yes.''

"I hear of him constantly. Why does he not attack us? How
long is he to go on preparing for this war?''

"We may know soon.''

"You have heard something?'' said Tennebriel eagerly. The
thought of another war, and one as terrible as had been promised, horrified her, but this waiting, this expectation, was at
times unbearable.

"Ottemar went to Ascanar. It seems there was a shipwreck
on Tannacrag. A small craft, but somehow it had made the
crossing from the far west.''

Tennebriel's eyes widened. "The *west?*''

"You have heard of the Deepwalks?''

Tennebriel gasped. "Yes, of course! But surely the ship

didn't come from there? Even our war galleys don't roam along that coastline.''

''The men in this ship had been *into* the Deepwalks. They fled, but their ship was destroyed on Tannacrag, and they were all killed, save one. And Ascanar had him.''

''Where is he now?''

''Somewhere below us in the palace. Fornoldur doesn't know where. He's under strict guard. Whatever ordeal he endured in the west and after made him into a madman. But something of his story was saved. He was brought here by the guardsmen, and Wargallow.''

Tennebriel looked thoughtful. ''Ottemar has been restless lately. In fact, yesterday his temper was very short. He hardly looked at the child. He was abrupt with me—''

''And he's upset the Law Givers.''

''Oh?'' Tennebriel was surprised. Otarus was rarely put out by her husband, and had been particularly supportive of him.

''Ascanar only gave up the madman for a price.''

''I can't believe he would be in a position to make demands on us. The Administrators are lucky to be alive. Many would have had them executed.''

Dennovia leaned forward, though there was no danger of her being overheard. ''The price he asked was his freedom— and that of all his followers.''

''Then Tannacrag has softened his head,'' sneered the Empress.

''But the madman is here.''

Tennebriel frowned. ''Ascanar traded this madman for his freedom?''

''It was the Emperor's express command. Before Wargallow and Otarus, he pledged his word on his seal. Already Ascanar and his followers are at sea, bound for southern lands. Tannacrag is empty.'' Dennovia tossed back her head, pleased that she had been able to shock her companion.

''Then this madman must be exceedingly valuable! Who is he?''

''Helvor. His master is well respected by Fornoldur and his guardsmen. He is Rannovic, formerly a Hammavar freebooter, now one of the Trullhoons' high ranking captains.''

"Rannovic," Tennebriel echoed. "Another of my husband's particular allies. They fought at sea against Eukor Epta's forces. And you say Rannovic was in the west? In the Deepwalks?"

"I can't find out why. Perhaps he was on a mission for your husband."

Tennebriel mused upon this. "Possibly. The Empire seeks as much knowledge as it can muster about the west. Ottemar wants to take a fleet and an army there, to carry the war to Anakhizer before he brings it to us. But the Deepwalks bar the way."

Dennovia's eyes flashed. "Then Rannovic has found a way through them. Helvor has been brought here and questioned—"

"By whom?"

"Wargallow."

Tennebriel shuddered in spite of herself. "Torture?"

"No. The man was mad, his mind locked in turmoil."

"You think that would deter the Deliverer?"

Dennovia looked angry, but she guarded her reactions carefully. "He is not that ruthless. Helvor had to be interrogated. His information is vital. There would be ways to take it from him without violence—"

"How?" Tennebriel was relentless. She knew how important Wargallow was to Ottemar, but wondered how much of a threat he could be to him if he so chose. Wargallow was far too self-contained for her to be sure of him.

"I know that Brannog's wife, Ruvanna, has certain skills. They say she was able to search the mind of a Child of the Mound, and draw from it such knowledge as she needed. And I have seen her shape elementals from the very mud of the sea bed—"

"Then did she question the madman?"

"I don't know."

"Perhaps it was Wargallow, with his killing steel."

Dennovia would have denied this, knowing the Deliverer no longer carried the steel hand. But she must not divulge that truth, nor say what it was he carried in its place. The safety of the Empire depended on the keeping of that secret, and she knew her life depended on silence. "No, I am sure he did not torment Helvor. But he had to learn what he knew of the west."

Tennebriel nodded. "I see. Then it may be that Ottemar will force the hand of his court. If there is a way through the Deepwalks, he will want to muster his army and sail."

"You don't approve?"

Tennebriel went to the balcony and looked out at the sea. The picture was one of serenity, a vivid contrast to the things which sped through her mind. "They won't let him go," she said.

Dennovia stood beside her. "The Emperor?"

Tennebriel sighed. "I know why he's so restless. This business explains it. More than ever he will want to take his forces to the west. Such action may well be approved, but if it is, the court will never permit Ottemar to go. He will have to stay here, to protect the Chain."

"You think he should go?"

Tennebriel turned to her with a thin smile. "His happiness concerns me. He and I are not lovers, Dennovia, you may have guessed as much. But we rule. Our first duty is to the throne, and to our son. But Ottemar's happiness is important to me."

"But if he goes to the west—"

"And faces its dangers? He would be more content to do that than sit here, chafing. That would destroy him. He should go."

Dennovia chewed her lip thoughtfully. "There is to be a counseling. In secret. These matters are to be discussed. I believe there are factions who would not support the sending of the navy and army to the west, even if there is a way through the Deepwalks."

"Has Fornoldur told you this?"

"No, no. He is only a party to so much. This is not something I have been told, but I've spent a lot of time in the company of Brannog and Wargallow." She had told and re-told her life in the east to Tennebriel. "I'm sure they have a different view of things."

"Different to whom? My husband?"

"Their answer is to go secretly to the west. Not with an army, but with a selected elite company."

"For what purpose? What could they achieve?"

Dennovia had said nothing about the rods of power, nor of Anakhizer's control of them. "They might find a way to the heart of the enemy before he discovered them."

Tennebriel considered it. "It would be a reckless journey. But in view of the past, I suspect the sort of exploit Ottemar would relish."

Dennovia shook her head. "He would wish to go, for certain, but—"

Tennebriel realized what she meant. "Of course! The court would be even less inclined to permit it. In fact, it would be forbidden."

"If it is decided that such a quest is to be undertaken, only those with particular skills will be chosen. There will be no room for anyone else. So even if he were not Emperor, Ottemar would have to remain." Dennovia had not said it unkindly, and Tennebriel did not turn on her angrily for saying what was the truth.

"No, you are right, Dennovia. Ottemar confesses he is no great fighter, and he does not possess skill with a sword, or with an axe or bow. He has no other power, not like the Earthwrought, or that extraordinary fellow, Brannog. Nor does he have the cold-blooded determination of Wargallow."

"You have no love for the Deliverer," said Dennovia, looking away for a moment.

"He frightens me! Oh, I know he is said to have killed Eukor Epta, for which I should heap praise on him, but—"

"Trust him, with your life."

Tennebriel seemed to be about to ask something, but before she had made her mind up to do so, Dennovia had moved away. She was studying the city below. "Why do you think your husband wants to go on this journey, however it is decided?" she asked abruptly.

Oh, I know why, Tennebriel said to herself. I know why Rannovic left Goldenisle, and who persuaded him to go. If the Hammavar is alive, and Sisipher is with him, Ottemar will go after them. If the girl is in danger, he will want to seek her out. But this is not for Dennovia to know. Ottemar and I have shown the Empire our union. He dare not make a fool of himself now. If Dennovia knew, how far would it go?

Dennovia broke into her musing. "He has every good reason to stay. And reason would dictate that he should."

"History may have something to do with it," said Tennebriel, groping for a moment at straws. "The Remoons have had their failures in the past. Ottemar's predecessor, Quanar, almost brought ruin upon the Empire. Ottemar is anxious to show himself to be equal to the crisis—"

"By putting himself at risk? After all that he has achieved? The Empire is stronger now than it has been for hundreds of years," said Dennovia, forcing home her point so strongly that Tennebriel felt her fabrication dissolving. She was no longer accomplished at subterfuge, whereas Dennovia had made an art of it. "He should not go," said Dennovia.

"Well, no—"

"Just as he was too quick to agree to Ascanar's release. He did so without consulting Wargallow or Otarus, and they were standing beside him when he pledged his word."

"He is the Emperor—"

"His enemies would murmur of the Remoon Curse. Does Ottemar's heart rule his head?"

Tennebriel gasped. The arrow of truth struck home. She could hardly conceal it from Dennovia. "I cannot speak of these things, Dennovia."

There was a brief pause, a silence that threatened to break open with secrets. Dennovia smiled. "You are not lovers, my lady. You have told me so."

"What do you mean?"

"He loves another, perhaps?"

"That is not my concern."

"It is easy to tolerate such things when one is indifferent. Men are ruled by their passions. Such things make fools of them sometimes. Such things make them cast aside duty, loyalty—"

She knows! "What are you saying!"

"Only that I understand such things in men."

Tennebriel almost told her then, almost spoke of Cromalech, but she said nothing, her lips tightening, her hands clenching, though not in anger.

"My lady," Dennovia went on softly, "I wish to go on this voyage, too."

As if the girl had completely changed tack and spoke of other things, Tennebriel gaped at her. "I don't follow you—"

"Whether a fleet sails, or whether it is one ship, I want to go."

Tennebriel laughed, breaking the tension. "Surely you're not bored with the city already!"

Dennovia smiled patiently. She looked away. "No, I can think of no other place where I would rather settle. I cannot imagine anywhere in Omara to compare with Goldenisle."

"Yet you want to go to the west?"

"Those who go may not survive. I understand what it is they will face there. I have seen something of those grim powers. It is because those who go there may die there, that I want to go. But not because I want to die!" She laughed nervously, but recovered herself. "How foolish you must think me!"

Tennebriel put an arm about her, suddenly understanding. "Does Fornoldur mean so much to you?"

Dennovia's eyes widened and she threw back her head and laughed, the sound echoing pleasantly around the balcony. "Fornoldur!"

"Why, yes. I'm sure he'd be picked to go, even on a single craft. He is one of the finest warriors we have." Just as Cromalech was—

"Fornoldur!" repeated Dennovia. "Oh, mistress, how little you know me! Fornoldur is my *toy*. I have used him, just as I have used others. To learn things. If I need information, I have to pay for it."

Tennebriel released her, not sure whether to laugh or frown.

"I was trained as a concubine!" Dennovia laughed. "And I will not pretend that it is always unpleasant. Fornoldur is a good man. He has given me pleasure. But I could never love him."

"Then who?"

Dennovia grinned wickedly and moved away. "He'll be on that ship that leaves for the west. And I wish to be near him."

"Who is he? Tell me, I insist!" said Tennebriel, her face lighting up. They were both laughing like young girls.

"Let us share our secrets," said Dennovia at last.

Tennebriel still smiled, but she felt an inner coldness growing. "Secrets? What do you mean?"

"Who is it that the Emperor loves?"

To her surprise, the question came as a relief to Tennebriel. She had assumed Dennovia would demand the name of her own lover, the dead Cromalech. What harm would it do to tell her of Sisipher?

"If I tell you, it must be our secret, Dennovia. There are those who know it already. But if I find out that you have given such knowledge to others, my anger will be hard for you to bear."

Dennovia nodded. "I ask only for myself."

"If you do manage to sail to the west," said Tennebriel, trying to excuse herself, "you would find out anyway. It is Sisipher, King Brannog's daughter."

"Ah. Then I had guessed."

"You knew?"

"No, but it seemed to fit a pattern."

"So tell me, who is it that has so besotted you?"

Dennovia suddenly scowled and Tennebriel could see for once beneath the soft exterior of the girl some of the hardness that must be there. "I'm not besotted with him! And he thinks little enough of me."

"Come, come. Don't make me guess."

"You may not approve my choice—"

"Dennovia!"

For once the eastern girl did not meet the gaze of the Empress. "You must never tell a soul. It is Wargallow's shadow. I have known him since the Direkeep. Harn Coldrieve."

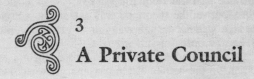

3
A Private Council

SHORTLY AFTER midnight, in one of the three private halls of the central palace, the counselors met, called together privately by the Emperor. Such guards as there were on duty had been detailed to stand watch outside the chamber's single door, admitting no one until the session was at an end. They had become used to these activities in the last month, knowing that they must be a prelude to war. After them there was always more preparation, messages sent out across the Empire, by sea and air. The day edged closer, the guards whispered, when it must begin. The city held its breath nervously, ill at east and restless.

In the small chamber, Ottemar's counselors met around the table. The room was not particularly well lit, as if the shadows could further privatize their talks and keep their secrets from the anxious ears of the outside world. Ottemar sat at the head of the table, his face pale, a little pasty in the glow of the candles, and his hands fidgeted with the medallion hanging from his neck, his eyes slowly taking in the gathered company. Otarus sat on his left, frail but determined and next to him were Renodas and Ulbric, his principal Law Givers. They were a little younger than Otarus, men in their fifties, but both of them had about them the look of stoicism that had been the mark of their loyalty to Goldenisle in the face of Eukor Epta's cruel administration. Renodas was tall, clear-eyed as an eagle, while by contrast Ulbric was a short, plump man, with a bristling mustache, his own eyes lined

31

and sunken, as if he were discomforted, although he seemed no less dignified than his tall companion.

Beside Ulbric sat the burly figure of Kelloric, now the ruler of the House of Trullhoon. Like the Law Givers, he was in his fifties, but unlike them, he was a warrior, a son of the sea, his face weather-beaten and full of grimness, as though he had known only war all his life. His left cheek bore a white scar to remind anyone who might doubt his personal involvement in the battles of the past that he was a man who led by example. He sat with his arms folded, a solemn stare fixed ahead of him as if at a distant sea horizon. Perhaps, Ottemar wondered, he thought of his cousin, Darraban, who together with his sons Andric and Rudaric had drowned in the Inundation, when the Trullhoons had almost been wiped out at a single stroke. Beyond him, at the far end of the table, sat the Deliverer, Harn Coldrieve, the only one of his people who Wargallow had brought with him here from the destruction of the Direkeep in the east, although it had been agreed that many more of the survivors would be admitted to Goldenisle. Though Coldrieve looked as cold and chilling as the killing steel he carried, he was utterly loyal to Wargallow and the Empire. His sharp face was unreadable, and if he knew himself to be the cause of speculation, of covert glances, he never let his feelings on the matter be shown.

Ottemar's eyes moved around the table to where Brannog sat, and even now, a month or more since he had come with Wargallow from Elberon, his presence still took the Emperor by surprise. Ottemar had first met him what seemed like an eternity ago, in the remote fishing village of Sundhaven. Brannog had, even then, been a formidable figure, a huge man, his body muscled and honed by the fierce seas he sailed, and although he had lived among a rugged people, he had stood out from them. But time had wrought remarkable changes in him, adding to his strength. Since he had become one of the Earthwrought, a King among them, he had undergone physical changes: he was yet a man, but there was an earthiness about him, a hardness, and his face had in its make-up something that spoke of the earth people, and of stone and rock. His hands on the table were massive, as if with a twist they could snap it. If he had once been dour and not prone to humor, he had changed in that way, too, Ottemar had noted. But he put that down to the girl who sat beside him, almost diminutive in his shadow: Ruvanna, herself blessed with the Earthwrought characteristics, now his wife. She had a mop of jet black hair, the envy of many of the women of court, particularly as she never had to attend it in the way that they did theirs, nor did she use paints and powder to enhance the shape of her eyes or lips. It was as though she had just walked from a forest, as a deer might, though the image enhanced her, added to her own strange enchantment. She was not beautiful, though pretty, but she had power, just as Sisipher had power, and it shone from her eyes, just as her deep love for Brannog shone like a nimbus about her.

If Brannog loomed over his wife, she was even more dwarfed by the other huge being beside her, who found it awkward to sit at the table as his companions did. This was Aumlac, leader of the Stonedelvers. He was a few inches taller than Brannog, but extremely wide, his shoulders far broader than any man's, and he looked as though he had been carved from solid rock and then imbued with life. His arms were proportionately thick, his hands huge. But his face spoke of intelligence, his eyes as sharp as those of Renodas, and it was almost as though he resonated with the power of the earth that was in him. He smiled briefly at the Emperor, and Ottemar took heart from the knowledge that Aumlac's people were among his most loyal subjects.

Next to him sat Harrudnor, ambassador of Ruan Dubhnor, the ruler in the new city of Elberon. He, like Kelloric of the Trullhoons, was a warrior, and he had proved himself worthy more than once in Ottemar's service. He looked to be a little nervous here, finding himself in company that he considered far above his own station, but Ottemar had privately impressed upon him the importance of his role, and the status of Elberon. Harrudnor, a tall, handsome fellow in his thirties, was, like Kelloric, happiest at sea, and he longed for the day when the plotting and planning and awful waiting would end.

The final member of the gathering was Simon Wargallow, who sat at the Emperor's right hand. He knew well enough

that many of Goldenisle's people saw him as a familiar
shadow, as though he had replaced Eukor Epta and was, like
the Administrator, a puppet master. But those who knew him,
and most of those here knew him well, trusted him, and not
out of fear. Of all the members of the council, however, he
alone sat with his hands well hidden.

Ottemar suddenly nodded, breaking the silence with a
cough. "I've called you together privately for what may be
the last time. What we decide here we may need to keep
from the Hall of the Hundred."

"There are developments?" said Kelloric, his arms still
folded, though his eyes twinkled as though he had caught the
scent of a battle. No matter how peaceful the Empire became, the Trullhoons and Crannochs would always remain
volatile people.

Ottemar turned to Wargallow, gesturing for him to explain.

"The last time we gathered," said the Deliverer, "we argued the merits of two possible strategies. Whether to carry
the war to the west with a full invasion force," and he looked
at Ottemar as he said this with a wry grin, "or whether to
send in a smaller force—"

"The navy was never readier," growled Kelloric. "Almost as strong as it was before the Inundation, and better
organized. Even since our last meeting, both the Trullhoon
and Crannoch yards have worked furiously. And Harrudnor
promises even more ships from Elberon." Once the burly
Trullhoon started speaking, it was not easy to stop him.
"Since Anakhizer *still* has not launched an offensive, which
is a mystery to me if he is such a force, then why do we
not—"

"Yes, yes," nodded Ottemar with a grin. "Your argument
strengthens, Kelloric. But hear Wargallow out, please."

The Trullhoon nodded patiently, though Ottemar knew that
the big man would not be able to contain himself for many
more days. He did not have the understanding of his cousin,
Darraban, the ability to bait a trap and wait, but his loyalty
was vital, and he had the trust of the Crannochs, having been
given the position of commander of the navy of Goldenisle.
There were other Trullhoons whom the Crannochs might not
so readily have accepted.

Wargallow nodded. "It is only the nature of the western terrain that has kept us back," he said, although he knew there was more to it than that. "To plunge an army into the Deepwalks without any real knowledge of the place might be our undoing. Possibly what our enemy waits for, though I don't think so."

"We know what Anakhizer wants," said Ottemar, and both Brannog and Ruvanna looked at him. There were things the council had not been told, secrets that only a select few were party to. The time to reveal them was now it seemed.

"The rods of power," said Wargallow, and he went on to speak about them for several minutes, explaining that Orhung of the Werewatch had carried only one of a series of them. "Anakhizer has them all," he told the gathering, and those who had not known looked at him with appalled expressions. "Except one."

"But such power," gasped Otarus, "could destroy all life on Omara with consummate ease!"

"As a unit," Wargallow agreed. "But Orhung's rod escaped Anakhizer's raid, and we have it safe."

"Here?" said Aumlac. "My Stonedelvers have told me how it was purloined by forces from the far eastern lands."

"It has been recovered," said Wargallow. "Very few of us know where it is kept, but you will appreciate, I am certain, that there are good reasons for this. It is safe, I promise you."

Kelloric grunted. He was thinking of the rumors he had heard that his aids had brought to him of certain smiths being employed privately, below the palace, reputedly by Wargallow and his henchman, Coldrieve. This would likely be something to do with that.

"What can this single rod do?" asked Ulbric.

"While we possess it, Anakhizer is loath to attack. But he will make every effort to find it, of course. Without it, his strength is weakened. And it can be used against him."

"From here?" said Ulbric, screwing up his face so that his eyes almost disappeared.

"No. As we said before, there is an alternative to sending out the war fleet. A small company, bearing the rod. An attempt to find a way to Anakhizer's lair, to drive home a single assault like a sword to the heart.''

Ottemar stared at the bare table before him. He did not favor this method of attack, and had said so previously.

"What are these developments?'' said Kelloric. "Just that we have the rod? If Anakhizer seeks it, surely it would be guarded better if we took our army and fleet with it to protect it.''

"In some ways I agree,'' nodded Wargallow. "But then it would be a simple matter for Anakhizer to mark our progress, especially once we landed. He would focus all his power on us. The outcome would be unpredictable. We could not be sure of victory.''

"And defeat,'' said Aumlac, his deep voice rolling around the stone walls like a threat, "would be final. Omara would be left unprotected. Even Ulthar's forces in the east would be at risk.''

"I yet fail to see,'' grunted Kelloric, "what possible chance a small unit would have of success. No one has ever traversed the Deepwalks. An army might.''

"It's the old sticking point,'' said Otarus. "But I believe Wargallow may have the answer.''

"There's a way in,'' said Wargallow.

Only Ottemar and Otarus, who knew this, did not react with a gasp or an expression of amazement. Once the company had settled, Wargallow spoke of Rannovic's ship and of the return of Helvor.

"Helvor was the last of them,'' he said. "He died, in spite of our efforts to save him. But there were, as Ascanar promised, times when he spoke clearly, almost lucidly, of the voyage to the west. A good deal of what he said was garbled, and some of it meant nothing. He used names and descriptions I could not make sense of.

"But Rannovic found a way into the Deepwalks. There is a river, and some sort of promontory that Helvor named the Claws. I have tried to sketch the details that he gave me.'' With his left hand he took from his robe a scroll of parchment, and in a moment he had spread it on the table. The company gathered around it. It was crudely drawn, but along its lower half was what Wargallow described as a coastline.

"The coast rises as a very sharp, overhanging cliff, topped with hills, an effective barrier to the Deepwalks for its entire length. But here, where the river cuts a way through it, is the passage Rannovic took."

Wargallow indicated a line he had drawn to represent the river. "There is a deep gorge, though how far inland it extends is not possible to determine. On either side is the impenetrable forest. As far as I can say, the river, which Helvor called the Fellwater, has its source under the mass of Starkfell Edge, the mountain range that forms the far barrier to the forest. Helvor ranted about the Gates of Anger." Wargallow had inked in a dark triangle at the base of the roughly drawn mountains, from which his Fellwater river emerged. "Rannovic's intention was to reach this place."

"What are these Gates of Anger?" asked Kelloric. "A way into the mountains?"

"We think they must be a system of caverns."

Aumlac was shaking his head. "You have not seen Starkfell Edge," he told them. "I have only glimpsed a part of it, but it is a colossal range, rising up to such a height that you must lean far back to see its upper edge. And there are mountains on top of that edge."

"But if the caverns stretch under them—" began Wargallow.

"For how many miles!" said Aumlac. "And what of the Ferr-Bolgan? The earth must writhe with them in such a place."

"Anakhizer is somewhere beyond Starkfell Edge," said Wargallow.

"The Edge is the limit of knowledge," said Aumlac. "In remote years my people might have known a little about what was beyond them in the far, far west. There may have been strongholds built there, though I suspect only in legend, and all that has passed down to us now speaks only of a void."

"The edge of the earth," said Kelloric. "I have heard tales of such a place."

"Anakhizer has chosen it for his refuge," said Wargallow. "No doubt because he feels secure in the knowledge that no man, no army, would dare attempt to breach Starkfell Edge."

"What happened to Rannovic?" said Ottemar. He had yet

to have the full report from Wargallow, though he had been tempted to go to him and demand it.

"He and a group of his followers—" Wargallow looked across the table at Brannog.

"My daughter?" said the huge man, his face lined with anxiety. Ruvanna's fingers closed on his arm gently.

Wargallow nodded. "Yes, she was with him. And Kirri-kree, the mountain owl."

"What happened?" said Brannog.

"The ship negotiated the gorge, but appears to have been attacked in the land beyond. Not by the forest but by Ferr-Bolgan and other equally vile creatures, followers of Anakhizer. Rannovic and one group had gone on into the forest, while Helvor and his men remained with the ship. It was evidently attacked and badly damaged. Helvor seems to have had no choice but to flee back to the coast, and it seems that he somehow fabricated a craft from the damaged ship in which to find a course back to Goldenisle. The nature of the land they had visited, the attack, and the return, half-starved, reduced the survivors down to one man, and he with little of his wits left to him."

Wargallow sat back, studying their faces as they looked at the map. Aumlac's eyes met his. "My people do not venture close to the Deepwalks. It is a strange land, hostile to all things that are not part of it. If the Ferr-Bolgan have penetrated it, they will have not done so easily, and every day they spend there will be costly to them. If Anakhizer seeks to bring his army through that land, he will not do so without heavy loss."

"Another reason," said Harrudnor, "why we would be best advised to keep clear of the forest lands." He looked at Kelloric, whose brows contracted in a thunderous frown. "We should let Anakhizer fight his way through the Deepwalks, and then, when he is attempting to marshall his forces to cross the sea, strike them with a war fleet, here—and here—and here." He jabbed at the map and its rough coastline.

Ottemar stroked his chin thoughtfully. "Yes, that is how I would see the campaign. Wargallow?"

"The reasoning is sound. And Aumlac is correct about the

losses our enemy would suffer if he tried to pass through the Deepwalks.''

"Is there no other way he could launch an assault?" said Otarus.

Aumlac shrugged. "He could go north, or south, and skirt the Edge. But it would take months. And he would still be faced with a difficult sea crossing. With that rabble of an army, it would be chaotic. No, he must come directly at us. He will not care about losses. The Ferr-Bolgan are barely above his contempt.''

"Anakhizer is a vessel, no more," said Wargallow. "A lens for what waits beyond. So I agree with Aumlac. His assault, when it comes, will be direct.''

"Then I move that we wait for him on the open sea," said Kelloric. "What ships will he use to cross it? Where is his fleet? Can he hew down trees in the Deepwalks and turn them into ships?''

The question met with silence for a moment. Until now, no one had asked it. Yet no one doubted that Anakhizer would be able to cross the sea to the Empire.

"Who knows what preparations are being made?" said Brannog. "Under the roots of Starkfell Edge, perhaps.''

"And there are the sea beings to consider," said Aumlac. "The issiquellen.''

"I am of the opinion," said Wargallow, "that we would imperil any fleet we anchored off the coast of the western lands. I would rather delay sending one until it has a definite enemy to attack.''

"And remain inactive!" cried Kelloric. "Sea and fury, Wargallow, our people are getting as short-tempered as wild dogs! If they don't see some action soon, they'll be difficult to control.''

Wargallow smiled wryly. "Yes, I realize that. My own people grew very restless while I was away from my lands; I know how inactivity under such stress can spread disaffection. But we don't have to be inactive. Let us send in the proposed small unit, with the fleet standing by, but well away from dangerous waters. If we can find a way in, we would take the initiative. Then if we can cut the head from the beast that snarls at us, we can cut up the body as it pleases us.''

"You think this could be achieved?" said Renodas. "A single strike? Who would go on such a journey?"

They were all looking at Wargallow, guessing that he would have already made his mind up on that matter.

"No more than fifty of us. One ship. Fifty could move with secrecy and speed. Less than that would be too dangerous."

"Horses?" said Kelloric, at once looking for flaws in any plan. "If you want a crew of fifty, you'll have precious little room for one horse, never mind fifty."

"No horses," said Wargallow. "Not in the forest."

"But you do have a plan?" said Kelloric.

"Of course!" Wargallow grinned. "I have been thinking over this war for a long time. But now that we have a key, albeit to a strange door, we have to use it. And we must decide now, tonight. And I am not sure that what we agree on should go beyond these walls until the last possible moment. Ottemar?"

The Emperor nodded. "Yes. Delay now favors Anakhizer. Let us hear your suggestions."

Everyone again sat, silent but attentive.

"Fifty of us," said Wargallow again. "Those of us who have certain skills, powers. Together we would be difficult opponents, even for Anakhizer. We would search for the Gates of Anger. They must lead, ultimately, to his hiding place."

"As Renodas said," put in Kelloric, "who would go? You would lead the party?"

Wargallow again nodded. "I would, and I would want Coldrieve with me." The Deliverer, who had said nothing since entering the room, made no sign of acknowledgment, his face absolutely impassive. "I would want Brannog with me," Wargallow went on. "With Earthwrought of his choice. Your combined powers would be invaluable."

Brannog felt Ruvanna's grip on his fingers tighten. "I would go, of course," he said.

"And would Ruvanna come?" said Wargallow.

Brannog scowled, his own arm about the girl. Whether or not he would have refused was not to be known, for she was quick to answer for herself. "I would insist," she said, trying to ignore the creeping terror that was already reaching for her.

"There are things you know about the Children," Wargallow told her. "We know they have fled to the west. Your knowledge would be important, Ruvanna."

"You would need Stonedelvers," said Aumlac. "With fortune you may get through the Deepwalks, but if you mean to go under the Edge, you'll need us."

"Yes, I would want you, Aumlac, and picked Stonedelvers."

"If you want the best ship in the fleet," growled Kelloric, though good-naturedly, "you had better consider me."

"Yes, I'd want both," agreed Wargallow. "And the bulk of the unit would be made up of the Empire's best fighting men. I would want you to pick them yourself, and all that I would suggest would be that you be diplomatic about who you took from which House."

Kelloric chuckled. "You think I'd fill my ship with Trullhoons! Well, I think I could find enough hard-bitten Remoons and Crannochs to swell a crew."

"And we would have the rod," said Wargallow. "By now Anakhizer will know it has returned to Goldenisle, but he'll not expect us to carry it into battle against him. That is why I place such a high value on surprise."

The gathering considered this in silence, which was broken by the Emperor. "I could hardly expect such a force to defend the Empire for me while I sat idly by," he said.

It seemed as though no one wanted to answer, or comment, even Wargallow, but Ottemar would not be deflected from his intentions, as though he had been holding himself in readiness throughout the discussion for this moment.

"You would wish to accompany the party?" said Brannog at last.

Otarus and his Law Givers were frowning in unison: they looked almost comical. "But, sire," protested Otarus. "You are the Emperor. Goldenisle dare not risk you in such a venture."

"My people would expect a strong leader," snorted Ottemar. "And besides, I've been on enough of these expeditions already. I've seen peril enough at Xennidhum and under Teru Manga.''

"Sire, I have to protest," said Otarus. "With the greatest of respect—"

"Protest!" snapped Ottemar, trying not to let anger override calmness. "You're not in any position to protest—"

"Otarus has the best interests of the Empire in mind," said Wargallow gently.

Ottemar turned on him, surprisingly short in his reply. "Do you advise me, or instruct me?"

Wargallow had expected this and kept perfectly calm. He had seen Ottemar under stress before. "Sire, I express no more than my opinions. I do not rule here."

"Of course not," said Brannog, sensing the potential explosiveness in this debate. Ottemar had always seemed to him a volatile man. Xennidhum had almost destroyed him, and though Brannog had been told how it had been Ottemar's strength of character that had led to the current union, he yet had doubts about him.

As if reading those doubts, Ottemar sat back. "I am tired," he apologized. "I know you all advise me, and advise me well. Goldenisle needs your combined service, but I have to repeat," he added with an effort, "that I would wish to be on that voyage, whether it is decided to send a fleet, or a single ship."

"If we fail," said Wargallow, "none of us will live. Solimar, who is yet a babe in arms, would be Emperor—"

"Tennebriel is not beyond managing the Empire, believe me," said Ottemar, but his smile was thin.

Wargallow covered his consternation. Talk like this would unsettle Kelloric and the Law Givers, especially Renodas, who had already voiced his doubts as to whether the girl had been a wise choice as a wife for Ottemar. The old fears of the so-called Remoon madness would be gnawing at him and any other doubters.

"I'm sure she is quite capable," Wargallow nodded. "You are fortunate to have such a wife. But there is no need for you to put yourself at risk in this matter."

Ottemar indicated Kelloric, Brannog and Aumlac in turn. "Yet you are willing to take those who are the rulers of their own people, or the commanders of their armies. Is Kelloric expendable? Or Brannog?''

''Ulthor Faithbreaker rules the Earthwrought,'' said Brannog.

''No one rules the Stonedelvers,'' said Aumlac.

''But you are Emperor over all of us, sire,'' said Kelloric, with a hint of impatience. ''I would be honored to have you with us, but surely it would be wiser for you to be with the court, here.''

Ottemar looked away from them. He had no strong argument to use against them. Did they *know* why he wanted to go? No, he had been careful about that. He could not tell them. Brannog would be appalled.

''But we are being premature,'' said Kelloric. ''We discuss the journey as though we have decided that it will be undertaken.''

''Must we discuss it further, or do we vote?'' said Aumlac, looking not at the Emperor, but at Wargallow.

''If we do go,'' said Wargallow, ''we take the best force we have.''

Ottemar kept his eyes on the table. Since Wargallow had come back from the east, a shadow had fallen between them, a keeping of secrets. Wargallow had the rod, but only Ruvanna and Brannog knew where it was hidden. Ottemar had been given a full account of the events in the east, and of the fall of the Sublime One, but the secret of the rod's whereabouts remained intact. It was a sensible thing, Ottemar knew in his heart, but it was yet another secret that isolated him. And now this! To be kept here, like a prisoner. Ah, but it was common sense, of course it was, he knew that. Wargallow was right, damn him. When had he ever allowed emotions and passion to interfere with his judgment!

''You had better vote,'' said Ottemar. ''Either send the fleet and deploy it wisely as Kelloric suggests, or hold it back while you send in your single craft.''

There were nods around the table.

''Very well,'' said Ottemar. ''If you wish to adopt Wargallow's strategy, place your right hands on the table.'' He had said it without giving it much thought; he glanced at

Wargallow, but the Deliverer nodded as though perfectly content with the suggestion.

Ottemar looked pointedly at Otarus, but he sat back, keeping his hands from the table. Both Renodas and Ulbric did as Otarus did. Kelloric looked as though he might change his mind, but he folded his arms with a grunt.

There was a faint tap as Coldrieve put his killing steel on the table. Kelloric stared at him briefly: why should he be a party to these councils? Was one Deliverer not enough?

Brannog and Ruvanna acted together, their right hands on the table. Aumlac's huge hand followed. Ottemar's gaze locked with that of Harrudnor. It had not been decided whether he would go, though it did not seem necessary for Elberon to be represented, fine warrior though Harrudnor was. A moment drifted by, and then Harrudnor put down his right hand, beside that of Aumlac.

Ottemar felt himself stiffen. There were two left to vote, himself and Wargallow, who only needed to vote his own motion for it to be carried. Ottemar sat back. "It should be the fleet," he said. "And I should be in the flagship."

Brannog was staring hard at Wargallow, as if suddenly afraid of something, and Ruvanna had become very still, as though there was some deeper meaning to the decision being made. Wargallow slowly brought out his right hand and put it on the table.

In the glow of the candles, his killing steel gleamed, the twin blades as polished as the finest blade. Brannog and Ruvanna gazed at it as though seeing it for the first time. Then they had recovered themselves, looking away.

"We go," said Wargallow, his voice as sharp as the steel he carried.

4

Two More Conversations

IT WAS late afternoon, and the city was as silent as it ever became during the day. It had been very hot earlier on, almost stifling, and the shutters were flung wide to let what air there was in. Wargallow, relieved that the day's talks and discussions were over, had come to his chambers in the tower that overlooked part of the bay. The docks were out of sight from here, but he could see part of the warehouse roofs. The Stonedelvers had done a miraculous job of repairing and rebuilding, and the people of Goldenisle were amazed by them. The Crannoch and Trullhoon Houses, which history had so decimated, were also rebuilding, and with the Stonedelvers and Earthwrought working here in the city, the future of the Empire looked to be sound, provided the threat in the west could be removed.

Wargallow sipped at the wine he had had brought to him. He rarely indulged in it, nor indeed in relaxation of any kind, but he needed to sit back for a few days, though time was short. Since he had returned here from the east, events had escalated, and exhaustion threatened all of the principal counselors. At least they were now decided on a course of positive action. The sudden strike, the picked unit, was the best hope of success, though who could say what it would meet in the west? The decision had been kept from the Hall of the Hundred, as secrecy was imperative, and although Otarus and his Law Givers had opposed it, they were now agreed on silence. Ottemar could have made things difficult had he decided not to agree with the vote. But such a thing would have been petulant. Instead, he had spoken out well. He had the makings of a fine Emperor, Wargallow thought. But this business with Sisipher was in danger of making a fool of him. At Xennidhum it had been different: the strange powers of the place had twisted the thinking of all of them. But to have clung to his obsession with the girl! If he were to control the Empire, to set an example to his people, he must not show weakness. The history of the Remoon Dynasty was littered with internecine strife, often built on adultery and indiscretion. As yet Ottemar had done well to keep his love for Sisipher in the shadows, and the Empire assumed him to be a constant husband, with an heir and a bride fit for any Emperor.

Wargallow gazed out at the motionless water of the Inner Sea. Ottemar's dissatisfaction was a problem that could not be ignored.

There was an unexpected knock on his door. Wargallow scowled at it, not answering for a moment. He had given strict instructions not to be disturbed, thinking he would sleep for a few hours. He sighed. If his guards knocked, it must be important. They knew him well enough.

He stood by the door. "What is it?" he said as patiently as he could.

"Sire, there is a lady to see you. I told her you were not to be disturbed, but she insisted that you would see her and be angry if I did not at least call you."

"Who is it?"

"Dennovia, sire."

Wargallow grunted, but then smiled in spite of himself. Dennovia! What could that raven-haired temptress be thinking of now? He had no desire to see her here. He sipped his wine, then reconsidered, unlocking the door. "Very well, send her in."

She was already waiting to be admitted. "I have to speak with you," she said, her eyes wide and beseeching. He almost laughed, but merely nodded to the guard.

Dennovia came in and Wargallow closed the door, sliding the bolt home again. His guards, he knew, would assume that Dennovia had come here to grace his bed, but whatever they thought, they would not speak of it to others. Coldrieve had selected his personal guards for him, so there was no need to question their worthiness.

Wargallow turned to Dennovia. He had not seen her for several days, and as he looked at her now he could see that life in Goldenisle agreed with her. She had dressed herself in silks that did her superb figure perfect credit, and her face was subtly made up to heighten her fine features. Wargallow could think of few men whose hearts would not thunder at the sight of this girl. It was as though her strong sensuality worked its power as a tangible force, almost hypnotic, and how well she knew how to use her art!

He was smiling. "You are happy here, Dennovia?"

She looked around the room. Typically of Wargallow it was dull, with little in it to brighten it. It was adequate, but for all its minimal furniture it might have been an outpost of Empire in the desert. She saw the wine.

"You drink alone?"

He laughed softly. "Would you begrudge me a little relaxation? It is very fine wine. Have some." He was about to pour her some, realizing he had only brought one glass. He looked about in brief confusion. Dennovia saw it at once and drew closer to him.

"Here, let me sip from yours. As a toast to your success," she said, her eyes sparkling. She took the wine from him before he could stop her and filled his glass. She sipped it and held it out to him. "To your success in the west."

He drank from the glass, wondering if it was sensible to do so. If Dennovia was here, she undoubtedly wanted something, and he felt sure it wasn't the pleasure of his company, though once, on the journey back from the east, he had wondered if she would cease attempting to seduce him. Well, she had seen in him a means to win true freedom, and had used the only means at her disposal to attempt to win it. But he had set her up well in Goldenisle, and had made her a Companion to the Empress herself. Surely she could not be dissatisfied with that. It was meant to keep her out of trouble, and yet still have her somewhere where she could be watched if need be. The things that she knew of the east were not things that Wargallow wanted shared.

"The west?" he said gently.

Dennovia grinned. "It was good of you to find me such an honored post here in the citadel. I've always been very grateful."

"You expected to be killed," he said bluntly.

Her eyes flared. "Yes, if I'm honest, I did. Your ruthlessness is well-known."

Wargallow laughed again. "My cold-bloodedness? My single-minded approach?"

She lowered her eyes. "The enemies you have known—"

"Have taught me all I know about ruthlessness, Dennovia. There are many views on war. Whether it is open war, with sword and steel, or a war of wits, of words. Evil is evil." He took more of the wine, then offered her the glass. "But you did not come here to insult me."

"Of course not!" she said indignantly. "You've been kind to me. Even though I had a hand in helping you—"

"You saved my life."

"Even so, I did not dare to expect your compassion."

"You were used to a different life, to Mourndark, the Dire-keep. No one knows how it affects people better than I do. But it's done. You have a new life. I have no wish to interfere in it. Serve Goldenisle well and you'll be rewarded. And keep the past to yourself."

She glanced at his right arm, which, as always, was hidden in his robe.

He had seen her eyes move to it and nodded. "What did you wish to see me about?"

"The war will begin soon. All the city talks of it."

Wargallow grunted. It had been agreed that the expedition would be a closely-kept secret, but that the war fleet would be prepared and that as many rumors about its sailing would be fostered as possible. Without that, the people would become even more restless than they were now. And Wargallow had wondered if Anakhizer had his spies in the city: if he did, then they would take him word of the preparations.

"Is it true," went on Dennovia, "that you are not sending a war fleet?"

For a moment he felt a cold breeze across his spine, but he did not show it. "The war fleet will muster, just as every

ally we have will muster. Ruan in Elberon, and Ulthor of the
Earthwrought, Korkoris and the Icewrought. The east and
south will be a fortress. And Goldenisle's fleet will be har-
bored in the Crannoch Isles.'' He stared at the wine glass as
if he had said more than he wanted to.

"But only one ship will sail?"

The cold breeze became a sudden chill. How did she know
this!

His eyes had given him away. "I should not know this,"
she said quickly. "I know it is secret knowledge. I have
shared it with no one, and the one from whom I got it does
not go far beyond the chambers of her master, the lord Kelloric.''

"It is dangerous knowledge, Dennovia. You must understand that—''

She nodded, lowering her voice. "It is safe, I swear it. But
is it true? I must know.''

"Perhaps it is.''

"Who will sail in the ship?''

He studied her for a long moment, and in her eyes he read
genuine fear. But for whom? Ah, he had it. She had a lover.
She had several, according to palace gossip. But there must
be a favorite. She feared for him! He might be chosen for the
ship. Fornoldur? Wargallow knew for certain that she had
been with him, and certainly Fornoldur would be high on
Kelloric's list of picked warriors.

"You know what I possess," he said softly, his face very
close to hers.

"Yes," she answered, her eyes on his mouth as though she
would inch forward to kiss it. "You told me once that if I
breathed a word of it you would cut me into pieces small
enough to feed every fish in the Inner Sea.''

"Believe it," he said. "Of all the things you learned, Dennovia, that is the one I would prefer you to wipe from your
memory.''

"It is as good as done, I swear it.'' Still her eyes were on
his lips. His left hand came up and touched her face. Its
softness took her by surprise.

"The ship is to go to the west. Anakhizer will not expect

such a thing. We have to find him before he understands what has happened.''

Suddenly something in him snapped and he took his hand away, turning from her, almost in anger at himself. ''There will be fifty of us, no more.''

''But it will be far more dangerous than the journey we made to the east, to Mount Timeless.''

''Far more dangerous,'' he agreed.

''But what chance will you have of success?''

He studied her again, his frown deepening. ''However small, it is our only hope. We act, or we rot and are swallowed. So if you came here to beg me to release one of your lovers from the crew, or to persuade me to some other course, you can save your breath.''

His words stung her, for he used them like a lash. ''No, no,'' she faltered. ''I didn't come here for that. I have had lovers while I've been here, it is true. You must not think ill of me for that—''

His face softened a little. ''I'm sorry. I should not have spoken so abruptly.''

''I came here to ask if I could—go on the voyage.''

Her words stunned him for a moment. Surely Fornoldur did not mean that much to her. ''Go with us?'' he echoed. He looked puzzled, then recovered his composure by laughing. ''Go with us? Are you mad, girl?''

''Not at all.'' She straightened, annoyed by his response. The color came into her cheeks and she drew herself up, ready to argue.

''But why?''

''I'm not safe here,'' she said simply.

Again he was puzzled. It must be the wine that was clouding his judgment. ''Are you honest in this?''

''Still you do not trust me. You never have!'' she snapped.

''But why come with us? Why are you not safe here? Who could possibly have threatened you? Do your lovers quarrel?''

''No one has any claim on me!'' she snorted, apparently furious that he should think of her as a common whore.

''No one here would dare harm you. I have seen to that.''

''What about the Emperor?''

He was visibly taken aback. *"Ottemar?* What are you talking about?"

"He desires me," she said, pouting. At any other time he would have been amused. But there was something strange at work here, some deceit. "He is trying to seduce me."

"Since when?"

"Ever since you brought me here. He has had private audiences with me and made it clear what he wants—"

His voice dropped. "You're lying. I know his heart."

"You must take me with you," she blurted out. "I can't stay here. Once you're gone, Ottemar will take me, by force if he must. It's only because you're here that he hasn't already."

Wargallow shook his head. "You're being very foolish, Dennovia."

"But it's true—"

"It's a *lie!"* he snapped, flinging down the glass, which shattered on the stone floor. "Why do you want to come on this voyage?"

She put her hand to her mouth and backed away from his fury, shocked by its power, its intensity.

"Give me one good reason. If you cannot, then do not come to me again. And keep in your chambers until I am gone, if you've any sense."

He went to the door, unbolted it and flung it open. With her head bowed, she left him without another word. He closed the door after her and went to the window. Why had she lied? Why could she possibly want to come on the voyage? For the sake of a lover? No! There was no man alive who could tame her, nor satisfy her needs. And what were they? he asked himself. Ah, but he knew only too well what Mourndark had planted in her mind, what thirst for power. The thought harried him for the remainder of the afternoon, and he did not get the sleep he had wanted.

Dennovia was furious with herself. What an imbecile! I should have known I could not fool him. Now he will suspect my every move.

She stormed down the corridors of the palace, watched by guards and servants alike, who were used to her presence now. She was not challenged.

It was a mistake to go to him directly! I should have known he would refuse me. He'll not let me go unless I find a reason with which to force his hand—

She stopped in her tracks. His hand! Suddenly she smiled to herself; then, as if realizing where she was and that people were looking at her, she laughed and ran off in another direction.

Eventually she came to the passages that led to the chambers where the Emperor had his residence. She was able to travel them without being questioned, for her position as Companion to the Empress accorded her that privilege. As she walked now, thinking frantically how best to act next, she saw the guard on the door of Tennebriel's rooms. The Empress was asleep and was not to be disturbed. Dennovia turned along another corridor. After a while another guard faced her.

She smiled at him. "The Emperor asked me to bring him word from his wife."

"He cannot be disturbed at the moment, my lady," said the guard, pretending to be unmoved by the beautiful girl.

"Oh, he seemed impatient—"

"If you'll give me the message, my lady, I'll see he gets it."

Dennovia pretended to be embarrassed. "It's rather too personal for that."

The guard studied her for a moment. "Wait here," he said. He entered the room behind him, closing the door, and after a moment reappeared. "You're in luck, my lady. He can spare you a few minutes." He let her pass, though she had to push past him, and he enjoyed the closeness of contact, his leer suggesting that she owed him a favor for his winning her this audience.

The chamber beyond was tall and luxurious, in complete contrast to that of Wargallow. There were drapes of rich velvet, divans and carved chairs, and the floor was a beautiful mosaic, its central point a fountain set in onyx and marble. Plants hung in rich profusion from baskets of beaten gold. Dennovia marveled at the opulence, the like of which she had never before seen. Stretched out on one of the splendid divans, wearing a simple robe and no sandals, was the Emperor. There were a number of charts spread out around him on the carpet, and a large flagon of wine on the ornate table at his elbow.

Ottemar raised his golden tankard cheerfully. He had evidently drunk more than a little wine. His cheeks were flushed, his hair uncombed.

"Lady Dennovia!" he called. Fortunately he was alone. "Come in, come in. It's all right, there's only me. And you're quite safe. I doubt if I can stand up, let alone seduce you, delicious creature though you are." He slurred his words slightly, grinning.

Dennovia sat herself on the couch opposite him. She knew his words to be bravado. A man in his position would not spend his energies on the women of the court. "You shouldn't say such things, sire."

"Why not? I'm the Emperor, damn it. I can say what I like, can't I? Do what I want?"

"Your cousin Quanar tried that, sire, and it didn't do him a lot of good, did it?"

Ottemar threw back his head and laughed. "Well said! No, no, poor old Quanar! Utterly mad. He would have been dreadfully amusing if it hadn't been for the fact that he was likely to lop your head off if you laughed at him. But no, I'm not suffering from the Remoon curse. I am merely inebriated, dear lady. But what is this message of import from my dear wife? Is Solimar well?"

"Both are resting, sire. I'm afraid I told your guard a lie. But please don't be angry with him."

"I see," he grinned, smothering a belch and swigging at his wine as if it were beer he quaffed. "Lies in court, eh? Can't permit such things."

Dennovia wondered if this would be a good time to speak to Ottemar. In his present condition, he might say anything. Later he would probably regret it. "I have heard, sire, that there is to be a ship sailing to the west."

Ottemar's face changed at once. He scowled, seemingly shedding all humor. When he spoke it was evenly and soberly. "Who told you this?"

"I am sworn to secrecy, sire. I know that the knowledge is to be kept dark. The lady who mentioned it to me had 'done so without realizing. She was not at fault, I swear it. And I will share my knowledge with no one else. But—there is to be a ship?''

"Against my wishes," he said, as though Dennovia were not there.

"You did not support this venture?"

"Oh yes, I *supported* it. In the best interests of the Empire. I do my duty for the Empire." He smiled again. "And whose interests do you have at heart, delectable lady?"

"Oh, that's easy, sire. And it is no secret. I have my own interests at heart."

"Excellent! But you're not plotting to overthrow the Remoons, are you?" he laughed again. "Let me see, weren't you an enemy of Wargallow's at one time?"

She smiled. This was a perilous game. He wasn't as stupid as he acted. He had once been called Guile; doubtless for good reason. "I was the slave of the Steelmaster, Mourndark. Not by choice. But I'm loyal to Goldenisle now. How could I be anything else?"

He eyed her mischievously. "Yes. But if your own interests clashed with those of the Empire, what then?"

"Do yours, sire?"

"My interests? I am not permitted to have interests other than those of state. I am an Emperor. All Goldenisle looks to me for leadership. I have a fine Empress, a son and heir—"

"But you do not have what you desire most," she said, risking everything. She had no choice, and there was little time.

He drew in his breath and looked across at one of the resplendent tapestries. "True, my girl. I do not have what I desire most." He took his eyes from the scenes of battle. "Is it so obvious?"

"I am a woman, sire."

"Yes, yes. And women know these things? What exactly do you know?" He sat up suddenly, his attention focused on her. He was far more sober now than she would have expected. "You were with Wargallow in the east. And Brannog was with you. What do you know?"

"I know what you desire."

"Does Brannog?"

"I think not. Or if he does, he does not speak of it."

Ottemar nodded. "And what is it to you? Do you have some message for me?"

She shook her head. "No, sire."

"Oh, then you have come to torment me?"

"No. I have come to help, sire."

"Help?" he said incredulously. "Are you trying to make a fool of me?"

Again she shook her head. "There will be a price, sire."

He sat back. "A price? Well, what is it you can offer me? I cannot imagine what you have that I should want. You are beautiful, of course, and I am sure that—"

Dennovia's cheeks flared. These men always leapt to the same conclusions! "I am not offering myself," she said coldly, but he merely shrugged as if the matter did not interest him. "You will not be on Wargallow's ship."

His gaze swung to meet hers, his eyes slitting. "Is that what they are calling it? Wargallow's ship? *Wargallow's* ship?"

"I, I just used it as an expression—"

"Yes, I'm sure you did."

"And you are not to go with him?"

"I would serve the Empire better, they tell me, if I remain here in Goldenisle."

"You would rather go, of course."

"Of course! You seem to know my reasons."

"And if a place were to be found for you on that ship—" She let the words hang between them like a promise of fulfilment.

He looked taken aback. "A place? By whom? Wargallow? Do you have influence over him? I cannot believe you have that power."

She tilted her head up defiantly. "No, not him. But there are others who sail."

"Wargallow will be in command. No one will be allowed to sail without his express approval. He holds the court very firmly. I ought to curse him for that, but damn it, he is the best hope we have of victory!"

"You could go aboard without his approval," Dennovia persisted.

"Be sensible, girl, how?"

"You could be secreted aboard."

His eyes widened. "Smuggled aboard? But who would be so foolish? If Wargallow knew of it, it would mean severe punishment. Not for me, I would merely be made to look ridiculous, and I could live with that. But anyone who smuggled me aboard, well, I doubt that they would be allowed to remain in the Chain if they did and were found out."

"I don't have the names of those who are to go," said Dennovia. "But will they not be your finest warriors?"

"Who do you have in mind?"

"Fornoldur, perhaps."

"Indeed? Yes, he would be a fine choice. And do you have influence over him?"

"There is nothing he would not do for me, sire. Absolutely nothing."

He nodded slowly. Yes, a woman of such voluptuous beauty would shape a lusty warrior like Fornoldur as easily as the Earthwrought molded the earth.

"Would he risk his life to smuggle *me* on board this ship?"

"He is ambitious, sire. I would tell him that it was with your approval. And that you have already written a pardon for him."

Ottemar sniffed, considering it. "Why should I not go to him in secret and order him to do this now? Without involving you?"

"He would refuse you, sire."

"Does he serve Wargallow better?" he asked angrily.

"On the contrary, sire. He is loyal. But some things are stronger than loyalty. As I told you, there is nothing he would not do for me."

He nodded slowly. She had a point. Men would stand on their honor. But where lust was concerned, and with a woman such as Dennovia, men were fools. Doubtless Fornoldur could be bought.

"Besides," Dennovia smiled sweetly, "if you refuse me, sire, I'll go to Wargallow—"

He chuckled, his dark mood lifting. "Yes, I'm sure you would. And if I agree?" He lifted his wine.

"My price is nothing."

"Yes, I'm sure. But can the treasury afford it?"

"I don't want wealth. I want precisely the same thing as you do, sire. A berth on the ship."

He put down the wine before he had taken another swig of it. His eyes met hers quizzically, but he could see that she was serious. "A berth? Is that all?"

"Yes, sire. I want to be on the ship, too. It is a small price."

He snorted. "Oh, and is it! And who is going to secret *you* on board? Am I to do it after I am safely below deck?"

"You'll have no direct part in it, sire. Except that you must convince Wargallow that I am to be included. First, before I make the arrangements with Fornoldur."

"But why? Why should you wish to go on a voyage that will mean incalculable danger to you? You know where the ship will make for. What lies in the west."

"I do."

"Then why?"

"I would rather not say."

"To be with Fornoldur?"

She would have denied it, as she had to Tennebriel, but she had regretted that denial since. It would have been perfectly convenient. She bowed her head sadly. "Yes, sire. I know it must seem foolish, but I would go with him. If you can persuade Wargallow to take me, I will make Fornoldur smuggle you aboard. I promise it can be done."

"It's an interesting proposal. The consequences would, in the end, be embarrassing, as I would be discovered. But it would by then be too late to return. And I rather think that Wargallow would want my presence on board kept a secret from the rest of the Empire, once he found me." He sat up unsteadily and scratched his chin. "But it won't be that easy, girl. For instance, what reason am I to give Wargallow? He will only take those who are trained fighters, or who have certain gifts or powers. There will not even be room for horses."

"You could tell him that you fear for my life because Tennebriel suspects us of being lovers and has threatened to kill me.''

He laughed. ''He's far too clever for a trick like that. And he knows me too well. He knows my weakness. If I go to him with a lie like that, he'll immediately suspect something else. Then he'll have my every move watched!''

The idea that had come to her in the corridor struck her again. She knew that it would be a dangerous ploy, but it would probably work, knowing the way that Wargallow would react to a threat. But her life would be at risk.

''There is another way,'' she said softly. ''We must play on the one thing that Wargallow fears.''

''Does such a thing exist?'' he said glibly.

''The theft of the rod of power.''

Ottemar paled. ''Oh, yes. We all fear that.''

''I know where the rod is kept.''

He gasped, unable to prevent himself. As far as he had known, only Wargallow, Ruvanna and Brannog knew this. And yet Dennovia had been in the east when they had found it. She could well be telling the truth. ''They did not keep this secret from you?''

''No. I am sworn to secrecy, of course. It is why Wargallow brought me to Goldenisle. To be sure of my silence.''

''And you know where it is kept?''

''I know that such knowledge would be dangerous if the enemy found it out. Disastrous to the campaign. I cannot even tell you—''

He held up his hands in horror. ''No! I have no wish to know. It is better that I do not. But how does this knowledge affect your plans?''

''You must tell Wargallow that you fear my nature. That you have found out, by chance, that I know the secret of the rod. He is already aware that I know this secret, but his fear will be that I will let others know. You must tell him that the only way to be sure of me, to watch me, is to take me on the voyage. I know that the rod will be on the ship.''

''But if I tell him this, he may want to imprison you here—''

She was shaking her head. ''All you will be doing is sow-ing doubt in him, though I'm sure there is enough of that

already. If he questions me, as he must, I'll swear loyalty
and secrecy. He will not kill me, sire, for he owes me his
life. No, he'll find a reason to take me.''

"You seem very sure of him."

"As long as I am on that ship, I can be no danger to him.
It is the one place where he can be sure of my silence. Simon
Wargallow is not a man who takes risks.''

Ottemar got up, stretching and wiping his eyes. "I think
I'll immerse myself in a hot bath," he said. "And later on
I'll go and visit my illustrious counselor. Unlike him, I've
taken risks all my life.''

Dennovia grinned, leaving him. Only when she got close
to her own rooms did she think about Ottemar's insistence
that she kept the secret of the rod from him. He was nothing
like as foolish as he sometimes appeared, she decided.

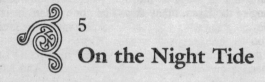

5

On the Night Tide

IDRAS KEMMIL, the harbormaster, studied the ripples of the tide as it gently lapped at the inner jetties of his impressive new harbor. You could take nothing from these powerful people of Aumlac's: they had performed miracles in the city, and none greater than their works here in the harbor. After the Inundation there had been little left of the lower city. It had been washed away as if it had never been. The Stonedelvers had no love of water and feared the sea, yet they had organized themselves and the men of the city, and lo! look what they had created. Now the proud ships of Empire rode at anchor in their dozens; war galleys, traders, fishermen, all manner of craft. And not just here, but across the bay, where a second major port had been built to take the main bulk of the war fleet. It was said that the Crannoch and Trullhoon islands had their harbors, too, and that Stonedelvers and Earthwrought had worked on them as welcome allies. Dare we dream of a new age? Idras Kemmil wondered to himself. The moonlight sparkled on the waters, gleaming like gold and the promise of treasure below them. And the Hasp! Open again, where once it had seemed closed up for ever. The narrow channel that was the only opening out into the sea surrounding Medallion Island had been choked during a series of avalanches during the Inundation, and the Inner Sea had become a lake. A few months ago the Stonedelvers and the Earthwrought, miraculous people! had finally cleared away the last of the mountainous debris. The Hasp was open again, its sides steeper and more towering than ever before.

The harbormaster stroked his dark beard, his instinct telling him that in an hour the tide would be full. Since the opening of the Hasp, many ships had gone out to the islands, and beyond. Vessels had come from the new satellite city of Elberon in the east, and others had made the long voyage from the smaller city states of the south such as Thuvis in Athahara and Deranga on Crotac. In the last few weeks a number of craft, some of them war vessels, had sailed away by night, often alone, like solitary marauders in search of unknown prey. The Empire was on the brink of war, and Idras Kemmil was a diplomatic man. He did his duty by the fine young Emperor. Such orders as he received from the palace he carried out to the letter. But there was not a craft in his magnificent harbor that he did not know and recognize, even if he did not always know its mission.

Tonight, he did know, there was to be a particular sailing. A solitary craft, as sleek as warship as the navy possessed, had been readying to sail on the coming tide. A dark ship, without a name, she bore no markings, no emblem of Empire, though the harbormaster knew from his instructions that she was under the command of the mysterious counselor from the east, Simon Wargallow. Like the Stonedelvers and Earthwrought, he and his Deliverers had emerged from the Inundation as beings of strange power. Wargallow himself had killed Eukor Epta, so the tales went, and there were many versions of that killing told in the city. Some said Wargallow had powers beyond those of ordinary men, some even said he could fly, but Idras Kemmil snorted at such a suggestion. His respect for the Deliverer was marked, however, and he knew that his work in restoring the Empire with Ottemar was held in the highest regard. The citizens of Goldenisle were wary of anyone with such power, but they respected Wargallow. No one could deny the remarkable ascent of the city after its near total destruction.

And now Wargallow was to sail to an unnamed destination, in utter secrecy. Idras Kemmil had guessed that it must be to the west, to carry the war to Anakhizer: he had safely seen Stonedelvers and Earthwrought aboard, and a good many

stout warriors—the best, in fact. And there were arms enough
to storm a dozen cities.

If the enemy had spies about (and who was to say he did
not?) they must surely be confused by now at the number of
craft leaving Goldenisle. Idras Kemmil glanced across at the
dark form of the warship. She would be fast, her oarsmen the
fittest in the Empire. Her sails were down now, but under
full spread with a strong wind they would carry her at a speed
no other craft could match. The best Crannoch and Trullhoon
shipwrights had argued over her lines, and now both were
justifiably proud of the result of their combined skills.

A single lamp shone amidships. Idras Kemmil nodded,
tasting the weak breeze. It would take oars to get the craft to
the open sea tonight. He walked along the jetty. The ale-
houses had long since shut down for the night, the last of
their revelers snoring off their excesses in their rooms, or in
some cases, the alleys, which were noted for it here. There
was a restless mood on the seamen these days, with war so
close. More brawling, too much womanizing, though such
things had to be put up with in the docks. No ship sailed yet
without her rats aboard. Idras Kemmil grinned to himself,
thinking back over his own colorful past. He was not totally
beyond the rashness of the younger men, but his post demanded a degree of dignity. He had not earned his position
without hard work, and he was not about to relinquish it with
the sort of indiscretions he had been guilty of as a young
oarsman.

From one of the narrow alleyways off the quay there came
a soft call. Idras Kemmil turned, surprisingly alert for such
a bulky man. Had it been a woman who called him? The
tavern girls were usually all taken at this late hour, and this
must be a new girl if she thought she could earn a coin from
the harbormaster! Grinning, he approached the mouth of the
galley, but the reflexes of years prepared him for any attack.
Heavy though he was, he made a dangerous opponent in a
brawl. Thievery was not unique here, but this was the navy's
end of the harbor, and the sailors thought badly of anyone
trying to slip their purses.

Idras Kemmil's thumbs tucked in his belt as he filled the
mouth of the alley, blotting out the moonlight. "Haven't you

got beds to go to?" he called, deliberately loudly. There would be guards patrolling the shadows further up the quay, though they would not come unless called. Wise to let them hear him, though.

"Idras?" It was a man's voice after all, low and secretive.

"Show me your face."

"Be quiet, man. I'll come to you, but keep your cudgel to yourself. I'm in no mind to have my brains spilled."

Idras Kemmil grunted, stepping back, watching, but his hands were ready to deal with any threat. Tonight of all nights was no time to have to deal with trouble.

A lone figure emerged from the pitch darkness. It carried no weapon, but looked as if a fight would not be foreign to it. These warriors had a bearing that was unmistakable. This was Fornoldur, one of the most respected guards of the inner palace. He was tall and strikingly handsome, his body lean but muscled.

Idras lowered his voice. "Fornoldur, what are you doing here at this hour?"

The guard nodded toward the dark ship. "I've a berth on that craft, but I'm late."

"She sails on the tide—"

"Aye, and I should have been aboard by now. Has the rest of her crew arrived?"

"As far as I know. Except for Wargallow and his captains. Even the Stonedelvers are aboard, which amazes me. They loathe the sea. It will be a hard crossing for them, wherever the ship goes."

"Quite so," nodded Fornoldur, though he would not be drawn to speak of it. He was watching the craft like a hawk.

"Forgive me," grinned the harbormaster, "but this must be an important mission. It seems to me that you are tactless in being late for it—"

"I had to say my goodbyes to a distressed lady—"

"Ah, and I trust she was worth it?"

"They always are, Idras."

"You think so? But then you are young yet. Well, what are you waiting for? I'll not detain you."

"I can't just stroll up to the ship, hail her and go aboard, now can I?"

"You are sure you have been assigned to her?" said the big man with a scowl, his bushy brows gathering together like a threat of thunder, though he knew full well that Fornoldur was a member of the select crew.

"Yes, yes, I've no papers to prove it, but one word with the night watch will confirm it for you."

"For me? Why should I have it confirmed?" Idras was enjoying himself.

"Look, Idras, if I go aboard now, I'll be bawled out by that moronic oarsmaster for being late. I should have been aboard two hours ago—"

"You should have thought of that when you were—"

"The last thing I want is to be thrust among the rowing oarsmen for the rest of the night. What I need is a good sleep. In the morning I'll row with the best of them."

Idras laughed gently. "You don't deserve any sympathy. She must have been rather special."

Fornoldur rolled his eyes upward. "Idras, you cannot imagine—"

"Maybe I can. My memory isn't that bad."

"So you'll get me aboard?"

The harbormaster snorted, scowling at the ship. "You mean in secret? How am I to do that? Toss you across the water?"

Fornoldur shook his head. "How many on watch?"

"Two or three at most. No reason to have an army pacing about up there. Your friend, Zuhaster the oarsmaster, and a couple of palace guards. I'm surprised you don't know them."

"I know them all, but with Zuhaster running the ship, I couldn't rely on them to turn a blind eye to my sneaking on board. Zuhaster is a surly bull. And I'm quite certain he'll work me like a dog."

"Why should he so favor you?" Idras grinned hugely.

"He's never quite forgotten that I dumped him on his great backside in a training bout once. Flat swords. He's none too quick with a sword. Mind you, let him loose with an axe—"

"Which is why he's going," nodded Idras. "He's split a few skulls in his time, I can tell you. Matter of fact, I fought with him years ago. Not a man to fall foul of."

"Which is why I want to get past him without his knowing."

"Won't he have missed you already?"

"Aye, but if I'm in my bunk when he finds me, he'll not be able to prove I was late aboard."

"So what am I to do for you?"

"Get him ashore. You can surely think of something."

"Oh, really? Shall I ask him about his wife? Or whether he thinks the morning will bring rain? The ship is about to leave, Fornoldur! Once Wargallow and the others arrive, it'll cast off. Zuhaster has all the information he wants."

"You'll be well rewarded, believe me."

Idras cocked his large head on one side. "Oh, and what have you got that could tempt me, young Fornoldur? I am not a wealthy man, but I am comfortable. I have a good post, which I would not jeopardize. I have my own small craft, a gem among boats."

Fornoldur put an arm around the shoulders of the harbormaster. "My dear friend," he said, "I appreciate your good fortune. What could I offer you?"

"And it would be amusing to hear you confronted by Zuhaster. It would take a lot to compensate for missing the sight of such a meeting," Idras chuckled.

"Your happiness is important to me, of course," nodded Fornoldur in a serious way.

Idras suddenly felt a change in the young man. There was almost a threat in his words. How could this be? Why should he have to resort to such a thing, when he must have known Idras Kemmil would be only too glad to help him make a fool of the odious Zuhaster? Was there some plot here that had yet to show its face?

"I would hate to think of you being deprived of the good things in life you have, Idras. Such as your boat."

"What do you mean?" A Plot? Against this ship, Wargallow's ship?

"*Eagle of Malador?* An excellent craft, I know it well."

Idras swallowed hard. "This is a threat?"

"No, no," said Fornoldur, smiling, but Idras could not rid himself of the thought. "I would hate to think of your craft at the bottom of the Inner Sea. Or your beautiful home, so close to the harbor—''

"I cannot believe you would—''

"I've many friends who won't be going with me, Idras. If they find out you've not helped me, they won't be pleased.''

Idras pulled free of the guard. "This is no way to behave!" he hissed. "You are a man of position yourself—''

"I don't want to spend the rest of the night pulling at an oar! Be sensible, Idras. Get Zuhaster down here so I can hop aboard behind his back. It can't be that hard.'' Fornoldur grinned, but the big harbormaster could not cure himself of the feeling that something was amiss.

"Damn you, get into cover. I'll fetch that oaf down. He has the brain of a sea cow, so shouldn't be difficult to fool.'' Idras grunted something obscene and lumbered off up the jetty toward the dark ship.

Fornoldur slipped deeper into the shadows, calling softly. "He'll do it, sire, but we have very little time. If Wargallow arrives now—''

"That's a chance we'll have to take,'' said a voice from the dark. "You'll be safe enough, I've promised you that.''

"Then we must move quickly, sire. Follow me.'' Fornoldur moved from the alley along the waterfront, and behind him the black-robed figure of Ottemar Remoon followed.

Idras came to the gangway up to the warship. Above him, leaning on the deck rail, the huge bulk of the oarsmaster gazed down balefully, his bald head shining in the moonlight like polished bronze.

"Ho there, Idras! Come to wave us off, have you?'' growled the bull-like figure. Two guards stood on either side of him, spears held rigidly.

Idras waved back as casually as he could. "I like to be sure all is in order when a ship leaves my harbor.''

Zuhaster snorted, wiping his nose on the back of his hand. "Want to see my papers, do you?''

"Of course not. I know your master. But I have something for you.''

"There's nothing we need, unless you've a couple of wenches stowed under your robes,'' Zuhaster laughed. The guards with him grinned.

Idras looked about him, but saw no one approaching. "I know it's a little late, but there are some charts I found—"

"Charts? What are you babbling about?"

"I was going through an old chest of mine. I found some charts, years old. To do with the western waters. They may be of use."

"Bring them up then! Kelloric'll be glad of anything like that. As far as we know, we're sailing blind."

"They're along the quay—"

Zuhaster swore crudely. "That's a lot of damn good. Hurry along, then. Wargallow'll be here shortly, then we're away. You can see the tide's nigh on the turn."

"Can't you come down and fetch them?" Idras called, but it sounded to him like a croak. He had to repeat himself.

"I can't leave my post, you buffoon—"

"It will take but a few moments."

Zuhaster swore even more crudely. He glanced at the two guards, whose expressions suggested that if there was anything of value among the harbormaster's charts, it might be worth having. Idras was an old campaigner, and although some of his waterside tales were on the tall side, enough of his past was known for the sailors to respect him.

"Why didn't you bring us these cursed charts before!" Zuhaster snapped, coming down the gangplank impatiently.

"I only just stumbled across them."

"Stumbled is right! Come on, then. Move your fat arse. Let's get these charts before the Deliverer arrives and kicks me off the ship for incompetence." He reached the quaking Idras and jostled him along the quay.

From the shadows behind a stack of beer kegs, Fornoldur and Ottemar watched the two figures walking rapidly along the jetty. Once Fornoldur was satisfied they were far enough down the quayside, he tugged at Ottemar's sleeve and they ran, bent double, as fast as they could for the gangplank. As they reached it, one of the guards pointed his spear at them.

"Hold your ground!" he cried.

Fornoldur looked up. It was a guard he knew, but not one of his closest companions. "It's me—Fornoldur! Quickly, let me aboard before that ogre comes back."

The spear did not waver. "Your late. And who is with you?"

"This is Jarrol," said Fornoldur. "Quickly, you idiot—"

Ottemar's face was hidden in a thick cowl. He leaned on the rail, heart thumping.

"What's happening?" came the sharp bark of the other guard. He peered down and saw Fornoldur. At once he chuckled. "Well, well, arrived at the last moment."

"Trennec, for the love of the Emperor, man, let us aboard—"

Down the quay, Zuhaster was looking about him suspiciously. Idras was acting remarkably strangely. Surely this was not some sort of idiot trap. He may well have charts, for he was as knowledgeable about the seas as anyone, but something smelled. Zuhaster turned, thinking he had heard a cry. He gasped.

"Tits of the Empress! What *is* going on back there!" he snarled. Idras tried to hold his arm, but the burly oarsmaster pushed him aside. He had seen the two figures climbing the gangplank.

"If that's Wargallow, I'm a—" But he never finished his colorful invective, for Idras had stretched out a fat leg to trip him. Zuhaster went down like a bullock, snorting and cursing loudly, fit to wake the entire quay. Idras chose that moment to duck into one of the alleys. Within seconds the maze beyond had swallowed him. Zuhaster, growling and spitting like an enraged lion, knew that he had no hope of finding him. He got to his feet and ran surprisingly quickly toward the ship.

Fornoldur had hauled himself up the gangway, right under the spears of the guards.

"Where've you been till this hour, you pair of imbeciles?" said Trennec. "It's all right, Verril, it's Fornoldur. Let him aboard. And Jarrol. But what's wrong with him?"

"Too much damned ale," spat Fornoldur as realistically as he could. "I've spent two hours looking for the stupid bastard. For the love of Medallion, get him below decks before Zuhaster claps eyes on him."

"You'd better move fast—he's coming across the quay now, and he looks about ready to crack a few heads." Trennec pushed Fornoldur past him and then he and the younger guard, Verril, bundled the disguised Emperor across the deck.

"Trennec," Verril blurted, "I hope you know what you're doing."

"Don't ask questions now. Just get those two out of sight. Move, man! You'll be repaid for this: we all need an alibi at some time. You'd do well to remember it."

Verril had the sense not to argue, too aware of the roaring from below on the quay, where Zuhaster was pounding the stone with his great boots.

"Trennec!" he howled, his war axe swinging overhead as if he meant to use it. "Trennec, who goes there!"

There was a movement further along the quay, and in a moment a number of horses came quietly across the cobble-stones. They drew up a dozen yards from Zuhaster, who turned to meet them with his axe still raised, as if to defend himself from assault. His face was leaking sweat, his eyes bulging. Steel rang out in the night as swords were tugged quickly from their scabbards, and to his amazement Zuhaster found himself facing a semicircle of blades as six mounted guards came slowly and silently toward him. They had moved like wraiths.

"Who challenges the Emperor's oarsmaster!" Zuhaster bellowed. On the deck behind and above him there was a scurry of movement. Trennec had been joined by a number of his colleagues, all with swords drawn. More lanterns had been lit and faces peered anxiously out at the night.

One of the mounted guards dropped from his steed and approached the big oarsmaster, ignoring his axe. "Perhaps you'll be good enough to explain what is going on," he said through his teeth.

Zuhaster lowered his axe slowly. "Skulduggery, I'll be bound." He swung round and stared up at the deck as though his gaze would burn a hole in it. "Who goes up there?"

Trennec stood on the gangway. "Only the guards, sir."

"Who else?" Zuhaster fumed.

"Only the guards, sir," Trennec persisted. Verril had returned, his face white, but he was committed to the deception now. "A number of them are here," Trennec added. "They heard the shouting."

"What shouting?" bawled Zuhaster. "There wasn't any shouting until I saw—"

"Are we to announce our departure to the entire island?" said a cold voice behind him.

Zuhaster turned, about to snarl out further abuse, but when he saw the dark robed man crossing to him, he felt as though his blood would ice over. It was Simon Wargallow.

"Lower your voice, oarsmaster, you'll wake the dead with your noise. What is wrong here? We leave as soon as we can cast off. Are we ready?"

"Your pardon, sire, but I—"

"Where is Kelloric?" said Wargallow curtly.

"I am here," came a gruff voice from the deck.

"Put out those lights. Get these men below, and make ready the oarsmen. I've deliberately waited until now to come to you." Wargallow glanced again at the quivering bulk of Zuhaster. "Perhaps I should have had a fanfare announce us, though I doubt if it could have been more effective than your oarsmaster."

"Sire, I—" spluttered Zuhaster, but to his amazement the Deliverer had a trace of a smile on his face.

"We're all on edge," said Wargallow softly. "Get to your task. I want to be far out to sea by the time the dawn arrives."

"At once, sire," nodded Zuhaster, relieved, for he had guessed that it was no spy who had come aboard his ship, but some fool of a soldier who should have been here far earlier. Zuhaster raced up the gangplank with stunning speed, though he did spare Trennec a withering glance as he passed him.

When Wargallow reached the deck, he turned casually to the scowling Kelloric. "Since Zuhaster is seeing double tonight, it might be an idea to have the ship searched. You have the name of everyone who is sailing with us. I suggest you account for them all. If you should find any stowaways," he added, "I further suggest you wait until we are well out across the Inner Sea. The water is said to be quite warm at this time of the year."

Trennec and Verril exchanged hurried glances once Wargallow and the rest of his party had gone below.

"You heard him," said Kelloric tersely. "I don't know what in fornication has been going on up here, but you'd better account for everyone on board. If there are any stowaways, they'll find me in no mood to be lenient."

Trennec bowed and divided up the duties with Verril and two others of the night watch, while others prepared the ship for leaving port.

Below deck, Trennec went first to the private cabin that had been set aside for Brannog and Ruvanna. He knocked softly and the girl opened the door.

"Your pardon, mistress," Trennec began.

"It's all right," came Brannog's voice. His face appeared. "Not a very auspicious start, eh, Trennec?"

Trennec swallowed hard. "No, sire. I have to say that Zuhaster is a little on edge. Please excuse his zealousness. It was—"

"Quite," Brannog grinned. "Spare me the details."

Trennec bowed and left, uneasily aware that Brannog and his wife both possessed unusual powers: they may well have understood everything only too well. Trennec knocked on the door of the only other woman on the voyage, the lady Dennovia.

She answered promptly, her beautiful face smiling at him. "Such an outcry," she laughed. "All is well, I take it?"

"Indeed yes, my lady," he said, returning her smile. "Just a couple of the younger guards a little the worse for their ale. I hope they didn't disturb you?"

"No more than necessary," said a voice behind the door.

Trennec entered the tiny cabin, to find himself confronted by the leering Fornoldur. He closed the door behind him. "Perhaps you'll explain what it is you're up to! This is no way to begin a voyage of this nature—"

"Oh, don't preach to me now," groaned Fornoldur. "I owe you a favor, and I'll not forget it in a hurry. Is the other fellow, Verril, going to be able to keep his mouth shut?"

"He's young, but an excellent warrior. Crannoch stock, like myself—"

"Must we have a discourse on genealogy at this hour?" said Dennovia.

Trennec bowed. "My apologies. Where is Jarrol?"

"The idiot has passed out," said Fornoldur. "But I've got him where Zuhaster won't set eyes on him till the morning."

"I had no idea he'd been chosen to come. Are there ale houses in the western lands?"

"Let's hope it wasn't a mistake," grunted Fornoldur.

Trennec heard the voice of Zuhaster down the passage and took his leave. He closed the cabin door behind him, and he heard it bolted from within.

"I trust the good lady Dennovia hasn't been disturbed?" Zuhaster growled in his ear.

"She was asleep, oarsmaster. I'm sure she'll be settled in her bunk again shortly."

"You'd better hope I don't find anyone on this ship who shouldn't be here. If I do, you'll join him in the sea, that I promise you."

Trennec inclined his head politely and went about his rounds. By the time he had completed them, the ship was moving smoothly across the Inner Sea. Wargallow stood at the rail, a solitary figure, but Trennec chose to deliver his report to Kelloric, who listened sternly for a moment and then dismissed him.

Wargallow heard Kelloric's approach, but his eyes were on the sea. "Ghosts, Captain?" he said, watching for the jaws of the Hasp.

"Everyone seems to be accounted for. But I'll know who it was that caused this—"

"Consider the incident closed. And no one is to be reprimanded. It's no way to begin such a voyage as this. If some of the crew were, as I suspect, baiting the oarsmaster, let them consider themselves lucky that they've got away with it this time."

Kelloric chewed at his mustache as if he would argue. "As you wish, Wargallow. You are in command here. Otherwise I'd have an accounting. If anything, it will have served to have Zuhaster work the entire crew harder. We've already crossed half the Inner Sea faster than any other craft has, I'll wager."

"Good."

Kelloric left the Deliverer to his thoughts and Wargallow

studied the dark smears ahead that were the hills above the Hasp.

Zuhaster had not been chosen as oarsmaster because he was a fool. He was unquestionably the best man at his trade in the navy, a good many captains had agreed on that. If he had seen someone who should not have been on board, there was no reason to consider him mistaken. And it did not take great powers of deduction to fathom who the intruder must be. Undoubtedly the warriors would rally to him, or at least, enough to keep him hidden, for part of the crossing, if not all. Wargallow had thought long on the matter before tonight. If he had left Ottemar behind, the Emperor might well have done something rash, possibly set out with a fleet too soon after this ship had left. And there was the question of his health: not his sanity, for Wargallow had no doubt that Ottemar was sane. But his discontent was obvious, and he had started to sink too heavily into depression, drinking far too much. It may be that here, on this voyage, no matter how dangerous, he would recover something of himself. The Empire was in safe hands: Tennebriel worshipped the child, Solimar, and would do nothing to jeopardize his eventual succession to power. So Ottemar was here, Wargallow was certain. Not mad, but driven by love, which itself must be a kind of madness.

Wargallow smiled to himself. It was a good thing to have the voyage under way in this fashion, though Kelloric was obviously furious. The warriors would enjoy the subterfuge, even if they had to sweat hard for their pleasure. They'd have chances enough to prove themselves later. He did not need Sisipher's gift of the telling to know that many of this crew would be making their last voyage. He turned his thoughts to his other passenger, Dennovia. She was the one who concerned him most.

He owed the girl a great debt, for he could never forget what she had done in the east. But what was she after? Power? She was devious, sometimes amusingly so. Transparent, and yet, not always so. She had wanted to come on this voyage, and he could not be sure of her motives. Ottemar had confronted him and insisted that she come, his determination to have his way even more marked than his determination to

come himself. He had said that the ship would be the one
place where she could be watched. If she had told Ottemar
that she knew where the rod was kept, who else had she told?
Surely she could not be a servant of Anakhizer. The thought
horrified him. Only that possibility, which he did not want
to accept, had forced him in the end to bring her, though he
knew only too well that she could only be a burden to him.

IDRAS KIMMEL leaned against the doorway, mopping at his
brow, his huge chest heaving. He was getting too old to race
about like this. But if Zuhaster had got hold of him, he would
have grilled him over a brazier to get the truth out of him,
old comrades or not. As it was, if the ship returned, there'd
be embarrassing questions to be answered.

But by now the ship would be out on the Inner Sea. Idras
had kept well out of the way. With a last glance along the
dark alleyway beside his home, he opened the door and went
in. As he did so, he did not notice the shape gliding across
the rooftops overhead. Blacker than the night, it swooped into
the open window of an old tower, one that had not yet been
restored and which had been abandoned in favor of more
important works. There were a number of such ruins in this
part of the city.

Within, a spindly figure stirred. As the aerial creature,
large as an eagle, alighted on the ledge of the sill, the figure
moved to it on all fours like a huge insect, silent as a spider.
From its filthy rag of a shirt it pulled a parchment it had
lately been scrawling upon. There was a leather thong at-
tached to one end of it and with a flick the figure dropped it
over the sinuous neck of the dark shape. It hissed a command, and the black wings spread once more. Like a spirit,
the creature was gone, high up, winging out over the bay, to
the west.

The figure peered out of the high window at the moonlit
waters far below. "Sail on, Wargallow," it whispered to itself. "There'll be a fine welcome for you. A fine, fine welcome."

PART TWO

THE
FORERUNNERS

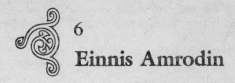

6
Einnis Amrodin

THE OLD Stonedelver opened his eyes, scratching sleep from them with a yawn. Bright daylight shone through the entrance to the cave and he raised himself up on his elbows. Had he slept that long? He could smell a fire, then heard the crackle of dry wood. For once he felt hungry.

A shadow crossed the entrance, and a Stonedelver entered the cave. It was Bornac, a huge fellow who had assumed responsibility for the well-being of the refugees, although his respect for the old Stonedelver was vast.

"Have I slept through the entire night?" said the latter. To most men he would have seemed large-boned and tall, but for a Stonedelver the years weighed heavily on him, in spite of the evident power he yet retained. His eyes sparkled, keenly searching out the land beyond the cave mouth.

Bornac laughed gently. His humor and his resolve had been priceless on this long flight from the madness in the mountains to the east of them, the range of the Slaughterhorn. "It's been a long time since you did so, Einnis. And not a day too soon."

"We were not attacked?" said the other incredulously.

"There were the usual cries and sounds of terror from the stone below. But we were not attacked. There are new lands in the valleys beyond the last of these mountains. The Ferr-Bolgan do not go there."

Einnis Amrodin, Stonewise of these people, went to the cave mouth. Beyond it he could see a group of Stonedelvers and Earthwrought squatting around a small fire. They were talking cheerfully, pointing, chewing on the meat of some animal they had caught and cooked. As a backdrop to them, the last of the mountains fell away to the west and to the south, and beyond them was a dense haze that obscured everything. But Einnis knew that in the west, no longer distant, was the towering barrier of Starkfell Edge, which even the Stonedelvers would find hard to climb or penetrate. Below the foothills in the south would be the fringe of the Deep-walks, their northern boundary. The choice of paths must be made soon. Although this place was a haven, it would not remain so; the mountains were full of evil these days, crawling with Ferr-Bolgan and worse. A night like last night, with unbroken sleep, was a rare thing.

"I am refreshed!" Einnis grinned, stroking his thick beard. "And that broth smells good."

"I'll fetch you a bowl at once," replied Bornac, delighted to see the Stonewise in such spirits. The journey had been tortuous, riddled with ambushes, more deaths, but they had come through. Whatever the future held for them, whatever grim places they would have to enter, they could hardly be worse than the trials of the Slaughterhorn range.

Einnis sighed. Let them enjoy the day. There have been so few where we could draw breath with any ease. His mind roamed back, as it inevitably would, to Rockfast. He could still feel the agony of the stone as Anakhizer had sucked up from the depths of the earth fires and power that had reduced it to a molten mass. How many Stonedelvers and Earthwrought had fallen at that frightful siege? Ianelgon himself, Earthwise of Rockfast, and Luddac, its king, both had been dragged to their doom by the swarming hordes of the enemy. The flight had been a procession of nightmares. The refugees had gone from one mountain to another, hiding in high places, only to be attacked by the Ferr-Bolgan, who had once kept away from daylight, but who now swarmed like insects, regardless of light, of fire, of death. How many months had it been? Some of the Stonedelvers had said it would have been better to have died at Rockfast, as Luddac had, but Bornac had scolded them for their words. It had not been easy to instill in these survivors a determination to come through. But to go where? How could they be promised a new home, here in this continent of horror? Starkfell Edge threatened only darkness: who knew what monstrous beings and powers dwelt there now? And to go down into the valleys, to the edge of the forest lands, would that be safer?

I must not let them see my despair, Einnis told himself. We have come this far. And Aumlac's folk got away. If they truly went under the sea and found the Emperor—but his thought broke off. If Ottemar Remoon had indeed gained his throne, what then? Would he return to the north, as he had said he would? To do what? Bring an army against Anakhizer? In these mountains? It would be annihilated. No one knew how vast the resources of Anakhizer were. The Ferr-Bolgan bred at a frightening rate. Only the sea contained them, but for how long?

Bornac brought the promised broth and Einnis sipped at it in delight.

"What do you think?" said the Stonedelver, studying the peaks above them as though expecting to see the enemy gathering. Like his fellows, Bornac was always alert, always ready for an attack. Even the children, and there were precious few of them now, lived this way, with one hand on a club or spear. "Dare we venture further west? The Edge looms beyond us."

"Aye, and the enemy's jaws, I fear," said Einnis.

"We could turn north, up into the frozen peaks and beyond. A cold place, but Anakhizer would have no interest in it. We could spend a few years there, trying to rebuild." Bornac did well to keep the defeat out of his voice.

"Is that what they want?" said Einnis, indicating his people.

"My father spoke of the frozen lands," replied Bornac. "He traveled there many years ago. Just to see. The stories he told me were not cheering."

"If we went north," said Einnis thoughtfully, "we could probably evade our enemies. But it is no place to grow. Even the stone is dead. We have little enough power between us to wake it. In a few years the place would become our tomb."

"Since we have won through to this place, there is more

hope among us. And with it a feeling of eagerness. Do you not feel it, Einnis?''

"Eagerness? To do what?''

"Search, attempt something fresh.''

"Go south? Into the forest lands? The Deepwalks?''

"Are they so bad?''

Einnis finished his broth slowly. It was better not to speak too openly of what he knew. "I cannot say. For centuries they have been closed to all but their own kind. I doubt that Anakhizer himself has been able to breach them. Should we go into them, we may not be welcome. Total mystery surrounds the forests of the south.''

"You fear them?''

"Of course,'' Einnis answered at once. "We should all do so. But do you think our people want to go down?''

"We look to you, Einnis. No one here would dispute your decision in any matter. We would not be alive now if you had not made us come away.''

Einnis nodded solemnly. It was true he had had to cajole and bully them into keeping alive, fighting for life instead of casting themselves into the doomed fray at Rockfast. But he had saved them for what? "What do they want, Bornac? I will not go against their wishes.''

The younger Stonedelver was surprised. Einnis had always told them what was best. He encouraged people to speak their minds, but he always drew on his own knowledge and instincts to point the way. His power, once remarkable, must have been greatly drained by the defense of Rockfast and the subsequent flight, but surely they had not deserted him altogether. "They are fighters,'' Bornac said at length. "Whatever we decide to do, they will thrown themselves into it with as much vigor now as they did at Rockfast; Anakhizer hasn't removed the spirit of a single one of them. And the children, Einnis! We fear for their sanity, but how quickly they forget the past and thirst for a new dawn.''

Einnis looked away. Does he think I have lost my spirit? Is that what Bornac is telling me? If he and the others think that, they will lose heart. "So a journey down to the edge of the forest would not fill them with dread, as it once would have done.''

"They wouldn't make such a journey lightly," Bornac said. "But there is enough in them to attempt such a thing. Knowing the terror that lies around us."

Einnis smiled in spite of his misgivings. A number of his people were looking up at him. Some of the children rushed to him, their hands gripping his robe gleefully, as if it would transmit magic to them, their voices shrilling.

"Careful, children," Einnis told them softly, bending to hug each one of them. "Sound carries far up here. Our enemies may yet be listening."

He went down with Bornac to the others. "Today will be our last in these mountains," he told them. He looked at Bornac, who grinned. "I've a mind to try different terrain. What do you say?"

All heads turned to him, and other Earthwrought and Stonedelvers emerged from the surrounding rocks, until the entire party of survivors, some hundred strong, had gathered. Gradually everyone spoke up, the women too, and Einnis listened patiently to them all. Some of the suggestions, especially from the bolder children, were extravagant and wildly impossible, but nevertheless Einnis heard them all out. At last, when all the possibilities had been exhausted, and there were in truth not many to be considered, Einnis raised his stone staff for silence. It fell at once.

"It seems to me," he told them, and every neck strained to catch sight of him, "that all paths before us are clearly marked, save one. Either we go onwards and fall at some time into the hands of our enemies, which I see as inevitable, or we travel the one path that leads to the unknown. There is a chance that such a path will not be dangerous. A slim chance."

"Which is it to be?" called a voice, and it could have been any one of them.

"I have always been scrupulous in my planning. Cautious, deliberate. At worst, instinct has guided me. It cannot do so now, unless it is to warn me away from our enemies. The Deepwalks may devour us. But we will only know that if we go that way."

To his amazement, there was a cheer, and soft cries of relief. It was what they had been hoping for! To escape the mountains, and try for another path, dark though it may be. Einnis saw Bornac give him a reassuring smile.

"Very well," nodded the Stonewise. "We go down." But the high spirits of his people did nothing to repel the fears within him. The Deepwalks had always been a name to conjure darkness. Even now he could sense their brooding shadows.

The decision had hardly been made before the journey down from the mountains began. Although they heard strange cries above them, as if the air was full of winged creatures they could not see, and though they glimpsed shambling movements high up on the snows, they were not obviously pursued. There would be some consolation in approaching the Deepwalks in that the Ferr-Bolgan were unlikely to venture there. Einnis and Bornac led their people down into the first valley, and there, far below them, they made out the first hint of vegetation, the limit of the great forest.

As though approving their choice of paths, the sun broke through the overhead mist, scattering it, and the company went further and further down the mountainside, realizing as they went that distance had played tricks with the landscape: the valley bottom was far deeper than they had thought, and even though there were scouts among them whose eyesight was as keen as any bird of prey's, the illusion remained. When they stopped at midday to rest the children and take some food, they looked back and up at a towering wall. The first peaks of the range that ended in the distant Slaughterhorn made them all gasp. To the west of them the thick wall of mist had for some reason not cleared, as though it had been fixed like a curtain; beyond it, Einnis knew, were the awesome specters of the Edge, a range more gigantic than the peaks behind him, which were like foothills before it.

"I can make out no movement on the higher slopes," Bornac reported, and several of his scouts agreed. A number of the Earthwrought had slipped underground, the first time they had done so for long months, and the reported strange currents of power under the earth, especially south of them where the first of the forest lands waited, but apparently no hint that the Ferr-Bolgan were close at hand.

"Should we go to earth?" Einnis asked them, but they

were all in agreement that it would be better to approach the Deepwalks above ground, where they could be better seen, and where they could watch things. To go below, they said, would confuse them, even the earth people, for the greater part of the forest was below ground, and where it grew, it completely controlled the earth. Even here, several miles from the forest edge, there were deep roots, probing the stone of the mountains, testing it, listening to its vibrations.

Einnis could sense that the Earthwrought were afraid of the forest, as if the company drew closer to a huge beast, a single entity that watched and listened to every footfall, every breath. If it intended to reject them, it would do so as effortlessly as the sea swallowing and disgorging a lone sailor. Even so, Einnis told himself, we are committed. We go on.

After a brief meal, the children were eager to move on, full of energy, only partially aware of the dangers ahead, but certainly aware of what waited behind them in the white peaks. Bornac pointed to an outcrop of sharp peaks that rose in the south east, thrust up from the deep green forest floor like some intrusive fortress.

"See, Einnis! Like an island of stone in the forest. Those peaks are bare. Do you think we should try and make our way to them?"

Einnis squinted in the bright sunlight. He could make out no details, except that the low peaks were oddly jagged, seemingly devoid of vegetation. He nodded. "If the forest treats us as intruders, it may be more tolerant of us if we went up to such a place. We will go that way."

They traveled along the valley bottom, deep into the afternoon, following the south bank of a lively stream which carved its way down from the mountains, bubbling and frothing like some spirit of the earth that was unaware of the strange forces gathered about it. The children loved it, dancing in and out of it, flowers adorning themselves, scolded by the women and sometimes the males, though any joy was welcome. As the afternoon wore on, Einnis saw the stream cut down to another, wider one which itself flowed south to the remote sea, forming the natural border to the Deepwalks. They would have to cross the larger stream just below the confluence, and then they would be before the very gates of the forest.

"When do we enter the forest?" Bornac asked him discreetly. "By night?"

Einnis glanced at the sun, which was already dropping to the western mists like a melting ball. There would be a few hours of daylight left. "If we enter the forest now," he decided, "we'd not make those peaks we saw before dark. It would mean a night in the forest."

"I'm not sure we'd be safe out here," Bornac replied with a frown. "It's all very quiet now, and I've no reason to suspect that the stone under us is hiding Ferr-Bolgan, but—"

"If they catch us in the open this time, they'll kill us," came a third voice. It was Graval, leader of the Earthwrought. He was relatively young, but experienced in war and as hardy a member of his race as any Einnis had known. His thick chin jutted, a challenge to add weight to his words.

"Since we have committed our destiny in the Deepwalks," nodded Einnis, "we must take our chance. But Bornac, Graval, have a care. Yes, yes, you don't have to look at me that way! I know you are careful. But we face the *Deepwalks*. No one has ever been into them and returned. Something in my innermost self tells me to stay away from them."

They all looked up the valley to where the trees began. They were packed, the first trunks visible as thick, gnarled battlements, and between them could be seen a wall of green darkness. They rose upward to a hill crest, a thick tide of greens and yellows, branches fused together. There were no birds in sight, and as the fugitives watched, they became aware of an appalling silence, as though sound neither entered nor left the forest. A mile across the river, it spread to the left and right of them, drifting into the distance as though it went on for ever, immeasurable as an ocean. All eyes turned from it, as if contemplating it were as dizzying as facing a god. The god did not speak, nor breathe, but it was alive, its power rich, infinite as a night sky. It merely waited.

"Cross the river," said Einnis, gathering his remaining strength. How his bones ached. If he sat down now, he would never want to rise again. "But I insist on leading us." He bent down and scooped up a handful of rich, dark earth in his left hand. In his right hand he carried his stone staff, long and bulbous at its top. It was veined, and to Einnis now, as he began a whispered chant, the veins seemed to come alive, gently pulsing in his hand. He strode down to the larger stream below the place where the smaller one met it; he did not attempt to step across their rocks. Instead he walked in to the freezing water. It did not hurt him; rather he took power from its iciness and its naturalness. He forded the stream, holding up his staff and the fist of earth, and the foam leapt and danced about him, waist high at one point. But he was as sure-footed in the water as on land, and his people went after him, even the children happy to cavort in the river and wallow like otters. Though the Earthwrought feared the sea, they were as one with rivers such as this, and Einnis walked up the far bank into the late sunlight, all his party with him, alive with fresh hope, eager to test the wall of forest that suddenly hung over them like the ramparts of a great castle.

Einnis had been soaked by the crossing, but the water, the earth he held and the power in the staff put back into him much of what the day's journey had taken out of him, so that for a moment he was able to face the new challenge with strength and resolve. He frowned for only a moment, for the stream from the mountains had spoken of evil up there.

Bornac stood at his elbow, Graval too. The people had fallen silent; the children understood the gravity of what was about to happen.

Einnis spoke to the forest as if addressing a warrior guardian, though very few of his words were understood by his people. He set his staff in the ground, which trembled as the stone bit into it, but the staff stood erect. Einnis threw down the earth before it like an offering and held out his hands, spreading his palms. Bornac and Graval saw the livid veins in them, glowing like fires. For an instant Bornac feared that the Stonewise was about to sacrifice himself in some strange ritual to the god of the forest, but he held his ground, gritting his teeth.

When Einnis had finished, he bowed his head, closing his eyes. No one moved. Even the children held their breath.

For a long moment nothing happened, and the only sound

was that of the river, bustling through the boulders. Then even that became muted, as if the flow of water had all but ceased. The forest did not seem to allow even as much as a breeze to penetrate it, for no leaf rustled, no branch creaked.

Everyone heard the earth groan. If it had been the earth. The sound came softly at first, but quickly built up, like no other sound they had ever heard. Tortured, twisted, it grated through each of them, an expression of pain, possibly of anger. And to most of them, it meant refusal.

"Are we denied?" gasped Graval.

Einnis had not moved. Neither had the trees. Like a painting, they were utterly still. The grinding died away as quickly as it had come, far into the distance, or so they thought.

"Dare we enter?" said Bornac softly. Some of the children were already whimpering, and terror quickly spread.

Einnis lifted his head. "The forest does not speak. Not as we do. But I understand it. It acknowledges us, no more."

Graval stepped forward, his club held up in readiness. "Then let it see me as I enter it."

Einnis would have moved to stop him, but the Earth-wrought was extremely nimble. He had dashed up the last of the slope and stood right under the first of the huge trees. Its trunk was as thick around as thirty Earthwrought, dwarfing Graval. Yet he stepped beyond it. At once he dropped his club, putting a hand to his head. Bornac would have rushed to him, but Einnis gripped his arm and held him back.

"Wait!" said the Stonewise.

Graval looked dizzy, reaching out, inadvertantly using the massive trunk to prevent him from falling. To the eyes of the transfixed watchers it was as though his hand sank into the tree, as though it must absorb him. But in a few moments he was free.

"Is it a test?" said Bornac.

Einnis shrugged. "I cannot tell. The forest hears me, but does not speak to me."

Graval began to stagger back from the forest, but as he did so, he pulled up short, suddenly stiffening and pointing over the heads of the mesmerized watchers. Bornac swung about to look, shuddering as he did so. Beyond the far bank of the little stream, emerging from a cluster of boulders, a score of shapes appeared. Howling wildly, they loped down to the stream. The children screamed, and the fugitives formed themselves into a protective ring at once.

"Ferr-Bolgan!" snarled Bornac. "Even here they follow us."

Einnis watched as more of the frightful beings came into view. It was no mere hunting party: there were scores of them, and now he could see the dark form of the being who controlled them, the herder, the garbed demon who drove them on with relentless will. Einnis felt his power sagging, his age crushing him.

There were cries of fear from the children, and the Ferr-Bolgan were quick to howl their glee at having at last run their prey to ground, and out in the open. Einnis and Bornac quickly moved to the front of their grouped companions, facing the enemy. Einnis felt his heart stagger at the sight of them. Now, even though the day was almost over, they could be seen clearly, their vile skins blotched, their great faces contorted with a bloodlust akin to madness. Their short tusks gleamed redly as though they had already dipped in the vitals of their enemy, and their long arms waved, claws extended like curved knives. They barked like wolves, teeth flashing, slavering, and the herder waved them down the stream. Quickly they rushed through it, churning its banks to mud.

Graval roared something above the awful noise, pointing to the edge of the forest.

"Retreat!" cried Einnis, thrusting the first of the Stone-delvers up the slope. As the Ferr-Bolgan horde began to emerge from the stream, their prey turned and raced away from them, right under the chilling shadow of the trees.

"Go in!" Einnis shouted. "We have no choice." He would have shouted more, but his people were panicking, afraid for their children. The stoutest of the warriors formed a barrier, lifting their clubs and weapons. Within minutes the first of the Ferr-Bolgan leapt forward, almost as large as the Stone-delvers, towering over the Earthwrought. Einnis swung his stone staff and sparks flew from it, suddenly awakened by the fury of battle. Two of the Ferr-Bolgan burst like fruit before its onslaught, but their horrible deaths meant nothing to their fellows.

Graval urged his people into the trees, and the children were taken in with the women. Even now the forest was silent and gave back not an echo of the frightful affray before it. Earthwrought and Stonedelver alike felt the cold embrace of the forest, almost numbed with the shock of it, but as they went in they turned their thoughts away from it, their prime concern the grim enemy without.

Bornac had smashed a number of the Ferr-Bolgan to the ground. He had never lost his hatred of them, his fury a vast reservoir of power on which he could draw. They were mindless beasts, but it did not prevent him from attacking them savagely, without a shred of compassion. Though his companions fought with similar ferocity, some of them were brought down, the Ferr-Bolgan sinking their fangs into them mercilessly, tearing at them like scavengers at a feast.

Quickly the retreat was completed, so that Einnis and Bornac were able to pull back and stand together under the first tree. For a moment the Ferr-Bolgan paused, waiting as one for their herder to instruct them. The dark-robed being came forward, his head covered, even his eyes invisible. The shadow that was his face turned up to see the forest. What manner of being was this? Einnis wondered. The herder raised a black staff and fire danced from it toward the vegetation.

Horrified, Einnis moved with dazzling speed, holding high his stone staff. It caught the stream of flame and drew it in, putting it out as a wave drowns a beach fire. Again the herder attempted to set the trees ablaze, but Einnis used his staff to protect them. As the third attempt failed, the herder turned and waved the Ferr-Bolgan forward. They came on afresh, howling, trampling the dead. Einnis uttered something that only Bornac heard, pointing with his staff. A white beam of fire crackled from it and struck the first of the Ferr-Bolgan. They burst into flames, the fire spreading among their fellows as if fanned by a wind.

The refugees cheered, but Einnis sank back against Bornac, exhausted. "I can do no more," he whispered. "If the herder yet has power, I cannot match it."

Bornac raised his bloodied club, ready to meet the herder alone if need be. The Ferr-Bolgan had drawn back, but the

fires were out. Again they advanced, slowly now, ignoring
the smoldering remains of their front rank. Death meant
nothing to them. The herder raised his black staff, about to
unleash more flame. As he prepared, the earth about him
opened up, abrupt as a yawn, and he toppled into it. Like a
speeding of shadows, the earth closed again, thudding shut.
The Ferr-Bolgan stopped in their tracks. Like beasts scenting
thunder, they lifted their noses to the sky.

Again the ground opened, and from it rolled something
dark and shapeless. It was the herder. He had been crushed,
pulped, now no more than a crumpled ruin. From the forest
there came a whisper of sound, like a cloudburst, and something hissed through the air. The Ferr-Bolgan were clutching
at themselves, plucking at the shafts that had materialized in
their gross bodies. Hundreds of arrows sang from the trees,
so many of them that they acted like scythes on the ranks of
the Ferr-Bolgan. The beast men screamed hideously, toppling
over or crashing in to one another. Within a few minutes they
had been struck down, a tenth of their number remaining.

With the death of their herder and the wholesale slaughter
of their forces, the Ferr-Bolgan became completely disorgan-
ized. They broke ranks and fled, crossing the river chaoti-
cally, some falling, trampled underfoot, until the last of them
ran this way and that to the lower slopes of the valley. As
evening fell, Bornac watched the last of them disappear.

"I fear they will return," said Einnis, holding on to Bornac for support.

The Stonedelver suddenly came to life, looking up at the
trees with fresh fear. "But what saved us? The forest?"

"Its inhabitants. Though they have not shown themselves."

Nor did they. The twilight shadows lengthened, and the
forest grew very cold, silent again, as though the unseen
archers had never been.

"Do we camp within the forest?" said Bornac.

"No. As near to the edge as we can. And there must be
no fires," said Einnis, though he knew they all needed some
warmth.

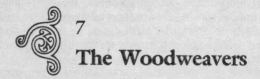

7

The Woodweavers

THEY DID as Einnis had instructed them and camped at the very edge of the forest, and although their guards faced the slope to the river, watching for the slightest hint that the Ferr-Bolgan would come again, there were a few who yet faced the forest itself. They had no fires, but although the moon was hidden by the bulk of the forest, there was faint light to see by, the glow of those Earthwrought who remained awake. The children, mercifully, slept, and one by one the adults drifted into sleep as well.

Bornac and Einnis took the first real opportunity, when the company was settled, to look at Graval. He was tired, and in the fighting he had sustained a bad cut to his right forearm. He had used earth to cleanse it, but he told them it pained him and would take a few days to heal. "There'll be a scar as long as a dirk," he said, his chin jutting out as if challenging anyone to tell him otherwise. Then he grinned. "A reminder of how many Ferr-Bolgan died out there."

Einnis touched the arm gently, feeling it with his long fingers, probing, sensing the veins. "There's poison in your blood yet. You might have died from the wound." His eyes opened wider and he touched the heart of the wound again.

"Is something wrong?" said Bornac.

Einnis shook his head. "Strange. Something in Graval's blood is eating the poison. Countering it. Graval, tell us what you felt when you first came into the trees. We saw you lurch—"

Graval nodded slowly. He had not had much time to talk until now. "I felt as though a score of eyes watched me, though I saw no one. And it was as though my every fiber was examined: a kind of fire coursed through my veins. It made me giddier than rough ale. I reached out to steady myself and the trunk drew me, almost as if it would—" He stopped, turning to the huge bole that was no more than a few paces away. In the dark it seemed an ordinary tree.

"Absorb you?" said Einnis.

"I seemed to be seeing *out* of the tree," Graval said at last, fascinated by his own vision. "My eyesight is good, and I feel the earth as all my kind do, but at that moment something else happened. I saw so much *more*. The whole valley was alive, every blade of grass *spoke*. And the Ferr-Bolgan were unmasked in their hiding places. I felt also a stab of revulsion, even greater than my own loathing of them. It was the *tree!* They filled it with hatred."

"What about the arrows?" said Bornac. "I have never seen so many. A hundred archers could not have unleashed them."

Graval shook his head. "I don't know. I was myself again when I came to you."

Einnis released his arm, which he had been holding throughout the conversation. "Something of the tree's power is in you yet. It works to save your life."

"Then the forest is not our enemy!" Graval said softly.

"We must be careful," replied Einnis, his brows knitting. "The forest loathes the Ferr-Bolgan and sees in them in great danger. Thus it has favored us. But we must take nothing for granted."

"The herder," said Bornac. "It used fire. But you prevented it from reaching the forest."

Einnis smiled grimly. "I think the forest would have shielded itself even if I had not. But perhaps it knows our hearts. I'm sure it does. We must hope that it will have pity on us. We cannot go back across the river."

"No," said Graval, with a solemn shake of his head. "The Ferr-Bolgan are gathering again, in greater number. They won't attack us while we're here, but if we leave the edge of the forest, they will destroy us all."

They watched the lower mountain slopes opposite them for a while, although they were lightless and forbidding, until both Graval and Bornac dropped off to sleep. Einnis rose, his body protesting, and forced himself to make a last tour of the camp. He was pleased to hear such deep snores, although not so pleased to note that some of the guards were also asleep. He would have berated them, but his own eyes began to grow heavy. In a moment he sat beside two of the Stonedelvers who were already snoring, their stone clubs beside them.

We're defenseless, Einnis thought, but it didn't seem to matter. The darkness drifted in like a warm blanket, the air full of soft whisperings that all was peace. His last glance at the forest deceived him, for it seemed as though the first line of trees had moved forward, suggesting that the company had erred and camped within the forest and not at its edge. But the dark closed over him.

GRAVAL OPENED his eyes with a grunt, his fingers automatically reaching for his club. They groped in the grass but could not find it. He sat up, alert as a wolf, but everything seemed in order. Other Earthwrought and Stonedelvers were waking, and the children were pestering their mothers for something to eat. The sun streamed through a canopy of rich green. Graval gaped. He stared upward, then around him. But they had not camped *in* the forest! He jumped to his feet. Others of the company were also staring about them, bewildered.

"What has happened?" whispered Engar, a young Earthwrought. "I can't find my war club. Neither can the others. Has Einnis taken them?"

"We have come deeper into the forest," breathed Graval. "Look, there's the entrance to it." He pointed some thirty yards through the great tree boles to where the grass slope fell away to the river. The entire company had moved into a small glade. No one appeared to be harmed.

Graval searched out the Stonewise. He was gazing deeper into the forest, although the great ferns and rich banks of undergrowth made it impossible to see far. The silence still pervaded everything, and the absence of birdsong or scurrying of squirrels and such creatures made the bright scene even stranger.

"How did we get here?" Graval said very softly. "I don't recall being moved. Did you—"

Einnis shook his head. "We all slept, even the guards. The forest has done this. I cannot think how, but its power is beyond anything we understand. It may be best not to question it. It has taken away our weapons, all save this." He held out his stone staff.

Bornac had joined them. "Do we go in further? Our people are willing."

Graval suddenly laughed and the sound rose up so that many heads turned to him. "My arm!" he cried. "Healed over. And I feel as though I could wipe away the Ferr-Bolgan with one blow of it. See, Einnis, what the forest has done."

Einnis did as asked and it was true, for the Earthwrought's arm had healed perfectly. Einnis touched the flesh. He could feel Graval's power, and something else. He tried not to frown.

"Aye," said the Stonewise. "When we have eaten, we go inward. But with caution. At best we are tolerated. I am not sure we were invited here."

"If only we could talk to someone," said Bornac. "The forest must be inhabited."

"No one knows," said Einnis. "There are only the myths to go by."

"Someone took our weapons," said Bornac. "Surely a tree could not do such a thing."

But no one replied. Einnis turned instead to the company, to find that most of them were ready to move on. The open ground beyond the forest held no less fear for them today than it had before nightfall. Einnis was amazed to see so many eager faces. His people looked refreshed for the first time in weeks. There were no signs of exhaustion, no ailing spirits. The level of chatter and excitement, yes, it could not be denied, excitement, was far higher than it had been at any time since before the fall of Rockfast. Even so, Einnis saw danger where his people did not. The Deepwalks had never been a friend to outsiders. They had not been hostile, but they had accepted no one. But then again, times on Omara

were changing. Perhaps Anakhizer's coming to power had
altered many things.

They organized themselves and began to march. As far as
Einnis and Bornac could remember, the peaks they had seen
previously were located somewhere to the west of them, and
unless the forest was particularly dense, they should reach
them in a day. At the end of the glade they found an opening
through the ferns, not a path, but enough of a gap to enable
them to move on into the forest. It was pleasantly cool this
morning, but still very quiet, though the company's inevitable
babble made up for that. The trees rose up on all sides, the
trunks incredibly thick, their twisted bark tapestried with
mosses and lichen, their first boughs high overhead, themselves festooned with moss and other growths, dense as great
curtains. Ferns grew in abundance, many of them having
seeded themselves in clefts in the trunks or in dips in the
branches, while higher overhead there was hardly a gap to
permit a glimpse of sky. Sunlight did filter down, as if through
water, highlighting a patch of thick grass or a rock that protruded from still more ferns. But even the stone was covered
in green profusion. Creepers wove their way intricately between the trees, dazzling the eye with their bright pink
blooms, while underfoot the carpeting of leaves was thick
and matted; fallen boughs and twigs set traps for unwary feet.
The scent of woodland plants came to the company like a
rich perfume, and although they thought they could hear distant sounds, whenever they stopped to listen, the silence
closed in. There was not even a hint of wind from high overhead, and not the usual soughing of branches. The Deepwalks closed out everything except the light, or so it seemed.

Yet Einnis knew they were being watched, no, studied,
with every step. Were they the first to come here? Perhaps to
this part of the forest, which must be its northernmost boundary. For how many hundreds of miles did it stretch? How
deep was it? At the moment they were moving slowly upward, but once beyond the ridge, did the forest fall great
distances downward to the very feet of Starkfell Edge? No
one dared even guess how deep a fall that must be.

There was a cry behind the leading group and Einnis
quickly went back to see what had happened. He found one

of the Earthwrought mothers staring out at a great clump of grasses, tears in her eyes.

"What is it?" he asked, surprised at his own anger.

"My child!"

"Where is it?"

"A few of them were playing at hunting each other—"

"I told you to keep them close to us!" snapped one of the Earthwrought.

Einnis calmed him with a look. "How long ago?"

"Moments. The others are back. But Lokar—"

"We'll search," said Einnis, indicating a number of Earthwrought. Bornac quickly set other guards to protect the company, then joined Einnis. They fanned out and entered the bank of ferns, calling Lokar's name softly. Within moments they were swallowed up by the tall fronds, which closed over their heads, shutting out more light. The smell of the forest floor was overpowering in here, pleasant but heady. Einnis soon realized that progress would be impossible. They would all be lost in no time at all. They must get back to the company. The child might have to remain lost, which was a cruel blow, but they dare not risk losing more of the company.

Einnis turned to find that the huge fronds had indeed closed in. He must have damaged some of their leaves on his way through, but he could find no trace, no clue to the way back. He thought he was stumbling in the right direction, but he found himself confused, snared in a web of terrible silence. He called out to the other searchers, but the ferns choked the sound, smothering it. He tripped and fell. On his stomach, he turned, peering through the thick fern stems. Was that movement he had seen?

He rose as quickly as he could, blundering through the fronds. They struck him, though softly, and he was sure he could go no further. Abruptly he was through them, staggering forward. He landed in a rich bed of moss in another tiny glade. Looking up, he saw an earth bank before him, with a number of stones lining the glade as if they had been set there. A tiny stream gurgled from the bank, splashing away into the ferns behind him.

On one of the flat rocks, face beaming, sat the missing

child, Lokar. But Einnis was not looking at the boy. It was the being beside him that took all his attention. It was no taller than an Earthwrought, and its body was dark, the color of the tree trunks; it seemed to have been grown from the wood of the forest, though this must be illusion. The hands, like an Earthwrought's, were large and knotted, and the feet were larger. The being wore a single garment about its loins which looked as if it had been woven out of leaves or other forest greenery, though it was as neatly made as any clothing. But the face pinned the attention. The hair was matted and wild, again more like a natural forest growth, with hints of green and yellow in it. The eyes were set deep in the lined face, which was whorled and crinkled like bark, and those eyes were very brown, their stare intense. It was the most unusual creature that Einnis had ever seen, and he knew at once that it was a spirit of the forest, for it had a feel of the Deepwalks to it, a oneness with everything around it, just as the trees and plants did. Seeing the creature standing there, absolutely motionless, brought home to Einnis just how much of an outsider he and his people were. Whatever empathy they felt for the forest, for the earth, they could never be as much of it as this extraordinary creature.

With as much dignity as he could muster, Einnis got to his feet. Only the creature's eyes moved. The ferns shook and another of the searchers burst clumsily through. He stopped when he saw the creature. Moments later, as if at a signal, the remaining searchers all appeared. Slowly they came to Einnis.

"Is the boy safe?" whispered one of them, but the question was unnecessary. Lokar looked up at the forest creature and grinned at him as if he were a companion of long standing.

"The child lost his way," said Einnis. "I hope he has not disturbed the forest with his games."

A flicker of the eyelids showed that the creature had heard. It looked at the Earthwrought and then at Einnis, who stood far taller. Lokar got to his feet and ran to the Stonewise, gripping his robe.

"I found him!" he cried. "He's called Svoor."

Einnis gaped at the child. Had he spoken with this creature?

"He's a Woodweaver," Lokar went on excitedly.

Einnis and his fellows were unable to suppress their amazement. The legends did speak of such beings, creatures who were said to exist in the Deepwalks and who possessed incredible knowledge and powers.

"I am Einnis Amrodin," said the Stonewise, with a bow. "My people and I have been forced to flee our home in the far mountains of the Slaughterhorn—"

"We know you," said a voice, and for a moment Einnis did not realize that it came from the Woodweaver. Its mouth had hardly moved, its expression unchanging. The voice was guttural, unlike any voice Einnis had ever heard before. It hinted at the groan of branches in the wind, or the whisper of gossiping leaves, and it was not possible to tell whether it held warmth or coldness.

"Was it you who saved us from the Ferr-Bolgan?"

The Woodweaver shuddered like a sapling stirred by a stiff breeze. "Do not use that name here. Yes, we saved you. We read you."

Einnis nodded, glad that his companions were prepared to let him talk for them. "We are most grateful. We understand that you have sheltered us."

"You are not of the forest."

"No. But we respect it."

"What do you desire?"

They know that much, Einnis thought to himself. But this was a time for diplomacy. "We are afraid to leave the forest while the—our enemy—waits for us. Would you consider guiding us to a place where we could leave the forest in safety?"

"Leave the forest?"

"We do not wish to intrude."

The Woodweaver still did not move. He did not speak for a long time. Lokar still grinned at him, as if he had already had a protracted conversation with him and all was well. Certainly he was totally unafraid of the unusual creature.

"You cannot leave," said the Woodweaver at last.

Einnis felt the touch of fear at the words, but kept it to himself. "What would you have us do?"

"You are not unwelcome."

Einnis relaxed a little. If they were to be kept in the forest, it might not be such a bad way to spend their days, knowing they were not to be chastised. "Will you guide us?"

The Woodweaver nodded, sleepily as an owl. "You were seen by the Star Watch as you climbed down from the mountains."

"They are your people?" said Einnis, amazed.

"The peaks that you saw and are making for are the home of the Star Watch. There are many Watches along the borders of the forest. Woodheart seeks knowledge of all that transpires beyond. The Star Watch looks north and to the ranges from which you came."

Einnis nodded. *So we were studied long before we came here! And how much of our thoughts are known to these people? Our hearts are true; we must not fear them.* "If you have read us, then you know of the terrors that are abroad—"

"They are known to Woodheart. But Woodheart would know more."

"Will you take me to him—" But as Einnis said this, he knew at once that he had made some diplomatic error, for the Woodweaver's expression hardened, as though an insult had been voiced.

"None go before Woodheart," came the growl.

"Forgive me. I am ignorant of your lore."

The Woodweaver was silent, but then nodded. "We realize. But you have knowledge of what lies outside. You must come to the Star Watch. And share."

"Gladly. There are many things you must know. Will you take us?"

"We will open a way for you. Do not stray from it. There is a Timber Maw close by." He said this as though speaking of grave danger. "Keep your children safely by you. Lokar has some wisdom in this now." The Woodweaver lifted one of his arms and pointed back at the fern banks. Whether through some release of power, or whether the opening had always been there, a narrow path became visible. "Go back to your people. Wait."

Einnis turned to speak to the Woodweaver, but he had gone, melding into the rocks and plants as if he had been an illusion. Lokar danced from the Stonewise to the fern path. "This way!" he cried excitedly.

The child's lack of fear was heartening, but Einnis could still not completely crush his own fears. He returned along the narrow fern path with his fellows and in a short time they had come back to the main company. There was a happy reunion between Lokar and his mother, and cries of relief from the others. Bornac and Graval were beside Einnis at once, and he explained what he had seen.

"A Woodweaver," said Bornac. "Then such beings do exist. But who is Woodheart? Their leader?"

"It is best not to name him, I think," replied Einnis. "I detected much reverence. The name suggests someone central to the forest."

"And what of this Timber Maw that was spoken of?" said Graval.

Einnis shook his head. "An evil, I think. But we are to have a path—"

The company was talking excitedly. Ahead of it now there was movement. The trees had not moved, but somehow the light shone down on to a path which wove through them, disappearing into yet more dense greenery. It seemed to lead in the desired direction. From beside it, detaching themselves from the bushes, a number of small figures appeared, silent as the air. They were Woodweavers and each of them carried a small bow and had a quiver full of arrows slung over his shoulder.

"The bowmen who saved us," said Graval.

One of the Woodweavers came forward soundlessly, hardly disturbing a leaf with his tread. Einnis could not be sure, but he thought this must again be Svoor.

"We will guide you," the Woodweaver said simply.

Einnis bowed. He could sense the presence of many more Woodweavers. If they decided on hostility for any reason, they could destroy every last Stonedelver and Earthwrought with ease. And there would be no escape down into the earth, for the Deepwalks throbbed with far more power below ground than it did above.

"I will lead," said Svoor and something in his manner suggested to Einnis that the Woodweaver wanted to walk with him. He welcomed the opportunity. Graval and Bornac did not object, themselves wary of the unusual wood people. Within minutes all of them, with the exception of Svoor, had slipped into the trees, and it was as if they had gone far away, though the company knew they had not.

Einnis and Svoor moved along the rising path, and although the Woodweaver was evidently as at home in the forest as any of its mighty trees, he yet looked this way and that, as though accounting for every branch, every plant. Did he fear enemies here? Einnis wondered.

For the first part of the journey, a gradual rise up into the even denser vegetation of the forest, crossing a number of tiny streams, there was little conversation in the company, and even the children were silent. Svoor said nothing and Einnis discreetly kept his own silence. Curiously, though, the forest had come to life, and they could hear the flapping of wings above, and the rustling of bushes as some creature ran from their approach. All the sounds they would normally have associated with a forest could now be heard, and they saw butterflies, spiders and other insects, as though the Woodweavers had given them leave to go about their work.

Svoor marched briskly, though not at a rate that tired those he led. Around mid-morning he stopped by a brook and indicated that it was a good place to rest and drink. His people appeared, bringing with them root vegetables of some kind and Svoor told Einnis they would be well advised to eat them. Einnis knew that if his people were to survive here, they would have to depend on the forest for their sustenance. He was the first to try the vegetables. They were bland but palatable.

As he sat with Svoor, refreshed, the Woodweaver began to talk for the first time. "Woodheart knows the enemy," he said.

"Has he attempted to enter the Deepwalks?"

"Through the Gates of Anger."

This reference meant nothing to Einnis, but he had no wish

to insult the Woodweaver or question him in such a way that
he would become suspicious. It was impossible to fathom the
creature, although the fact that Anakhizer was a common
enemy had so far saved the company.

"The enemy seeks to send his angarbreed through the
Deepwalks and to the east, beyond Sea Scarp," said Svoor.

"Has there been conflict?"

"Aye, and there will be more. None are permitted in the
Deepwalks unless Woodheart decrees otherwise."

"Where is the enemy?"

"Under Starkfell Edge. And in your own mountains.
Woodheart has felt the death of your stone homes."

"Rockfast?" said Einnis softly. Sometimes he almost forgot that the citadel had been turned to rubble, the stone murdered.

Svoor appeared to understand. "Your sorrow courses
through earth and stone to Woodheart. And through Woodheart to all the Deepwalks. The trees sorrow with you."

"Forgive me, you know that I am a stranger here, but I
must ask you this, Svoor: is Woodheart your ruler? You must
not take my question as an insult. I ask it from ignorance. I
have only respect for your people and for your realm."

The Woodweaver looked away, as though in communion
with the vast forest about him. "Only those of the Deepwalks
may know Woodheart. But I ask you this: what do you see?"
His gaze took in the huge, stately trees and the profusion of
plants that clustered between them, the shimmering colors.

Einnis began to describe each tree, but Svoor stopped him
gently, politely, "You see many, many things. I see only one.
The Deepwalks. Point to a tree, or a single leaf, point to a
strand of web, or to my people, or to me, or to a single arrow,
and you point to the Deepwalks. We are the Deepwalks. Each
is of the whole. Not apart. Do you understand?"

For the first time since he had been with the Woodweaver,
Einnis smiled. "I do."

Svoor put a gnarled hand to his chest. "I have a heart and
feel its beat, as you do, and as the children of the earth do.
And as Men do."

"You know of Men?"

Svoor nodded. "Woodheart listens to all Omara."

"Then the Deepwalks has a heart," said Einnis. "Just as we all have."

"You understand. The life that unites us all and courses its power through us, every leaf, is Woodheart."

Like a god, thought Einnis. And the forest is one organism, one being. His eyes suddenly widened as a greater vision came to him. Just as Omara is! One world, with each stone, each creature, each plant, a part of it.

"I have spoken of the Watches," Svoor was saying. "Through them the forest learns. You are a Stonewise, in whom power focuses."

"That is true."

"Your knowledge is deep. Have you no Earthwise with you?"

Einnis looked away, closing his mind to the death of his close friend, Ianelgon, who had fallen at Rockfast. But Svoor must have read these things in his mind.

"Woodheart sorrows for you," said the Woodweaver.

"What knowledge I have, and whatever craft my people master, is yours to share," Einnis told him. "We cannot return to our lands."

"They will be of much value," said Svoor. "These are things you must tender to the Star Watch. When you have done so, you will be Absorbed."

Again Einnis felt a ripple of unease, though he told himself not to be foolish. "What does this mean?"

Svoor rose, ready to move on again into the endless forest. "You will be accepted. You cannot leave, therefore you will be Absorbed." There was no menace in his voice, and yet Einnis would have preferred to know exactly what the Deepwalks planned for his people.

8
Landfall

RANNOVIC STOOD in the prow of his sleek vessel, scanning the horizon eagerly, his eyes taking in every wave, every blemish against the bright sky. The sails billowed behind him, the ship leaping forward with each gust of wind, spearing for the west. His crew had not used the oars for many days, and the men were in a lively mood: the return to the sea had lifted their spirits immeasurably. Since the fall of Teru Manga and the brief war with Eukor Epta's alliance, the terrifying Inundation of the city of Medallion, they had been on edge, unsure of their future in the new regime of Ottemar Remoon. Rannovic, now confirmed as a Trullhoon of the highest esteem because of his service to the Emperor, had the trust and confidence of his men, his Hammavars, who had been accepted at last in their ancestral islands, having for so long been excluded from them as freebooters. It seemed that the new Emperor would bring fresh union to the Empire, for his allies were far spread, and he had even succeeded in bringing the Deliverers under his banner, as well as the rebels in the east, the men of Elberon. Hammavar ships were now Trullhoon ships, no longer engaging in skirmishes with Empire ships, for the days of piracy were over. Some of the younger Hammavars, Rannovic knew, were restless, thinking life dull without the occasional conflict to keep them alert. Yet there were other forces to contend with these days, and other reasons why the union of the Empire was vital. Having fled the horrors that destroyed Teru Manga, they at least understood that much. Even so, they were eager for something positive to do. It was one thing to be able to establish new homes in the Trullhoon islands, but they wanted to be at sea, employed usefully.

To Rannovic's amazement it had been the girl, Sisipher, who had provided a solution to their frustration. It had been several months after Ottemar had been enthroned: he had married the Crannoch woman, Tennebriel, and she had been big with child when Sisipher had sought out Rannovic at his quarters on Medallion. The big Hammavar would have preferred a home in the Trullhoon islands, but the Trullhoons had been cruelly decimated in the flooding, most of their leaders drowned or killed. They needed new commanders. Rannovic was embarrassed but honored when he was chosen: now he had not only been welcomed back into the Trullhoon fold, but he was chosen to be one of its main spokesmen. He had the confidence and trust of the Emperor and, more significantly he thought, that of Simon Wargallow. But the responsibility worried him. It would be best, he constantly told himself, when the war began. Then he would be able to turn his attention to the enemy, and all lingering thoughts of internal differences would be forgotten. For the moment, he was based on Medallion, and he watched its rebuilding with amazement.

Sisipher had come to him one evening. As always, the sight of her took his breath away. She was not what men would have called beautiful, and yet there was that about her which drew the eye and made the girl the center of attention in any group in which she moved. Rannovic had seen her beside the Empress, the stunning Tennebriel, whose own looks made her the envy of every woman who met her. But Rannovic would have chosen to spend one day with Sisipher rather than a week with Tennebriel. Sisipher's eyes were strangely compelling, as if there was a power in them, and certainly, Rannovic mused with a wry grin, they had power over him. From the moment he had first seen her on Cromalech's war ship, he had desired her, and with a passion that surprised him. She had made it clear from the same moment that she had only scorn for him and his advances, and had taken the wind from his sails more than once. For a long time he had assumed she loathed him, though he had come to understand that she did not; it may have been indifference, little more, and he wondered if he would rather have had her hate.

When she had come to him that evening, she had asked him to dismiss the servants and the guards that he was now duty bound to have about his residence. He knew at once that there was a sadness on her, and it took great self-control for him not to mention it, or to attempt to comfort her. He knew so little about her, or what moved her, but like any man caught in love's web, he thought of rivals. She had spent much of her recent life with the Emperor, shared peril with him. Did she love him? Marriage to him had been impossible, of course. In fact, so the story went, it had been Sisipher herself who had suggested to Ottemar that he marry Tennebriel, thus cementing Crannoch, Trullhoon and Remoon in a rare union that would do more than anything else could to strengthen the Empire. If Sisipher did love him, what act could have been more painful to her?

Rannovic made her as comfortable as he could. He had decided no longer to press his own feelings on her, either here, or elsewhere. Although he had become a man of position and power, she had always known him as a rough barbarian, or so he would have seemed to her in his freebooting days. She would, he assumed, never be able to think of him as anything else.

What she had asked of him that peaceful evening had shocked him. She wanted to leave Medallion and travel to the west, to the land of the Deepwalks, a place of mystery and terror from which no one had ever returned. And she wanted to go in secret, because she knew neither Ottemar nor Wargallow, nor any of the Empire's counselors, would permit her to go. Was she mad? he had asked her.

"Anakhizer is there, somewhere," she had argued. "And one ship might get through."

He had known from the outset that he would go. If she had asked him to row her across the ocean alone, he would have done so. Inwardly he cursed himself for such utter foolishness. He had made a stand against the venture.

"You know the Emperor would veto such a voyage," he had told her, trying to scowl. "Yet still you ask me. Why?"

"Who knows the western seas better than you?" she had replied, but for once she had not been able to meet his gaze.

"No one knows the coastal waters of the west. There are no charts. It is not why you ask me. I understand very well why you ask me, Sisipher." *Because you know how easy it is to use me.*

He had embarrassed her, but it was as it should be: he dare not lose his dignity entirely before her. If he did so, she was lost to him for always. He had waited for only a moment, then laughed in his loud way. He had lifted a golden chalice. "To be honest, girl, I am not made for sitting in such high places. I've a mind to go back to the sea. Though not as a rebel. I have no wish to see my people outlawed again. No, but I'll go as a scout, a seeker after knowledge. Ottemar needs that."

"Then you'll sail, in secret?"

"Aye. And with the best crew that ever sat at oars."

"How soon?" She had not been able to keep the eagerness from her voice. "It must be within the month."

He had seen it then. Within the month, before the child was born to the Empress. Sisipher could not bear that. He knew it as he knew the sea, and he had bowed, promising that they would leave within the week, which they had.

And now they were far away from the Chain. Rannovic saw the smudge of land ahead: his lookout had been right and the western continent loomed. The meeting with Sisipher on Medallion was far in the past, or so it seemed. They had left by night, and only when they were beyond the outer islands of the Chain were they missed. Rannovic's men were exultant to be at sea, and as the weather had been indifferent, neither too calm, nor too tempestuous, they had sped quickly on their way, light-hearted and inflated with zestful confidence. As the west drew closer, they were quieter, realizing that they were coming under the shadow of a land of myth. It was impossible to laugh fears away altogether. What was it, they whispered, that the witch wanted here? Rannovic knew that they called Sisipher a witch, though not if they thought he could hear them.

Although there had been no gulls following them for the last few days, a sudden rush of wings made him look upward. It was the huge white owl, Kirrikree, the bird of the east who was Sisipher's constant companion. From his place high on the mast he had launched himself, going on ahead to study the coastline. Rannovic did not fully understand the girl's relationship with the bird, but he knew that in some way she communicated with him. Already there were several stories circulating about the owl and his so-called magical powers. Some said he had great strength, and that he had once carried Wargallow bodily from the jaws of death. Such stories were bound to come out of these difficult times, he imagined.

Rannovic wanted to call out to the bird as he went, his spirits soaring with the beat of those wings. As if in response to him, Sisipher appeared at his side.

"He'll be glad to find land," she said softly. "He has never been at home over the sea."

"He is very loyal. You are fortunate to command such valuable servants."

She had become used to his manner and smiled. On this voyage she had quickly learned that he was no fool, and a man who had the respect of his crew, some of whom needed firm handling. But the sight of land troubled her. "I don't command Kirrikree," she insisted. "And this is your ship, Rannovic. The crew jump to your orders, not mine."

He grinned. "Then shall I have them turn us around?"

She frowned. "In some ways, it would be for the best."

His own smile dissolved. Her troubles dug into him, barbed. How he longed to soothe them without offending her. "You think we may have been rash in coming here?"

She nodded. "*I* have been so. I wanted to leave Medallion, and I could think of nowhere to go that would serve the Empire. Only here." *And I've been a fool to drag these men from safety, just so that I could run.*

"There's no resentment on this ship," Rannovic told her, watching distance swallow the white owl. "Sooner or later, we would have come this way. Since the enemy is in the west, we must seek him out. With you or without, ships would have come."

"It's not too late to go back—"

He shook his head. "We're here. And we'll look. Besides, Ottemar is far too cautious. Oh, I understand the dangers. I lived in Teru Manga long enough. But we need to learn what Anakhizer is doing. The west is very quiet. Unnaturally so."

Later that day they came closer to the western shore. Kirrikree had not returned, but Sisipher told Rannovic that she was still in contact with him. He had found a coast that was rugged, a long line of jagged cliffs that overhung the sea in a unique fashion, so that they looked even more unscalable than the most difficult cliffs of Medallion itself. The owl had apparently flown over the cliffs and found a range of low mountains beyond. Passing over them, he had lost contact with Sisipher. She was not unduly alarmed, assuming that the owl was searching for a kill, in which case his thoughts would become his own. But it was a long time before she heard from him again.

When the ship at last reached the coast, Kirrikree's observations were confirmed. The cliffs that rose up were particularly high, as if the sea bed had been twisted in a massive faulting, snapped in half and heaved up. The cliffs were indeed overhangs, so much so that their upper ledges were like vast platforms stretching out over the sea for as much as a quarter of a mile. Rannovic was wary of taking the ship in too close. Quite apart from the dangers of rockfall, there were the currents to consider.

"I cannot imagine how we are to land," he told Sisipher at the bow. "I've never seen the like! Even the Teeth to Medallion's south would be easier to negotiate! There seems to be no entrance, unlike Teru Manga."

"Kirrikree has reported none yet." Sisipher shuddered as she studied the striated cliffs and the clusters of thick shadow below them. They were like an impregnable fortress, hostile and menacing. There was not a bird in sight, and not a hint of bush, scrub or leaf.

For days they sailed southward, under the frowning cliffs, which offered no hint of variation, as though they would go on to the very ice fields without a break. Sisipher tried several times to contact Kirrikree, but it was as though the huge cliffs acted as a barrier to everything, closing his thoughts out. She was reluctant to do so, but she briefly sought to look with her power into the land, but again there was only a shadow, no indication of life, no murmur of sound, no suggestion that beyond the cliffs there would be anything but darkness.

"There must be life there," said Rannovic one morning. "Even if it is corrupt."

"I can't tell," she said. "It's screened." She seemed to have shrunk into herself, humiliated by the coastline, defeated by it. The crew were also intimidated, and their old restlessness returned. There were petty arguments and even a scuffle or two, though Rannovic stalked among them like a bull and threatened to toss overboard anyone who couldn't keep his patience.

He said nothing to the girl but he was anxious about the ship's supplies. They had water enough for a few more days, and less food. The would have to land soon. But where?

Relief did come eventually, though not from the inhospitable cliffs. A large island loomed out of the morning mist, and though it was steep-sided and in places sheer, it had a number of coves with vegetation that seemed to be normal. The ship was anchored in a shallow bay facing the open sea, and a party ashore soon found fresh springs and edible fruit. Later in the day they killed wild pig, and that evening the entire crew celebrated. Rannovic was relieved, sitting on a fallen log, watching the men as they danced about a campfire.

"Let them enjoy this," he told Sisipher, who looked uncomfortable at the possibility of attracting attention to the ship. "Unless they do, we'll not go on in the right mood. These men are fighters. And they'll need to be, I fancy, if we do get on the mainland."

They returned to the ship for the night, though the singing went on for a long time. Sisipher fell asleep shortly before dawn. When she woke, the ship was sliding through calm waters, the crew working the oars effortlessly and without complaint. She went to the deck and found Rannovic beaming at her, delighted about something.

"Our faithful owl is back," he said, pointing to the rail.

Sisipher clapped her hands and rushed over to the great white bird, gently stroking his wings. Those of the crew who saw her nodded to themselves. The owl had become a good omen.

"I have been over the mountains," Kirrikree told Sisipher, though she alone heard his voice.

"And the Deepwalks?"

"I did not fly too close to them. They are beyond the mountains that crest the coastal cliffs. They are well named, for they are indeed deep, but how deep I cannot tell you. They drop away, a fathomless green, down to the mist and cloud that forms the base of yet another line of mountains. But mistress, you cannot conceive of what this other edge is like. It rises beyond imagining."

"Starkfell Edge?"

"I cannot describe it. It is a wall built by gods, hanging over the world. For miles it rises, up, ever up, out of sight. Even though it was far to the west and I did not go there, it seemed huge. I turned south along the smaller range, which is called Sea Scarp. These cliffs behind us are not endless, as we feared. They soon slope away to a headland, and once the ship has sailed around this, there is a wide bay. It forms a break in the cliffs and in the center of the bay there are strangely formed dunes, shaped like mighty claws, and from out of them runs a river. This is the Fellwater. It has chopped its way down through a mighty gorge, thrice the height of the cliffs of Teru Manga, perhaps more. I did not follow its course inland, for it is watched."

"By whom?"

"The mountains rise up on either side of the gorge. And in each of them are Watches. The servants of the forest are in them, though I did not see them. I heard them, and caught certain names, such as those I have given you. Nothing escapes the eyes of these Watches."

"Did they see you?"

"The forest knew of my presence long ago. And it knows the ship is here. I think there is nothing this forest does not know."

"Is it hostile?"

"I cannot read its thoughts. They are closed to me. It sent winged servants to watch me, but they did not attack. They were not unlike eagles, though smaller than the great eagles of Medallion, such as Skyrac. I outdistanced them, but they did not seem inclined to pursue me. There is something else they fear, though I did not get a clear image of it. They call it the Shadowflight.''

"Do you know what it could be?"

"Only that it is a darkness in the sky."

Sisipher called Rannovic to her. He had kept away out of respect for the owl and his relationship with Sisipher. He nodded to the bird, wishing that he, too, could converse with him. Sisipher told him all that Kirrikree had imparted to her. At once Rannovic had parchment brought and began hurriedly scratching out a map for his helmsman, Helvor.

"Where should we land?" asked the latter, a burly, dark-bearded man whose rugged looks belied a sharpness of mind. He looked directly at the owl as if expecting a verbal reply.

"Kirrikree says we could get ashore in the bay," said Sisipher. "But we would be out in the open, like voles on a bare rock." The image of a winged predator swooping down, claws outspread, was in all their minds. "He says we would do better to sail through the Claws and into the gorge. It would be very difficult for anything to attack us there."

"He thinks we'll be met with force?" said Rannovic.

"He doesn't know. But I think we must assume we will be targets and unwelcome."

"I agree," sniffed Helvor, scratching his thick beard and running his hand back through his hair. If he had been much larger, Sisipher thought, he would have been almost as large as a Stonedelver. How she wished Aumlac and some of his companions were here. But she must not rue their absence: Rannovic's crew were as capable a team of fighting men as she could have wished for.

"As far as Kirrikree could tell," she went on, "the Fellwater runs out of Starkfell Edge. It cuts through the forest."

"Once through the gorge," said Helvor, "where next? A safe berth for my ship?"

Rannovic chuckled and clapped an arm around him. "Aye, we'd better find somewhere for your beloved ship, eh, Helvor? You'd never sleep knowing it was in peril, never mind the crew."

Helvor grunted. "Men are expendable. Ships are unique." But he grinned back. Rannovic knew he was as dependable as the next man, and loyal to his fellows. Most of the crew were pure Hammavar.

"The ship could be berthed safely at the far end of the gorge," said Sisipher.

"What should we do then?" said Rannovic. He had become serious again, and not only Helvor watched the girl, but also other members of the crew; she was conscious of them all hanging on her words. They had almost arrived: what should they do? With a sudden stab of shock, she knew that she had not thought beyond this point. She tried not to let it show in her face.

Rannovic came to her rescue. He knew instinctively what was going through her mind. "Someone dwells in the land beyond the gorge," he called to the crew. "We know that our enemy is here. We must look for signs of him." He glanced at Kirrikree. "Does the owl know?"

Sisipher shook her head. "He learned nothing of Anakhizer or his servants."

"Then the forest may be inhabited by those who would oppose him," said Rannovic. "I say we should try to find them."

Sisipher nodded, her confusion evaporating. "Yes. It may lead us to the enemy. We may find something out about his plans."

"I'll go to the skies once more," Kirrikree told her.

"Where will you go?"

"To see what I can learn about the forest. And Starkfell Edge. I think, mistress, it would be best if you do not try to follow my flight. Close your mind. We do not know what feeds upon it."

Although reluctant to cut herself off from the owl again, Sisipher agreed. Shortly afterward, Kirrikree flew off and was soon lost to view as he soared over the lip of the cliffs high above.

The ship went south, finding the promised headland the following day. Eventually, in the sweeping bay beyond, they saw the massive dune banks of the Claws and knew that they had reached the mouth of the Fellwater. It was a huge relief to get clear of the overhanging Sea Scarp, and at once the mood of the crew altered.

Although the bay was calm, it was deep, the water a rich green, shot through with clouds of rust-colored water from the mouth of the Fellwater, as though a giant bled its life blood into the ocean. A number of the crew muttered about movement below the gentle waves, but though there was much pointing and scanning of the waters, no one saw anything that could be positively recognized. Sisipher recalled the issiquellen, wondering if they would be here, if they could be following the ship.

At dusk they anchored off the mouth of the river. Vast dune banks rose up on either side, topped with bristling grass as tall as a man, and beyond them there were the lower cliffs, covered in forest. The coast here was in contrast to Sea Scarp, for there was a profusion of animal and bird life. Shapes wheeled in the twilight sky, birds hunting, though none came out into the bay to investigate the lone ship. Inland could be heard a chorus of insects, and the crew listened to it with a sense of relief, as though the familiarity of such sounds brought with it more comfort than the dead silence of the Scarp, where there seemed to be no life, and nothing to encourage it.

In her cabin, Sisipher slept fitfully, her dreams threaded by visions from her past, and the shadow of Xennidhum, which had not troubled her for a long time, returned to plague her as though its black heart beat stronger than ever. And she imagined Anakhizer looming over, larger than Sea Scarp, watching and laughing, spreading madness. Once, awake for a while, she thought she sensed a huge shadow spreading high above the ship. She drove the awful image from her mind and thought of Ottemar, or Guile as she would always call him to herself, and of how the shock of realizing that she loved him had first caught her unawares. He had an empress now, and would soon have a child. The thought tormented her, far worse than the shadow she thought she had sensed, far more than the western threat. She could not close it out. Would it be a son? An heir to rule Goldenisle one day? Tennebriel could give him that, where she could not. But it had come to them so quickly! No sooner had he married the girl, than he had—

She cursed herself for her weakness, but she did not sleep

again that night. Rannovic's men prepared early the next day, rising before the sun. The red haired Hammavar stood with his hands on his hips, face thrust out almost in scorn at the landscape beyond. They were through the dunes and now faced a gash in the towering rock wall that was the mouth of the Fellwater. Sisipher smiled to herself when she saw Rannovic. Somehow he was able to smother his own doubts about this expedition. Could he really be so impervious to the terrors lurking in the land beyond those cliffs?

"We're going in," he told her, almost casually, though she knew from experience that the preparations would have been thorough. Weapons were held at the ready, and the men would be listening to every sound, poised to defend the ship. They were as taut as bowstrings, alert and quivering, though with a kind of fascinated excitement and not fear. The ship moved forward, oars dipping silently, hardly making a splash as the crew pulled the vessel through water that was like glass. Up on the cliffs, the birds wheeled, indifferent.

The cliffs rose up, suddenly assuming an awesome scale, and as the ship slipped between the first of them, shadow swallowed it and the cold closed in like a fist. The water swirled under the hull, sluggish and dark, though there were no rocks to tear mercilessly at the timbers. Carefully, tensing, they moved on. The cliffs leaned back a little, hinting at even greater size, and in some ways they were not unlike the secret entrances to Teru Manga, although there were not the dreadful tidal drags of that northern land to contend with. Rannovic thought briefly of how Sisipher had made a fool of him before his men in Gondobar's time, but he let it pass.

"This is all too simple," he whispered to her. "This land is like a pack of sleeping hounds, or worse. I wish we had Aumlac's folk with us. The Stonedelvers would see into those walls, as would Carac's Earthwrought."

Sisipher nodded uneasily, her mind clouded. In a while they came through the first of the cliffs into a wider area that the river had scooped out of a softer band of rock. Beyond it narrowed again. This strange configuration of the shores occurred a number of times, until the ship came under the brows of the largest cliffs yet, the entrance to the great gorge that had been sliced down through the scarp. The passage looked too narrow to take a ship, but as the craft closed on it, Rannovic saw that there would barely be room. Enough for one ship, but not enough for two to pass. He ordered the ship forward and Helvor nodded, his face as grim as war.

Once in the channel, the cold intensified and the sun, which had been behind them in the east, was lost to view. Apart from a few rays of light, it was as though night had come again. An appalling silence settled on them, muffling the dip of the oars. Rannovic called for firebrands and a number were quickly lit. The shadows receded, but not far. The walls closed in, now rising up so high that they appeared to meet overhead like a pointed vault. It was as though the ship traveled deeper into an ever darkening tunnel.

No one spoke for a long time, and there was no more than an occasional whisper. Sisipher tried to concentrate on the black stone, but it told her nothing. The river, which must once have been a raging torrent, slithered along like a vast serpent, bloated but content, silent and patient.

"Is the sky yet above us?" said Rannovic, gazing up at darkness.

Sisipher nodded, sensing light where he did not. "It is yet a gorge."

All that day and most of the night they wound onward, taking turns to sit at the oars, for they dared not let the ship rest in this place. When, a few hours after dawn, they heard a break in the silence, the raging of water ahead, they were all relieved, whatever it might mean. Too long in this numbing hole would have dulled the edge of the hardiest of them. They came to a section of the gorge that twisted dangerously, swinging the waters from one side to another, so that it was more difficult to steer the ship, but Helvor was content to have something challenging to do. The crew became so involved in their work that they did not notice the growing light ahead of them. Sisipher pointed to it.

"Then we'll soon be out," Rannovic grunted.

At last they were beyond the gorge, and the river widened. Its banks were yet steep, their tops thickly matted with vegetation that was as profuse as tropical growth and impossible to see into. Trees spread their branches in an embracing canopy over the dense undergrowth, and the sound of birds echoed between the rocks.

"The Deepwalks?" said Rannovic, glancing at the girl.

She nodded, but did not speak, as though she visited a land that was sacrosanct.

Rannovic was looking back at his crew, about to give them a noisy cheer, but his breath left him in a great gasp as he saw the gorge from out of which they had lately emerged. Its walls shuddered, groaning deep under the earth, then moved gently as if afloat, toward each other. In moments they had come together with a crack like thunder. Men leapt up, swords at the ready, and birds took to the skies with cacophonous shrieks.

The mouth of the gorge was sealed.

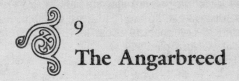

9
The Angarbreed

RANNOVIC AND his crew studied the rock walls closely for a long time, but there was no further movement, and around them all the silence closed in. Yet nothing happened and the expected attack did not come. Several theories as to how the rocks had closed on themselves were argued, but at length Rannovic called for the ship to move on up the Fellwater. Soon after it began to move, the sounds of the forest on either bank started afresh, though in them was a uniqueness and a lack of the familiarity that had been in the lands outside the gorge.

The ship had not traveled far upriver when it became clear that it could go no further: there were far too many obstructions in the water for a large craft. Broken trees poked upward with eager, spiked branches, and overhanging boughs threatened anything that passed. Helvor pronounced that the ship would have to be anchored, and when they saw the tributary swirling in from the east bank, it seemed a natural place to steer the ship. The banks of the river were steep and slippery with mud, and it seemed as though the ship would be safe from any attack from the shore.

Sisipher was grimacing at the turgid waters. "I cannot guess what is in the river," she said. Both the Fellwater and its tributary were an ugly color, dark and impenetrable. It seemed unlikely that either could support life, but they could not be certain.

The ship was secured, partly under an overhang, a minia-

ture of the Sea Scarp overhang. Rannovic called for the
smaller boats to be lowered, and he arranged for a few men
to remain with the ship, under the watchful eye of Helvor.
Until they knew they were relatively safe in this alien land,
the big helmsman had no desire to leave the ship, fearing its
loss. Rannovic was doubtful about leaving any of his party
behind, but Helvor's plan was sensible.

"We'll follow this tributary as far as it will take us," said
Rannovic. "And we'll bring back what news we find."

"If you're not back in a week," said Helvor, scowling
meaningfully, "do we return to the Chain?" It was a stan-
dard Hammavar understanding. In the past they were famed
for their voyages of daring, but they had their own codes. If
Rannovic could not meet the accepted deadline, he would
have to assume Helvor would be gone.

He laughed. "Aye, Helvor. But you'll have to prize open
the gorge first."

Helvor would have echoed his laughter, but none of the
crew had been able to relax since the unnerving movement
of the gorge. Unless it reverted, the ship would never leave
the inner lands.

With a few last words, Rannovic and Sisipher led the party
away up the narrowing tributary, their six boats pulling quietly through the water, all eyes fixed on the overhanging vegetation above them. It was tangled and thick, indicating
nothing of what might be within it, and as they went deeper
into a narrow gorge, the sounds above became muffled and
distant. An occasional shadow flickered by overhead, a bird,
but moving too quickly to be seen. The men fingered their
swords, the oarsmen studying the water ahead and behind,
certain that an enemy of some kind must be preparing an
attack.

While Rannovic's party moved up the river, Helvor put his
remaining men to work, shouting at them, barking orders. If
he had let them sit around idly, he knew, the gloom of the
forest would have soon overwhelmed them, so he worked
them hard. They examined every rope for wear, then hauled
down the sail and set to work repairing it. As the hours
passed, the men became more absorbed with their tasks, and

although the forest was constantly watched, it gave no sign of being hostile, or of disgorging an enemy upon them.

That night, darkness closed on them quickly, the sun masked by the forest late in the afternoon. Helvor insisted that only the minimum of oil-lamps were lit. The forest became increasingly more silent and the drone of insects fell away. Even the water seemed to drop its voice to a whisper. There was no breeze, the air turning cold. Most of the men were drowsy, having labored hard throughout the day. They began to fall asleep, Helvor with them. Those who were on duty at the prow and stern of the ship also found their eyes getting heavy, with only the darkness to study.

When the boat began to move, the guards were not at first aware of it. Along the bank it slithered, its anchor and ropes severed, until Rordas at the stern realized what was happening. He gave a shout and leapt amidships, waking others. Swords flashed in the faint glow of the lamps, and the men were all up and racing to the sides of the ship.

"Our lines are cut!" swore Helvor, bristling with rage. But they could see no one. "Throw out a fresh anchor," he shouted, the forest muffling his voice. The order was quickly obeyed, but no sooner had the spare anchor hit the water and sunk below it than the line went limp. It was hauled in, its end cut, though on closer examination it seemed to have been bitten through. By now the ship was out in the main river. The men tried to see the walls of the gorge, but the night was like a black fog.

"Use the oars! Come on, you oafs, move, *move!*" Helvor snarled, his voice laden with anxiety. There was no more than a handful of men aboard. They might be able to halt the ship with oars, but the current was dangerously swift. Eight long oars hit the water, and for a moment braked the ship, but then, one by one, the oars shattered, splintering as if they had been wedged in jagged rocks below the surface. What *was* below? Helvor's mind cried, as his ship lurched and swung about, wallowing helplessly. It was midstream and abruptly struck something, a sand bar, perhaps, though Helvor could not understand how a sand bar could be here in such a swift river, caught in between its rocky banks.

His crew looked at him helplessly and he saw terror crawl

over their faces. He waved them into a rough circle about the
rails, knowing that an attack must surely be imminent, and
it must come from the river.

Helvor himself was looking upstream, though in pitch
darkness it was difficult to make out any detail. There was
movement, however, and he saw at last the sweep of oars.
Another craft! Narrow and with a long, pointed snout, it was
bearing down upon them like a huge runaway log. It had no
sails and was as black as death. There were shapes within it,
and spears poked up at the night sky, but Helvor could see
no faces.

He yelled to his men, telling them to be ready to take the
blow of the ram. The river had swung his ship round almost
deliberately, exposing its side to that oncoming point. With
startling speed, the dark ship came on, its ram crunching
home like a giant spear, ripping into the guts of the Hammavar ship. Timbers snapped and the deck crumpled. Helvor's men were barely able to hang on, almost pitched
overboard as the enemy vessel ploughed right through their
ship.

Helvor raised his sword, screaming with indignation and
fury, and at once he found himself faced by a dozen warriors.
They were wearing thin metal armor, black as the night, their
helms dragged down over their faces so that only their eyes
were visible, though they were the eyes of beasts, feral and
hungry. They made no sound, striding forward with the speed
of insects, chopping at Helvor, their curved blades whistling
as they almost cut him apart where he stood. Behind them
there were other larger beings, great, bloated creatures with
huge heads and elongated fangs. They carried no weapons,
but their arms were long and they had massive hands,
equipped with claws instead of fingers, and they seemed to
be ripping blindly at the air before them. Helvor knew them
for what they were, the hated Ferr-Bolgan, spawn of Anakhizer. But the black-armored devils were unknown to the
Hammavars. The ship was full of them, and beyond them all
stood a cloaked figure, hooded and silent, a herder, driving
them on as remorselessly as the ship's ram.

Helvor had no time to take in anymore. A blow to his head
knocked him across the leaning deck. His feet slipped from

under him and he was down. He was only half aware of the
world slithering away from him, then he had fallen into the
wounded belly of his ship. On the deck the black-mailed
warriors chopped down the other sailors easily. One leapt
into the river but within minutes was screaming as something
under the water took hold of him and tore him apart.

RANNOVIC'S BOATS had not gone far up the tributary of the
Fellwater before he realized that the river would turn back on
itself and lead to the hills above the gorge. "Away from the
forest," he told Sisipher. "Though if we go up into the hills,
we should be able to scan what's below us."

"Yes, I think we should try and see how the land lies. If
we enter the forest with no clear idea, we could be lost almost
at once," she agreed. Again she considered her folly in
bringing them to this place. It had been one thing to follow
Korbillian and the others to the lands of the east, but they
had possessed power, strength of numbers. This land bristled
with a different kind of terror.

Late in the day they had to take the boats ashore, for there
were falls up ahead. The forest had not thinned, the trees crowding together and collecting shadows as if they were precious.
But the right bank was less densely packed, the trees a little
sparser, and the men could see through them and up the slopes
to the woodland that skirted the foot of the hills. Rannovic suggested they go upward, moving away from the river. They found
a place for the boats, cutting down branches to cover them, and
when they had finished, Sisipher was surprised at how well they
had disguised them. She doubted that the forest would be fooled,
though she still had no way of measuring its capabilities. She
knew there was life in it, probably watching eyes, but she could
not single anything out.

The party began the journey through the trees. They were
thinner here, not particularly tall, as though this part of the
forest was apart, a section not linked to the main forest across
the river, the true Deepwalks. The men were cheerful, some
of them saying aloud that if this was the feared forest of
legend, it was not so bad. But Sisipher said nothing. It was
evening as they moved high up on the lower slopes of the
hills, approaching the edge of the trees, and Rannovic sug-

gested they camp at their limit rather than on the open slopes. This was done, though Rannovic would not permit a fire. The men grumbled as they ate their dried fish and fruit, but they knew there was good sense in their leader's instructions.

Darkness spread quickly. Sisipher and Rannovic went up beyond the camp, studying the rocky terrain for a while. It seemed little different from the slopes of Malador on Medallion, or the lands above the forests of King Strangarth in the east.

"Does it tell you anything?" said Rannovic gently, knowing that she had powers beyond those of ordinary men. Here, alone with her, he felt those powers stirring him, wishing that he could break his vow with himself and speak his mind to her. But he did not.

She nodded to the peaks that rose up, stabbing at a sky now filled with stars. "My powers are an odd thing, Rannovic. They ebb and flow like the tides. I might control them better if I did not fear them. There are times when I sense things, but have to draw back from them. At other times I want to use the power like a sword. To be honest with you," she added, turning to him with a smile that, ironically, struck him like the thrust of a blade, "I would be happier if I were free of them. Once I thought they had been cleansed from me."

Had she been any other woman, he would have pulled her to him and comforted her. But he spoke as warmly as he could. "I'm sure we'll be glad of any powers you have in this land."

She nodded again to the high peaks. "See up there. Something is watching us, just as Kirrikree promised. The hills have eyes. Not just for us, but for everything. The Deepwalks have set their own guardians about them."

"Is that where we will go?"

"In the morning." She nodded. "I think—" But her head snapped round as though the woods below were full of howling.

Rannovic's sword leapt to her defense and he covered her at once. "What is it?" he hissed, though he had neither heard nor seen anything.

Sisipher had gone icy cold. Her hair felt tight to her scalp as she watched the motionless trees. "We must go higher," she said through her teeth.

"Are the men in danger!"

"No. Their camp is not threatened. But beyond—" She said no more, gripping Rannovic's arm. With surprising nimbleness, she went up the slope, threading through the boulders and scree, Rannovic hard put to keep up with her. In a while she came to a huge outcrop and went around it, climbing up on to it as if it were a balcony. Rannovic went after her, watching every stone as if it would turn into an assailant.

Once on the rock outcrop, he gasped. The view, in spite of encroaching night, was staggering. Directly below them was the forest through which they had come. But beyond it, rising up in an endless dark stain, were the Deepwalks. To the right, the rocks fell away to another small gorge, and it was from this that the tributary of the Fellwater emerged. Beyond the bulk of the Deepwalks it was impossible to see much, only the varying degrees of darkness, but Rannovic sensed something awesome there, something of such magnitude that he had to turn his eyes from it.

Sisipher was looking at him, her own expression ghastly. "We must go back!" she whispered fiercely, as if afraid that her words would be carried out over the listening land.

"What did you hear?"

"There are certain things that touch upon my powers as if they were exposed nerves," she said. "The Fellwater is that way." She pointed. "And evil is gathering. I hear the name, angarbreed. And there are Ferr-Bolgan."

Rannovic groaned. "What about Helvor! Are they near him?"

Sisipher stared at the distance, shuddering as if she could see every detail of what occurred. "We must go back to him. Rannovic, there are *thousands* of them, like an overturned anthill."

He turned and leapt down from the rock immediately, not even waiting to see if she was behind him. But she was just as nimble and within minutes was at his heel. They burst into the camp together, rousing the men with their shouting.

"To the river! At once!" Rannovic boomed, careless of who or what heard him. The camp erupted as every man belted on his sword and threw off his sleeping cloak. With desperate speed they raced down through the trees, some tumbling over but rising at once, heedless of danger, anxious to get back to their companions. Rannovic did not mention Ferr-Bolgan, but the mere fact that the ship was imperiled goaded them on.

They came to the place where they had hidden the boats and Rannovic supervised their refloating, men leaping into them and paddling frantically. It took but a few minutes to have the entire party back on the river, though Rannovic and Sisipher found themselves bringing up the rear.

"How close are they to our ship?" Rannovic whispered, leaning over the girl.

"I cannot tell. The Fellwater runs far away through the Deepwalks to the very base of Starkfell Edge."

Rannovic shivered at the name. Was that what he had sensed, towering over the world beyond the forest? Could anything be so vast?

As they were rounding a tight bend in the river, something bumped into their boat, protesting as wood scraped on wood. It was a half sunken tree, and although it did not crush the side of the boat, it knocked it almost to the bank. Rannovic cursed roundly, yelling at his rowers to right things. The other boats were already out of sight around the bend.

Something splashed in the water, a sudden gushing as if rocks had been exposed by a retreating tide, and a swirl of water swung the boat out of control a second time. One of the men was flung outwards, hitting the river with a convulsive splash. The crew were all shouting, not knowing whether to man the oars or drop them for their swords. But no attack came, and the boat shot forward, straight into the undergrowth, which accepted it willingly, wrapping tendrils around it. An old branch snapped overhead, dropping like a spar, and the men barely had time to leap aside.

Rannovic swore, chopping at the branch with his sword, but the wood rang like metal and his arm shook. "Cut us loose!" he ranted. But the forest was not prepared to release its prize so easily. The minutes dragged by as the men cut into the undergrowth. Some of the oars were lost, others were damaged. They could not move their boat.

"We must go ashore," said Sisipher.

"How far away are we from our ship?" said Rannovic, nothing else mattering to him.

"Several miles. I doubt if we can reach it by night. Not through the forest."

Rannovic peered about him, but the trees crowded in like giants, shutting out all light and sound. "Which bank is this?"

"We have crossed," said Sisipher. "We are in the Deepwalks."

HELVOR FELT the burning knife driving into his head. He tried to cry out in protest, but his voice came out as a dry rattle. Painfully he opened his eyes, though the lids seemed to have been gummed down. The first thing he became aware of was the cold, lapping at his chest; the lower half of him was completely numb. The knife in his skull withdrew, but it left a throbbing that threatened to blind him. Light splashed over him from somewhere above, a ragged sun. A hole had been punched in the hull of the ship. He groaned as he saw the destruction about him. Somehow he had fallen inside the crippled ship, draping himself over a chunk of timber. Daylight had arrived, and with it had brought a new silence. He hauled himself up on to the leaning inner deck, learning as he did so that none of his bones were broken, though his entire body felt bruised. Blood matted his hair and beard and he scooped up the cold water to revive himself. His sword was gone.

He managed to work his way up through the innards of the ship to the deck above. The sight that met his eyes made him gag. None of his companions had survived, as far as he could make out. Their bodies had been cut up mercilessly like beef, though a butcher would have been more careful in his work. Blood splattered everything, clotted about severed limbs, and eyeless heads gazed moronically upward, severed from their trunks. The Ferr-Bolgan and their spider-like fellows had ripped into the men with utter abandon.

At first Helvor was numbed, thinking that it would have been better if he had perished with them, but he thought of Rannovic and the others. If they should come back, with no ship! As quickly as he could, he began to go over the ship, hoping that something could be done. It was then that he saw the true extent of the carnage. He sank to his knees, his head in his hands. For there, flung this way and that about the lower wreckage, were the longboats. The men *had* returned. And like Helvor's men, they had been sliced apart, ripped limb from limb by the enemy. Some of the dreadful being had also been killed, but Helvor could not bring himself to look at them. He could find none of the black-armored beings, only the Ferr-Bolgan. Swarms of flies had taken over the scene.

The ship itself shuddered, as though sorrowing with Helvor, and he knew that it would inevitably go under. It would be best if it did, for it could not possibly be refloated here. The ram had cut it almost in two and it was holed in numerous places down in the hold. Let it be a fitting coffin, then. With a last glance at its horrific contents, Helvor leapt from the deck into the river and struck out laboriously for the shore. If something below the water came for him, well, let it.

But he made the shore, dragging himself up its slippery mudbank and into the trees. Sinking down, he sat and stared at the river. Had any of them escaped? How many of the enemy had there been? The thoughts churned over and over, his head throbbing painfully, and the day flowed by as quickly as the water before him.

It was eventual movement on the water that caught his attention, much later in the day. A craft was coming downriver. Helvor dropped to his belly in the grass, watching, his body shaking at the thought of more Ferr-Bolgan. But it was one of the boats. It must have been caught in the mud or in the fallen branches beside the river, and somehow it had worked itself loose. Now it swirled down the river toward the main gorge.

Helvor's years of training and struggle for survival in Teru Manga prompted him now. He glanced around quickly, saw no one, no sign of the enemy, then rose up, plunging into the river. He timed his swim perfectly, intercepting the long boat in midstream, his hand groping for it and hanging on desperately. To his horror he heard the hiss of metal and a sword chopped down, embedding itself in the rail inches from his knuckles.

"Hold your steel!" he gasped, this time his voice sharpened by his terror. In a moment he found himself staring up into two bewildered faces. They were men of Rannovic's party. As the boat sped on to the gorge, they hauled the helmsman aboard.

"Is this all that is left!" Helvor gasped. There were nine of them, all wounded and exhausted. They shook their heads, unable to say anything. Helvor crawled to the prow of the longboat, suddenly remembering where they were. The river was entering the gorge. This escape by boat was not such a fine idea, for the walls of the gorge had closed. He was about to warn them, to stir them, but he saw the gorge ahead. It must be an illusion! The opening was as it had originally been. His cry brought two of the others to his side and they confirmed that he was not dreaming this. Like huge doors, the walls of the gorge had opened.

"Then this black land has had its fill of us," said Helvor. "See how it spits us out." Moments later they were in the gorge, the boat racing along, the huge walls closing in, bringing the darkness and the cold. Helvor looked back to have a last glance at the once proud ship he had brought across the ocean. Again he was shocked by what he saw. The crippled wreck was moving, already swinging round to enter the mouth of the gorge. It, too, was being ejected from the land of the forest.

As Helvor watched its broken corpse following his own escape, he had already begun to formulate a vague plan of repair, of salvage, and of possible escape from this hellish continent. Night was endless. Sisipher had warned Rannovic that any attempt to move through the forest would be almost impossible, especially at night.

"Almost, but not absolutely. Then we go on. I'll not let my men die while I sit here." He refused to say any more. Sisipher understood his bitterness and understood his resolve better. But she would have preferred to wait until dawn, when they would be fresher, even though none of them would have slept.

For her, the hours were nightmarish. The coming of the Ferr-Bolgan and the unseen angarbreed was like the advance of the sea, and she heard its waves breaking in the distance. Rannovic kept asking her what was happening, but she only shook her head. She sensed the spilling of blood, the release of pain, but she dare not say anything that would infuriate the men. If they had known the worst, they would have plunged into the forest regardless, to be lost in no time.

When dawn came, it hardly penetrated the thick canopy overhead. Sisipher knew that not only had they moved a short

distance from the river, but they had gone north instead of
west, where the ship was moored. Each time they tried to
force their way westward, the trees closed, or the ground rose
sharply. Exasperated, they had to stop and rest. Rannovic
looked appalling, fearing the worst. The humor that had set
him apart from other men had abandoned him. Sisipher put
a hand on his broad shoulder.

"I am sorry," she said quietly.

"Have we lost them?" He did not look at her, instead
watching with anger the thick undergrowth, the dipping
branches, obscuring the way ahead.

"We may not find out. Had we taken the short route to
Starkfell Edge, up the Fellwater, we would have been over-
run. The forest knew it."

Rannovic scowled at the trees. "Does it have its own
mind?"

"It is alive. Our coming took it by surprise, I think. The
Fellwater is an evil part of it. It tried to warn us, to spare
us." The words came haltingly to her, as though she were
trying to read them in the foliage around them.

"*Spare* us?" He did not look at her, face haggard.

She took her hand away as if he had burned it. "Yes.
Strange that our longboat should run aground and be trapped,
held. If we had gone on, back to the ship—"

"Then what?" he challenged her. The remainder of the men
had gathered. Every man demanded an answer with his eyes.
Sisipher felt their sudden distrust, their uncertainty. Even Rannovic, so hurt by the events of the night, questioned her.

"They are lost, aren't they?" he said coldly.

"I fear it." She would have said more, but there was
movement in the trees beyond them. They turned, still on
edge, and found themselves confronted by the strangest being
they had yet seen. They knew of the Earthwrought, and had
been amazed by the skills of the little people, and for most
of them, this being was closer to an Earthwrought in appearance than it was to a man. It was of slimmer build, but its
skin, if skin it was, seemed to have been hewn from solid
wood, knotted and gnarled. The hands were long and powerful, like clubs of wood, and the face was bizarre, expressionless, with deep-set eyes. It carried a short spear and a

round shield made of wood, the center of which was inlaid with a green emblem. It watched the men without moving, statuesque as a tree, and although they held their swords as if to fend off an attack, they did not feel threatened.

Sisipher went to it and bowed slightly. "I am Sisipher," she began.

"You are known," came the creature's deep, gruff voice. "And these others."

"Whom do you serve?" said Rannovic, standing beside Sisipher as if he would use his sword at any moment.

The creature did not seem inclined to answer him at first, but then it gestured with its strange arms to the forest. "I am a Woodweaver. I am of Woodheart."

This brought gasps from the men, for Woodweavers were creatures of myth. Rannovic indicated the creature's shield and spear. "You are garbed for war—"

"There is danger in this part of the forest. You are not safe yet."

"Yet?" echoed Rannovic and would not be mollified by Sisipher's look. "Where are my men?"

'Woodheart saved those that could be saved—"

"Why us? Why not all of us?"

Sisipher winced at the Hammavar's hard words. She could see that the Woodweaver would not answer. "Because of me," she said at last, afraid of a battle here.

Rannovic glared at her. "You?"

"The forest sensed me. It trapped us, our boat. Something of my power attracted it. But it was too late to save the others. Rannovic, I did not plan this—"

"You must follow me," interrupted the Woodweaver. "This part of the forest is evil. There was much killing in the night."

Rannovic closed his eyes, his hands white.

"We must go with him," said Sisipher.

"This business does not end here," said Rannovic. "By my sword, I swear it."

10
Grimander

KIRRIKREE SWEPT upward on one of the powerful thermals exuded by the thick green depths of forest below like the breath of a giant. He had come further inland, to see if there was somewhere that the ship of Rannovic could be safely berthed. He wondered even now if this voyage had been wise. It was one thing to speak of surprise, of finding a way into the Land of Anger in secret, but quite another to do it effectively. The world below was strange, its secrets hidden from above as darkly as they were hidden from the outside world. There was no guarantee that the Deepwalks would have any sympathy for their cause, no guarantee that they would be other than hostile. Sisipher had allowed her heart to rule her head, and Kirrikree, who would never pry, never use his gift to communicate without consent, found the girl's mind closed off regularly these days. Since the Inundation and the enthronement of Ottemar, she had shut part of herself away. And she had come here to escape. Should the owl have told her? It was not wise of her to use Rannovic, who would have refused her nothing, Kirrikree knew, although the big Hammavar knew Sisipher's mind better than she realized. Kirrikree had once hated Ottemar, or Guile, as he had justifiably been known. But during the flight from Teru Manga and after, the owl had learned a new respect for the man who was destined to be Emperor, just as he had come to respect Simon Wargallow. But how much more sensible it would have been for Sisipher to have turned from Ottemar, and looked more

130

closely at the redbeard. Rannovic was full of bluster and
bravado, but there was a nobleness about him, and had Sisipher returned only a part of his love for her, he could have
brought a richness to her life she had not previously known.
Perhaps in time the girl would see him as he was. For the
moment she was confused, her mind tormented not only by
her sense of loneliness and loss, but by the shadows that
deepened, reaching out like a fog from this western fortress.

Kirrikree closed his own mind to those shadows. They
seeped like madness across the world, twisting everything
they touched. In all of the Empire's men this strangeness had
rooted, making them reckless, prone to impulsive acts. Wargallow himself did not seem to be free of this curse. Where
once he would have been clinical and intractable, now he
was unsure. He had become a man of mercy, which was a
blessing, but even he did not know how insidiously Anakhizer's powers worked, eating like disease at the innermost parts
of the Empire.

Movement below took Kirrikree's eye, and he swung down
at once, concentrating fiercely as if homing in on a kill. The
river wound like a dirty, mottled snake through the dense
forest, broken only by the occasional fang of rock or protruding tooth of old trunk. The owl could smell evil, and his
claws came out as though in a moment he would have to use
them.

Ferr-Bolgan! Scores of them, tramping through the undergrowth. And with them there were other creatures, dark,
spindly beings, black-armored and feral, stronger of mind,
swifter of foot. Angarbreed; they were under the command
of a herder, one of the gray-garbed beings. Sisipher had told
Kirrikree that they were renegade Children of the Mound,
refugees from the far eastern lands, weakened but nevertheless still powerful enough to drive their armies forward. Kirrikree had fought them in Teru Manga and had seen the way
in which the Ferr-Bolgan flowed forward like a tide under
their prompting.

The owl swerved in the sky, sensing the herder's probing
mind. It was like a stab of pain. But it had not found him
out: he closed off his own mind to it instinctively. Turning
from the river, he swooped over the edge of the Deepwalks.

Should he return to the ship and warn its crew? But they knew the enemy was here in force. It would be a while before the Ferr-Bolgan were near them, although the evil creatures seemed to be making for a camp of their own in the forest, on a wide bend where there were few trees. There would be time enough to explore further before swinging back to the coast and Rannovic.

He had no wish to travel over the Deepwalks. They stretched to the north and west of him, endless, lost in misty distance, dropping away to the west, sloping steeply as if falling forever into some unimaginable pit in the north. Behind him the sun was gathering its strength and now it speared its rays through the mist, gradually unveiling more of the mysteries of the landscape. The Fellwater had chopped its way with evident power through the rising slope of the outer lands of the Deepwalks, cutting for itself a gorge that went deeper and deeper as it wound to the sea, ending in the towering cliffs of the outer scarp. From the air it looked almost as if the river defied gravity, flowing in the wrong direction.

Kirrikree had spiraled up high above it once more. He could see far ahead, and the vast shadow that was Starkfell Edge suddenly confronted him. Its presence almost stopped his flight, filling him with a sudden dread. How could it be so staggeringly huge! Like a colossal wall, it rose up and up, mile upon mile, its sheer cliffs hanging outwards, their top edges way over the land below. And as if their height was not enough, a range of immense mountains rose from the upper ledges, lost in cloud and distance far overhead. Kirrikree was made dizzy merely by looking at them. He circled, unable to keep his eyes fixed on the stupendous cliffs, almost as though he had come face to face with a god, whose gaze meant madness. And yet this range must be passed somehow, for Anakhizer's fortress was somewhere beyond it in the Land of Anger.

For the moment Kirrikree would have to follow the river. Perhaps it emerged from the foot of the Edge, and worked its way outwards from an inner labyrinth. It would have to be looked at. Kirrikree flew on, trying not to allow his eyes to be transfixed by the wall ahead. As he flew on, it rose up higher, while below him the Deepwalks dropped further and further away, their lowest reaches obscured in green shadow, down at the very feet of the Edge.

It was a deceptively long flight, emphasizing still further the sheer immensity of Starkfell Edge. Already it rose up so far that the mountains were out of sight, the upper cliffs leaning out over Kirrikree like a gigantic hand about to close around him. He concentrated on the river, which glistened in the sunlight. He flew downward, sensing the forest, crouched like an impossibly huge beast about to spring for him. It was silent, ominously so, but no attack came. The lower reaches of Starkfell Edge beckoned, smooth and glassy, though higher up there were banks of vegetation burgeoning out from the walls, so thick and vast that they themselves were like forests.

At last Kirrikree found himself flying between two outcrops of wall toward the back of the Edge. Below him he could see the river emerging from the wall before being swallowed by the lowest part of the forest. And as he had expected, there were caves at the very foot of the cliffs. Like great gaping mouths, they stretched across a wide area, and from them tumbled a number of violent streams and rivers, all merging almost immediately into the deep channel that was the Fellwater.

When he dropped lower, well under the terrifying overhang of the Edge, Kirrikree realized that the caves were infested with Ferr-Bolgan. He flew as low as he dared, uncertain what other allies these monsters might have, and found a ledge some fifty feet above the uppermost edge of the cave. Dozens of voices clashed below, and he could feel the intense weight of countless minds, jumbled and confused as the waters that spilled out from the belly of the cliffs. Although the Ferr-Bolgan were numerous, there were almost as many of the black-clad beings, and the organization amongst the latter, their strict and orderly way of going about their business sent a shudder through the body of the huge owl. They were an army, and they were no rabble. Anakhizer's preparations were no longer haphazard. But something else about the dark beings sent a warning through Kirrikree, some faint chime of memory: had he seen them previously? No, surely that could not be. Yet why this familiarity?

It came to him as abruptly as an eddying gust and the

understanding shocked him. Like him, they were not native to Omara. They had been bled into this world, but from what darkness? If Anakhizer had summoned them, *drawn* them through the fabric of the world, they were an even more terrible threat. And what else could the renegade do?

As Kirrikree looked to the river, he felt another sudden twinge of panic. Stretched on the banks, resting, were scores of issiquellen, the creatures of the sea who had swarmed into the waterways of Teru Manga. It seemed that, as with the Ferr-Bolgan, the daylight and open air no longer deterred them. Their forms were unmistakable: Kirrikree would have known them in utter darkness. Although they seemed to be in some ways like men, they had much paler skin, squamous and with a fish-like translucence that hinted at the organs beneath. They had elongated, spatulate fingers, their arms webbed to their sides. Though their eyes were seemingly blind, opaque and misty, Kirrikree knew they saw clearly enough, and he knew their hunger for the kill would drive them to war without fear. They, too, looked to be well-organized, waiting for whatever command would send them forward in waves toward conquest. Wargallow and Ottemar must hear of this! It was what they had feared and predicted, but still they must be told.

Rannovic must not try to enter these caverns, no matter how far under the Edge they extended. Kirrikree had seen enough for now. Silent as a cloud, keeping as close to the rock walls as he could, he flew upward in a tight spiral, away from the milling host of the enemy, away from the caverns that he had heard his enemies call the Gates of Anger.

How was Rannovic to get past Starkfell Edge? No man could climb it, not only because of its steepness, its dizzying overhang, but also because of its immensity. The Stonedelvers, or Earthwrought? Stonedelvers had once lived here, had they not, or at least somewhere beyond the walls? Before they had been driven out from the north and had made their stand at the Slaughterhorn. But could even they climb this infinite cliff, carrying men with them? Could Earthwrought delve their way into it? How far must they go?

As he flew higher and higher, Kirrikree felt the growing impracticality of the task. Not only was Starkfell Edge higher than belief, but it must also be countless miles deep, and he knew from accounts that it stretched from the far north down the spine of the entire continent to southern seas. More and more he was forced to conclude that the only way to Anakhizer would have to be through the Gates of Anger. But that would mean a ferocious battle on the lower slopes before them. And of course, secrecy would be impossible.

The air had grown noticeably thinner. Kirrikree realized that he had probably flown higher than he had ever flown previously, and still the crest of the Edge was high overhead. He had begun to think that he must abandon the idea of reaching it, when eventually he was over the lip. A barren waste confronted him, sprinkled with snow, devoid of life. A cold blast of wind tore down at him like the angry scorn of the mountains, and he struggled for a moment to keep his balance. He alighted on a broken rib of rock, and under his claws it felt cold and icy. He studied the sudden upsweep of the land before him. The mountains loomed above him, almost as unbearable a weight as that of the Edge. They were also vast, thick with snow, their peaks lost to view. If anyone had somehow scaled the Edge and stood here at its rim, they would only have had a fresh range to climb.

Another cold gust of air rocked the owl. This was no realm to remain in. There was a feeling of hopelessness in its winds. It was almost as though Omara herself had risen up in protest, forbidding entry into the jagged peaks. There could be no possible way through them.

Kirrikree wasted no more time in studying them. With a beat of his wings he took to the sky, gliding downward, searching for a glimpse of the remote sea. The day was cloudless and from this great height he could look down like a god on the world. He half expected to see the distant Chain of Goldenisle on the horizon, so high he was, although he could see the far reaches of the sea, glittering invitingly beyond the coast and Sea Scarp.

As he dropped, reveling in the pleasure of flight, he became newly aware of the immensity of the forest. Like an endless blanket, rucked up to the east, it stretched on either side of him as far as he could see. Even from this height he could sense its intelligence, its awareness. There must be a way to communicate with it, to make it and its inhabitants realize just how dire a threat was gathering in the mountains. Perhaps it already knew: it must surely be aware of the intruders below.

The forest's details gradually became more clear. Kirrikree could see that north of the Fellwater it rose up very sharply, so that its lower slopes were practically sheer, having given rise to the name, Deepwalks. The dense foliage was so tangled and interlaced that the character of the forest was impossible to scrutinize. How tall were its trees? What plants grew within it? Who lived there? These and a score more questions went through Kirrikree's mind as he flew steadily lower.

He was about to begin a slow curve that would have taken him parallel to the Fellwater and away back to the coast, when he felt a sudden strange pull, like the drag of a tide. It was impossible to say what had caused it, but it came again, a tangible thing. Drawn to its source, he flew north east, straying further over the Deepwalks. Somewhere far beyond was their heart, but whatever was there was hidden in a thick swirl of mist that rose upward like steam, blending somewhere in the west with the heights of Starkfell Edge.

Swooping still lower, Kirrikree suddenly found himself gazing beyond a drop in the greenery to even greater depths. Somewhere beyond was the source of the strange power. Like a voice calling, it lured him. Steadily he circled, torn between returning to the coast and searching out whatever it was below that so beguiled him. It did not seem a hostile power. Not at first. For an instant a vision of Ternannoc, his home world, flashed on his inner eye.

The green ocean of forest divided abruptly, and he was flying directly above a huge opening, the sides of which were sheer and scarlet, like the walls of a vast plant. The pit fell away to a brilliant, red center, the sides of which throbbed with orange veins. Up from the funnel came a sudden gust, a stench so nauseous that Kirrikree almost plummeted, out of control. He veered away from the gigantic plant, and only when he managed to get back above the green layers of forest was he able to right himself and think clearly. Still the power of the thing below him pulled at him, gaping like a mouth, as if it would suck in anything that came near it.

Dazed, Kirrikree was on the point of alighting in some high branches, when a rush of wings deterred him. Several shapes rose up like black ghosts, smaller birds, their beaks flashing, scarlet as the plant, but they eyed him only for a moment before darting low over the forest ceiling and disappearing beyond yet another cliff crest. Kirrikree attempted to pierce their minds, to read their thoughts, but to his horror found that he had struck at something else, something far more complex and bizarre. The great circle of redness beyond him was alive, its own mind a sudden thunder, a wild howl. Kirrikree beat at the air in sheer panic, winging away above the forest. He had to put as many miles between himself and that atrocity as he could.

As he flew, his sense of direction deserted him. He was far lower than he ought to have been, he knew, but as he attempted to rise, he saw that his flight was being tracked. Overhead there was a dark cloud, swooping lower. It was made up of countless birds, and their wings glittered and flashed in the sunlight like knives. Ravens. Hundreds of them. They had been summoned. And they meant to attack him.

He was tired, only beginning to realize now how much his flight up to the Edge had drained him. The birds were fast, and as they began circling him, preparing to launch their attack, he knew that he would not be able to outfly them. Moments later the first of them speared in and he met it with a flick of his talons that ripped it open and sent it tumbling down into the upper forest. But the assault became a rain and he was fending off those scarlet beaks from every direction.

It was not long before he understood what they intended: to herd him back to the gaping plant-being. He also knew that if he remained in the air, he would never survive. With a final slash of his talons, he dropped like a stone, threading through the upper branches, twisting like a vole as he swept down, finding a way perilously quickly deeper into the trees. The host of ravens followed him on all sides, but for a while they could not get at him. Those that did were cut viciously for their efforts.

In spite of his size, Kirrikree sped quickly into the forest, dropping still lower until he was below the great spread of branches that coupled to form a dark canopy overhead. Eventually it was the closeness of the trees that undid him, for, as he swerved to avoid the darting attack of three ravens, the edge of his wing clipped the top of a young sapling and he plummeted. Before he could right himself in the still, silent air, the ravens crashed into him, and the great owl struck the ground in a flurry of white feathers. At once he felt something in his left wing snap as he struck a sharp boulder. Quickly he rolled, finding himself pressed up against another of the mossy rocks. He put his back to it, trying to ignore the sudden shafts of pain in his wing.

A score of the ravens fell from the trees and formed a half circle about him, their cold eyes fixing him. He opened his beak and hissed at them. Let them come, he thought. At least while I am here they are limited in what they can do. They may have shared his thoughts, for they held back. They waited in silence, as if expecting a signal. The forest listened, the huge trees grouped like an audience, patient as time, unmoved by the grim spectacle at their feet.

Kirrikree's pain increased. The ravens knew he was damaged. He felt his strength ebbing. I must not sleep, he told himself, silently repeating it to himself.

A raven made a sudden dart forward, but Kirrikree's talon came out like the claw of a cat, ripping feathers from the black bird, making it call out in a sound that grated in the forest. But each time the owl used his talons, the pain in his wing worsened.

He became aware of something else in the skies, far away, another cloud. More of the ravens? But those here were aware of this vast shadow, and its distant presence disturbed them. Some of them flew back up to the branches. The entire flock sat in silence, listening to the shape that passed far, far above. Then they began to leave, hardly concealing their panic. Kirrikree could not read their garbled thoughts properly, but he sensed that they had gone to guard whatever part of the forest it was they seemed to consider their particular territory. They feared the distant shadow far more than they did this crippled owl.

Shadowflight, their minds said. Then the last of them was gone.

Kirrikree shuddered. He had no idea how deep in the forest he was. As he watched the motionless trees, he began to realize he was hungry. He had killed earlier in the morning, long before his flight up to the Edge, and now he needed something to sustain him. But how could he catch anything in his present condition? Should he stay where he was until the next day, his back safely protected by the rock? It was mid-afternoon, and he doubted that he would find anywhere much safer for the night.

So he waited, his head nodding, sleep drawing him, offering to numb the worst of his pain. His head dropped, and then jerked upright. He had heard something. The thought of the awesome shadow overhead came at him like an arrow, but whatever thing it was, it was far away. He pressed himself back to the rock, gasping at the effort. The curve of the rock hid him and he kept as still as he could.

Into the narrow glade before him came a strange figure. Slightly smaller than an Earthwrought, and a little less stocky, it was gnarled and dark brown, seemingly sculpted out of the very wood of the forest. It had a mass of thick hair, tangled and leafy, and its long arms ended in hands that were knuckled and whorled. Some of its thoughts drifted across the glade, and Kirrikree sifted them. The creature was a Woodweaver, and a very ancient one, and it appeared to be moving about randomly, with no particular quest. It carried no weapons, but tucked in its belt and poking from the pockets of its thin shirt were a large number of feathers of varying sizes, most of them dark. Kirrikree guessed that it was looking for somewhere to spend the night.

The Woodweaver sat on one of the rocks in the glade and scratched at its wrinkled face, yawning. Then it put its nose in the air as though trying to catch a scent.

"Ravens," it said aloud in a hoarse voice. It jumped up nimbly and began searching the glade as a dog would have, dropping to its belly. Kirrikree understood that its eyesight was poor, probably because of its age. It was coming toward him but had not seen him. Then it came across feathers from the fight of earlier.

"Yes, yes. Been a fight. Ravens, indeed. Black blood."
The Woodweaver poked a number of the feathers into his belt
as if they would make trophies. He came on, now on all
fours, and in a moment had found one of the white owl feathers. He sat up with it and turned it over and over in his
peculiar hands, sniffing it and holding it up to the light.

"What is this? *White* feathers? See how it catches the
light!" It seemed to him to be an item worthy of reverence.

His back was to Kirrikree now, and the great owl knew
that he had but a few seconds to decide on his next act. He
could rise up and dig his claws into the shoulders of this
creature, demanding whatever he wanted of it, or he could
be more subtle. Elsewhere he would have had no hesitation,
and the Woodweaver would have been his prisoner in spite
of his wing. But these were the Deepwalks and something in
the strange being had evoked warmth in the bird.

"If you like the feather, there are more."

The Woodweaver almost toppled over as he heard the words
in his mind, as clearly as if they had been spoken aloud. He
looked about him, hunching up as if fearing attack. "Where
are you?" he called aloud, eyes squinting.

When at last he found Kirrikree, he sat back in awe, unable
to move. The great owl could feel his terror, as if the creature
saw death itself before him. "What manner of thing are
you?" gasped the Woodweaver.

"I am an owl, surely you can see that," Kirrikree said
again to his mind. "Do you not have owls in the Deepwalks?"

The Woodweaver nodded violently. "Yes, yes. Of course.
But you are so large! Almost as large as myself. But where
are you from?"

"From far away," said Kirrikree, not prepared to say more
for the moment. "My name is Kirrikree."

"I am Grimander. I am a Woodweaver. And what's more,
I'm an *erratic*. Have been for nearly eight years. Passed my
three hundredth year nearly eight years ago. Does that surprise you?"

"Then you are privileged, I suspect?"

'Yes, yes," nodded the Woodweaver with great pride. "I
still serve Woodheart, naturally. We are all of Woodheart.

But as an *erratic* I move about the Deepwalks as I choose. If Woodheart wants me to do something, though, I'm only too pleased to obey. Otherwise, the woods are mine. In a manner of speaking," he added, peering about to see if anyone else had heard him. But he turned back to the huge owl and tried to study him more closely. "You're injured," he said. "I can feel your discomfort. And it is in your words you send me."

"My wing," said Kirrikree. He described his flight from the ravens.

"Ah, yes. You must have been flying too near to the center of the forest. That's Woodheart's realm. The Ravensring is that way, though they fly out from it on patrol. Something strange crosses our skies at times."

"Who is this Woodheart? Your ruler?"

"In a way. He is at the heart of the Deepwalks. And all things in and of the forest are of Woodheart. The forest is the body, and we are the life blood."

"And those not of the forest, like myself, are not welcome."

"Woodheart protects us. The Ravensring is a circle of moors that protects the center of the forest. Anyone or anything trying to cross the Ravensring would be in a rare dilemma, I tell you. Yes, yes, there are a good many ravens there. Usually they kill."

"Then I'm fortunate," said Kirrikree.

"How bad is the injury?"

"Bad enough."

"Shall I look at it for you?" Grimander drew in a breath and for a moment looked a little pompous. "I have some skill in healing, you know."

Kirrikree could sense that this was something of rare importance to the strange being, something personal and far deeper than Grimander would say. "I'm not of the Deepwalks. But I have not come as an enemy."

Grimander was on his feet, quite nimbly, scratching his tuft of beard and then his corona of hair. "You've come a long way from your home, wherever that may be. Why have you come? Are you lost?"

"No, I came in search of your forest. And those who threaten it."

"Threaten it?" Grimander crackled, hopping about, himself a little like a bird. "No power in Omara threatens Woodheart." But he looked up through the trees.

"Oh, but it does."

Grimander stiffened. "The dark things that fly far above us—"

"Do you know of the Ferr-Bolgan?"

Grimander snorted. "Ah, them! Yes, yes. Crawling about under the Edge. They have done so for many years. The mountains must be alive with them, like maggots. But not here. Woodheart would destroy them."

"Do you know who rules them?"

"*Rules* them? No one rules that plague."

"Then it is well that I have come. You have much to learn. And if you serve Woodheart as well as you say, you had better take me to him."

Grimander shook his head vigorously. "No, no, no. Impossible! I can't do that. No one goes to Woodheart. Not just like that."

"His counselors, then?"

Grimander frowned, pondering this as though it were a particularly difficult problem. "Hmm. I must think about this. Yes, yes. But your wing—"

"I'd be glad of help."

"You did say earlier, that if I, if I liked your feathers—"

"I can spare you a few," agreed Kirrikree.

"Wonderful! But you will not hurt me, eh? Those talons—"

"No, Grimander. I will give myself into your hands."

The words must have been well chosen, for Grimander caught his breath at them. He bowed solemnly and in a moment had begun a careful study of the owl's wing. To Kirrikree's amazement, the little creature was extraordinarily gentle, his clumsy-looking hands completely belying the skill that was in them. Grimander was able to feel every sinew in the damaged wing, each minute muscle. He located the exact nature of the broken bones, and used soil to rub into the feathers. Kirrikree was surprised to find that it did not irritate him, but dulled his pain. He had been unable to fold his wing up properly, but by the time Grimander had finished, he could do so.

"You must have it bound to you. It's folded as it should be, but it needs to knit." He disappeared into the wood, where evening drew a rich orange glow over the trees, and came back a short while later with leaves and a handful of trailing bindweed. Carefully, expertly, he set the leaves about the wing and then bound them in place with the string-like plant.

"I have asked Woodheart to bless this work," he said. "Though he will know you are not of the forest. But as one who can heal, I give of my skill." He glanced at the forest as if defying some ancient law. "It'll be a week before you can even begin to fly again."

"I am curious," said Kirrikree, "that you have shown me such kindness for a few of my feathers." Grimander had already selected those that he wanted.

"Yes, yes. But I also expect you to tell me a good deal more about why you are here and what you want. I may be an *erratic,* but my first duty is still to Woodheart."

Kirrikree was about to do as the Woodweaver asked, when Grimander silenced him and told him they ought to make themselves safe for the night. "This part of the forest is far too close to one of the five Timber Maws. Sometimes their servants are abroad at night, though what shape they take, no one can say."

Kirrikree would have asked more about this, but it was evident that Grimander wanted to get away. Slowly they went from the glade, Kirrikree uncomfortable traveling on the ground, though he had no choice. At least the pain in his wing had receded almost entirely.

They were silent as they threaded their way between the huge tree boles and the thick coils of root, until, with the darkness gathering very swiftly, they came to a rise, topped by another mighty giant of the forest. Between its immense, serpentine roots there were a number of openings, one of which turned out to be an entrance into a sort of burrow. This proved to be Grimander's home. Kirrikree had never been under the earth in his life before, and a dozen fears rose up in his mind at the thought of what it must be like.

"There will be food," said Grimander, gently leading the owl between the roots. In the end it was the owl's hunger which overcame his fear.

Inside, it was not so bad, more like a nest than a home. There were leaves strewn thickly about, and dried grass and a profusion of feathers. Grimander later explained that of all the things in the forest that lasted, feathers were particularly enduring, and there was power in them of a sort, long after they had become detached from the birds to which they belonged. He also had a number of stones which seemed to ooze their own light, enough to see by. Grimander left Kirrikree to examine them, returning later with a dead rabbit dangling from his hand.

As they shared it, they talked of many things, of the evil in the west, and of Rannovic's ship.

RANNOVIC HAD not taken his eyes from the wall of forest on either side of them since the march had begun. For an hour the party had followed the strange figure of the Woodweaver guide, hardly a word spoken, though in all their minds were the same thoughts. Sisipher, Rannovic noticed, was cool, almost detached, and if there was any fear in her, she hid it well.

"We're moving still further from the river," said the big Hammavar. He glared at the crowding trees, which were like great sentinels on watch. They spread a thick canopy above, as complete as the vaults of a palace and the sunlight beyond was bright enough to light up these deeps, but not before it had been filtered through a thick down of vegetation. There were banks of scarlet, pink and yellow flowers, towering bushes that would have dwarfed many an eastern tree; the undergrowth was tangled, some of it higher than those who passed through it, and all plants grew in utter profusion, the air thick with pollen. Direction and distance meant nothing here, and time seemed a fixed point, although the Woodweaver moved as unerringly as an Earthwrought through stone and earth.

Sisipher called to their silent guide. He had not looked back once on the journey, moving ahead with surety, but always at a speed that would not take him far ahead of the company. He came back now, facing them with his peculiar expression, gnarled hands on hips as if he might be annoyed at being interrupted.

"How far are we from the Fellwater?" said Sisipher.

The Woodweaver pointed into the trees to its right. "Many miles."

Rannovic thrust forward, face red. "I have a ship there. And many men—"

"Too dangerous to go there," said the Woodweaver.

"I cannot abandon my men!" Rannovic snapped, his words choked by the vastness of the forest. He felt belittled by it.

"If you went there," replied the Woodweaver expressionlessly, "the angarbreed would kill you. Woodheart has called us all away from the forest about the Fellwater. It is pronounced a forbidden place. Great evil has come there, and there will be a reckoning."

Rannovic turned back to his men. They were haggard, worn out, their spirits in tatters. Like him, they were men of the sea, not of these tall green vaults. They had put away their swords, but yet they gripped their hafts nervously. If Rannovic had ordered them back, they would gladly have gone, even though no path was visible.

"My people will search for your companions," said the Woodweaver.

Rannovic whirled on him. "When? How soon?"

"There will be word. When we reach our destination."

Sisipher put a restraining hand on Rannovic. She could understand his deep concern. In a sense he felt that he had betrayed them. "We had no choice, Rannovic," she told him. "We have to trust this Woodweaver."

He grunted, though her words gave him little comfort. "And where is this destination?"

The Woodweaver hardly moved. "Since you have come to the Deepwalks in peace, you will not be made to suffer. Woodheart understands you. You are to be Absorbed."

ON ONE of the steep banks that leaned out over where the company passed, a lone figure listened, trying to catch the words. It could not see the figures clearly, but had guessed that these must be Kirrikree's friends. Now, as Grimander heard the Woodweaver speak, he turned and scuttled away into the tall grasses as fast as his bent legs would carry him. It was a short journey back to his home.

The white owl was outside, sitting on top of a boulder, preening himself, his wing strapped firmly to his side. His head bobbed up as he heard Grimander approach and the eyes stared, saucer-like and alert.

"Kirrikree!" Grimander called as loudly as he dared, as if afraid that other ears might catch the name.

The owl could sense that the Woodweaver was greatly perturbed.

"I've seen them! Your allies," gasped Grimander. "One of the Woodweavers, a warrior, is taking them into the forest."

"Then I must go to them—"

"Wait! I must explain." Grimander stood breathlessly, searching for satisfactory words. "Something terrible has happened. You remember how last night we spoke of the Timber Maw?"

"Yes. One of the five that are spread around the Deepwalks—"

"Yes, yes. They draw into them many things. Things that die, things that are good for the forest, things that give sustenance." He was dancing about, his own arms waving frantically, and Kirrikree would have been amused but for his own anxiety.

"What of the Timber Maw?" His own vision of it hung before him still, like the fall into oblivion, the night that followed death.

Grimander became very still. "Your friends are being taken to the one beyond us."

"Why?"

"To be given to it."

"*Given* to it?"

"It is a form of honor, Woodheart understands them, their wish to warn him of the dangers to him. He will bless them by taking them into him. They are to be Absorbed."

PART THREE

THE
DEEPWALKS

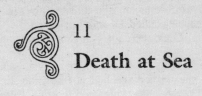

11
Death at Sea

DENNOVIA FELT the pitch and heave of the ship as it ploughed steadily through the seas to the west. They were a week out from the Chain, and though the good weather had not broken, there was a strong gust from behind them, and the waves were mounting. Dennovia tried to sleep, but the movement of the ship kept her awake, unlike her companion, who slept like one dead in the bunk above her. She wished she could go to Ruvanna, who had worked some particular spell over the Earthwrought and Stonedelvers the first night of the voyage, for they either slept at night or dozed during the day, torpid as hibernating animals. The sea was usually bad for their kind, but Ruvanna's powers had made the crossing easy for them, even now during the roughest part of the journey, Ruvanna sat with them constantly, tending them with remarkable care.

There was a soft knocking at the cabin door, and Dennovia groaned to herself, knowing who it would be. She had deliberately ignored Fornoldur on the voyage, telling him before it had started that she would have to do so if she was to avert the suspicions of Wargallow and the others. But during the nights he had insisted on trying to get in to her cabin, and he was becoming very foolish.

Dennovia went to the door, glancing across at Ottemar, but tonight he was deeply asleep, exhausted by the voyage. He had been very quiet on the voyage, saying little and spending most of his time in thought so that Dennovia almost forgot he was with her. So far he had not been discovered, but he had promised her that he would announce himself to Wargallow and Kelloric as soon as the west coast was sighted. By then it would be far too late to have him sent back.

"Who's there?" called Dennovia.

"Dennovia? Open the door." It was as she had suspected. Fornoldur.

She smiled briefly. It had been so easy to snare him, although now she wished she had not been so accomplished. "You cannot enter," she whispered to him. "My companion is not asleep."

"You're lying," came the answer. "You wouldn't have answered the door if he had been awake."

"Go away."

"Not until you open the door."

"You cannot meet me until after we have landed."

"I must see you now."

"Go away," she hissed.

But he knocked again. "If you don't open the door, I'll let it be known who's in there."

"He'll have you executed—"

"I don't think so," came the hoarse whisper. "Not if I go to Wargallow."

She thought it over. She had no intention of allowing Fornoldur his way with her: that was over with. But she had to keep him silent. She dare not risk Wargallow's fury. If he found out her part in this, he would probably have her flung overboard.

"Hurry, Dennovia. If I'm seen out here, I'll have to explain myself."

Frowning, she slid the bolt and let him in. He was very quick, closing and bolting the door behind him at once. He grinned at her hungrily, and for a moment there was something strange in his expression.

"You'd better hurry," she told him. "He's asleep, but only fitfully. If he finds you—"

He smiled, dismissing the Emperor. "Then let's not waste time." He reached for her, but she slipped away from him lithely. It amused him.

"Must it be a chase? Wouldn't you rather we made no noise?"

"What do you want?" she snapped.

He raised his brows. "A brief embrace—"

"You don't think I would couple with you *now*? With the Emperor a few feet from us?"

His grin widened. "Why not? Come, Dennovia, I've thought of nothing but you since we left the Chain. I can't contain myself any longer. He sleeps like one drugged."

"You must go back," she insisted, avoiding him again.

But still he smiled. "You wouldn't have let me in if you had wanted to be rid of me."

"You delude yourself," she told him. "This is no time to behave like a fool. Wait until we get ashore."

"Then what? You think I want to go into those forest lands? Do you?"

They had spoken of this before. "You intend to remain on the ship?"

"Some of us will have to. And in time, when it becomes evident that the main party isn't coming back—"

"You're sure of that?"

"The Deepwalks swallow all those who enter them. And they'll swallow this party, powers or no. Those of us left on the ship can sail when we please. Just as I promised."

"You also promised to leave me alone until we reached land."

He chuckled, and his apparent lack of concern disturbed her. In the past he had been far more discreet. "You know how much I desire you," he said. "Surely a single kiss would not be too much?"

She eyed him warily, still keeping her distance. "With you? A single kiss?" She smiled, but shook her head.

He moved forward swiftly and this time caught her wrist. With a jerk he had pulled her to him. Her eyes widened in anger and she beat at his face with her free hand.

"Don't!" she hissed at him, but he laughed, trying to kiss her. She twisted away, but he caught the back of her head and turned her face to him. As he bent to kiss her, she saw his eyes and choked back a scream. They were wild, filled with a lust that she had not seen before, something red and evil, as though a kind of madness had gripped him. It made her more determined to beat him off, but her strength was useless against his. Slowly he thrust his lips to hers, and they were burning, his tongue probing out obscenely, pushing into her mouth. His hand pulled at her shift, tearing it and exposing her breasts. At once he was squeezing them, but roughly, brutally, with none of his former tenderness. He had become bestial, careless and utterly absorbed. With a desperate slash of her hand she dug at his face, her nails biting into the flesh. It served to hold him back for only a moment. He gazed at her, face inches from hers, a string of spittle dropping from his lips, his eyes blazing with terrible lust.

She screamed.

He ignored it, dipping down to seek her lips again, his hands probing for her, trying to push her thighs apart as he bore her backward. He did not hear the movement on the bunk behind him.

"Fornoldur!" grunted Ottemar, barely awake. But he saw what was going on. He climbed down, almost toppling over as the ship cut through another large swell. He reached out and gripped the shoulder of the guard. "Have you lost your senses, man!"

Fornoldur swung round, his face crimson with fury. Blood ran from the cheek that Dennovia had slashed, and he growled like a beast.

Dennovia broke free of him, clutching her ripped shift to her, tears in her eyes.

"What are you doing!" Ottemar snapped, trying to keep his voice low. "This is no time to be—" But he did not finish, for Fornoldur had launched himself, hands spread out like talons as if he meant to grip the Emperor's neck and strangle him. Ottemar was still only half awake, but he managed to lurch aside. Fornoldur whipped round to face him.

"Fornoldur!" Ottemar said again, but the man was past all reasoning. Ottemar suddenly felt cold. He knew then that whatever power seeped from the west had reached out and found the guard, had probed his weakness, his lust for the girl, and was using it now to sow confusion. Tennebriel had once described to Ottemar how her old servant, Ullarga, had been possessed, and how she had died horribly because of it.

Fornoldur had abandoned all stealth and subtlety. He charged, wielding his fists like clubs, and again Ottemar managed to duck out of reach. Fornoldur almost crashed into the girl, and her arm came up, white in the pale glow of the storm-lamp. There was a gurgling sound, suddenly choked off, and Fornoldur thumped on to the deck.

Ottemar straddled him, wishing he had some weapon to hold at his neck, but there were none in reach. He used his knees to clamp the man down and he looked up at Dennovia. "'Get help! He'll need chaining. He's possessed.''

But she was staring at her hands, ignoring his plea. His eyes followed hers, and he saw the knife for the first time, dull in the lamp glow. There was a rasp of breath from the man under him, and Fornoldur shuddered before going very still. Ottemar gripped his hair and pulled back his head. The throat was cut and blood ran steadily from the fatal wound that Dennovia had inflicted.

She dropped the knife, appalled at what she had done. "I didn't mean—'' she began, her eyes filling with fresh tears.

Ottemar was on his feet at once, an arm going around her. "No, no. You did what was best, girl,'' he said, a little dazed. He stared down at the body of her former lover. Only then did he hear the knocking on the door.

"Quickly, you must hide!'' Dennovia told him, trying to recover her composure. "I'll try to explain this—''

He shook his head. "No. The time for deceits is over.'' He went to the door. "Who's there?''

For a moment there was no answer, but then a familiar voice, that of Wargallow, answered. "Open the door. I am alone.''

Ottemar did so at once, and Wargallow entered as swiftly as Fornoldur had done, closing the door behind him. He faced Ottemar reprovingly. Dennovia had moved back into the shadows, but Wargallow glanced at her, nodding.

"This can be explained,'' Ottemar began.

"I heard a scream, as did a good many more of the crew,'' said Wargallow. "I had assumed it was Fornoldur molesting the girl, and not you. You've done some stupid things in your time, Ottemar,'' he went on, his voice hardening. "But this!'' Could the girl possibly have been telling the truth when she said Ottemar desired her? But that was ridiculous, Wargallow told himself. It was only then that he saw the blood on Ottemar's hands.

What madness had been performed here? His eyes took in the cabin, alighting at last on the body of the guard.

Quietly Ottemar explained what had really happened.

Wargallow examined Fornoldur: his throat had been cut expertly. This was no chance strike. Dennovia had learned under Mourndark how to do such things. The Deliverer gazed at Ottemar. "He's dead," he said bluntly. He went to the girl. "You were a fool to let him in here—"

"You did not see him, how he acted!" she protested, trying to explain how Fornoldur had suddenly become a monster. Ottemar confirmed it and Wargallow's face tightened.

"Then it was the work of Anakhizer. This madness he sends is a threat to us all."

"You did not seem surprised to see me," said Ottemar. "Or had the girl already told you I was aboard?" He looked accusingly at Dennovia.

"No one told me," said Wargallow. "It was an easy thing for me to fathom. I could have had you put ashore before we left harbor. Your clumsy subterfuge didn't fool me."

"Then you sanction my coming?" said Ottemar, forcing a grin.

"I'm not convinced you acted in the best interests of the Empire."

"Dennovia is not to be blamed, nor punished," Ottemar suddenly said. "I forbid it."

Wargallow bowed, though he was smiling as he did so. "It would seem unreasonable to punish someone who has so recently saved your life."

Dennovia was shaking her head.

"Oh, make no mistake," Wargallow told her. "Whatever Fornoldur had become, he would have killed you both, easily. Anakhizer is far more adept at using people than you ever were."

Dennovia gasped as he said it, but before she could retort there was an outcry on the deck, so loud that they all heard it clearly. Ottemar and Wargallow exchanged anxious glances.

"Stay here," said Wargallow. "You can announce yourself in the morning. Wrap up that corpse. I'll have it fetched later. And keep out of sight."

Ottemar would have objected, but he felt that he had caused his friend enough problems for one night. He nodded.

Wargallow left them, thinking as he went about Dennovia. Why had she wanted to come? And why had Ottemar aided her in her cause, adamant that she should be brought? But Wargallow had no more time to speculate as he reached the deck. A number of guards were milling about, weapons to hand. Wargallow confronted the formidable bulk of Zuhaster.

"Sire!" he growled above the noisy bluster of the wind. "We've lost two of our men."

"The sea?" said Wargallow coldly, but he saw at once that it was not that simple.

Zuhaster swore. "I think not, sire. Something stirs in the waters. We have tried to see them, but it's too dark."

"Keep the men away from the rails."

"Aye, sire." Zuhaster moved away swiftly for one so large, his war axe gleaming.

Wargallow was joined by Kelloric and the Deliverer, Coldrieve.

"Issiquellen," said Kelloric softly. "I've not told them, but my men understand well enough."

"Have they tried to board us?"

"Aye."

"How many?"

"Just a handful. These waters are bound to be patrolled. The coast is a few more days' journey off. With this following wind, we've made good speed. What was the trouble below?"

Wargallow scowled, his eyes meeting those of Coldrieve. "Some stupidity with the girl—"

"Dennovia?" grunted Kelloric. He had not wanted her aboard.

"Yes. You were right to question her coming."

"I know the men on a voyage like this. Like dogs. And that one is a rare woman. She'd test the chastity of a god—"

"Fornoldur has made a fool of himself for the last time. He tried to force her—"

"From what I hear," said Kelloric, "Fornoldur would not have had to force himself. They have been lovers for some time."

"That partnership is ended," said Wargallow stiffly. He would have said more, but a shout near the prow dragged him and the others forward. One of the men was pointing out at the waters. Storm-lamps were raised, casting a dancing glow on the sea for a short distance. In the light the men could see a dozen heads above the surface, light gleaming in the bulbous eyes. As Kelloric had said, these were issiquellen.

"Our coming will be known," said Wargallow above the wind.

"But we are relying on surprise," said Kelloric.

Brannog joined them, watching the sea ahead as if he could read its every contour clearly. "Wargallow," he said. "There are scores of them ahead of us. You'd better wake and arm the entire crew."

"You think they mean to board us?"

Brannog shrugged. "They prefer to be in the water, just as my people prefer to be on land. But I don't think they can be here merely to watch us."

"Could Anakhizer have sent them?"

Again Brannog shrugged. "They're his vermin. But these are their waters. We may have come on them by chance."

There were more shouts, from the stern of the boat, voices raised against the din of the wind and the furious flapping of the great sails. Brannog was gone at once.

"Watch the waters ahead," Wargallow told Kelloric, and he and his men did so warily.

At the stern, Wargallow found another group of men. Some were bloodied, a wounded colleague at their feet. It seemed that the issiquellen had indeed attempted to board, some dozen of them.

Brannog gazed back at the dark seas, shaking his head. "They mean to attack in force. The seas are filling with them."

Wargallow considered for only a moment, then nodded to himself curtly as if he had weighed a number of decisions. He gripped Brannog by the shoulder. "Can you handle this ship without a crew?"

Brannog frowned at him. "In this wind?"

"How many men do you need?"

"For how long?"

"A short while. Just keep the wheel steady and the ship on course."

"A strange request."

"I want every other man below, out of sight, save myself and Coldrieve."

"With the issiquellen ready to swarm over us—"

Wargallow shook his head. "No, I don't think so. Can you handle this ship alone? For a few minutes?"

Brannog nodded. "But why?"

"Then take the wheel, at once. Zuhaster! Get your men below. Quickly, do as I say." Wargallow raced off to the prow, where Kelloric and his men were yet watching for movement. "I've given the wheel to Brannog, just for a short while. Take your men, the entire company, and get them below decks, out of sight."

"Are you insane!" gasped Kelloric. "The issiquellen—"

"Please do as I say."

For a moment the two men eyed each other in the gloom, Kelloric warring within: this was his ship, no matter whom he carried, and he was being relieved of its command. For what reason? This was lunacy. Every man should be here on deck! Brannog was a fine seaman, but was he to sail the ship single-handed? Had Wargallow lost his senses?

"You must put your trust in Brannog and myself," said the Deliverer. Like a silent shadow, Coldrieve stood behind him. "And what we bear."

Kelloric grimaced, but nodded at last, signaling for his men to follow him. They filed below, and as they did so, Zuhaster leaned close to his leader.

"Mutiny is an ugly word, sire, but there is madness in the air tonight. It smells stronger than salt. What can three men hope to achieve?"

"Perhaps they know how to speak to these sea beings," said Kelloric. "I admit a battle would be costly. We may lose the ship. We had best put our faith in Wargallow."

Zuhaster grunted, prepared to obey Kelloric without further argument. But he felt a sudden grip on his shoulder.

"But tell me, oarsmaster, what do you know of the scuffle below deck? The woman, Dennovia."

Zuhaster's great face creased in a frown. "It was the shouting on deck that awoke me, sire. Was there trouble?"

"Go and look. If you find Fornoldur, bring him to me. He

may be one of the Emperor's guards, but while he's on my ship, he's under my command, damn him!''

"It will be a pleasure, sire. Where should I look for him?''

"I suggest you start with the lady Dennovia's cabin.''

With a final leer, Zuhaster went to do as bidden, the peril on deck momentarily forgotten.

Brannog had taken the wheel; he found it easy to handle, the ship responding well to his seamanship. She was a superb craft, he reflected, probably one of the finest ever to sail out of Medallion. Kelloric would be furious at having had control taken from him, even for a short time, though he would know that Brannog would sail her with care. But what in the name of the seas did Wargallow intend? *Speak* to the issiquellen? Surely he would not dare try. But nothing seemed beyond him.

Wargallow and Coldrieve stood in the prow of the sleek craft, studying the heaving seas. The wind roared in their ears, almost deafening them. They knew that their enemies were before them, the waves thick with them. And they did mean to take this ship, swarm over it, drown it. Whether or not Anakhizer had deliberately sent them did not matter now. They must be stopped.

Brannog tried to see what the two figures were doing. He thought he caught a glimpse of steel, a faint blue radiance. The rod of power? They had it with them? If so, no wonder Wargallow had sent the crew below. Brannog recalled the night on Medallion when he and Ruvanna had gazed stupidly at Wargallow's killing steel, wondering what had become of the perfect hand that had replaced it. There had been whispers on Medallion of how Wargallow and his inseparable colleague, Coldrieve, had spent much time with the Emperor's smiths, and it seemed to Brannog now that the secret of those hours must lie here. Wargallow had a new hand of steel, the twin-bladed horror of his former days. Thus the rod of power was hidden again. Until now.

Brannog could see the Deliverers leaning out over the water, their silhouettes limned in a gentle blue radiance. Still the ship cut through the waves, the spray bursting on either side of the prow as it rose and dipped, its course never wavering as Brannog held the wheel, in complete command of the vessel, at one with the wild elements. The storm seemed to rise in pitch, but nothing turned the ship aside. The waters were alive with issiquellen, and already they were preparing to climb aboard.

Power spread from the Deliverers like a bolt of fury and there was an abrupt flash of vivid blue, ghastly as heavenly lightning. The pure heat shot down into the sea, igniting it from below like sunlight. All around the ship the water suddenly turned to a dazzling, radiant whiteness, the searing light spreading outward as if from an explosion. Brannog closed his eyes to the freak daylight as if he had suddenly been confronted by the sun. But he heard the screams above the howl of the raging wind. He squinted at the waves, seeing power flood down into them, flattening them, burning up the bodies of all who were in the water. The light tore downward, searing the issiquellen, burning them up as if they had been submerged in molten lava.

For no more than a minute did the awesome power crackle about the ship, which itself was immune to it. Brannog felt his mind wrenching, and he shuddered at the escape of power. Mercifully it shut off. The white light went out, a snuffed candle. Darkness raced in, deeper than before. The ship sped on, through seas that had been made calm. And all around her the bodies floated, scores of them, broken, charred, destroyed. It was as though a huge nest had been flooded to douse a fire.

Wargallow and Coldrieve staggered toward Brannog, their hands hidden, their faces white, streaked with perspiration.

"So you carry the rod yet," said Brannog, his mouth dry.

Wargallow nodded. "I take no joy in this slaughter. I wanted no one to know the truth of the rod. But Anakhizer will know." He looked at Coldrieve, who as ever, remained impassive.

"There'll be no survivors to swim to him," said Brannog.

Wargallow nodded tiredly. "I'll fetch Kelloric."

Below them, Zuhaster had obeyed Kelloric's orders and had gone straight to the cabin of Dennovia. The oarsmaster's blood still boiled when he thought of the first night of the voyage. Somehow Fornoldur had made a fool of him, and he was certain that Dennovia had had something to do with it. He had sworn that he would have his revenge for that, and this might give him an opportunity.

Loudly he knocked on the door. In a moment he heard Dennovia's voice.

"Captain's orders, my lady," he boomed. "You've to open up."

The door opened slowly and Dennovia's face, paler than he remembered, gazed up at him. "Can you not be a little more discreet?" she said softly.

He lowered his voice without thinking, instantly obedient. Who could possibly refuse any command of this divine creature? No wonder Fornoldur had made a fool of himself over her. She let him enter, closing the door behind him.

"Are you alone?" she asked.

"Aye," he nodded, puzzled. She seemed to be expecting him.

"Well, he's there. Hurry. I can't stand having him here any longer."

Zuhaster frowned deeply, following the line of her finger. She was pointing to a thick blanket which had been used to bundle something up. When he went to it, his frown turned to an expression of shock. "What is this?" he gasped, glaring at the girl.

She looked at him in horror, as if seeing him for the first time. "Did Wargallow not send you?"

"Wargallow?" He looked about in confusion, then suddenly pulled the blanket folds apart. The face of the dead Fornoldur gazed up at him, the lips drawn back in an accusing rictus.

Zuhaster leapt up, pulling a short sword from its sheath. "By whose hand did he die!" he growled, full of ugly suspicion.

"Who sent you?" repeated Dennovia.

In the doorway a figure had appeared. They had not noticed him open the door and stand forbiddingly behind them. It was Kelloric and his face was as cold as the steel in his hand. "I sent him," he said through his teeth. "And if you cannot explain Fornoldur's death to my satisfaction, you'll join him in that cheap shroud."

Suddenly the entire cabin was lit up in brilliant white light by something outside. The air crackled as power danced through it, and they all felt their hair stiffening. In the dazzling glow, another figure was revealed in the cabin, a man who had been hiding in the recess of its far wall. Zuhaster had snatched up his axe in a reflex action, brandishing it and the sword as though he would assault the man without more ado. But Kelloric's voice cut through the air like a knife.

"Be still! It's the Emperor, or his ghost!"

The searing light died, although it seemed to have been with them for an age before it did so. It took them a long time to adjust to the darkness.

Ottemar had come forward. "No ghost," he said. "I am Ottemar Remoon."

Zuhaster bowed and shuffled back, embarrassed by the display of weaponry. "Sire, your pardon. I had no idea—"

Kelloric also bowed, but his confusion was clear on his face. "There is a madness aboard this ship," he breathed, but not so low that Ottemar did not hear him.

"There is indeed," said the Emperor. "Guard yourself against it. And against rash acts. Our enemy will test every one of us as he tested Fornoldur."

Kelloric and Zuhaster both stared again at the ghastly dead face, and though they saw a fallen colleague, they saw something else, a grim, dark something, a crawling evil.

High above the ship, circling in the folds of night, the black creature of the air watched as the brilliant light below went out, like a fire doused by a wave. The wind tried to bring down the dark bird, but it was too powerful and flapped away casually. It had seen enough. It flew onward and upward, until, in the heart of the night, it saw above it the vast darkness that was its goal, the silent Shadowflight. There was news for it, for the rod of power that had been misplaced was no longer missing.

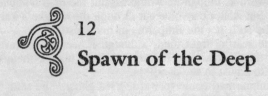

12
Spawn of the Deep

WARGALLOW HAD called together a special gathering, and it met in his narrow cabin as the dawn was breaking. The sea remained calmer, the gusting winds of the night having died away as if they had witnessed enough when the issiquellen host had been smitten. The ship was back in Kelloric's hands, Brannog having been relieved shortly after the Deliverers had performed their strange rite. On the deck and at their stations, the crew were uneasy, sensing that the events of the night had far more to them than anyone was prepared to say. Word had spread that Fornoldur was dead, and there was much speculation as to how he had died.

Ottemar was not present when the meeting began. Wargallow sat with Coldrieve, and beside them was Brannog. Ruvanna remained with the Stonedelvers and Earthwrought, though Brannog had spoken with her. Kelloric insisted that Zuhaster joined him at the table, and there was no objection.

"There is an unease among the men," said Wargallow. "I can understand why. Last night it was necessary to make use of the rod—"

"It is not that which has aroused the men's unease," said Kelloric.

There was a knock at the door. Dennovia entered, and behind her was Ottemar. The girl kept her eyes on the table, but Ottemar nodded at Brannog, whose surprise was obvious. Coldrieve looked on as if this was no more than he had expected.

162

"He's here with my agreement," said Wargallow. "I know what we planned on Medallion, but I wanted the Empire to think we had left him behind."

"And do you rule the Empire?" said Kelloric tersely. Coldrieve looked at him sharply, as though marking him. Kelloric was aware of the glance, himself masking his thoughts.

"He does not," said Ottemar. "But be advised by him, Kelloric. We are at war. One man cannot rule alone. And you are as much a part of the command as any other. I depend upon you as much as I depend upon Wargallow."

"Then why did you not think it fit to share your confidence?"

"There's a sickness aboard the vessel," said Wargallow. "And it has been sown by our enemies. Something that works at us when we least expect it, turning in us like a knife—"

Kelloric banged a fist down on the table. "All the more reason for us to trust each other!"

"I agree," said Wargallow.

"Then let us be open! I understand why you thought it sensible to keep the Emperor's movements secret, but I never thought it wise to agree to his coming at all. I apologize for my bluntness, sire, but your absence will cause anxiety—"

"The Empress is a very capable woman, Kelloric," Ottemar smiled. "She will maintain order in my absence, be assured."

"Just so," nodded Wargallow.

Kelloric grunted. "You'll understand my own concern."

"It is war, Kelloric," repeated Ottemar. "Our mission is not an open one. We need to sow confusion."

"I see that. But why is the girl here?" Kelloric nodded at Dennovia, his expression clearly one of scorn. "What powers does she have, other than to twist the minds of men—"

"There is no need for that," cut in Brannog. "Your anger is unnecessary, Kelloric. It is fuel to Anakhizer."

"If you say so. But tell us why she is here. I cannot believe she was brought purely as a chattel."

Ottemar's brows contracted. His own anger seemed to be contained with an effort. "You think she came to accommodate me?"

Kelloric looked away. "Of course not, sire. She was Fornoldur's woman—"

"You think she was brought merely to keep him company?" said Wargallow.

"It would have been a poor reason. Why was she permitted aboard without prior consent?"

"She had my consent," said Ottemar.

Dennovia stood up, her cheeks flushing. "I am no one's chattel! I was brought because I am considered to be a threat to you all."

"In what way?" snapped Kelloric before anyone else could interrupt.

"I knew where the rod of power was hidden. Wargallow would not let me remain behind. Not where Anakhizer could find me. I am safer here, and because of it, so are you all. You think I wanted to come!"

Wargallow did not react, but he admired the girl for her deceit.

Kelloric was glaring at him. "This is true?"

Wargallow nodded. "The Emperor himself told me of his concern. I had no desire to alert anyone of our suspicions. But Dennovia speaks the truth. You know that she was with me in the east."

Brannog was nodding. "You should know, Kelloric, that Dennovia brought Wargallow from the edge of death."

"I have heard the tale," said Kelloric, though frowning. "Because of it I had assumed she had a special place—"

"I have not," said Dennovia coldly. Her back had stiffened, and there was a hauteur about her. "I would have been left in Elberon long ago were it not for the knowledge that I have."

Kelloric looked away, seemingly satisfied, but his expression remained serious.

Ottemar gave again an account of how Fornoldur had attempted to assault the girl and how he had died for his actions. He told them how the sudden transformation had come over Fornoldur, the way in which something far more evil had manipulated him.

"Perhaps," said Kelloric afterward, "I owe you both an apology, sire."

"It has not been a satisfactory night," said Ottemar. "I would have preferred that you learned of my being here more appropriately."

"You'll understand," said Wargallow, "that we wanted as little known about the rod as possible. Anakhizer will be searching for it with every last vestige of his power."

Zuhaster was nodding thoughtfully. "Aye, sire, but have you nor alerted him to it by using it in the night?" He had spoken his thoughts aloud, coloring as he realized, but Wargallow nodded calmly.

"It may be. I regret that I acted in secrecy. I sent you below because we had no choice but to use the rod's power. The sea was brimming with issiquellen. It was unpleasant work, but for the rod, all too easy to destroy the sea people."

"Then Anakhizer must know precisely where we are!" said Zuhaster, his color draining.

"Perhaps not," said Brannog. "Although the issiquellen have come under Anakhizer's banner, there are many of them in these waters. It is more likely they came upon us by chance. It would have been in their nature to attempt to capture us. I think if they had known we had the rod, they would not have dared attack."

Kelloric almost smiled at that. "Aye, Brannog! That is a wise surmise. They would have fled to their master, warning him—"

"As it is, they perished," said Wargallow. "All of them."

"Then the voyage remains a secret one?" said Kelloric, brightening.

"I don't know. The power that was released may have repercussions. The sea felt it, and the skies. Be sure that Anakhizer is bending his every effort to finding us."

Kelloric grunted, satisfied. "The crew must be told, everything. I want no unrest. No gossip. And they'll mourn Fornoldur. He was a popular man, and a good warrior."

"I will come to the deck," said Ottemar. "I trust that it will give the men fresh heart."

"It's better that they know the truth of the matter, sire," said Kelloric. "Naturally the men will be honored, though the responsibility will weigh heavily on them."

He's not content, thought Wargallow. But he is in no position now to take issue.

The meeting was at an end, though the mood had altered little for the better. As they began to leave, Wargallow called Ottemar back so that they were alone.

"I know only too well why you have come," Wargallow told the Emperor bluntly.

Ottemar grinned. For a moment he looked more like the man he had been in Elberon, in the peaceful days after the fall of Xennidhum. "You didn't think I'd be able to sit on my throne, gathering dust while you and my picked warriors came out here—"

"You are no warrior," said Wargallow, though not unkindly. "Sire."

Ottemar laughed. "No, though I use a sword far better than I once did." It was true, for he was reasonably accomplished.

"Perhaps I'm being unfair," said Wargallow. "You thought yourself a coward once. But you're not lacking in heart."

"Once I was quite content to keep well away from combat. A quiet life would have been perfectly acceptable—"

"But not now?"

"As the Emperor?"

Wargallow walked to the door, listening. Coldrieve was outside, though, a guard against eavesdroppers. "It's Sisipher, isn't it?"

Ottemar's face clouded at once. "Is it so obvious?"

Wargallow studied his friend, one of the few men in his life that he had ever felt remotely close to. "To me."

"Does Brannog know?"

"I'm not sure. He's aware that Sisipher left Goldenisle because of you. Whatever he suspects, he says nothing on the matter."

"I'll not rest until I find her, Simon, I swear it—"

"It is best if you don't speak of it, even to me. The task of this crew comes first."

"You *knew* I boarded the ship in harbor?"

"I don't claim to be a genius for having anticipated it. You gave up wanting to come too easily, in public at least."

"Yet you knew why I came."

"Yes, I knew. Your head is ruled by your heart in this matter."

"Then why did you allow me to come? You could have prevented it."

"Yes, I could have. But if you had remained on Medallion, what would you have become? Would you have resigned yourself to disappointment and got on with the business of ruling, today, when the Empire needs a firm hand more than ever?"

Ottemar stared at him, unable to answer.

"I doubt it. In the short time that I was away from you I could see that you'd begun to neglect your duties."

"You exaggerate—"

"I tell you these things as a friend, Ottemar. Remember that. You'll have praise enough at court, but not from me, unless you earn it. And what is the result of your folly? A good man has died. Fornoldur was caught up in this intrigue. This path you have made."

Ottemar cursed under his breath. Wargallow was right.

"I won't dwell on it, Ottemar. But look at the truth. Your own ruthlessness. Well, I'm sure you'll be more usefully employed here than at home."

"Are you?"

"As you said, Tennebriel will look after your throne."

"You do not trust her?"

Wargallow smiled. "Don't you? You should. She worships Solimar. She will let nothing interfere with his succession."

"I cannot believe she wants me dead."

"No, no. She'll keep the throne secure. But you—"

"You have plans for me?"

"Only this. That you do not let your infatuation for Sisipher weaken you—"

"That is no kindness—"

"Anakhizer deals in madness, Ottemar. Love can be turned to madness easily. You saw the result of Fornoldur's desires."

"Are you so expert in these matters? You who have never—"

"If I stand outside these things," Wargallow answered coldly, "then perhaps I see them more clearly. Your love will make you vulnerable."

Ottemar would have retorted but Wargallow cut him short. "Tell me one thing. I see now that you had help from Dennovia in boarding us. I assume that in exchange for her part in this romantic bargain you agreed to convince me she should also come. You did it eloquently enough."

Ottemar nodded sullenly.

"What reason did she give you for wanting to come?"

"To be with her lover."

"Fornoldur?" said Wargallow, eyes narrowing. "And you agreed?"

"I had some sympathy for her—"

"Yet her love," said Wargallow, pronouncing the words with a sudden chill, "did not prevent her from putting a knife into him—"

"It was not Fornoldur she killed! Had you seen what he had become—"

I did not see that, Wargallow told himself, but I did see the way in which he died. Had Dennovia loved Fornoldur deeply, she would not have been able to kill him so neatly, for the cut had been expert and very swift. "Then you persist in your belief that she came so that she could be with her lover? For that she risked the consequences of my anger?"

Ottemar looked hard at him, trying to read the answer in his face. "Why else?" But his voice wavered.

Wargallow nodded slowly. "Yes, why else."

Coldrieve suddenly appeared in the door, allowing Zuhaster entrance. The oarsmaster stood with his chest heaving as if he had been in a battle. "Apologies, sires, but you must come above at once! Please hasten." His face was such a mass of anxiety that both Wargallow and Ottemar followed him without question. Privately both were glad that the conversation had ended when it had.

On deck there was confusion. Many of the crew were leaning on the port rail, pointing to the southern horizon. The sea was relatively calm, broken only by a few white curls of foam. There were gulls in the sky, wheeling with the thermals, but they kept clear of the ship instead of following it. Otherwise everything seemed to be normal.

Wargallow looked askance at Zuhaster. "Well?"

"There have been several sightings, sire," he replied, and from his face it seemed that he was afraid of something.

"More issiquellen? The seas here are bound to—"

It was the shadow of Brannog that cut Wargallow off. And beside him stood Ruvanna, who had left the sleeping Stone-delvers and Earthwrought for a rare moment. She looked out at the sea as if she saw far more below its waves than any of the men around her. Her fingers interlinked with those of Brannog.

"Do you feel nothing?" Brannog asked the Deliverer.

Wargallow studied the sea. It was no different. He shook his head.

"Something from its deeps is coming this way," said Ruvanna. "It is far away yet. But I think it seeks us."

"What have the men seen?" Wargallow asked Zuhaster.

But Brannog pointed to the horizon. "There have been water spouts. Large waves, though they have not reached us, as though the sea had sucked them back under itself."

"I think the rod has attracted this thing," Ruvanna said softly to Wargallow. "Brannog has told me it is here."

"What is it that comes? Do you know, Ruvanna?"

Brannog answered as softly as his wife. "You recall our journey across the Silences to the east? Korbillian was forced to summon a storm in the desert to dismiss what came."

Wargallow saw in his mind the vast, rolling dunes as they had moved inward like creeping tidal waves. Again he looked out to sea. Could something as terrible be here, in these waters? Brannog's grave face affirmed that it could.

"The rod?" whispered Wargallow.

Brannog shook his head. "This thing is drawn to it. Perhaps it would welcome its power. Dare we risk such a thing?"

Wargallow shuddered. The rod's power was two-fold. It could destroy, but it could also create. Zoigon, who had forged the rod for him could have absorbed the power into himself and become a god. Whatever was out in the deeps of the ocean could also be capable of doing such a thing.

"No, I dare not use the rod again." Wargallow swung round on Zuhaster. "Oarsmaster! Get every man to the oars! At once. How far are we from land?"

"We should be in sight of it by the next dawn," said Zu-haster.

"To late. By nightfall."

Zuhaster gasped. "Sire, you'll burn the men up—"

"Try. At once."

The oarsmaster gazed out to sea. Whatever was out there had evidently filled the Deliverer with a fresh dread, in which case it must be something worthy of great fear. Zuhaster turned to the men. A number of them had recognized Otte-mar, who had himself been listening to part of Wargallow's conversation with Brannog and Ruvanna. The Emperor now used his sudden appearance, which the men greeted with as much pleasure as surprise, to urge them to do as Zuhaster was bidding them.

"Speed is essential," he was telling them.

Shortly afterward the ship gathered speed as every available man sat at the oars. They pulled with a new gusto, talking excitedly when they could about the abrupt appearance of the Emperor, deciding that he was not, as had previously been hinted, the coward some would have him.

Kelloric came to Wargallow and Brannog at the port rail, hiding his annoyance at having Zuhaster's last orders countermanded, though he accepted the new urgency. In silence they watched the sea.

Throughout the morning the ship raced on across the western sea. From time to time the watchers had glimpses of disturbances on the southern horizon, where clouds had gathered, together with what seemed to be fog banks. Waves rose and dipped, but never came northwards, as if some barrier prevented them. By mid afternoon the oarsmen were getting very tired. Their brief rest periods were no longer enough and Wargallow agreed that they must be extended. The ship moved forward slowly, catching what little wind there was.

"Will we make landfall by dusk?" Wargallow asked Kelloric.

"I doubt it. But if the men can manage another long pull, it will not be far into the night. Though we'll not be able to land. Have you thought of that?"

"The cliffs?"

"Aye. We were to sail down the coast to this place named

the Claws. Whatever it is that comes, it is from the south. We shall have to pass it."

Brannog shook his head. "No," he said with finality. "Though I do not know the coastal waters, it is certain that they are very deep, dropping sheer to the ocean floor. If there were a shelf below the coast, we could hug the scarp and go past whatever this thing is. No, we will have to try and land before it reaches us."

"Is that possible?" said Kelloric anxiously, his eyes yet fixed on the darkening horizon.

"The Stonedelvers will help us," said Brannog stoically.

Kelloric nodded, wondering about this big seaman, who had become a man of the earth, the world below the surface. He and his wife were more like the earth and stone people, as if they were changing and becoming one with them. Yet Brannog still remained a master of the seas. He had handled the ship with stunning ease during the events of the night, as if he could have continued to do so alone until the dawn if necessary. And the crew thought highly of him for it. Probably they held Brannog in higher esteem than anyone else on the voyage, even Ottemar, who was to most of them as yet untried. Kelloric was still not sure if he thought it a good thing to have the Emperor on such a dangerous voyage; he had heard too many rumors that he was a reckless man, unlike the calculating Wargallow. It would be a very bad time to lose the Emperor, though Kelloric tried not to think of disaster.

Night fell abruptly, lending afresh urgency to the efforts of the crew, for though the pursuit was invisible by day, the thick darkness brought with it a thousand phantoms. The men bent their backs with renewed vigor, the miles speeding by.

Shortly after nightfall, three shapes flapped down from the skies, alighting on the upper cross beam of the mast. Ruvanna was brought up from below, smiling as she saw Skyrac, Aumlac's fierce war-eagle, and two of his companions. A number of them had flown on ahead of the ship from Malador.

"Can you speak to them?" said Wargallow, instantly beside Ruvanna. She wondered if he ever slept properly.

"Not as well as Aumlac can—"

"Then wake him. Bring him here."

Ruvanna would have protested, but she knew the serious-ness of their plight. Aumlac loathed being on water, but if Skyrac had news, they must have it. She went below and brought the Stonedelver from his sleep. He was on deck, peering at the night, before he fully realized it. But when he saw Skyrac and his companions, his face broke in a grin and he forgot about the movement of the ship.

"How far is land?" was his first question.

Skyrac reported that it was no more than an hour's flight, which Aumlac guessed to be about three hours by ship. But as he listened to Skyrac's report of Sea Scarp and of how difficult it would be to take a ship close to the shore, and of how the massive cliffs overhung the sea, almost impossible to scale, the huge Stonedelver found his attention drawn to the sea. He stood by the rail, gazing like a sentinel at the darkness.

"Do you not hear it!" he gasped.

Wargallow listened, but heard only the sea. Somewhere out in the night it sounded as though there was a storm, or waves pounding an unseen reef.

"We are hunted," said Aumlac. "From below—"

"We know," said Ruvanna. "Which is why we must get to land."

"But the ship is too slow!" protested Aumlac. "We need to be like Skyrac if we are to outrun what comes."

Wargallow looked up at the eagles. They, too, were study-ing the darkness to the south, their eyes flashing in the light of the ship's lanterns.

"The men have given everything," said Kelloric grimly. "They cannot be pushed any harder. And if it is to be a battle—"

"A battle!" cried Aumlac. "Against what comes?"

"My friend," said Ottemar, emerging from the shadows, "you find us at a loss."

"Ottemar!" said Aumlac, bowing at once. "I did not know you were with us. This is a difficult plight—"

"You'd better ready your warriors for a fight."

Again Aumlac shook his head. "I'll ready them, sire, but

not for war. You need fresh oarsmen. I will fetch them for you." With remarkable agility he went below.

"Stonedelvers?" said Kelloric. "The sea is no friend to them."

"They will row for me," said Ottemar proudly.

"If we survive this voyage," said Ruvanna, "men will speak of it for many years to come."

When Aumlac returned to the deck, he had a dozen of his Stonedelvers with him and as many Earthwrought, the whole company, in fact. None of them looked very alert, having been in an unnatural sleep. But whatever their feelings about being awake on a moving ship, they hid them and looked eager to get to the oars. Zuhaster could hardly believe his eyes as Aumlac led them down to the rowing deck. And he looked even more astounded a few minutes later when the ship suddenly lurched forward.

"My crew," he told Wargallow and Kelloric, "are the best the Empire has. Not only do they fight harder than any other warriors, but they row like ten men. But *these!* The stone men and the earth people! They shame us." For all his bluster, he looked delighted.

"Shame has nothing to do with this," Wargallow told him. "They have power, Zuhaster. They draw it up from the very earth, or perhaps from the sea, as Brannog does."

Zuhaster nodded, leaping away. Moments later he was sitting at one of his own benches, bending his back with the new crew. His men were glad of a rest, and seeing the extraordinary strength of the Stonedelvers and Earthwrought, they cheered them on for all their exhaustion.

Wargallow scanned the night. It gave up none of its secrets, except to remind him with fresh sounds that the pursuit drew ever closer.

It was a little over an hour later, with the fresh crew still rowing mightily, that a watcher on the mast shouted down that land was ahead. It was closer than they realized, looming out of the darkness.

Aumlac sent one of the Earthwrought to the prow. Again, the being ignored the fact that he was on water, which would normally have terrified him. Instead he studied the cliffs ahead, seeing them as clearly by night as a man would have by day.

"There is nowhere fit for a landing," Kelloric told Ottemar and Wargallow. "As the eagle reported, the cliffs are very high and they hang far out over the sea. And there is nowhere we can take the ship in. The seas are not that rough tonight, but even so, the swell will dash us to pieces on the foot of that scarp."

The ship yet moved forward, Kelloric giving the order that it must not get in too close.

Wargallow grimaced. "Our only hope is to get ashore. And there is very little time."

As he watched the seas beyond them, the ship gave a sudden shudder, as though it had struck something below it. Oars snapped out in the waters and there were curses from below. The ship swung round, and more oars broke. Aumlac appeared at the head of the stairs.

"Are we aground?" bawled Kelloric. His men were dashing about, trying to organize the ship's defenses.

Aumlac shook his head. "Something is below us—"

"The pursuit?" cried Kelloric. His sword was out, but as yet he could see no enemy on which to use it.

"I cannot say," called Aumlac above a sudden roaring of the waves. The sea had become very choppy, the ship rocking violently.

Brannog was leaning out far over the port rail, heedless of the dangers. "No, it's not the pursuit, I'm sure. I can hear something beyond us. It still comes on from the south."

"Then what is it that has us? Sand bars?" shouted Wargallow.

Brannog shook his head. "No, I told you there is no shelf here. Just a sheer drop."

Again the ship lurched, now being dragged forward quickly as if caught in a rapid tide race, its nose righting, aimed at the cliffs. They rose up darkly, blotting out the sky with their own deeper shadows.

"We're being sucked in to the land!" someone shouted. Everyone seemed to be on deck, weapons gleaming, though still there was no assault.

Ottemar edged closer to Wargallow. "I fear you may have to use the rod again."

Wargallow shook his head. "I dare not."

Brannog staggered back from the rail, his face white. Ruvanna went to him, her arms about him as she pressed herself close to him. "What have you seen?" she asked.

He hugged her. "Something huge has wrapped itself about the hull. It is pulling us to the land. And it is *of* the land."

Wargallow barely heard him above the din of voices and roaring waves. Panic spread like a fire. "Explain yourself!" he cried. Beside him, Coldrieve had his killing steel at the ready, watching the sea for the first sign of the enemy.

"Some sort of growths," Brannog shouted back. "I cannot see clearly. They have their own purpose."

Wargallow glowered at the precipitous cliffs, which now hung right over the ship, hundreds of feet above it, dwarfing it. He had his own killing steel out.

There was a tug at his sleeve and he turned to find himself looking into the eyes of Dennovia. She was shaking her head, but the sound of the waves, which now seemed to be breaking on all sides of them, drowned out her words. The face of the cliff raced to meet them, and they braced themselves for what must be an inevitable impact and the destruction of the ship.

13
Sea Watch

THE ROAR of the waves mounted; added to it now came a cracking of the rocks ahead, a deep groaning as if the overhanging cliffs could not bear the sudden massive onslaught of the seas. Water boiled and sheets of white foam flew back from the rocks, drenching the crew of the ship as it arrowed for its inevitable destruction. As the prow was about to crumple into the stone, another rumble like deep thunder shook the wall and a tall crevice, darker than the night sky, appeared. The stone was moving, unless it was an illusion caused by the violently shifting seas. A great wave lifted the ship and hurled it forward, but it did not disintegrate: instead it shot into the passage, waves leaping up on either side, cascading over it in fury. Behind the ship something rose up from the churning water, a thick shadow against the tumult. It was gray and bulbous and it glistened as the water poured off it in huge cataracts, while the seas about the cliffs raged as if filling with molten lava. The crevice in the cliffs opened out, and although the Stonedelvers gazed into its darkness, they could not understand what was happening. It was widening, like immense doors being forced open by the sea, the cliffs pulling back to provide a channel for the ship. The sea dragged at the ship's hull, heaving at it and then driving it further down the passage. Darkness closed in as the rocks overhead nodded together.

Many of the crew had been knocked to their knees by the impact of wave and spray. Wargallow clutched the rail, Dennovia wedged between him and Coldrieve, her eyes wide with fear, like a child caught in its darkest hour. Aumlac, amazingly, stood firm in the stern of the ship, watching the awesome thing that had risen from the deeps of the ocean. As the ship rushed deeper down the stone maw, this thing had heaved forward against the line of cliffs, but whatever it was, its colossal bulk would not permit it to pass into so narrow a channel. Instead it now pushed up against the rock face, sending another line of mighty waves in pursuit. Aumlac shouted to the crew to prepare themselves, but as the first wave came at them, the ship was hurled forward even more quickly than before, scraping the sides of the channel, splintering its timbers. A number of men were flung like twigs into the sea, lost at once.

Onward the ship plunged, until at length the gap widened and the ship swirled out into a circular cove, closed in by walls that rose up dauntingly all around it, seemingly as sheer as glass. There was a narrow half-moon of beach and in a moment the ship ran aground on it, the hull grinding into the pebbles, protesting. Kelloric knew at once that her back was broken. As if to emphasize their plight, another great wave rode in and struck the ship, almost punching it over on to its side. Several more men were flung out into the foam, though these were able to haul themselves up the beach to the relative safety of the rock walls.

Wargallow and the others were looking back up the channel. Like a tall gash that opened on to pitch darkness, it taught them nothing about what lay beyond it. This power from below the sea was still trapped outside the passage, though the sound of its monstrous movement against the outer cliffs came clearly to them, and the waves continued to race down the channel. But for the moment the ship was able to withstand them.

"What was it that dragged us here?" said Kelloric. "Did you not feel it? It was not the sea."

Brannog studied the foaming waters. "The land brought us here. And it opened to receive us." He said no more than that, his huge arms around Ruvanna, who nodded solemnly. She, too, was silent.

As the dawn broke somewhere high up beyond the rim of

the cliffs, the waves began to last to ease, until they became no more than a procession of peaks and troughs. The men who had been pitched ashore were safe, though eager to clamber back into the distressed ship.

Aumlac had not taken his eyes from the passage to the open sea, as if in dread of seeing something emerging from it. As the first light etched some of the details of the stone there, the Stonedelver shook his head. "I cannot see beyond it to the sea. It is twisted and shadowed. But it is clear that we must not go back that way."

Kelloric was haggard in the dawn glow, hair plastered to his scalp. "The ship needs extensive repair. Many of the timbers on the port side are broken. I'll need fresh timber if I'm to have the ship seaworthy again. It could be weeks."

Aumlac nodded, looking up at the walls that dwarfed them. He, too, looked exhausted, his bulk somehow diminished by the ordeal. His Stonedelvers and Earthwrought had gone to shelter below deck, and he knew that most of them would take days to recover from the events of the night, for they fared badly on water. The cliffs of this cove were of hard rock, scornful. Certainly no man could scale them. Aumlac wondered if he would be able to do so himself.

Wargallow saw his anxiety. He spoke quietly to him. "Is there a way up?"

Aumlac darted a quick glance at him and then away. "I cannot read the stone clearly. Its secrets are well hidden from me. There is a deliberate darkness that clings to it. And a silence. But it lives."

Brannog pointed to the waters of the cove. He yelled a sudden warning as the surface broke to reveal something that gleamed and shed water, a slick, globular mound, some thirty feet across. It was moving through the water with incredible speed, aimed at the defenseless ship. In the pale light it was sickly green and brought with it an almost overwhelming stench of decay, the reek of countless dead fish.

It would have reached the ship in minutes, but there was another movement in the water. Something else coursed through it at stunning speed, breaking it and writhing like a thick coil of rope. As it moved, it thickened, abruptly meeting the first intruder some fifty yards from the ship. Again the water boiled, foam cascading upward as the two forces met. As it fell, the two shapes could be glimpsed through a mist of spray, wrapped about each other like two leviathans of the deep. The green of the outsider contrasted vividly with the white of the serpent-like creature from the land, but as they fought it was impossible to see which of them had the best of the exchanges. It became apparent that the coiled creature from the land stretched back to the rock walls like a cable, and as the light improved, the watchers on the ship realized that it was some kind of immense root. The cliff bases had cracked open around the cove, and a number of these awesome cables now wormed out under the water, attacking the intruder. And the roots rose up through the walls of stone like pillars.

Brannog pointed high upward. "This is what brought us here! It is beating back the thing from the deeps, beyond the outer cliffs."

Beside him Ruvanna had closed her eyes, as if cutting off her mind to sounds that no one else could hear.

The waters heaved, the contest terrifying, until the combatants dipped below the surface. It became abruptly very still. For a long time there was silence. Wargallow looked about him to see most of the crew at the rail, hypnotized by events beyond them, though fear was chalked upon every face.

Across the cove there was an abrupt crash as something hit the walls at the entrance to the passage. The rock walls were slowly closing, trying to pulp whatever it was that had rammed itself between them. The water heaved, creating fresh waves, and then all fell silent. After a while the immense roots appeared briefly, then withdrew across the cove. Whatever it was that had come up from the ocean floor had been repulsed.

The crew were bewildered. "What was it that saved us?" they called.

Both Brannog and Aumlac were shaking their heads as they stared up at the tall cliffs. "What manner of life must be up there?" Aumlac murmured. "What is this land we have come to?"

Ottemar, who was with the crew and who had watched the

staggering conflict in the center of the cove, and whose face was no less pale than any of the others, pointed to the beach. "We had better get ashore. There has to be a way up."

Wargallow again turned to Aumlac. "Is there such a way?" "We are exhausted. Our powers will need time to recover."

Now that the water was calm and the cove had become something of a sheltered harbor, the beach itself, though small, offered a better place to rest than the broken ship. There were a few provisions left, and it was agreed that a makeshift camp should be set up as close to the rock wall as possible. Once the men had eaten and dried themselves out, their spirits began to rouse. The Earthwrought and Stonedelvers remained the most shaken by the journey, many of them falling into a deep sleep, but Wargallow was content to let them do so.

Ruvanna watched over them like a mother with her children. She could sense something ominous in the land about them, even though it appeared to have saved them from the sea dweller. "I felt the ferocity of the land's hatred for that thing," she said. "As furious as a storm. But still we must not assume we are favored."

Wargallow was with Ottemar, watching Kelloric and his sailors as they examined the ships. "We should not spend too much time on the ship," said the Deliverer. "Our path lies to the land."

"I would rather know that we had a ship waiting for us should we need one," replied Ottemar. But Wargallow said no more.

The day passed quietly. When evening came, it took them all by surprise with its suddenness, but they were glad to continue their rest, most of them still very tired. Three men had been lost in the flight through the passage, all of them Kelloric's warriors, and his men sang softly in memory of them as their fires burned low.

The following dawn brought with it a warm day and skies free of cloud. Aumlac had recovered his energy, though a cursory study of the rock walls showed him that they were no more willing to render up their secrets to him or to the Earthwrought. When he turned from them, it was to find

Wargallow standing at his side. The Deliverer looked fresh, as if the events of the past few days had left no mark on him, no weariness, and the Stonedelver wondered at the discipline that could so set a man apart. The other Deliverer, Coldrieve, was no less composed. Perhaps, thought Aumlac, it had something to do with the rod of power. But where was this thing? Few of the company seemed to know. But, Aumlac reflected, that was a good thing.

Wargallow again asked his question. "Can a way be found?"

Aumlac was about to answer when the rocks seemed to murmur deep in their beds, like a great beast stirring in its sleep. The Stonedelver stood back, automatically using himself as a shield to protect Wargallow. A number of the Earthwrought suddenly materialized, responding to the sounds in the stone as though it had spoken to them. Wargallow watched, fascinated, and before he had realized it, he saw an opening in the cliff base, a tall crevice, wide enough to receive a man or a Stonedelver.

"Aye, there's a way up," grinned Aumlac, and the Earthwrought nodded, as if they could see into the very heart of the rock face.

But Kelloric, who stepped forward to join them, was not so easily convinced. "It could be a trap." He did not relish the thought of entering the earth, nor did his warriors, who were primarily seamen.

Wargallow shook his head. "We've not been brought here to be eaten by the rock."

"It will be safe," Aumlac told them.

Gathering the last of their depleted supplies, the company began the ascent, entering the narrow cave and finding a rough-cut stairway that rose sharply, high up into the cliffs. It was a long climb, made mostly in silence, and although there was no hint of animosity in the rocks about them, the men felt cold, exposed. They thought of the great roots that must thread this silent domain. Even the Earthwrought were reluctant to pry into the dark or to commune in their strange way with the stone. It allowed them all through it under sufferance, not committed to them, as if a greater power had commanded it to be tolerant against its will.

Daylight broke above them at last and they emerged, relieved, high above the cove. They had come out on a sloping bank that dropped away gently into a thickly forested area. On all sides of them there were huge trees, protected from the strong sea winds by the upper reaches of Sea Scarp, which jutted at their backs. None of the company had seen the like of these immense trees before, although Aumlac whispered that there were tales of how the Deepwalks were full of far greater growths than these. They spoke of timelessness, of an indomitable will, and in their way they were a reminder of the smallness of the creatures that stood and gazed up at them now, humbled by them.

As the company studied the barrier of trees, looking for a possible way through them, the silence was broken by the creaking of branches and a distant murmur of leaves, the strange, slow conversation of the forest. A number of the company slipped their swords from their sheaths, taking up an alert, semicircular formation.

"Be careful," warned Ruvanna. "Do not antagonize this place."

"What are these trees?" said Wargallow softly, but she shook her head.

The trees before them were massive in girth and had huge roots that seemed to reach over one another in profusion, dropping down into the earth, buckled and twisted. They had formed an impassable tangled wall at the rim of the clearing. None of the company wished to venture near them for fear that they would spring to life like saplings, or writhe as the roots down in the cove had done.

As they watched, there was eventual movement. Scores of shapes drifted into view in silence, rising up from behind the roots and beyond the line of first trees. They were small beings, a rich green, as if wrapped in the leaf and mold of the forest, and their faces could not be seen, except for their white eyes. They seemed blind, but the creatures had a vision of another kind, for the Earthwrought could feel it probing them and their minds. They were too substantial to be illusion, yet they drifted, silent and almost mournful. One of them moved up on to a large root, his eyes fixed on the company, his arms folded beside him like green wings. When he spoke, his voice was strange, a blend of wind and sea, as though the ocean had taken an elemental voice.

"We are the North Sea Watch. We preserved you from the deep dweller at Woodheart's command."

Aumlac leaned toward Wargallow, saying softly, "I have heard of the Watches. They are protectors of the forest."

Wargallow bowed. "I am Simon Wargallow, adviser to Ottemar Remoon, Emperor of Goldenisle."

"You are known," came the soft reply. "You are each of you known. Which is the Emperor?" The being looked directly with his white orbs at Ottemar as he asked, the question apparently superfluous.

Ottemar smiled, inclining his head. "We are grateful to you and your ruler."

"You have brought a great evil to the shores of this land," said the forest being. Although it was impossible to tell from his voice if he was displeased, it yet seemed that he had not come here to welcome the company.

"The deep dweller?" said Ottemar, wondering what else these creatures knew.

"Yes. Fortunately it has gone back to the realms from which it came. It is not used to shallow water, nor to light. Both cause it great agony. Had it remained near the surface for a longer time, it would have died in considerable pain. Yes it pursued you in spite of this, its hunger voracious."

Ottemar glanced at Wargallow, but the Deliverer's expression warned him to be discreet. This was not the time to disclose anything of their purpose.

"Yet you attacked it," said Wargallow. "Or your servants did."

A sigh gusted through the ranks of the Sea Watch. "We are the North Sea Watch. We serve Woodheart and attend his will."

"Then Woodheart attacked this creature?"

"The roots of the great trees did this thing. To drive the evil away from the shores of the Deepwalks. All outside powers are driven away from the forest lands. They are not welcome here."

"We come to you in peace," called Ruvanna. Brannog had

an arm on hers, afraid that her boldness might bring wrath upon them.

Still the creatures hovered by the roots, not yet a threat. "You are not of Woodheart," said their leader, and again there was a rustle of sound from the Sea Watch.

"You have told us," said Wargallow, "that Woodheart commanded you to save us. If we are not welcome here, why has he done this?"

"We do not question Woodheart. It is for you to answer us."

"What do you wish to know?" said Ottemar. "Though if we are all known to you," he added, with a wry grin, "your questions would seem unnecessary."

"You are a strange gathering. Men, Stonedelvers, Earth-wrought. And Deliverers from the east. In our skies, also, there are eagles from the lands of the far north, the Slaughterhorn range. And other strange things have been seen in our skies."

Ottemar's expression altered at once. "Other birds?"

"The dark clouds from the west, the Shadowflight. And the great white owl. It sought out Woodheart's secrets until the ravens brought it down."

Ottemar looked as if he had been struck. "Kirrikree—"

"Is the owl alive?" said Brannog.

"It is." But the creature said no more of this.

"Who else is here?" said Ottemar and Wargallow inwardly cursed his impetuousness.

"There have been many intrusions into the forest lands of late," was the reply, and there was a hint of annoyance in it. "Woodheart is displeased."

"Who is this Woodheart?" snapped Ottemar.

The silence that followed was one of shock. The Sea Watch were very still, but something passed among them, a mental breeze, as though Ottemar had spoken a curse. It was a long time before he had his answer.

"Woodheart is all things in the forest. We are all of Woodheart."

"Their god," whispered Wargallow. "Have a care how you speak of him. They may yet attack us."

Ottemar glared at him briefly, but turned back to the Sea

Watch. "We have no desire to offend your—Woodheart. We are here on a matter of extreme urgency. The evil being that you beat back from your shores was nothing to the evil that threatens you—"

"Such evil that gathers about Woodheart seeks that which the deep dweller sought. It is known to Woodheart. It is like a blazing fire in the deeps of the night, a shout in a silent cave." Again the Sea Watch stirred, either in annoyance or fear, it was not possible to detect which.

"Then," said Wargallow, "Woodheart knows the power held within it."

"Why have you brought such a thing to the Deepwalks?"

Wargallow looked about him at his colleagues. Brannog and Aumlac nodded to him, and then Ottemar also nodded. "To use it on the evil that gathers in the far west. To free our people and those of the forest from the threat of oblivion."

This seemed to have met with no response, but again the Sea Watch stirred. "You are a danger to all life while you possess this thing. Woodheart does not wish you ill. But as long as you are in the Deepwalks, you draw evil to Woodheart. You cannot remain here."

"What of those who came before us?" said Ottemar.

"Many have come to the Deepwalks over the years. Some have perished. Others have been favored and have been Absorbed."

"Absorbed?" said Aumlac. "What does this mean? I know that Stonedelvers have been known to stumble into your lands and have never returned."

"Woodheart takes life into himself. Life gives life."

Ottemar paled, his hand tightened on his sword. "What are you telling us? That they have been sacrificed!"

At this there was a murmur among Kelloric's warriors, but they kept very still, watching the Emperor.

"Woodheart listens to the world," said the leader of the Sea Watch. "Nothing on Omara is a mystery to Woodheart. The earth and seas whisper their secrets to him. There is much harm beyond our shores, and in the mountains. Woodheart denies this harm entry into the forest. Those that are allowed into the Deepwalks are blessed, for Woodheart Absorbs them into himself—''

''What happened to those who came with the owl!'' shouted Ottemar, taking a step forward. Kelloric and Zuhaster were surprised at the heat in his voice, but they also wanted an answer to this.

Around the heads of the Sea Watch there came an abrupt cloud, seemingly of large, brightly-colored insects, and like bees they hummed, wings flashing. Wargallow took them to mean danger and he put a restraining arm on Ottemar.

''Let none of this company be harmed,'' the Deliverer called. ''We mean no harm, but if anyone here is harmed, there will be retribution.'' His words struck home, but he regretted them almost at once.

''Answer my question,'' Ottemar called to the forest creatures.

''Aye,'' called Kelloric, and in the clearing his voice seemed to ring out. ''Let us have an answer.''

''Where are those who came with the owl?'' said Ottemar.

''There is no answer for you here. Our duty is to watch the western seas. Our eyes are turned outward from Woodheart. We hear a little of the events of within. We saw the ship that came. Many of its crew were killed by the evil ones along the river of darkness.''

''The Fellwater?'' said Wargallow.

''So it is named. Some escaped the massacre and fled into the forest.''

Kelloric and Zuhaster exchanged pained glances, and their warriors murmured at this grim news.

''Those who survived have been Absorbed, just as those who came to the north were Absorbed.'' The creature looked with such deliberation at Aumlac that the Stonedelver jerked as if he had been slapped.

''The north? Who came to the north?''

''News came to us from the Star Watch; those of us who look north to the mountains there. Stonedelvers and Earthwrought came to the edge of the Deepwalks. Like the men who sailed up the Fellwater, they were pursued by Ferr-Bolgan and the Broodmasters. They were permitted to enter the forest.''

Aumlac gasped. "Could this have been Einnis Amrodin?"

"Aye, so he was named," said the forest being.

"Where is he now?" said Aumlac.

"I cannot say, not knowing."

"Absorbed?" said Wargallow, the word like a shadow.

"That may be so."

"And the Ferr-Bolgan?" persisted Wargallow. "Have they, too, entered the forest?"

A ripple of unease drifted through the Sea Watch and the cloud that hovered among them also seemed disturbed at the mention of Anakhizer's spawn. "They amass at the Gates of Anger, below Starkfell Edge where the Fellwater gushes forth. And with them are a multitude of the angarbreed and their Broodmothers and Broodmasters. Those you name herders."

"The Children!" exclaimed Ruvanna.

"They travel along the Fellwater, but those which attempt to go into the forest are destroyed. Yet their masters have no desire to challenge Woodheart. They wish merely to pass through the Deepwalks, along the Fellwater to the coast."

"To what end?" said Wargallow.

"It is your Empire, your lands they covet. Woodheart is not important to them. They plan an invasion."

"Woodheart is not concerned?"

"Woodheart has preserved the Deepwalks since time began. There have been many wars in Omara, many great evils. Terrible powers have been unleashed and much sickness and strife has riven the world. But Woodheart has preserved the forest against all this. And will do so again."

Ottemar scowled. "Then the Ferr-Bolgan will be allowed to pass? Ignored?"

"They are not of Woodheart."

"And what of us?" said Wargallow. "Are we to be allowed to pass through the forest?"

"For what reason?"

"We seek Anakhizer."

"Only Woodheart can answer you."

"Then we will speak to him." It was a demand, not merely a statement, and the Sea Watch seemed to understand this.

Kelloric was not eager to cut into the exchange again, but in the silence he did so. "My wrights have looked hard at my ship. It is badly crippled. If we are to sail in her again, we will need to cut fresh timber.''

"Timber," echoed the Sea Watch, as though a greater curse than before had been hurled at them. "No tree of the Deepwalks must be touched! Evil to those who speak harm to the forest.''

"No harm is meant," said Wargallow. "We would have been content to sail along your shores and up the Fellwater in pursuit of both our allies and our enemies. But that is no longer possible. If we are to reach Starkfell Edge, it must be through the forest.''

"That is for Woodheart to decide.''

Ottemar glowered at the forest creatures, infuriated by the deadlock. "And as we pass," he said coldly, "we will seek word of those who went before us. Those who are dear to us, and who, like your trees, are not to be harmed.''

The leader of the Sea Watch bowed. "Woodheart will know these things.''

"When are we to know his decision?" said Wargallow.

"It is not for me to say—''

"Then we will begin our journey into the forest at once," Wargallow told him. "In peace. We have no time to delay.''

There was evident anxiety among the Sea Watch, but they began to drift away, as if swept aside by a gentle gust of air from the sea far below. It appeared there was to be no dispute, and within a few moments the entire company had gone as if they had melted into the very trees.

Kelloric's men were ready to follow, swords drawn, but Aumlac stayed them briefly. He clambered up one of the large roots and stood above it, gazing ahead into the deep green shadow.

"Woodheart dare not risk impeding us," said Ottemar.

"It would not be wise to use the rod," said Wargallow. "But the forest must fear it.''

He heard Dennovia speak, her voice clear in the motionless air of the clearing. "No, you should not use the rod. It is as they told us. Like a beacon. Anakhizer must not find us. If he did so, we'd be finished.''

Brannog nodded. "Aye. We need the help of the forest. It can conceal us. How better to travel in secret?''

Kelloric murmured assent. "Perhaps we can turn its loathing of the Ferr-Bolgan to our advantage."

"We must try," said Wargallow. "But for now it seems that it treats us as a threat to its own security. We will have to watch each step we take. It may yet attempt our destruction."

As one they gazed beyond Aumlac, but the trees had become a wall, like a solid barrier, a fortress of stone, locking out all those who would seek ingress.

14
The Ravensring

IT SEEMED for a time that the way onward was to be barred, but after a while, when the silence had become as dense as the forest, there came a sudden gusting of wind over the tops of the trees, and a creaking of boughs as if they had filled with invisible beings. Sunlight angled down between two of the greatest trees and it seemed then that the barrier had been no more than a conspiracy of shadows, for there was a way through, a trunk-lined corridor winding downward as if into a vast lodge.

Thus the company began the march into the Deepwalks, picking its way carefully over the roots and knuckles of stone. Aumlac warned them all not to use a sword or knife on the vegetation, for fear that the forest would seek reprisals. Brannog and Ruvanna led the Earthwrought, their faces grim; the little people did not feel the oneness with the earth and stone that usually came as a second nature to them. Instead it was like a darkness, deep and brooding, closed off from them, though it sensed their every step. Aumlac's folk were similarly cut off from the rock, as though it studied them but returned nothing of its thoughts. But it was the trees that had the strangest effect on the company. They rose up majestically, their fantastic branches twisting this way and that, clustered with bizarre growths, festooned with clumps of rich green moss and lichen. The higher branches interwove like the crossbeams of a palace, not quite blotting out the sunlight. In places the forest was gloomy, chill, but now and then great shafts of sunlight cut down to its floor, and in them danced a thousand motes, creating a shimmering haze in which butterflies flashed and the air was thick with drifting seed. The undergrowth varied: in places it was thick, for huge fronds speared up, higher than some of the trees that were common in the eastern continent, and in other places the forest floor was all but bare, though cluttered with branches like snapped bones and scattered mounds of leaves. The company followed what seemed to be a dried-up stream bed, the land veering downward from the high ridge of Sea Scarp like a tunnel underground. It was an illusion, a trick of the trees, but the impression remained one of menace, or at best, one of being manipulated.

A number of sounds in the undergrowth made it clear that there was much life in the forest, but very little of it showed itself. Creatures scurried along the branches high above, almost invisible, and birds could be heard flapping far above the highest banks of leaves. Aumlac confirmed that Skyrac and his companions were somewhere above, keeping near to the party, but the green verdure made it difficult for him to communicate with them.

The company had been moving deeper into the endless trees for a number of hours, when Wargallow called a halt. They were in a widening gully and were able to spread themselves out along its steep banks, eating their dwindling provisions. Fresh water had been found, and the Earthwrought were at least able to pronounce it drinkable.

Wargallow took Aumlac to one side. "Have you any idea which way this path is taking us?"

"West," said the Stonedelver at once. "But perhaps a little to the north of it. That much Skyrac has told me."

"The forest no longer seeks to prevent our passage. I would have expected a protest of some kind by now."

"Aye, but it hears and feels our every move."

"The Sea Watch?"

"No, they went back to the high scarp. I mean the trees. This is a strange land indeed. The Deepwalks are like some vast creature, with a thousand eyes. Every tree, every leaf trembles with life. Cut one branch and you cut the whole. Whisper in the southernmost deeps of the forest and the northernmost trees will hear you. Speak to a rock here, a sapling there, and your words will be known throughout the forest. No one tracks us, for there is no need. Every footfall we make is carried the length and breadth of the Deepwalks.''

"It resents us?"

"Who can say? It will not speak. I cannot read its rocks, nor can the little brethren. The earth is cold to us."

"Well, we can do nothing about that. As long as we can reach Starkfell Edge and go beyond it, it will not matter."

"What of the others?"

"Others?"

Aumlac frowned, lowering his voice. Wargallow knew precisely what he meant. "The Trullhoons. And Einnis Amrodin, my Stonewise."

"You wish to search for them?"

Aumlac's scowl deepened. "You would consider them lost?"

"What do you suggest? Without the help of the forest, we would search endlessly, until we fell where we stood. The forest is boundless. And I suspect there are parts of it better left unvisited."

"So you would have us move on to the west with all speed?"

"Our prime goal is Anakhizer's stronghold. With all haste."

While the Deliverer and Stonedelver talked quietly, Ottemar was with Kelloric and Zuhaster. All of them eyed the forest in trepidation, as though expecting to see something rush from it to attack them, or as if they would at least discover a huge pair of eyes gazing down from out of one of the massive trees.

"You heard the Sea Watch, sire," said Kelloric. "They said the others had been Absorbed. What does it mean if not killed? There can be no point in searching for them. I value Rannovic as much as any of us. But this forest means to destroy us in time. It is as though we were creeping through cages of sleeping wolves. When they wake—"

"Your men are more content at sea," said Ottemar. "These wooden walls invent illusions for us all. But the owl is alive.

If Skyrac could find Kirrikree, he may yet lead us to any survivors.''

Zuhaster coughed politely. His unease in the forest was particularly marked: his companions swore he had been conceived at sea, and born between islands. "What of our goal, sire? In the west. Dare we tarry to search?''

Ottemar's brow clouded with ill-suppressed temper. "Would you abandon them?''

Zuhaster drew back, heavy jowls quivering. "Of course not, sire.''

Kelloric silenced him with a glare, but he understood his oarsmaster well. "Perhaps, sire, it would be better if the company split up.''

Ottemar frowned, but then he nodded for Kelloric to go on.

"Wargallow has this rod of power. He needs few men to support him. Since he wishes to come upon Anakhizer secretly, he would do better to have as few in his company as possible. Let him go westward with Coldrieve and a handful of others. Let Aumlac go north in search of Einnis—''

"You would remain with me to seek out Rannovic?''

"Aye. But let us first seek out this Woodheart. Skyrac will find his lair for us. We do not have to go to him with our swords raised. He must know we do not come as enemies.''

Ottemar nodded slowly. "There's merit in what you say, Kelloric. Wargallow has power enough to keep himself secure.''

On a lower part of the bank, Dennovia had asked to sit with Ruvanna and Brannog and they had made her welcome, sharing their dwindling food with her.

"It may not be wise to search for food here,'' Ruvanna said. "But we must have fresh supplies soon.''

Brannog was talking softly to a number of the Earth-wrought, and while he did so, Dennovia moved closer to Ruvanna. The latter was much changed since the journey into the mountains of the far east and the seas beyond them, when her powers had been at the flood. She had declared that these powers were receding, but with Brannog she yet seemed to share some secret earth skills that were at least as great as those of her people. Since she had become Brannog's mate, she had grown very close to him, as if the two of them were able to converse without speaking for much of the time. Their love for one another shone clearly, no longer hidden by the circumstances of their early plight, and Dennovia envied this love. Once she had brought distress to the earth girl, and Dennovia wondered if she would ever be forgiven for that. Ruvanna seemed indifferent to her, as if her thoughts did not matter. She and Brannog had not made any fuss about her being on this voyage, though their unease at the death of Fornoldur could be read.

"Why are you here?" Ruvanna said softly, so that only Dennovia heard her. "I have often wondered. I would have thought that life on Medallion would have suited you perfectly. This voyage and journey can provide you with no comfort."

The unexpectedness of the question completely caught Dennovia off her guard. "I—I was brought against my will," she began.

To her further surprise, Ruvanna laughed quietly, and for the moment some of the strain of the journey left her face. "You were a gifted liar once," she said.

"Wargallow dared not leave me behind," Dennovia insisted. "I know of the rod."

Ruvanna's hand came out and caught at Dennovia's wrist, casually but with such strength that Dennovia drew in a sharp breath. "Don't think to betray him," Ruvanna said mildly. "If that is your goal."

Dennovia gaped at her, wincing as Ruvanna released her. "What are you saying?" She rubbed at her wrist. "To whom would I betray him?"

"I don't know. But I have seen avarice, greed for power. If that is what you seek, have a care."

"You can't believe I came here for my own ends! To *this* place?"

"There's no other reason that springs to mind," said Ruvanna, with a smile and Brannog turned from his conversation, seeing that Dennovia was evidently annoyed.

"What is wrong?" he said softly.

"Nothing," sniffed Dennovia, rising and leaving them, her anger coursing hotly but impotently through her.

"Why did Wargallow bring her?" Ruvanna said to Brannog.

"He is a man who does not like to take risks," he said, but wondered as he had done since the night the ship had sailed.

As Dennovia walked away, she saw Ottemar making for Wargallow and Aumlac, and the Emperor's face was troubled, as if he, too, was angry about something. She knew what it was that twisted inside him. Sisipher may no longer be alive. Even if she were, Wargallow had no intention of wasting time in a search for her. What would Brannog have to say about that? There would be a conflict over this issue soon, Dennovia knew it. The silence of the forest, the oppressiveness of its tunnels, served to stretch the patience of them all. How futile this expedition had become!

Wargallow rose to meet Ottemar. He knew that the Emperor was about to confront him and could tell by his face, his irascibility that he had reached some kind of decision that would cause disunity. In the background, Kelloric and his warriors were stirring, closing ranks. Coldrieve sat apart, as did the Earthwrought and Stonedelvers. It was as though all parties had moved apart. In this, Wargallow sensed impending disaster, a further madness at work.

He was prepared for the worst, but before Ottemar could speak, a sound came out of the forest, distant but clear. It came again, a long, musical note. Once more it sounded, closer this time, the sound of a horn, though unlike any other the company had heard. And it struck a chord deep within all who heard it, alerting them, sharpening their minds.

There was no movement in the forest, and yet the air trembled with a kind of anticipation. Everyone had stood up, listening intently as if craving the horn's call again. They were as silent as the forest, and then the horn answered their longing, closer yet. With it now came a thrumming of hooves, and presently on the ridge above them, racing through the trees, they caught sight of a single horseman. The beast it rode was tiny, a stout pony, but it moved through the huge boles with tremendous speed, fierce as a gale. The rider was crouched over his mount, light green cloak flapping out behind him like a vapor, and he lifted his head to sound again his horn. Neither the face of the man nor the horse's head could be seen clearly, for in their wild race they were no more than blurs, but they hinted at specters and images of the inner eye.

Within moments they had gone; all heads had turned, eyes fixed on the place where they had disappeared.

"There's a legend," said Aumlac to Wargallow. "The Horn Moot. The forest is said to call to its creatures, gathering them. The riders of the Horn Moot go out through all the forest."

"Did you see the speed at which it rode past us?" someone cried.

"The legend says that the riders are elemental beings, fashioned from the breath of the forest, with which they sound the horns. They will be heard throughout the Deepwalks. No creature will miss them."

"Then it was not meant for us?" said Ottemar.

"Your pardon, sire," said Aumlac. "But I think that it was. Woodheart has decided that we should come before him after all. Perhaps to judge us before his folk."

Wargallow grunted. "We welcome a chance to exchange views. Well, Ottemar?"

The Emperor looked momentarily startled. "Why, yes. Of course."

Wargallow looked up at the ridge. He wondered if the timing of the rider's arrival had been significant. It had undoubtedly been timely.

Soon afterward the company moved on, and it seemed as though the way became easier, less cluttered. From time to time the distant horns could be heard, encouraging them, although the sounds were strange, like voices of the forest, some of them deep, some shrill, but always demanding.

If they had expected to come across the forest's secret quickly, they were disappointed. But they did find fruit that was edible and root crops, as thought the forest had opened itself to them a little. For three days they moved onward, down to the bottom of the sloping valley, and then up the steeper slope of another. It became almost dangerous, the trees less huge, but clustered together thickly, as if they marched on across the world to its very edge. The horns periodically guided the company until, shortly after dawn on the fourth day, they say daylight streaming in from beyond the trees. It showed them a stretch of moorland, a curving dome where only banks of heather bloomed. Apart from an occasional gray rock poking through this purple profusion, the moor was open, curving upward and out of sight.

"This must be the highest part of the forest," said Aumlac. "Its crown." As he spoke, they saw through the sunlight a cloud racing down upon them from the north. "Skyrac and the eagles!" Aumlac pointed, and within moments the great birds of Malador came winging downward. Beyond them, in a tumultuous flock, were more birds than any of the company had ever seen before. Countless thousands of them circled, beginning to fill the sky overhead as if in readiness for an attack.

"Get into the forest," called Wargallow, and already the company was on the move, glad to be back in the shelter of the trees.

Skyrac, the huge eagle, flew overhead and alighted on a broken branch above his master, his companions following him quickly. All the birds looked exhausted. Overhead the ravens swarmed like disturbed bees, though for some reason they did not enter the forest. Like a black curtain they shut out the light.

Aumlac spoke to Skyrac, nodding, then turned to his companions. "This place before us is the Ravensring. It is indeed a crowning area of moorland. It reaches around the highest part of the forest in a circle, and at its heart is yet more forest, a central region that is forbidden to everything but the ravens and servants of Woodheart. All those who attempt to cross the Ravensring are attacked, usually killed, by the raven swarms."

"Then beyond the Ravensring is where Woodheart dwells," said Brannog.

"Aye," confirmed Aumlac. "The eagles tried to penetrate that central mass. They were fortunate to come away alive. See, the moorland is open to the sky. The ravens are as innumerable as the leaves of the forest."

Wargallow faced him grimly. "So how do we reach Woodheart? Do we make our way below ground?'' He pointed to the Earthwrought.

Aumlac shook his head, horrified by the suggestion. "It would be far more dangerous than an overland crossing, I fear. We should abandon the quest for Woodheart, and move on to the west—''

"The horns have summoned us," said Wargallow. "Or must we ignore them?''

"We cannot," said Aumlac's folk. "We will be driven to the Horn Moot. Those who do not attend will be marked, hunted.''

Ottemar cursed loudly, waving his sword at the skies. "What is this foolish game the forest plays! If we are to attend this assembly, why are we attacked!" He gestured at the swirling ravens, though they had drawn back, taking to the higher air.

"Wait," said Brannog. "Are they not leaving?" It became evident that they were, for the darkness eased as the raven cloud flew back across the moorland. As quickly as they had come, they were gone. And as the last of them disappeared, the sound of a horn came floating across the moor, as enticing as ever.

From over the crest of the moorland, three riders galloped on silent hooves, the feet of their small steeds blurring in the heather as they came on, splitting their formation and arrowing across the moor, one to the left, one to the right and one directly toward the company, like spears hurled by a giant. This latter hornsman brought his steed to a rearing halt, put his horn to his lips and gave a long blast that rang out over the forest. He waited, the steam rising from his horse in a white cloud, obscuring him, his green-cloaked body misshapen by the garment. The horse seemed hardly less ethereal, as if it might rise up on wings and follow the ravens. The rider waited.

"Keep the company together," Kelloric called back to his men, and they moved out as a body on to the exposed moor, led by Wargallow and the Stonedelvers. The Earthwrought brought up the rear, but even here they were no more at ease with their surroundings than they had been in the forest. Behind them it crouched, watching like a predator, and what

horizons could be glimpsed were deep green, hinting at endless ranks of trees. Skyrac and his eagles flew low overhead,
watching for a return of the ravens.

The hornsman wheeled his steed in a swirl of air and trot-
ted it in absolute silence over the cushion of heather. The
sunlight was warm up here, and although the sky was cloudless, there was the threat of cloud higher up, the top of the
moor blanketed in white. Wargallow urged his companions
on as quickly as he could, but the distance between them and
the rider never closed. Like something from a dream, the
hornsman drifted upward. The cloud higher up drifted back
a little, like a sluggish tide, though only to reveal further
heights of moorland. But thrusting up from them could be
seen a circle of standing stones, gray and glistening. Like
statues they gazed down emptily at the oncoming company.
The Earthwrought were stunned by them, as if they approached a gathering of demigods.

Aumlac pointed off to the distant left, and from the lower
slopes of the moor could be seen another party climbing the
heather path. The figures were too far away to be identified.
Moments later a cry turned the company's attention to the far
right slopes, where yet another company was climbing up
through the heather. Each party was guided by one of the
hornsmen.

Brannog let out a sudden gasp of astonishment.

Ruvanna squeezed his arm, trying to see what drew his
attention. "What is it?" she said, feeling his excitement
coursing through her.

He pointed to the group from the right, but did not speak,
as if his mouth had gone dry. Ruvanna's grip tightened as
she stood on her toes, craning her neck. But the figures were
still too far away for her to see them.

The three companies converged on the standing stones,
and the riders suddenly raced on ahead, regrouping and
plunging up into the rolling cloud. Wargallow's company was
the first to reach the stones, which towered over them, some
thirty to forty feet in height. They had been carved subtly,
almost as if they had been grown, some of them having what
could have been faces, others which were more representative

of thick boles of trees, covered in whorls and markings, like grains of wood.

Brannog passed through two of them to meet the oncoming right party, and as he did so, the first of its figures emerged from the mist. It was a girl with flowing dark hair, and as she saw Brannog, her face lit up in a mixture of amazement and joy. She rushed forward and Brannog raced to her. He scooped her up in his huge arms, swinging her round like a child, laughing aloud so that his voice rang back from the gray sentinels.

Ruvanna felt the warm tears on her cheeks as she slowly went forward, watched by the rest of the company, most of whom were baffled by what was happening. But Ruvanna knew who the girl must be. As she went to meet her, she noticed the Emperor. He stood with a peculiar expression, one of relief, but of uncertainty also. He did not move, as though rooted, but his eyes never left the girl that Brannog held.

Brannog swung Sisipher back to the ground, his arms about her. He suddenly looked across to Ruvanna. "Ruvanna!" he shouted, his voice rich with joy. "Come here!" The silence of the stones was broken by that cry, and the Earthwrought felt a shiver of exultation, wanting to cry out with their king.

Ruvanna felt a stab of relief as she ran across the heather. She pulled up short of the two figures, her eyes held by those of the girl that was Brannog's daughter. Only now did she understand just how deeply she had feared this moment, this meeting. Sisipher, however, smiled through her own tears, a rich, welcoming smile. She held out her hand. Ruvanna took it at once, and it was as though a stream of power coursed through them both. For a while it was unnecessary for them to speak, but then Brannog embraced them both, laughing aloud to the skies. In that moment the anguish of his past seemed to be flushed from him, leaving him speechless, released.

Wargallow spoke to Ottemar, who was yet silent. "Keep your head," he whispered. "There is Rannovic. Go to him. Welcome him."

Ottemar snapped from his trance and waved to the red-headed figure. "Rannovic! Well met!" Both the Emperor and Kelloric strode down through the stones to meet Ran-

novic and his surviving Hammavars, and although they cried
out heartily, Ottemar could see that something had hurt them
cruelly, for their faces spoke of it.

Rannovic bowed before the Emperor, then took his hand.
"Sire, we are both pleased and shocked to find you here.
This must be some miracle—"

"I could say the same. I feared you dead, Rannovic."

"And Kelloric," said Rannovic, grasping the hand of the
big warrior. Like giants they pounded each other. "A strange
land for us to meet again." Their men were mingling, talking
rapidly, exchanging stories already.

Rannovic suddenly straighted, as if he had forgotten something. "But, sire! The Empress—has she—"

Ottemar nodded. "I have my heir, Rannovic. A son. His
name is Solimar, and he thrives."

Before he could be stopped, Rannovic swung round and
shouted out to his men. "Hear this news! The Chain is
blessed! The Emperor has an heir, a son!" As he shouted,
his eyes caught the look upon Sisipher's face and he had to
look away, abruptly realizing the pain he had given her without a thought. His men were about him, smothering him and
the Emperor as they shook his hand and gripped his arms
in the traditional salutes. Ottemar held his head proudly, as
though his happiness could outweigh that of Brannog himself. But within he felt the fire of the blade. The joy of seeing
Sisipher alive was seared by this celebration, which would
cut her more deeply.

Wargallow watched the coming of the other company from
the left slopes. Aumlac had already gone with his Stonedelvers and Earthwrought to meet them, for those that came
were of their kind.

Coldrieve stood at his master's side, apparently unmoved
by the reunions. "They appear like ghosts," he said. "Is that
the northern Stonewise, Einnis Amrodin?"

"I believe it is," said Wargallow. "It may be that the
forest shows us a kindness after all."

"Unless this is a trap. We are much exposed here. Could
this be the ceremony they spoke of?"

"Woodheart must know that whatever his power, he could
not match that of the rod. I cannot believe he would force us

to unleash its power." But Wargallow wondered what purpose the forest had in gathering them.

Aumlac and his followers met with Einnis Amrodin and their reunion was as emotional as that of Brannog and his daughter, and Kelloric and the Hammavars. They held each other and spoke of the wonder of finding each other again, and the children danced about, reading the joy of these new friends and feeding on it. There was much laughter and singing as they came up to the great circle of stones.

"Einnis, how have you kept them together?" said Aumlac, trembling with pride.

Einnis grinned, his eyes moist. "You should thank Bornac for that, and Graval, two of the stoutest hearts one could find." He introduced them to Aumlac and the latter bowed to them.

"We knew each other briefly in happier times, I think," he told them.

"Aye," grinned Bornac. "And we would have been doomed more than once on our trek from the Slaughterhorn range had it not been for Einnis and his will. We came to the Deepwalks in desperation."

"I should never have left you," Aumlac began.

Einnis dismissed this with a wave. "Nonsense! You had your own duty. You must tell me of it. I have so much to learn from you, Aumlac. Although you will be surprised to hear what things the forest has taught your people during our sojourn here."

"But—it must have been for months!"

"Aye. Sheltered by beings known as the Star Watch. At first we thought we were to be sent to a sacrificial death, to a Timber Maw." They had been approaching the standing stones and as they came under their shadows, Aumlac introduced Ottemar.

"No longer a renegade in search of allies," Ottemar laughed, shaking Einnis by the hand. "I promised you I would find you again."

"So you did, sire. And now you have your crown." Einnis bowed. "It is an honor to meet you again. You once saved the life of Aumlac, and for that alone my people will ever be in your service."

Aumlac could not hide his surprise. He was not ashamed of Ottemar's deed, but he had not yet had time to speak to Einnis of it. How could the Stonewise know of such a thing? But Einnis smiled at him discreetly, as if to say, ah, there are many things I know of that will surprise you.

"And this is Simon Wargallow," said Aumlac, introducing the Deliverer.

The latter inclined his head politely. "An auspicious day for us all. We had despaired of finding you alive."

"The forces at work in these lands are deeply strange. To reach their heart, their mind, is as difficult as it is to speak to the roots of a mountain range. But they have heard us, I think." Einnis bowed. "Woodheart has studied my people for many months."

The companies combined, taking great comfort from being united. They drew further strength from the huge stones, as if somehow they had found a sanctuary here in the forest, a high place where they would be safe. As the sun rose to its zenith, they gathered about the central area, sitting so that they could hear each others' tales. Even the stern seamen of Kelloric were moved by the discovery of the folk of Einnis, so that before long the three companies had truly become one. But a quiet fell upon them all as they knew it was time for decision.

Ottemar and Wargallow were invited to speak first, to explain what had befallen the Empire before and during the Inundation, for the people of Einnis knew only a little of this. Wargallow talked of events in the east, of the razing of the Direkeep, of the fall of the Sublime One and of the rise to power of Ulthor Faithbreaker, Warlord of the Earthwrought. There were many cheers among the little people at this news, and as many tears. Ottemar told of the plan to come to the west, to seek out Anakhizer before he could muster his armies and sail across the ocean to carry war to Goldenisle and beyond. He and Wargallow spoke of the rod of power, though guardedly.

After they had finished, Sisipher took up the tale of how she and Rannovic had entered the gorge to the Fellwater and how disaster had befallen them quickly after that. They described how they had been led away from the Ferr–Bolgan and the angarbreed trap and readied for what they took to be a ceremony, that of Absorption.

"We thought we had lost Kirrikree," said Sisipher. "He had flown far across the Deepwalks, trying to learn what he could of the lands beyond us. Only when I heard his soft voice did I realize the peril we were in. Kirrikree had been injured, a wing broken, but he was saved from a lingering death in the gloom of the forest by Grimander, one of the Woodweavers. And Kirrikree had seen the Timber Maw to which we were being taken." She described the huge plant-like creature just as the owl had described it to her. "Kirrikree and Grimander were planning our means of escape from our Woodweaver guards, but we were diverted to a high stone outcrop in the forest and kept there. Although Kirrikree and I spoke to each other throughout my incarceration—for such I judged it—it was not possible to escape that place. I doubt if the Stonedelvers themselves could have broken free of its cold stones."

Beside her, Einnis was nodding, as though his own prison had led him through a similar experience. "My people and I were admitted into the forest far to its north. Woodweavers led us to the peaks known as the Star Watch. We, too, were promised the ceremony of Absorption, though something in the words frightened me. Each time I tried to question our hosts about it, they were reticent. Then one day I learned that it involved a Timber Maw. There are five such things, spread about the Deepwalks. They draw into them all life that is not of the forest, and most of the life that dies here. As a furnace produces heat for the metalsmith to shape his work, so do the Timber Maws produce fresh energy for the forest, Woodheart's power."

"Yet you avoided this horror?" said Wargallow.

"Aye. We were imprisoned, as Sisipher and her companions were. I felt the stone as though it were reading us, probing our hearts, for there was vast power within it. I see now what happened. Woodheart realized that he could not ignore us all, our gathering fears. Three companies have come to him in what is, for him, a short space of time. Separately we came, but with the same dire message."

"All speaking with one voice, one heart," added Sisipher.

"Aye," Einnis nodded. "Thus Woodheart paused, and thought. And now he has brought us here."

"You know his purpose?" said Wargallow, speaking for everyone. "Are we to meet him at last?"

Einnis smiled. He had heard of the determination and drive of this darkly clad man. "We shall never do that, I think. But he will hear more from us. And you will hear the deep knowledge which it has been my privilege to receive from him."

"He has spoken to you?" said Wargallow.

"His servants have done so. They had imparted to me much of the lost histories of Omara. Through this knowledge we are able to comprehend the true nature of what it is that Anakhizer's masters intend."

The sound of horns alerted the entire company, which rose as one to gaze up the far slopes to the highest parts of the moor. Cloud obscured everything up there, and from it rode a score of hornsmen. Each carried now a pennant, whipping in the breeze, a long streamer of green, symbol of the undying forest. The riders arranged themselves in a semicircle, facing the host among the stones. Beyond them were more figures, tall, spindly beings who moved down the slope awkwardly as if movement was foreign to them. They were horned, their faces masked, oddly shaped, and they brought with them an atmosphere of power which spoke of trees and of the deep earth and of the roots winding beneath it.

Behind them the cloud drifted apart briefly, and in its folds could be glimpsed a colossal root, scores of feet thick, suggesting by its awesome presence that the tree above it must stretch up unimaginably into the heavens. Every member of the company gaped at the sheer size of the root, but the cloud swirled over it jealously, covering it again.

"Could it be Woodheart?" murmured more than one voice.

Einnis shook his head. "No. It is one of the guardians. Woodheart is yet beyond them. But we go no further than these stones." He pointed to the tall figures as they descended, escorted by the wraith-like riders. "The voice of the forest comes to us through these envoys. The Horn Moot begins."

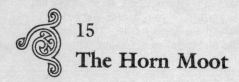

15

The Horn Moot

WARGALLOW WATCHED as the silent figures, soft-footed as ghosts, came to the slope beyond the ring of stones. There appeared to be no malice in them, but he sensed their power, the power of the ages, of endurance, the power of the forest. Einnis Amrodin had gone to join them, speaking in a low voice as if he had already enjoyed conversation with them or their kind. Wargallow felt something tugging at his mind, and he glanced up at one of the tall, gray stones. He felt a shock of pleasure as he did so, for he recognized the white shape almost hidden on top of the stone.

"So you found us," came Kirrikree's voice in his mind, and there was a hint of amusement in it.

Wargallow was also able to speak mentally to the bird, for he was one of the few men permitted to do so. "It seems we have all been brought together by this forest. Do you know why?"

"Einnis understands these things better than any other. Now will be a time of learning." Kirrikree said no more for the moment, and as Wargallow turned to look again at the envoys, he noticed at the foot of Kirrikree's stone a strange being. It was his first glimpse of a Woodweaver, and it peered back at him as if it knew him.

"He is Grimander," said a gentle voice at his side. It was Sisipher. "A great friend to Kirrikree. See, he wears his feathers with unusual pride."

Wargallow inclined his head slightly to the ancient Woodweaver, though he could not be sure if the little being saw. Einnis, meanwhile, lifted his hands to the company for silence. At once the murmuring among those gathered in the circle of monoliths died away. Brannog, Ruvanna and Sisipher stood together, watching intently, and every eye was upon the Stonewise.

Out on the moor, at the edge of the forest, scores of figures materialized in eerie silence as if the air had fashioned them. They were Woodweavers, and those who had not seen their kind before marveled at their strangeness. The forest people waited in silence, rank upon rank, watching the figures beyond the stones with Einnis.

"Woodheart recognizes the terrible peril that besets us all," began the Stonewise. "The Deepwalks and Woodweavers, the Chain of Goldenisle, the lands of the east, Earthwrought, Stonedelver, all of us. For countless centuries the forest has been a closed world, permitting no one and nothing to interfere with it, though it has studied the world outside it and knows far more of what happens across Omara than any of us would have dreamed. Woodheart has read our hearts, our fears. He shares them. Thus he has given me knowledge to share with you. You must listen while I speak of the true nature of the danger that threatens Omara and the worlds beyond it."

Ottemar grinned as he saw the Earthwrought and Stonedelver children huddling up to each other, fascinated by the words of the Stonewise, though his own men were no less transfixed. Omara's beginnings were the source of a thousand myths.

Einnis spoke again, as if the envoys used him as their voice, their vessel. "Long, long before Omara gave life, long before Omara was given life, there was an ocean of darkness, measureless and timeless. In this vast gulf there was power, energy, a dream of life.

"In the primal darkness, the power developed and formed itself into entities, though at first they were no more than minds, dreaming, floating in their very dreams. If the primal ocean of darkness was the host, then these first powers were its parasites, feeding on its raw, unformed power. They learned how to generate power of their own making, giving to this raw energy form, although it was chaotic and without order. The primal powers were whimsical, amusing themselves purely for pleasure, for they knew of self and nothing more. There was confusion and disorder for unthinkable eons. We shall name them, Primals.

"And yet, in time, a kind of order did impose itself, splitting off from the Primals. They had become isolated and individual, unrelated to each other. Indeed, if they came into contact, they annihilated one another. But the more powerful of them, the secondary powers, evolved in a separate way. There was one essential change: the Primals remained nonphysical, while the newer powers took physical form.

"And the first physical form was Omara."

There was a whisper of awe that traveled through the entire gathering; Wargallow, Brannog and all the host felt it and with it a strange coursing of power, like the current in a river, or the tide of an ocean. There was unquestionable power in the words of the Stonewise, as though he had put his hand upon the heart not of the forest, but of the world itself, and they all felt its vibrant beat.

"Yet the growth had only just begun," went on Einnis. "Omara evolved in two ways. She diversified and gave birth to countless life forms: we see many of the results about us. But Omara also developed in a second, more complex way. In order to protect herself from the Primals, Omara split herself and created a chain, a linked sequence of Aspects." As Einnis spoke, the tall envoys indicated the ring of stones about the gathering, and all those who were within them studied them with a new insight, even the children, who had been concentrating hard on the difficult words of the Stonewise.

Einnis smiled as he saw heads nodding and heard the children explaining to the younger ones. "The chain," he repeated. "It is thought that each Aspect of Omara has its own, lesser chain, linking through the principal chain, so that all form a globe of linked Aspects.

"Why should Omara evolve in this way? It was because if a Primal threatened Omara, it had to focus its energy on one Aspect, one link in the chain. Thus, although separate from each other, the Aspects depended on each other for survival.

Should one link be broken or damaged, the other Aspects could repair it.''

Wargallow and Brannog looked at one another, each knowing what the other must be thinking, of the grim destruction wrought by Korbillian's race. Word of that was yet to follow, they knew.

"The Primals also diversified in that they linked themselves to one particular Aspect each. Opposite forces balance each other, and thus there was an equilibrium in such an arrangement. There was a Primal for each Aspect: any other arrangement would have meant imbalance, the annihilation of the Primals and the Aspect. It would seem that there was a kind of harmony. Each Aspect had its dreaming Primal, but both existed separately, content to develop physically or otherwise. Omara remained the prime Aspect, the heart of the chain.''

Einnis paused, turning to the envoys. They bowed to him, as though in praise of his words. Wargallow wondered if they had come from Woodheart, who must be as old a being as any other on Omara.

Kelloric was close by and he spoke, his face troubled. "These are matters of great weight, are they not? Can they not be simplified?''

"They will be,'' said Wargallow softly. "Be patient. This is knowledge that will shape the destiny of us all.''

Einnis waited for the murmurs to die down, then spoke once more. "Omara's bond with the life she has created is very strong, and such power as she possesses exists in all her life forms, Man, Stonedelver, Woodweaver, Earthwrought, and all others. These are Omara's blood, her children. And this is true of all other Aspects, for their blood runs in their creations, their children.''

Blood from the earth and blood to earth return, thought Wargallow, but quickly drove the grim words from his mind.

"Certain focal points of power developed on Omara,'' said Einnis. "Just as they did on other Aspects. On Omara these were centered on the Sorcerer-Kings of old and also here, in the Deepwalks, the oldest part of the world. In Ternannoc, power centered on the Hierarchs.''

And in the water Aspect of Zoigon, thought Ruvanna, remembering the sad being of the Bay of Sorrows, it was the Seraphim.

"Each Aspect is the god of its own life forms."

Once again there were murmurings among the host. No one would have disputed the words of the Stonewise, handed down from the powers of the forest.

"Although the linking of the Aspects is vital to their defense, there was originally no contact between their life forms. Omara understood that such contact would mean the chance of other accidental contact, such as the contact of Primals, so perilous to the safety of all Aspects. So for millenia the life of Omara knew nothing of life in Ternannoc, believing itself unique.

"However, the Sorcerer-Kings, masters of great power, discovered through their arts, the forbidden paths to the other Aspects. They followed them."

"With catastrophic consequences," said Brannog quietly, and a number of those around him looked at him.

It seemed as if Einnis and the envoys had heard him, for they, too, looked his way, though not with reproach. "Just so," said Einnis, with a long, slow nod of his head. "Catastrophic. There were two major consequences. Firstly, the Sorcerer-Kings attracted the attention of the Primal that was linked to Omara. And secondly, they were unable to prevent other powers like themselves, such as the Hierarchs of Ternannoc, from learning the secret of the Aspects. The Sorcerer-Kings relented, of course. But because they attempted to hide their error, the Hierarchs' knowledge was incomplete.

"They performed a great Working, the greatest single act of significance in Man's history. We know only too well how terribly wrong this Working went. It released a stream of consequences, of unimaginable chaos. It broke the chain of Aspects. The power that was released was mindless: it traveled like a virulent plague, rupturing many Aspects, obeying no law, and causing destruction on an immense scale. It left many Aspects isolated, and some of them were destroyed.

"There was an exodus from Ternannoc, its source, mostly to Omara, and this exodus became the first contact between life forms of different Aspects of any scale. It weakened the power of the Aspects so seriously that it damaged the equilibrium between Aspects and their linked Primals."

And, mused Ottemar, it led to Korbillian's bravery in Xennidhum, where he used his given power, that of the Hierarchs, to divert the awakened Primal of Omara into Ternannoc. There it had clashed with Ternannoc's Primal and the two had destroyed each other. Ternannoc had become little more than a cinder.

"The Hierarchs of Ternannoc," Einnis was saying, "mostly combined to attempt to atone for their errors. Who does not know of the war in Xennidhum? But there were other Hierarchs who could not face their sins and fled them.

"One of them is Anakhizer, and he is here, beyond Starkfell Edge. When he knew that the power of his fellow Hierarchs was used up at Xennidhum, sacrificed by Korbillian, he conceived of his plan to take Omara for himself. He knew that the Sorcerer-Kings were a spent force. But after the disastrous Working, the Aspects were so badly damaged that the Sorcerer-Kings did certain things to protect Omara from any possible intrusion by dark powers. They sealed Omara off from other Aspects. They were helped in their work by the Seraphs of the Water Aspect, who gave them the rods of power; these enabled the Sorcerer-Kings to protect the fabric of Omara from attack through their guardians, the Created, or Werewatch, keepers of the rods.

"In the wake of the chaos of the Working, a number of Primals are no longer tied to an Aspect, thus they have more choice of movement in the limbo that exists between Aspects. Although Korbillian rid Omara of the Primal that was linked to her, he left her open to others. And Anakhizer, in his greed for power, has woken one of these and focused its attention on Omara. Foolishly, Anakhizer thought to control this Primal.

"Woodheart understands what it is that the Primal intends, for he has knowledge of the lands beyond Starkfell Edge. The Primal intends to metamorphose into a physical entity by possessing Omara. By absorbing Omara's life forces and all life on her, the Primal can become a new, dark Omara. It will create new life forms of its own, the like of which cannot be contemplated."

For a while Einnis allowed his audience to digest his words, his last, horrifying statement.

"Anakhizer is now merely a vessel," he went on at last. "A lens for the power that uses him. And there are other creatures which have become the instruments of the Primal. Through them the Primal will absorb all Omaran life into itself, through the stolen rods of power, for their use is two-fold. They destroy and store life, and also they discharge this stored power in greater destruction.

"Yet to attempt the translation of all Omaran life would take the combined power of all the rods that the Sorcerer-Kings owned. Otherwise there would be an endless war and possibly a direct confrontation between Omara and the Primal. Whichever triumphed would do so at a staggering cost."

Wargallow was conscious that a number of anxious glances were aimed at him, but his face remained impassive. Woodheart must surely know that the last rod of power was here, the rod that Anakhizer craved in order to effect his own grim working of power.

One of the envoys spoke for the first time. Its voice was deep, like an echo from the darker parts of the forest, and in it was the power of the elements, of storms, controlled but fierce. "Omara listened to her children and heard the voice of the Sublime One in the eastern mountains, exhorting her to sacrifice all life that came from beyond Omara, the refugees, thus diverting the Primal into the husk of a world that Ternannoc has become. Woodheart knows of this, and knows also that Omara rejected this betrayal. Omara has put aside the dictates of history. In the past the Aspects were kept in ignorance of each other, but now salvation lies in their sharing power, the sharing of the life of all Aspects."

Ruvanna and Brannog held each other as the envoy's words rolled over the gathering like thunder. Zoigon had known this, which is why, thought Ruvanna, he had chosen Wargallow to receive the power of the lost rod. And perhaps it was why, at last, after centuries of introspection, the Deepwalks had allowed them in.

"Omara," said the envoy, "is soon to attempt a working of her own. She will concentrate her power into a repairing of the chain of Aspects. You have wondered why Anakhizer has delayed his offensive for so long. It is because he is waiting for Omara to begin her working. When she does, she will be at her most vulnerable.'' The envoy indicated the ring of great stones. ''Though the stones here do not move, the Aspects have their own cycles of movement, their own courses, just as the stars do above us. Soon the time will come when Omara must begin her work. If Anakhizer and the Primal that uses him are to be thwarted, it must be before then.''

The envoy fell silent, as did Einnis, and they were grouped like trees, motionless and solemn. Wargallow went to them, turning to face the gathering. He saw the great numbers of Woodweavers beyond the circle on the moor, all listening attentively. They accorded him the same attention as they had Einnis and the envoy.

''We have come to you from Goldenisle with one purpose. To find the lair of Anakhizer beyond Starkfell Edge. We have with us the one rod he yet desires.''

The reaction to this was a controlled one, but there was no doubt in Wargallow's mind that the news he had given the Woodweavers was sensational to them. Sisipher also seemed stunned.

The envoy spoke. ''Woodheart understood that the rod had come here. What do you intend with it?''

Wargallow's eyes never left his audience. ''It can either be used to destroy the other rods, or to command them. I have learned much about the rod since discovering it, and I know that if all the rods are turned upon one another, they will wipe out each other's power. We must get to the others before we are discovered.''

''Anakhizer cannot watch the Deepwalks, only their borders,'' said the envoy. ''Though the rod is safe within Woodheart's domain for now, you would be discovered the moment you left.''

''Anakhizer will not expect us to send a small company through the mountains to his lands—''

The envoy drew in a deep breath, his form shaking as he did so. ''You intend to pass Starkfell Edge? How can this be?''

Einnis was frowning. ''Aye, how would you achieve this?''

"Our original intention was to follow the Fellwater to the Gates of Anger—"

From his high place on the monolith, Kirrikree gave a cry, opening his wings like white clouds on either side of him, for Grimander's work with the broken one had repaired it. Though Kirrikree spoke to Wargallow, there were others who heard him. "I have been there and seen those stark caverns. They are choked with our enemies, with the Ferr-Bolgan and the angarbreed."

"Woodheart knows of this," said the envoy. "An army could not win its way through those gates. Not if a hundred ships of your navy brought it."

"What, precisely, are these angarbreed? We have not encountered them in the east."

The envoys seemed to tremble for a moment, but their leader spoke again. "It is feared that Anakhizer uses the rods of power to create these monsters from the very stuff of the darkness beyond Omara, that which seeps into her through her damaged walls. Once the Werewatch would have sealed such ruptures, but since their fall, Anakhizer has sucked in the darkness, and in his forges has created an army, a swarm of servants. And they flock to the power of the survivors of Xennidhum, who command them. Your armies dare not challenge them at the Gates of Anger. They must not entertain such a venture."

"I have flown to the very rim of Starkfell Edge," said Kirrikree. "Not even Aumlac's folk could climb it. I was greatly taxed just to fly there."

"Then there is no way through the Edge?" said Wargallow. "Must we go to the north or to the south to journey around it?"

Einnis was shaking his head. "North? No, we have come from there. The lands crawl with Anakhizer's vermin. As with the Gates of Anger, an army would not be enough. Not if you brought the hosts of Goldenisle, the east and Ulthor himself. I fear that it will be the same at the southern end of the Edge."

"There is no time for such journeys," said the envoy.

Wargallow could feel the disappointment of the gathering,

even of the massed Woodweavers, as though the entire company had for a moment caught a glimpse of crushing defeat.

"Anakhizer dare not attempt to enter the Deepwalks," said the envoy. "Save along the Fellwater. Woodheart will repulse him."

Einnis shook his head. "For how long?"

"Aye!" called Brannog. "No matter what great powers Woodheart possesses, can they prevent the eventual flooding of the world?"

"The rod would be safe here," said the envoy. "Without it, the Primal would be forced to resort to another kind of war."

"Imagine the carnage!" cried Einnis. "Those who were not here in Woodheart's sanctuary would suffer terribly, even if they were able to stem the flow of the angarbreed."

Several voices rose over the babble of debate in the stones, but a small figure forced its way through the front ranks and came before Wargallow and the tall envoys. It was Grimander.

He squinted up at them, his gnarled hands bunched, his expression a mixture of rage and impatience. "Who says there's no way through the mountains!" he shouted, and in the shocked silence that followed, he shrank back as if he had performed some embarrassing misdeed.

"Grimander," breathed the envoy, though there was a hint of remote thunder in his voice.

Yet the Woodweaver raised himself proudly. "Yes, I am Grimander, the *erratic*. Woodheart has granted me certain freedom, and through it I have come to learn many things. Many things."

"You know of a way through the mountains?" Wargallow said at once, fixing the ancient figure with a hawk's stare. But who was this creature? He was very old, possibly senile.

"He's no fool, Simon Wargallow," came the calming inner voice of the white owl. "And sharper than many a blade."

"I do know of a way," affirmed Grimander, no longer awed.

"Name it," said the envoy, the command clear.

"There is a way that extends deep under Starkfell Edge. I

have glimpsed it, in the western deeps of the forest. In the place of hurt."

The envoy said nothing in reply, but Wargallow sensed that Grimander's bald statement had shaken him and his fellows. "Well?" said the Deliverer. "Woodheart must know of this place."

The envoy nodded eventually, but he looked down upon Grimander as if angry that the Woodweaver should have mentioned it. "It is not wise to speak of it."

Grimander shrugged. "Not wise, no. But you spoke of the Gates of Anger. I've seen them, too. And they're impassable. So how else is anyone to go under the Edge?"

"What is this other passage?" said Wargallow, ignoring the envoy's unease.

Grimander made to answer, but he was forestalled by the envoy. "I will tell of it, though it would be better to consider other ways." He locked glances with his two companions, who had not yet spoken, and they nodded, though in them now there seemed to be some pain, an uncertainty. "We have known that evil lurks under Starkfell Edge for many years. Woodheart has made the forest safe, although there have been a few breaches made in his defenses. You know already of the Fellwater, which flows out from the very mountains, bringing with it their dark spawn. But there was once another issue from the mountains, lost in the murk of time. Something seeped out from them and sank down into the lowest part of the Deepwalks, a trough under the mighty brow of Starkfell Edge. A marsh was born there, a black, foul place, shunned now by the creatures of the forest, for it lies down at the very foot of the Deepwalks, ringed in by healthier tracts of forest, its far wall the sheer cliffs of the Edge. It is called Gloomreach. It is a blight on the forest, but being remote is left to itself. It has been contained for millenia, and is no threat to Woodheart."

"You have been there?" Wargallow asked Grimander.

The latter screwed up his face even more. "Aye! Down through its filth we went. Across it to the crack in the stone face. One of Woodheart's mistakes—"

"Be silent!" cautioned the envoy.

"Let him speak," said Wargallow. "What mistake?"

Grimander looked sheepishly at the envoy, but nodded. "Aye, an error. Woodheart sends his roots deep under the earth and stone. Sought to look under the Edge. But when he opened it, out spilled that filth. And though Gloomreach is contained, still the crack is open."

Wargallow faced the envoy, the silent mask. "Surprise must be our weapon. Is this way Grimander speaks of passable?"

"Nothing is known of what is beyond, except that great evil must lie there. It once did Woodheart much harm."

Wargallow would not let this be. "The Gates of Anger are impassable. Is the way beyond Gloomreach the same?"

The envoy did not answer.

Aumlac appeared out of the throng, his face grave. "Our legends speak of Gloomreach." He looked at Einnis, who nodded hesitantly. "The opening in the rock face may provide us with a way under the mountains, but how are we to cross the marsh?"

Again the envoy made no answer. But Grimander tugged at the Stonedelver's fingers. He peered up at the giant figure. "Woodweavers could do it."

"And do you speak for them?" said the envoy.

Grimander muttered to himself, avoiding the gaze of the three figures.

"There is to be a Woodhurling," the envoy told him, and among the Woodweavers there was a shout, like a war cry. When it had died down, the envoy raised his arms. "There is news that the Ferr-Bolgan and the angarbreed, goaded on by their Broodmasters and Broodmothers are ready to swarm out along the Fellwater. They will make for the islands beyond our shores and begin their last preparations for the invasion of Goldenisle. With them are gathered multitudes of the issiquellen, the sea people."

"What is the Woodhurling?" said Wargallow.

"Woodheart will no longer tolerate the passage of Ferr-Bolgan through the Deepwalks, and would see the Fellwater purged of them and their allies. The Woodhurling goes to the banks of that black river." Again there was a shout from the Woodweavers and they lifted their wooden shields and struck them with their spears, the sound like thunder in the trees.

Wargallow looked amazed. "You would send the entire Woodweaver army? But the Emperor can have a fleet sent—" He looked at Ottemar as he said this, and the Emperor nodded vigorously.

"My ships are ready," he said. "One command and the eagles will fetch them for me."

But the envoy shook his head. "There is no time. As soon as the Horn Moot is over, the Woodhurling begins. Few Woodweavers will not go on the march."

"Then *I'll* lead the way across Gloomreach!" said Grimander rebelliously. He waved his fist at the sky. "I may be too old to go on the Woodhurling, but I'll—"

He was cut short by yet another voice. This time it was the burly Hammavar, Rannovic, who came forward. He bowed slightly to Wargallow and the Emperor. The Deliverer recalled this fierce sailor, whose prowess in past battles had been well noted.

"Sire, may I speak?"

Ottemar nodded.

"Most of my loyal Hammavars were killed on the Fellwater, slaughtered in a surprise attack by the angarbreed. There are a dozen of us left, the pride of our House. Does the envoy put a price upon us?"

For a long moment the envoys said nothing, their masks shutting off anything they may have felt. "A price?" said their spokesman. "We do not understand you."

"Come now," said Rannovic with a familiar, huge grin. "Surely a dozen stout Hammavar freebooters would be enough to freeze the bowels of a hundred, a thousand of your enemies!"

"State your meaning, Rannovic," said Ottemar as patiently as he could.

The red-bearded giant looked at Sisipher, but she turned her eyes from him. "Why, I would offer my services, sire. Let me and my Hammavars go with the Woodweavers. Let us take our revenge upon those who murdered our brethren."

Sisipher did look at him as he said it. She seemed about to protest, but he was quick to cut her off. "We will prove our worth at this Woodhurling. To our Emperor and to Woodheart. You have spoken of unity: then you shall see it!'' He laughed. ''And our foes will tremble.''

His warriors raised their swords as one and repeated his cry.

''This does not seem an unreasonable request,'' said the envoy. ''Who would deny him the right to avenge his slain?''

''I do not think—'' began Ottemar, but again he was cut short by the huge sailor.

''Mind you, I'll not be bought cheaply!'' Rannovic laughed.

''Bought?'' echoed the envoy.

''I'll go on the Woodhurling gladly. And I'll be an axe in the hands of the forest folk. My warriors will be an iron fist to beat back Anakhizer's filth. But we ask one thing in return. Not as a price, but as a favor for our Emperor and—his company.'' Again he looked at Sisipher, and the meaning of his look was not lost on her, nor on others.

''What would you have?'' said the envoy.

Rannovic turned to him, his beard bristling. ''Give him enough Woodweavers to guide him through Gloomreach to the place beyond. Spare the best you have and I'll fill the breach in their ranks with Hammavar steel.''

''It is a noble gesture,'' said Einnis.

''Gesture!'' snorted Rannovic, turning on him. ''This is no gesture! My people are proud, Stonewise. We are men of honor. What we give you is our bond, our greatest gift.''

Brannog was scowling, and Ruvanna looked as though a cloud had crossed her path.

''You cannot refuse him,'' Wargallow told the envoy. ''Not unless you would insult the Emperor and his people.''

''You are bent on this journey through the marsh lands?'' the envoy asked Wargallow.

Wargallow studied Ottemar and Brannog, their faces suddenly drawn. ''We were once told we could not go to Xennidhum and live.''

The envoys shuddered as if moved by a sudden gust from the Edge itself. ''Very well. Since this is your path, we will select those who will guide you.''

PART FOUR

STARKFELL EDGE

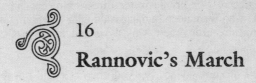

16
Rannovic's March

It was not long after noon when the Horn Moot came to its close. A long discussion followed, and although the talk was of the dangers of the potential journeys they must take, the excitement that ran through them all was palpable, fired by a fresh purpose.

Rannovic gathered his men about him and spoke of his plans. He gave Kelloric and his warriors an account of what had happened at the Fellwater, and of the loss of Helvor, whom they had guessed to be dead. Kelloric told them of their helmsman's brave journey back to Goldenisle and of how he had been responsible for the Emperor's coming to the west. Helvor's death came as a blow to the Hammavars, though they had long feared it.

Alvar, Rannovic's second in command, glared out at the southern horizon. "You spoke well for us, Rannovic. To go back and avenge them will be an honor and a pleasure."

Rannovic nodded, knowing that his men were united in this. But he, too, looked away, hiding his inner turmoil. As though his thoughts had taken on material form, he felt a touch at his arm. Sisipher stood there.

"Should I think you brave or reckless?" she asked him softly, gently guiding him away from his men to a place between two of the great stones. "I've never quite known which of the two you are."

For once he did not smile, watching silent trees of the Deepwalks.

"Is your revenge so important?" she asked.

"You know something of the Hammavar pride."

"Yes. I should do after so many months—"

She glanced back briefly in the direction of her father and Ruvanna, who were deep in discussion with Ottemar and Einnis Amrodin. "You knew why I wanted to leave Goldenisle."

"The Emperor—"

"Yes. I did not say so, but you knew. I could not remain there and see him, his beautiful bride—"

"I understand all this." Still he did not meet her eyes. "Perhaps you will understand why it is I wish to leave for the south."

She gripped his arm. "Rannovic, you must not do this thing for me, or because of me."

"I had hoped that as time went on, you might put something of your past from you and think of a new life. Even after the strange times we have spent in this land of mysteries, I thought—"

"I felt only scorn for you once," she said. "You assumed you could take me by force and make me your woman in Teru Manga. My gift showed me what was in your mind."

Her words did not shame him and he smiled, recalling their first meeting. "Aye! The Hammavars were pirates then, living on our wits. You have taught me something of tact. If you can read my mind, then you must know what is in my heart."

She winced. "Well, it is true that I love Ottemar. It has hurt me to see him again."

"I saw that in your face when he met us—"

"But his duty lies in Goldenisle. With his son."

Rannovic drew in his breath. "It was careless of me to shout it out—"

"No, you did your duty," she said without remorse.

"And what is your duty now?"

"I shall return to Goldenisle."

He turned to her at last. "My path lies in the south. I am committed to it. If you can see the future, you'll see me there. But when this business is done, I shall look for the passage to the west. Unless you would have it otherwise."

"Rannovic, I do not love you—"

He put a hand on her shoulder, but tenderly. "No, I have lived with that for too long. Love is not something to be commanded. But if times were not as they are, if we could think of ourselves and not this war, I would take you on the high seas, and show you parts of Omara that would win your heart. Who knows what would happen then?" He smiled.

She nodded, but her own heart was saddened. "I dare not even think about this journey we must make to the west. When you return from the Fellwater, wait here by these stones. But don't follow. Whatever lies ahead of me, I wish it kept in darkness."

"You'll return here?"

She drew in a deep breath. "Yes. And although I cannot promise you anything, and there must be no pact between us—"

"I demand nothing—"

"No. But if we meet here," she went on, putting her hand on the gray stone, "I will go with you after, on the high seas, far from these lands."

She withdrew her hand and at once he put his own hand over the place where her palm had been. The stone felt warm to his touch. He turned to speak, but she had left him, rejoining her father.

Rannovic went to his men, and now saw that a dozen or more of the Woodweavers had come to them. "Rannovic!" called Alvar. "Here, look what they have brought us!" He held up two round shields, both made of wood, and the Hammavar leader took them and studied them with interest. The craftsmanship was stunning, for although the shields could not have been hewn from a single piece of wood, it was impossible to see where any joints had been made. There was also inlaying which seemed as if it had been grown, veinlike, fused into the wood, and although the shield was small but heavy-looking, it felt exceptionally light. The device upon it was obscure, but it hinted at roots or branches, spreading from the central stud.

"Watch!" called Alvar. He pointed to a place on the heather about twenty yards away where a shield had been set up by two or the Woodweavers. Another of the strange folk handed a bow to Alvar and he drew it back as far as his bulging muscles would allow. When he released the arrow, it sped with the force of the wind. The shield deflected it and it shot across the moor. The shield was brought to Rannovic, who examined it closely. There was no mark upon it.

"That arrow," said Alvar, "was a fine one. It would have gone through the hearts of three men in line, I swear it. But you see, it could not even scratch this shield."

Rannovic turned to the Woodweavers. They were grouped about him, waiting for his reaction as if anxious that he might condemn their workmanship. But the big man grinned, then laughed aloud. "Well, well. Here's a shield that would stop a bull! There's magic in it."

He had never seen a Woodweaver laugh, but there was no doubting the pleasure in the faces of the forest people.

"The arrows, too, are unique," said Alvar, handing a few of them to Rannovic. "They might as well be cast in metal! What tree they are cut from, I could not say."

Two of the Woodweavers came forward, faces typically solemn. "It is wood blessed by Woodheart, from his sacred groves. For the Woodhurling. He has given of himself for this purpose."

Rannovic bowed to them. "Then we are in Woodheart's debt for these. But we shall repay him with the heads of our enemies."

The amassed ranks of Woodweavers raised their own weapons, all hewn and shaped in wood, and called out something that sounded like a salute. It rolled along their columns, shaking the earth, and Rannovic realized just how large an army was gathered there. Up among the monoliths, the rest of the company looked down, surprised to see such a transformation in the Woodweavers, who now seemed far less aloof and suspicious.

Sisipher was with her father, who seemed troubled by something. "You think Rannovic should not go?"

"A man has to choose his own destiny when he can. And so, it seems, must a woman," he said gravely.

Sisipher had argued with him over this before, but she did not smile, instead looking at Ruvanna, who spoke to the envoys beyond them. "What is wrong, Father?"

He put his arm about her. "Not wrong. But my heart is a little heavy. Ruvanna will not be coming with us."

Sisipher frowned. She could not imagine the girl allowing fear to prevent her following Brannog anywhere.

"She has good reason," Brannog said quickly. "For she has great powers of healing. Though her other powers are not what they once were, her gift for healing remains strong. And Woodheart needs her."

"Woodheart? Is he ill?"

Brannog shrugged. "I think he feels the hurt given to him by the ills that beset his borders. There is more to this Gloomreach than we have yet discovered. I think it has pained him greatly, and yet does so. Ruvanna would not desert us, but we must all do what is best for Omara."

"Duty," she murmured, but nodded as he looked at her. "Yes, Father, I understand. It is noble of her to do this."

"Sisipher," he said hesitantly, "I'm not a man to speak my feeling—"

She took his hands and squeezed them. "You think I disapprove of her? No! I need no gift of telling to read your love, nor hers. It is blessed by Omara, Father."

"And by you?"

She hugged him. "Of course! By me."

While they spoke, Wargallow and Ottemar were with Ruvanna and the envoy. The latter gestured to a party of oncoming Woodweavers who were led by a stocky figure to whom Einnis bowed in recognition.

"Here are the guides that were promised," said the envoy.

"Woodheart honors us," said Einnis. "I see that Svoor leads them."

The Woodweaver bowed, his face no less solemn than Einnis remembered.

"This is a dangerous plan," said the envoy. "You must not fail."

"We'll begin at once," said Wargallow. "Our followers are fresh. We've many days travel ahead of us."

"You seek Gloomreach?" said Svoor, almost disapprovingly.

"And a path through it," said Wargallow.

"Indeed?" said Svoor.

"It is the will of Woodheart," said the envoy.

"For Omara," said Ottemar, with a wry grin.

"I will take the children and the mothers to safety," said Ruvanna.

"They are to remain in the Deepwalks?" said Svoor. "That is good. You will need your wits about you if you are to pass through Gloomreach."

"Not all of the women will be staying," said Sisipher.

Svoor frowned as if she had said something untoward.

"You have your duty," the envoy told him.

Sisipher left with Ruvanna to help her gather the women and children of the Earthwrought and Stonedelvers. "This parting saddens me," said Ruvanna. "Doubly so. Brannog, and you—"

"I'd like to try and look ahead, but the west fills me with dread—"

"Just look after him," Ruvanna smiled.

"No doubt he and the others will fuss over me as usual, being the only woman—"

"I think not," said Ruvanna, looking around her. Her eyes fell on a solitary figure standing some distance from Kelloric's warriors.

"Oh?" said Sisipher, puzzled. She followed Ruvanna's gaze. "Dennovia? She's a mystery to me yet."

"When you leave, I think you'll find she is with you. But I cannot tell you why. Wargallow is behind this. She may be a prisoner."

They said no more, for Brannog came to them, arms outstretched.

The farewells began soon afterward. As the main company began their journey off the Ravensring, Rannovic joined the ranks of the Woodhurling. He could still not guess at how many of the forest dwellers there were, and as they now maintained silence, sound was no guide. The last of the goodbyes were brief, for no one wanted to prolong them. As the Woodhurling went down into the embrace of the forest, only Rannovic looked back briefly; he could not see clearly, for the mist on top of the moor was already billowing downward. His last glimpse was of a gray standing stone, aimed up at the sky, and in his mind he took it to be the one under which he had vowed to meet Sisipher again.

The Woodhurling was led by two Woodweavers, Raal and Gurd, and at first it was impossible to tell the difference between them, either in their solid looks or by their deep voices. Their expressions, too, were notably grim, set like those of the Earthwrought, and they glowered about them at every tree, every leaf, as if suspicious of them. They were, Rannovic and his men already knew from their contact with them over the past few months, attuned to the forest in a remarkable way, as if in mental communication with it. Although the Hammavars could never be at ease in this place, or indeed in any forest, no matter how small, they understood the Woodweaver bond with the Deepwalks, being men of the sea. Their own bond with the seas and oceans, not something they could easily explain to anyone unfamiliar with them, such as a Stonedelver, was not unlike that of the Woodweaver for his forest home, nor for that matter, the earth home of the Earthwrought.

As they moved on into the forest, the trees grew taller, closing in above like gigantic sentinels, their branches forming a great vault through which the afternoon sun filtered. Though the ground was choked with rich vegetation, fallen logs and curling bracken, the Woodweavers moved through it with effortless speed, not needing a path, relying on an inbred sense of direction. The power of the Woodhurling was in them, like strong mead, or fire. Rannovic and his men often paused to look ahead to some vast expanse of nettle or copse nestling under the giant trees as if sure they could never penetrate it, but somehow when the army reached it, they moved on through almost as easily as the Woodweavers. The woods remained very quiet, and if the Hammavars had not known otherwise, they would have thought no more than a handful of the Woodweavers accompanied them.

They rested by night beside a dark pool, but the waters were good to drink, icy cold but vividly refreshing, heady, and the Hammavars felt strengthened rather than tired. There were no fires lit, for this was one of the first lessons they had learned in the forest, that it was a prime fear of the Deepwalks and their people. The Ferr-Bolgan and angarbreed used it on their ships down on the Fellwater, keeping the forest at bay, and furnaces had been seen glowing beyond the Gates of Anger, though little was said of that dire place.

Alvar sat beside Rannovic, watching the last rays of sunlight fading above them. He handed the bearded giant a slice of the root he had been chewing. "I swear this stuff becomes more palatable with every meal," he grunted. "Either it's possessed of its own magic, or we're changing into something else."

Rannovic managed a grin, accepting the food and chewing on it. "The earth people eat an equally strange crop from the underworld," he said. "And it seems to me that Brannog is not as other men."

"Aye, you're right," said Alvar. "He was a sailor, you know. Now he's like a man chiseled from stone, with much of the Earthwrought in him. And in his mate, Ruvanna. A strange creature. They say she has power."

"Omara has bred strange children."

Raal and Gurd had been making an inspection of their forces and they emerged from the forest like wraiths and sat with the two Hammavars. They were like twins, inseparable, and as each spoke, the other watched, as if waiting for an error so that he could correct it with a word of his own.

"It will take us three days to reach the Fellwater," said Raal.

"At least," nodded Gurd.

"The attack will be at night."

"There are many of them. Since you were there, many more have come out of the mountains. They intend to go with the water vermin to the islands."

Rannovic nodded, knowing that they spoke of the issi-quellen.

"They outnumber us twenty times," said Gurd.

"Perhaps more than that," said Raal.

"Perhaps. But Woodheart has prepared the Woodhurling. He is ready."

Rannovic glanced at Alvar. He had already wondered what the forest would do to defend itself, knowing that Anakhizer's forces were vast. And he knew that somehow Woodheart had been unable to rescue his companions. But even this army of

Woodweavers would be inadequate to meet Anakhizer in open battle. Rannovic had expected the battle to be one of attrition.

"Sleep peacefully," Raal told him. "Dreams will not trouble you this night."

His words were accurate, for when the Hammavars awoke early the following morning, they felt uniquely refreshed, their blood singing in their veins.

Alvar leapt up as though he had come from his favorite bunk and he waved his axe in the dawn light. His fellows were no less jovial, and Rannovic felt a peculiar elation on him, as if he had eaten something that had made him eager to begin the affray.

"I vow the forest floor's the best bed I've yet known!" Alvar was laughing. "Even at sea I was never more comfortable."

The Woodweavers about him smiled to each other, and Rannovic cuffed him on the back. "Then let us give the forest our thanks. Come, you Hammavar dogs, let's hear you open your mouths! Sing out!"

Raal and Gurd gaped at him, not knowing what to expect. For a brief moment Rannovic wondered if perhaps the singing might be an affront to the dignity of the forest, but he began the song anyway, and in no time his warriors were singing it with him, lifting their rich voices to the branches high above. They sang as they marched and the Woodweavers listened, rapt, glad for the forest. Afterward they asked quietly for another song, and for the first part of that day's journey, the Deepwalks rang to the Hammavars' singing as if there were three score of them.

The journey through the Deepwalks passed in a kind of dream for the Hammavars, and although the paths they trod were often deep, the trees crowding them, the verdure strange-hued and whispering, it was as though the forest blessed their passing, infusing them with wonder and strength. As they neared the end of their journey, high above the Fellwater, they felt the anger of the forest, the loathing for the things that invaded it.

It was evening when the Woodhurling reached the last ridge and looked down at the river. It gleamed like oil in the fading light, black and sinuous, a stark contrast to the greens and browns of the woodland. Like an open wound, it ran thickly, and there was no sign of life upon it, no hint yet that the angarbreed craft were out in force.

"They'll be here with the dawn," said Raal, pointing up the river to the first of its many bends. Beyond it, miles away, the Gates of Anger would soon vomit out the army, the first black wave.

Gurd snorted. "Hurry," he said simply, and the Wood-hurling moved with fresh speed along the ridge above the northern bank of the Fellwater. Nothing had been said about tactics and what the Woodweavers intended to do when they met the enemy, but Rannovic guessed that the battle had been planned in some detail. Woodheart, he felt sure, had given thought to this for many months.

Through the night they moved, never tiring, ever silent, and the Hammavars felt their own strength soaring, as if Woodheart flooded them with a new resolve. The ghosts of their murdered companions sailed this grim river, and the thought of striking a blow to avenge them spurred on the men, lending a unique skill to their acquired forest craft, as though they had been walking the avenues of the Deepwalks since childhood.

The first eastern rays speared the trees when they stopped their march. They had climbed a steep bank, some hundred yards or more higher, when they discovered a ropeway that linked two great branches. From below it would not have been visible, so cunningly was it blended, and already ivy and moss had spread with such profusion that the bridge seemed as though it had been grown rather than woven by the forest folk. Far below it was a tributary of the river, and Rannovic gasped as he recognized it. It was the one he and Sisipher had taken when they had left their ship to go in search of the inhabitants of the forest. They were at the end of the long gorge that led to the open sea.

Raal confirmed Rannovic's thoughts, and in a moment the crossing of the bridge began. The Woodweavers were star-tlingly agile, swinging out over the bridge with the skill of spiders, as effortlessly as if they were on the ground. The Hammavars, being adept at rope-climbing, were equally at ease on the bridge. The crossing was swift, the entire Wood-hurling camping soon afterward. They were at the apex of the gorge.

"In a few hours," said Raal, "our enemies will be here. Already the issiquellen have been swimming up the dark river. Did you not sense them?"

Rannovic shook his head. "There are many?"

"Aye. Beyond the gorge, in the bay. We cannot go down there to fight them. Yet if we inflict a heavy defeat on the angarbreed here, the sea folk will be like a beast without a head. They rely on the leadership of the black ones and the Broodmasters from the Land of Anger. Without them to lead, the issiquellen will never invade your islands."

They rested for two hours. Alvar and the Hammavars spoke with Rannovic between their stolen sleeps. "Is this the *only* route from the west?" said Alvar. "If it is, what size will this army be? The gorge is narrow, but can it be held?"

"Aye," nodded Sturmvor, a hardy warrior who had served beside Rannovic since they were children. "We may toss down an avalanche, but we cannot go down and hold the gorge, not from the river."

"I am sure," said Rannovic softly, as if speaking some prediction he had heard in his dreams, "that the forest will help us. Woodheart will guide us. He is ready for this on-slaught."

When the battle began, an hour later, they were all to remember his words.

The Woodweavers were the first to know that the Ferr-Bolgan were coming, a gray tide on the river. The word trav-eled like a swift breeze through the entire Woodhurling, now invisible in the bushes that grew thickly above the gorge. The Hammavars drew their swords and axes, their shields at the ready. Each looked to Rannovic, but he shook his head. "We wait."

They could see little from this distance, assuming that Raal's folk had the river watched closely, but they were soon able to hear the coming of the enemy. Words were impossible to distinguish, but there were calls and shouts, all in strange voices, and other, terrible sounds. The Hammavars closed their minds to the memories of the day in Teru Manga when the Ferr-Bolgan had attacked them in force, driving them from the citadel, pouring like rats from the depths of the rock, irresistible and merciless.

After a while, Alvar grew impatient. "They're past us! The first of their craft are in the gorge! We should act."

Gurd appeared beside him as if by magic. "Woodheart has them. And there is no mercy in Woodheart on this day of retribution. Our hour will be upon us soon." He slipped away as easily as he had come.

Rannovic was concentrating on the ground about him. He could feel it, sense it *listening* to the passage of those unseen horrors below in the gorge. His mind made a sudden leap then, to the time he had first passed through the gorge, turning back to see—

"The gorge!" he gasped. "Do you not feel it, Alvar?"

Alvar grunted. "It moves. As it did—"

"Aye! As it did after us. *And closed!*"

Now it was easy to feel the grinding of stone, the drifting of huge weights of rock. Woodheart was closing the trap. He had been waiting for this day. Rannovic looked about him and for a moment it was as if the forest had pressed in to witness this. Through the lower trees he could see the huge ones below, and it was as if they had marshaled themselves on the banks of the river, on both the north and south banks. Their branches swept down, great elongated claws that trailed into the water, with briar banks dragging at the flow.

The first of the screams rose up, followed by a tremendous thundering sound as the walls of the gorge smote each other, closing on the massed apex of the Ferr-Bolgan and angar-breed. From his high vantage point, Rannovic could see the low craft of the enemy, many of them striking each other, the confusion rife. Countless dark shapes were in the water, thrashing, and those that tried to get ashore were swallowed up by the foliage as if by lurking predators. The Woodhurling held itself in check, like dogs on leashes, waiting, waiting.

"It is time to go down," said Raal at long last, and with no more ado, he waved the first ranks of his warriors forward. The Hammavars went with them, but not one of them shouted out a battle cry or curse. They moved with the speed and silence of the wind. As they came to the river bank, they saw the immensity of the havoc that Woodheart had wrought. Dozens of craft had been overturned on the river, which was choked with them. Up out of the water sprang thick roots, groping tendrils, white and bleached. Cracking like whips, they smashed into more of the oncoming craft. Ferr-Bolgan and angarbreed alike were swarming like ants over their crippled fleet.

A wave of them struggled to the bank, but the Woodhurling unleashed a hail of arrows, killing a score in the blinking of an eye. Something sucked the corpses under the water as another wave tried to reach the shore. There were more arrows and on the opposite bank the enemy fared no better, unable to breach the thick curtains of green that seemed to strangle all those who tried to cut into it.

Still more craft came down the river, for they would not heed the chaos before the gorge, as if by sheer weight of number they could force their way through their own dead and dying. But Rannovic could see the gorge: it was closed, its sides slammed to like colossal doors, and at their feet there swirled a bloody tangle of the slain. How many had been pulped inside that crushing trap?

He had no time to deliberate, for the first of the enemy had slipped by the rain of Woodweaver arrows and the fighting began. Swords cut into them, and now each Hammavar shouted out the names of their fallen comrades, remembering them. The Ferr-Bolgan, crazed with terror, were like animals, rat caught in a trap, and they fought without skill, blindly and clumsily. The Woodweavers slaughtered them and the Hammavars soon took no pleasure in the bloody butchery that followed.

They had to move further up the river, for the banks were becoming impassable, so thickly did the enemy fall. Even now their craft came on, for Anakhizer had indeed launched his first great wave. But Woodheart had no mind to let them pass.

Raal fought his way to Rannovic's side. "We must move back to higher ground. There is danger there, for they have brought one who makes fire."

Rannovic nodded and called his men away from the carnage. They came in silence, chests heaving, and to his dis-

may, Rannovic saw that two of them were down. But he had
no more than a moment for remorse as the flight up the banks
began. Woodweaver archers cut into the pursuit, and the Ferr-
Bolgan were again driving out on to the water. It heaved and
boiled like the sea in a storm, thick with issiquellen corpses,
sucking down yet more craft.

The Hammavars reached the crest of a ridge, turning to
defend it, though the enemy had fallen back. They paused to
regain their strength, and as they did so a startled cry swung
Rannovic round like a blow. He was in time to see two of
his men flung back by a tall, cloaked being. He knew it at
once: a herder, which the Woodweavers called Broodmasters.
Sisipher had known these monsters, for they were the Children of the Mound, devils from the far eastern realms, from
Xennidhum itself. A number of Woodweavers raced for it
like hounds, but they were struck down by an invisible hand,
their shields snapped.

Rannovic faced the dark being, seeing only its scarlet eyes
as he raised his sword. He called his men away, and they
were wary. It was this creature that Raal feared, for it carried
fire, the one thing that Woodheart also feared.

Gurd and Raal burst from a thicket, covered in blood,
though not their own. They seized on the situation at once
and made ready to attack the Broodmaster. But its gaze was
fixed on Rannovic, its hate molten.

"Woodheart sees you," Raal told the intruder, but it returned his words with a thunderous growl, full of fury. It
swung an arm and there was a sizzling burst of white light
that struck at one of the nearby trunks. At once it burst into
flame. The Woodweavers who were nearest rushed at it,
smothering it, and Rannovic watched in horror as they sacrificed themselves to prevent the spread of the fire. A dozen
arrows flew at the Broodmaster, but none of them struck it.
All shot past as if they had been mis-aimed.

Rannovic knew that he was facing death. He could have
turned, even now, and fled that thing, for Woodheart would
have pulled it down in time. But he would not run. Nor would
his remaining men. Alvar and Sturmvor nodded to him, gripping the shields they had been given. Between them they
would take this abomination.

There was no signal, but they had fought as a unit for many years. They sprang at the enemy, and more light and fire crackled in the glade. A dozen Woodweavers raced in like striking serpents. The Broodmaster was met in the center of the glade. Rannovic's sword glancing from its skull, another Hammavar axe biting into its side. It howled maniacally, flinging off its assailants as a bear throws off wolves, but they attacked it again. This time Rannovic penetrated its defense and his sword point dug deep into its vitals. He felt a surge of black power blasting up from his enemy, through his own sword, and he was tossed back like a doll of straw.

The Woodweavers tore into the dying Broodmaster with abandon, and at last had destroyed it, though a score of them were charred and dead. Beside them lay the body of Alvar, smoking and bleeding. Sturmvor was on his knees, holding a frightful cut in his side. He crawled across the grass to the tree bole where Rannovic was sprawled.

Raal had survived the wild fury of the fight, and as a dozen of the angarbreed blundered into the clearing, he rallied his Woodweavers and sent them scattering back down to the river, where, along with their allies, they were cut to pieces.

By the time Raal came back for the redbeard, Rannovic was up on his feet, though reeling like a drunkard. There were tears in his eyes, but he grinned through his pain. Sturmvor had fallen, his face pressed to the grass as if in prayer to Woodheart.

"I need a fresh blade," said Rannovic. "Come, hand me Alvar's axe. The work isn't over yet."

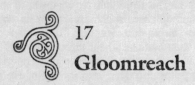

17
Gloomreach

As THE company left the Ravensring for the west, led by Svoor and his Woodweavers, morale was far higher than it had been previously. Einnis Amrodin and his people had lived under a shadow at Star Watch, unsure of their future, for at that time the talk was of the Absorption Ceremony; although Svoor and his companions had not been unfriendly, they had been distant. Now that the Horn Moot was over, however, their attitude had changed, and although they would always seem a reserved race, they had accepted Woodheart's ruling that the company was comprised of allies who must be helped. They were less inclined to be respectful to Grimander, who explained that they were all jealous of his status, although no one had confirmed that being an *erratic* was in fact as prestigious as the old Woodweaver made it out to be. He did not travel with the Woodweaver scouts, instead keeping close to Ottemar and his party. Kirrikree had again met Skyrac and his eagles, and they circled overhead, ever watchful. Of the ravens there was no sign, but it was understood that their prime function was to patrol the Ravensring.

Brannog tried not to let his own spirits flag, for although it was a joy to be reunited with Sisipher, he felt the parting from Ruvanna deeply. It was a blessing, though, that the two women had not only accepted each other but had struck up an immediate bond. Sisipher had fallen silent as the journey began, and Brannog wondered if she was again troubled by the gift that had once been such a burden to her, the gift of telling, of seeing into the future. But he had noticed her with Rannovic. They had been together here in the Deepwalks for a long time; had the bond between them grown during those months? Had she set aside her childish notion of loving Ottemar? She had almost ignored the Emperor, having no more than a few words with him since the dramatic meeting at the stone circle. Should I ask her outright? But no, it was never his way. There may be an opportunity eventually.

Zuhaster and the warriors brought up the rear of the company, their weapons always drawn, watching the skies. The huge oarsmaster had no love of this country and would have been far happier back at sea. He listened to the idle chatter of his men. By and large they were in good heart, with allies about them and the knowledge that the forest was not, after all, determined to kill them. But the sea seemed almost as remote as the stars.

Kelloric walked beside the oarsmaster. "I did not like to see Rannovic and the Hammavars go from us," he said quietly.

"No, sire," agreed Zuhaster. "The men wondered about that. It was a noble gesture, of course, and we should be glad to have such allies as these forest dwellers. But this is no time for division."

"When we spoke before the Horn Moot, I thought it was. But we should hold them together in this venture. The Emperor never questioned Rannovic. In a way it seemed as though he was glad to be rid of him, or do you think I imagine this? Speak honestly, Zuhaster, you have sailed in my ships long enough to know my loyalty to the throne."

"There's talk, sire, of the girl, Sisipher."

"Let me hear of it."

Zuhaster had lowered his voice, as though the forest, which they had again entered, could hear each word. "The men are glad to have Ottemar here to lead us. But it has always seemed strange to them that he should have come, thus endangering himself. This expedition hangs by a thread, and from the sound of the land we seek, the dangers are immense. We're not complaining for ourselves, but should the Emperor be here?"

"It's the girl, isn't it? You think so?" said Kelloric grimly.

"As I say, sire, there's talk. And was in the city. And what of this other girl, Dennovia? A strange business. Does she have powers that we don't know about?"

"She's of value to Wargallow. I suspect myself, and you had best relay this with great care, that she does. She's from the east, from the Direkeep, so who can tell what she is capable of? Since she is here, she is here for a reason. We have no choice but to trust Wargallow."

"The men fear him, sire. But they are obedient."

"Everything he has done has been for the Empire. But he is a ruthless man. He will make sacrifices for his goals. On such a journey as this, perhaps it is best that such a man leads. But I would have been happier if we had not lost Rannovic."

The forest swallowed them, and as they moved westward, they dropped ever downward, steeply, into a thicker mass of trees, where the sun could not directly reach down, the air cool, the undergrowth more tangled and alien. But the Woodweavers guided them easily, opening a way. There was no birdsound, no flutter of wings, and although the wind occasionally stirred the branches overhead, no sound from the forest itself.

During one of their periodic rests, Sisipher sat with Dennovia. Even here in this shadowy realm, after a journey of miles, the dark haired girl from the east looked strikingly beautiful. Sisipher had been musing on why the girl was here and, like Kelloric, she assumed she must have a gift of some kind, other than her beauty.

"I know a little of your time in the east," Sisipher told her. "Will you tell me more?"

"Of course," smiled Dennovia, delighted to have the chance to talk at all. Ruvanna had never been a friend to her, perhaps because she had not trusted her. "Though your father could tell of those days better than I could."

Sisipher grinned. "Not so. He'd be too modest and probably leave out most of the events in which he played a part."

Dennovia nodded. "Yes, you're right. He is a modest man. He has no idea of the respect he commands. Of all those I have met since my freedom, he is the most remarkable." Her eyes dropped and Sisipher wondered if there was something Dennovia was hiding, but she let it pass.

"I understand you were a prisoner?"

"In the Direkeep," Dennovia nodded, and for a time she talked of her past. Sisipher listened intently, unaware that others were also listening to the voice of the girl from the east.

Meanwhile, Wargallow and Coldrieve were surveying the forest ahead of them. Still it dropped before them into an even deeper green trench of silence. Einnis had joined them, with Aumlac and Bornac and some of the Earthwrought. Grimander, too, was with them, himself fascinated by the outsiders, of whom he had heard so many rumors.

"Long, long way down," he said, chuckling. "You see why the forest gets its name."

"Does anything live down there?" said Aumlac.

"Aye. Full of forest life. But everything has moved aside for you. The Woodweavers command it. There's no danger. Woodheart won't permit it. But as we go lower, the forest is unwell."

"Unwell?" said Wargallow sharply.

"Aye. At the very bottom is the sink of Gloomreach. Diseased, full of pain. Woodheart has cut off that part of himself, trying to be free of the darkness. Woodweavers have not been there for many years. Only me."

"What did you find?"

"Evil. Darkness and despair. I did not linger. But I saw the place. Ah, we warned him. But it is enclosed now and will not spread. But we'll pass over it. With care."

"Who warned who?" said Aumlac. "Woodheart?"

Grimander screwed up his face, shaking his head, but he would not elaborate on his puzzling statement.

"Give us something to fight," growled Bornac. "Ferr-Bolgan—"

Grimander silenced him with a slow shake of his head. "The Ferr-Bolgan wouldn't dare come near the place. You'll see none of them, nor the angarbreed."

Later they moved on, and around them the undergrowth thinned until the forest floor was almost devoid of it, a sloping bank of earth where odd mushroom-like plants grew, and where there were tiny burrows, but no animals to be seen. The trunks of the trees were thin, conveying an impression of emaciation, their bark very dark, splotched with mold, and the trees rose up straight, their branches beginning high overhead. It had become a permanent twilight realm, soundless and cold, and it was not an easy place to take heart.

At last, four days from the Ravensring, they saw a company of Woodweaver scouts clambering up the slope from the darkness below. Svoor led them, and came to Wargallow and Ottemar with a stiff bow.

"You'll see Gloomreach in under an hour. It is silent, motionless. But even as we looked, we felt it. It has been listening to us."

Ottemar frowned. How dangerous a crossing would this be? Perhaps it would be better to have some knowledge of what was beyond. Kirrikree? Or Sisipher. Should he ask her? He had hardly spoken to her since the meeting on the moor. She had almost ignored him. Was she angry at his coming? Did she realize that he had only come here because of her? How could he possibly speak to her with so many ears about him?

Yet as the journey downward continued, with slow and painful care, he spoke softly to Wargallow. "We have to find out more about what awaits."

"Yes, we cannot risk a blind crossing."

"Perhaps Sisipher will look ahead for us. I'll speak privately to her."

Wargallow gave him a critical look, but only for a moment. He nodded.

Ottemar went back to Sisipher and spoke clearly and openly, as if he were addressing one of the warriors. "Come, Sisipher, walk with me for a moment. I need your advice. Where is the owl?"

Sisipher was acutely aware that her father was watching her, as were many others, but she smiled pleasantly and went with Ottemar. They walked some yards from the company, and Ottemar pointed downward.

"You are well," he whispered so softly that she almost did not hear him.

"We must not speak—"

"I came to this forsaken land for one reason only."

"We have already talked of this, months ago—"

"When I saw you were alive, I wanted to embrace you before them all."

"Ottemar, you must not go on." She, too, pointed to the lower forest, as if they were discussing it. "Our work is below us."

"Why did you flee the Chain?"

"You know why."

"You should have remained—"

"And watched your wife grow? How soon you filled her belly—"

His face had gone ashen, but he could not rely, searching for the words that would explain the sorrow of Tennebriel, and his own.

As they spoke, Grimander, who had curled up into a ball as he often did and sat gazing ahead of him, heard every word, his ears far sharper than those of the company around him. He did not mean to pry, but to him it was as if the Emperor spoke in his ear. Ah, so there was one mystery solved! Grimander had thought it strange that an Emperor, ruler of such a vast realm as that of Goldenisle, should come here and risk his life in this wild venture. Well, the Woodweavers would know it now, as would Woodheart.

"Since you have learned this secret," came a voice inside Grimander's head, "you had better keep it safe." It was Kirrikree, somewhere above the canopy of branches.

Grimander spoke silently back to the great owl. "I will. But you had better tell your mistress to guard her tongue."

Kirrikree did exactly that, discreetly warning Sisipher that she was overheard. She colored and gazed more intently at the lower forest.

"What is it?" said Ottemar, sensing her withdrawal.

"Unless you wish to discuss the journey, I have nothing else to say."

He could see that she had locked him out, at least here. "There is one question, though I hesitate to ask it. But it is, I suppose, my duty to do so."

"Then ask."

"Can you see?"

The coldness took her, and the forest closed in like an alien thing, as if they had already passed from the protection of Woodheart. But Ottemar touched her arm gently.

"No. Forget that I asked." He turned away and strode back to the others.

He found himself meeting the level stare of Coldrieve. If he knew anything of Ottemar's weakness, he did not show it, nor would Ottemar have expected pity or sympathy from him. He seemed far colder than Wargallow, and was aptly named.

"Have you learned anything, sire?" said the Deliverer.

"She once had a gift, though one could say it was a curse. But it will not help us here. The forest people will have to guide us."

"We should attempt to cross without resting," said Svoor. "It will be murky and unpleasant by day, but when night comes, nothing will penetrate the darkness. I doubt that the Earthwrought light will shine for us." He turned to Graval with an apologetic bow. "Though I mean no insult by this."

Graval, who had been listening attentively, nodded. "No, Svoor. You are right. We feel this earth under us. It is dark, brooding like a mind that has lost its way, knowing only the dull and constant throb of pain. How deep this evil must be!"

Aumlac and Bornac murmured their agreement and even Einnis looked drawn and weary beside them. "It is a madness that saps the power of us all, but I fear we must endure far worse if we are to pass under Starkfell Edge."

"Let us go on swiftly," suggested Svoor, anxious to be away, and it was agreed.

Sisipher had returned to Brannog. "What is it?" he asked her, aware of her distress.

"Nothing, father. Just a glimpse of what lies below. The anguish of the land here. Gloomreach—"

He would have said more, but perhaps this was not the time. He had not spoken of the Emperor, not sure how to do so. If there was a deep bond between him and his daughter, it must be hidden. Now, in such a time of peril, they dare not reveal it to the company. Brannog had already sensed that the warriors were acutely conscious of their Emperor's danger in being here. They considered him brave, but few would have seen his coming as a wise decision.

Downward they went, mindful not to slide on the dark earth, which was packed hard, carved by the rain. There were few roots protruding, and no vines, no creepers. Overhead the foliage was still tangled, dark and forbidding. The Stonedelvers and Earthwrought had to help the others to descend, while the Woodweavers led the way. Grimander was sniffing at the air like a weasel, as though every scent that came up from below brought with it a new hint of menace. Then the slope became less pronounced, almost leveling off into a narrow ridge. Beyond it there was a sheer drop and a clearing.

Svoor pointed to the drop. Through the narrow trunks, the company could look down to the sink that was Gloomreach. There were dark green banks of foliage below, and rotting trunks poked up from the mire, sharpened and splintered, aimed like weapons at the company. The twisted trees had their limbs entwined where they had fallen, locked like silent combatants, disfigured and broken by others that had fallen, or snapped. Moss and lichen crawled over everything, while the floor of Gloomreach looked as if it might be safe, though Svoor warned of its many hidden pools.

A particular stench rose up from the place, hinting at decay and dissolution, and a deep silence pervaded every foot of that lifeless domain. The sun reached down and dabbed at the open areas of the mire, yellowing further contortions of fallen trees, or dancing on a pool that was clear of reed or clinging bloom. And far beyond, at the limit of vision, was a gray shadow, rising upward like a bank of thunderheads, half veiled in vapors, Starkfell Edge. The company studied it, each of them wrapped for a time in his own thoughts.

"How do we cross?" Wargallow asked Svoor. "Will we need a craft?"

Svoor's wrinkled features twisted in what may have been a smile. "No craft you could call to mind, sire. But craft of a type. The Woodweaver craft." Without another word, he waved his colleagues over the ridge, and they slipped like spiders to Gloomreach. The remainder of the company watched, fascinated.

Svoor and his people alighted on a huge log, and within moments they were working with its wood, though what they were doing was impossible to see clearly. In a short while they had somehow bound together, using the slippery creepers of the mire, this log and another, pointing them forward into the morass ahead.

"Ah," sighed Aumlac. "I see it now. It is like a bridge. See how quickly they work!"

Graval grinned beside him. "Aye, they're as quick with wood as you and I would be with earth and stone."

Einnis called for them to make a rough stair down to the mire and at once the little people and the burly Stonedelvers leapt to obey, pleased to be able to do something positive. Working with the dark loam of the forest was not easy for them, for it did not shape in their hands as other soil would have, but they constructed a path for the company to use. In an hour Wargallow, Ottemar and all the rest were down on the first of the logs that the Woodweavers were diligently binding together.

Sisipher, who had been fascinated by the progress of the forest people, suddenly looked up to see a flutter of white, and in a moment Kirrikree winged down through the thin, sickly branches and alighted on a bough a few yards from her. Grimander hopped eagerly to his side.

"You've found a loyal friend," Sisipher told the owl.

"I owe him my life," the bird replied, and she sensed the warmth in her mind as he spoke.

"Have we far to travel across this wilderness?"

"If you journey through the night, you'll reach Starkfell Edge by dawn. Skyrac circles above. We will search ahead, but it is not always easy to see down into this place. There are pockets of mist, thicker than sea fog, and in other places a kind of darkness that shifts from place to place."

"I know the way!" said Grimander, speaking in both their minds. "I'll go to Svoor." He hopped away, nimble as a youth in spite of his age.

"How has he been here before?" said Sisipher incredulously. "It is the most dismal region I've yet seen."

"His memories of the place are not fit to be shared," said Kirrikree. "And something of his own history is tied up in it. But he knows how to reach the mountains." The white bird flew upward again, glad to be in open sunlight, and Sisipher watched him disappear over the thinning trees.

By evening the company had advanced well into Gloomreach. Shadows gathered about them as they threaded carefully over the moving logs and dead timber that the Woodweavers had constructed tirelessly for them. On either side the mire had become a thick, oily excrescence, dotted here and there with banks of reed, fused in dark clumps. Gases escaped from the surface, curling in strange, flickering emanations, like horrible masks. The broken trees further out were like watchers at the edge of light, crowding each other, readying for a sudden rush that never came. After the sun went and twilight spread over the mire like a plague, the Woodweavers worked on.

"It is no place to rest," Svoor had said. "Be vigilant at all times."

"Your people must need help," said Einnis. "Can the Stonedelvers not help with the trees they are moving?"

"No. We cover our presence in the water. Should any of you do so, it would bring hunters. There is life here."

Svoor had not said any more than that, but every member of the company clutched a weapon, even the girls. Sisipher had shut her mind to the awful darkness around her, afraid to test it. Dennovia was no more than a step behind Wargallow and Coldrieve, neither of whom had spoken for hours. They were set on this course, she knew, seeing nothing else but the final goal.

The company had an unexpected ally that night, for the moon suddenly rode out from cover, dispersing the clouds about it and flooding Gloomreach with pallid light. Fallen trees were daubed in silver, and objects that jutted up from the mire were like supplicant arms, frozen in time. Still the silence gripped everything, the passing of the company muffled and distant to its own ears.

Svoor materialized in front of Wargallow like a wraith. Behind him his Woodweavers had suddenly balled together, shields and weapons ringing the front of their working.

"What is it?" said the Deliverer.

"Prepare for the first defense of the road," said Svoor, his normally gruff voice betraying fear. "We are found."

Wargallow had no time to reply, for ahead of them, out to their left, the mire erupted, flinging waves of much and reed aside as something burst to the surface. The moonlight could not depict it for them. Whatever it was, it splashed down on the mud and shot forward as if propelled by great strength. It crashed into the woven road beyond the Woodweavers, and the entire fabrication shook. There were shrieks from the men behind, and shouts that some of them had tumbled into the mire.

Zuhaster bellowed orders, seeing one of his men struggling in the mud. He bent and held out his axe haft to the man, but something cracked through the air like a whip, a wet rope, it seemed, but with a clawed hand. Those cold fingers closed on Zuhaster's weapon and with an awesome strength jerked him bodily from the log. With a howl of rage and terror he hit the mire, at once sucked below it. The men were yelling together, swinging their blades at the unseen enemy. More of the long arms from the mire snaked out, and in the poor light it was impossible to chop them back.

Kelloric had seen the oarsmaster go under and swore vilely. But there was no possible way to help him. The Woodweavers raced along the logs and wherever they saw the hands of the marsh, they thrust their spears at them, the mud boiling. Whatever it was that had struck the front of the road had dived under it.

Svoor waved the company on. There was a thick clump of vegetation ahead, like an island, and although the logs did not quite reach it, the leap across was not too difficult. Wargallow and Coldrieve helped the girls to get over, and as they did so, another attack on the road came. Something rose up under a section of it, sending more of its defenders into the mire, and some of Svoor's folk fell with them. There followed a terrible splashing and churning of the water, and as the mud flew, the rest of the company hastened to the clump of island. Once upon it, they took a position defending its highest point, a hump that overlooked the mire on all sides. They ringed it, the girls in the center, though Sisipher protested.

Kelloric stood shoulder to shoulder with Wargallow, face

writhing with fury at the loss of so many. "You must use the rod! It is the only way to clear the way for us."

Wargallow met his blazing stare, his own eyes cold. "You saw what it dredged up from the ocean floor. What would it bring upon us in this hellish place?"

Kelloric would have argued, but the din from the mire abruptly ceased. A single shape flopped up the island like a landed fish, but its movements ceased as life leaked out of it. It was a Woodweaver.

"Zuhaster!" someone shouted, the voice ringing out over the mire. But there was no reply.

Svoor emerged from the shadows, covered in filth. "We are safe here for a short time."

"How many did we lose?" came Ottemar's voice.

"I fear at least a score," said the Woodweaver. "They have brought us a respite."

"Then let us remain here for the night," suggested Wargallow.

Svoor shook his head. "We dare not. These islands move of their own volition. And they have strange appetites. We must begin on the road again." He was gone as quickly as he had come.

"Zuhaster gone!" Kelloric groaned. "I saw him go under. Are they sure there is no sign of him?" But the huge oarsmaster was not to be found.

Soon Svoor's folk were calling for the company to begin anew the crossing, and they did so with great trepidation, in spite of the return of the silence. The island slipped away behind them, almost as though it had, as Svoor had said, swum away. Whatever it was that had attacked the log bridge, it had withdrawn.

An hour later there was another peril to negotiate. Ahead of them there was a spread of trees that had woven themselves into a tall barrier. The Woodweavers leapt up into the lower branches, using their weapons to cut a way into them, but as they did so, the branches, thin as wire and thick with spikes, began to whip back into place, curling and tightening. Several of Svoor's folk were choked, and it took the ferocious attacks of the Stonedelvers to hew a passage through the branches. The company was forced to clamber up over the marsh now, wriggling through the criss-cross of branches. Below them, in the depths, something else stirred.

"We cannot use the log bridge again," called Svoor. "We must build on to this copse. If it thins, we cannot."

His prediction was accurate. An hour on they came to a wide expanse of Gloomreach. The only way across it would have been by a log road. But from the platform of thorny branches above the mire, the company knew that something waited eagerly for them under the surface.

"There are many of them," said Svoor. "It is as though all of Gloomreach closes in on us."

"How far to the cliffs?" said Wargallow.

"Dawn is an hour away," said Svoor. "As it strikes the upper crags, we should be at their feet. But how to get across—"

Einnis called the Stonedelvers to him, himself resting on a thick bough that stretched out over the marsh, fifty feet above it. "I do not like to think of communicating with this abominable place," he told Aumlac, Bornac and the others. "But there are masses of reed out there that float and drift. Let us command them. Our wills are strong. They may yet serve us."

"It would be dangerous," said Aumlac. "But I agree that we try this."

The others nodded and together with the Earthwrought they used their mental powers, stone and earth, dragging at the humped shapes out in the night, until at last Grimander was hopping up and down like a child, pointing.

"One comes, one comes! In response!"

"Can there be a *mind* in that thing?" said Kelloric.

Sisipher heard him. "No. But there is earth and stone, and something in them, no matter how debased, responds to the earth people."

"Memory," murmured Grimander in his obtuse way.

The company watched as the vast shape floated close under them, and at a command from Svoor, they began dropping down on to it. When they were all on the strange island, the Stonedelvers and Earthwrought again used their powers to guide it across the mire. It had barely moved out from under the trees, when every branch shook. Another denizen of

Gloomreach approached. Like a huge spider, its dark shape rose up over the skeletal trees, and it began to clamber slowly and unnaturally to the place where the company had been. The island moved away sluggishly and the Woodweavers unleashed a hail of arrows at the bulk of the creature above them. It reached out a pale, flexible appendage, nearly resting it on the edge of the island, narrowly missing it.

There was a sudden cracking of branches, a snapping of rotten wood, and the huge bulk plummeted downward through the thorns to hit the surface of the mire. At once something else rose up, black and obscured, wrapping its own rubbery limbs about the thing that had fallen. A terrific thrashing followed, with numerous trees toppling over and waves of thick mire lapping at the retreating island. But the company pulled away.

Ahead of them they saw more fallen trees, some of them of staggering girth, and jutting rocks. The latter were the first they had seen in the mire, though they were no more inviting than the rest of the foul terrain. The filth swirled about them, whirls and eddies visible like the currents in a river, and they knew that other creatures swam below, waiting for a chance to attack. Behind them the battle died abruptly, and moonlight splashed over a landscape that was again silent and lifeless.

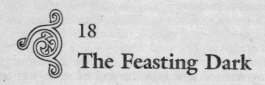

18

The Feasting Dark

THE PROGRESS of the island across the mire was slow, although it was mercifully not attacked from above or below. Sisipher had tentatively sought out Kirrikree and the eagles but they did not answer her.

Svoor pointed ahead to a long patch of darkness against the night, itself like a shore line, or possibly another, wider island. "We can begin constructing a new path. it will take us to the foot of Starkfell Edge."

Wargallow nodded, but as the island drew closer to the thick banks, shapes rose up from them, black and sinuous, globular heads weaving from side to side like those of huge serpents. The Woodweavers drew back in alarm and Aumlac tried in vain to see what the eyeless creatures were in the clusters of weed.

"Whatever they are," he said, "they stand between us and the exit to Gloomreach."

A shout from the rear of their island made them all turn. They could see other thick shapes coming across the mire from behind them, larger than trunks, blunt snouts raised above the dark water.

Kelloric glared at Wargallow, but the Deliverer ignored him, guessing his thoughts. "Ring the island," said the Deliverer. "And keep it moving."

They came closer to the shore, and the shadows thickened, scores of the creatures eager for confrontation. Arrows and swords alone could not defeat them, and Wargallow tried not

252

to think of the rod. It would be used if there was no other choice, but its use would focus Anakhizer's attention directly on them. To venture under Starkfell Edge without the element of surprise would be an act of suicide.

The mists that shrouded the land ahead seemed to shiver for a moment, and then they took on a fresh, paler hue. Several of the weaving shadow-beings drew back. High overhead there was a gleam of light, and for the first time the company realized how high the wall of stone was beyond them. Starkfell Edge rose up almost vertically. It was the dawn light that had etched it for them. They had to bend back to see the highest part of it, for it rose sheer, mile upon mile, its top hidden by the mist.

Light speared fresher rays from the east behind the company, and as it did so there was frantic movement ahead. The shapes were ducking down into the mire, hissing as they did so. As the faint light reached them, they fled, creatures of the dark.

Svoor grinned, thumping his shield with his sword. "The dawn defeats them! See, they sink down to their lairs."

Moments later the reed island bumped against the bank and the company was able to disembark, though with trepidation. The ground here was much firmer, if pocked with sinks and mire-wallows. Svoor and his fellows flanked the company, watching out for predators as well as searching for a solid path. Graval and the Earthwrought were utterly confused by the ground beneath them. It shifted and flowed in places, and could not be read, and though there were stones in it, and in some places great boulders that must have fallen from on high, even the Stonedelvers were unable to read anything from them. Only their despair. It was a land soaked in misery and pain.

Dawn streaked the far eastern sky with golden bands, shredding the clouds. It gave new meaning to the height of Starkfell Edge, and every member of the company stood in awe of the sheer size of the cliffs.

Grimander hopped out of the fading mists, pointing behind them to the rocks. "The opening is not far, but guard yourselves well," he cried. "There is no dark like the darkness below."

Kirrikree and the eagles came out of the heavens, alighting on a fallen tree. "You must hurry," the owl told Sisipher. "From either side of the cliffs there are other enemies gathering. These, unlike the beings of the mire, do not fear the daylight."

"Ferr-Bolgan?"

"No, we have seen none of them. But these go upon two legs. Do not ask me to describe them to you. If the company moves quickly, they can be avoided."

"Will they follow us into the mountains?"

"No," said the owl simply and Sisipher sensed there was more he wished to say.

"What is it?"

"Mistress, I do not think the eagles and I can be of use to you in those places."

She read then his masked terror, felt its extremity. Skyrac and his companions were likewise afraid, and a grunt from Aumlac beside her confirmed it.

"We cannot ask them to come with us," he said to her gently. "They could achieve nothing."

She nodded. "Of course. You must remain outside," she told Kirrikree.

"It shames me to ask this," said the owl. "But there should be watchers at the portal for a while. The eagles and I will deter any possible pursuit."

"Wait for a short time only," said Aumlac. "Then you must go back to the Ravensring. Search for news of the Woodhurling. There will be important news for the Empire." He had been addressing his eagles, but Kirrikree heard him. It was sensible advice.

"We cannot fly over the Edge," the owl told Aumlac.

As they spoke, Grimander led Wargallow, Coldrieve and Einnis Amrodin across more heaped trunks, past lakes of black, treacle-like liquid. It was as though the lower stones of the cliffs had bled, their wounds leaking thick, coagulating pools that stank of decay. No plants grew here, nor mold, and what trees poked through the muck had long ago perished, frozen like stone, lifeless as bleached bone.

When they came upon the opening that Grimander had promised them, its size surprised them, for it was little more than a tall split in the rock that they might not have noticed in passing. From its mouth there dribbled more of the dark blood-like fluid, clinging to the rocks about it. They threaded around it, coming under the massive wall. The fissure was some twenty feet high, wide enough for two men to pass abreast. The sun was unable to penetrate it, so that it rose like a jet black sword slash.

"Can this lead through these walls to the land beyond?" said Ottemar incredulously.

Both the Earthwrought and Stonedelvers shook their heads, unable to read anything beyond a depth of a few feet. The Woodweavers had gathered themselves together, afraid of the crack as if something dire would thrust out from it.

Grimander alone smiled, hopping from one foot to another like a young boy. "Aye, aye! Deep and deep it goes. But it goes on to the Land of Anger. I know this place. And it remembers me."

"How far beyond have you been?" asked Wargallow, wondering if the old Woodweaver was after all, a little mad.

"No further than that door before you. I was not permitted," he added, screwing up his face. "But others have." He turned to Svoor and the Woodweavers. "This is the place where the Wood Healers were lost."

His words meant nothing to the company, but the Woodweavers were clearly disturbed by what he had said. Svoor came forward, not only a little frightened, but angry. "You talk nonsense, Grimander. The Wood Healers are known to have traveled far to the south of the Deepwalks, well beyond the Fellwater and the southern edges of the range."

"They did, they did! Some of them were lost, while others came here, against Woodheart's will. They went below, and only a few came back."

"What could you know of them?" said Svoor almost scathingly.

Einnis stepped between them, thinking they would be at each other with fists if they kept this up. "I have heard whispers of the Wood Healers. You must explain their mystery to us, or be silent, Grimander. We have no time to waste in argument. Our enemies are closing in upon us."

Grimander screwed up his face, adding yet more years to

himself. "It was so long ago. I was a child, well, old enough to leave my home and travel with other adventurers. I came across the Wood Healers by chance. I wanted to become one of them, but I was far too young and inexperienced. It was not easy to become a Healer, and it took much testing—"

"You exaggerate," snapped Svoor. "They were an elite body."

"I was their guide for a time," said Grimander huffily. "There were parts of the Deepwalks I knew and they did not."

"What were they?" said Wargallow.

"High servants of Woodheart," said Grimander, with unfeigned reverence. He knew he had an audience and he relished the power he had over it. "Tenders of his very roots, for the roots are the life. They spread, it is said, below all Omara. And there came a day when Woodheart sought to delve under Starkfell Edge."

"The Wood Healers were opposed to such a dangerous thing," said Svoor, adding to the history. "They warned Woodheart that he should not do this."

"But he went in spite of them," nodded Grimander. "And he told the Wood Healers not to follow him, no matter what dangers he encountered. And he opened up this wall, splitting the rock from which Gloomreach spilled. To his shame—"

"Be silent!" cried Svoor, offended.

"He was wrong to do it," said Grimander, ignoring the angry looks of the Woodweavers. "And there was further tragedy. I knew of this place and the Wood Healers asked me to bring them here, so that they could go in search of the roots."

"Woodheart forbade them to go!" said Svoor. "Yet you helped them—"

"Woodheart decreed that Gloomreach was forbidden to all his servants. And the way into the mountains most of all. But I wanted to become a Wood Healer," said Grimander with a sniff. "So I brought them here. To this place of agony."

"But you did not go beyond?"

"They would not permit me to go with them. I waited with other, younger numbers of their company. We fought off the

creatures that beset us. And when the Wood Healers returned, after many months, few of them were left. And of
those, some were no longer themselves.''

"What did they find?" said Wargallow.

Grimander nodded slowly. "There is a way through."

"And the Wood Healers?" said Svoor, less angrily.

"They tried to spare Woodheart pain. His shame meant
nothing to them. But they could not bear his suffering."

"They have passed into legend," said Svoor. "None have
been seen in our forests for many a long year. My father
spoke of seeing one once."

"There may be a few of them left," said Grimander. "Who
can say? The Deepwalks are vast, are they not?"

"You did not go with the survivors?" asked Einnis.

"No. The company broke up after they emerged. Some
died on the return to the forests. Others had decided to go to
the Timber Maws, to give themselves to Woodheart. They
would not make me one of them, nor create any new Wood
Healers. I went on my way. Woodheart, you see, has not
chosen to prevent me." He turned to the fissure and shook
his gnarled fist at it. "My years are many, and there may be
but a few left. But this time I will enter."

Einnis put a comforting arm around him. "Who is to say
you were wrong? You acted for Woodheart, not for yourself.
To serve him—"

Svoor was nodding. "Your desire to be a Healer," he said,
with a meaningful glance at his fellows, "had nothing to do
with greed."

Einnis smiled. "This company may not have the skills that
the Wood Healers had, but we do have other powers."

"That you have," said Svoor. "Though the Woodweavers
have none that can usefully be put to work in yon place."

"Then you will not follow?" said Einnis.

Svoor shook his head, speaking for all his companions.
"Woodheart has charged us, through his envoys, to bring you
across Gloomreach. But we are forbidden entry."

"You have guided us with honor," said Ottemar, before
any of the others could object. He bowed before the Woodweavers. "I am indebted to you and to Woodheart for your
part in this. But when you return to your forest, do not think

that this business is ended. Whatever has befallen Rannovic and the Woodhurling at the Fellwater, the war is not over. Not while Anakhizer rules in Anger. Go back and prepare. Marshal every defense you have. The storm will break, and when it does it will surpass all those that have gone before it.''

Svoor and all the other Woodweavers bowed low. "This shall be done, sire. Before Woodheart we vow it.''

Then, with little more than brief farewells, the Woodweavers went out from under the shadows, melting again into Gloomreach, already searching for a way back to their forest lands.

Ottemar grinned, though he could not ignore the cold bite of the air from the stone walls above. "We had best enjoy the sunlight while we may. Will we have light beyond?''

Graval looked doubtful. "Svoor told us that our bodies will not give light in this place. We had better take torches with us. There is dead wood aplenty in the mire.''

An hour later the company entered the crevice, a good many of them holding firebrands. Silence dropped over them, as if they had burrowed several miles into the rock face rather than a few hundred yards. Above them the fissure had widened so that its top was out of sight. Soon the ground twisted away downward.

Aumlac felt a massive weight over him, oppressive and exhausting, as though the very mountain ailed. Einnis, too, for all his great skill as a Stonewise, could not fathom the walls, the distances. He felt weakened, almost crippled, by the burden of the stone, and it was so cold, uninviting. The Earthwrought were no less disadvantaged, their spirits eroded, so that a glum silence draped all the company.

Sisipher had moved closer to Ottemar, and in the shadows his hand clasped hers. She would have pulled away, but could not, not in this awful place. But she would not speak. Brannog was in front of them, following the two Deliverers and Kelloric, while Dennovia had chosen to keep as close to Brannog as she could. He was silent, though it was because he thought of Ruvanna, glad that she had not come to this place of despair. He spared little thought for the beautiful girl beside him, now almost forgotten as the procession moved on, though from time to time Coldrieve looked back at her, his face as impassive as it always was.

Somewhere deep under the heart of the mountains, days later, the company heard the first sounds of their underground journey. They were in a low-ceilinged cavern, the slope gentle and smooth, when they heard ululations echoing from somewhere far behind them. Their torches had shown them a number of narrow tunnels leading away from theirs, and although Grimander had no idea what these were for or how they had been caused, he was adamant that the correct way to go was along the particular channel they were yet following. Einnis wondered if there must be some scent, some hint of forgotten power that the Woodweaver could detect, but he did not ask him.

Swords scraped in the gloom. Some of the carefully-rationed firebrands were lit now to create a glare. The sounds from behind them were intermittent but chilling, filled with menace and a suggestion of madness, as though the creatures that made them were no less vile than those that had wallowed in the sinks of Gloomreach.

"Should we stand and fight?" Kelloric called to Wargallow. "We'll not be able to run and defend our backs for any distance. That way we'd lose too many. There must be a chamber where we can organize a proper defense." He loathed the thought of being trapped in the dark, unable to meet a foe head-on, in a clean battle.

"We must keep moving!" shouted Grimander from ahead, his voice echoing from the dark stone. "If these things come upon us, it will not go well for us."

Again the company moved on, breaking into a gentle trot, and although the howls from behind them remained far off, they seemed to be drawing closer. As time wore on, the howls drew nearer yet, and in them was a ravenous hunger that could not be mistaken. Grimander would say nothing of what they might be, though the company guessed he must know something of them.

There were other sounds from ahead of them, though these differed from the frightful sounds behind. A wind seemed to roar in the distance, as if tearing across the peaks of the range instead of below its roots. Grimander nodded to himself, but he would not be drawn into discussion.

"Einnis," said Wargallow. "Surely you must be able to tell us something about these forsaken stone tombs? What wind can that be?"

"I cannot say. But it is made by air and stone, not creatures such as the things that track us. We should go on, though what we may have to face, I can only guess at."

They did move on, but shortly they were forced to tear strips of cloth from their clothing to bind up their ears, all of them, for the winds from beyond rose shrill and piercing, drowning out completely any sounds from behind.

Then from out of the dark something struck, swift as light, but yet unseen. Men were torn from their place in the line of march, and although their companions struck out, they drew no blood. Whatever it was that had come so near to the company, it smothered itself in darkness, and the fluttering brands that had fallen were snuffed out quickly. The stench that blasted the company was awesome, as if a vast pit had opened in the earth around them. They ran, panic grabbing at them, and men fell, only to be snatched by the invisible death from behind. Great shrieks and screams of fury came from the pursuers, but still Grimander said nothing of what could be there. He urged the company on. Their torches abruptly lit up a wide bridge that reached over a chasm to more darkness beyond, and the wind tore upward from this chasm, defying all known laws as if it spewed up from a rent in the very fabric of the world. Wargallow wondered if that was what it was, a gash in the wall of the Aspect.

The company raced over the natural span, and as they did so, ripped by the fingers of howling wind, Aumlac and the Stonedelvers remained at the rear. "Whatever follows us," he yelled, his voice almost torn away, "must not cross this arch." He and his companions formed a line across the end of the bridge. They spoke words known only to their race and to the stone, though no one could hear them. Perhaps, thought Wargallow, the stone will not hear either. Einnis joined them, realizing what they were attempting, the breaking of the bridge. But the alien stone held. It would not bend to the commands of these intruders.

As they worked, something began to crawl over the far end of the span, slithering forward on a fat belly, grossly bloated arms flailing like some dweller of the seas dredged up on their shores. There were no eyes, just a long gash of a mouth, yards wide. Behind the monster there came others, no less repulsive, alien to light, pawing at the way ahead of them. Einnis held his line of Stonedelvers with difficulty, for to look upon these things was to court insanity.

Einnis struck down with his staff at the stone and it splintered, cracks zigzagging out from where he had smitten the rock. Again and again he did this. He averted his eyes as the things clambered or hopped on to the bridge, the leaders sliding over it. The Stonedelvers themselves closed their eyes, keeping up their chant, trying to put more power into Einnis's working. Again he struck the stone.

A fat, clawless paw from the first creature flapped upward, reaching inexorably for its victim, when suddenly there was a great cracking sound which cut through the abusive roar of the wind. Einnis jerked backward, breaking the line of Stonedelvers. They tumbled back on to the path beyond the arch, gazing at the stone. Einnis had been successful, for a great chunk of bridge dropped away, and in a moment others fell with it. The weight of the obscenity on the bridge weakened much of what was left and seconds later there came a deafening screaming as it and others plummeted down into the hungry darkness below. Einnis dragged at his spellbound companions, and moments after they rejoined the company.

"Away, away!" he shouted, for the roar of the wind had not declined. Beyond the chasm, scores of shapes wriggled, choking the corridors there, seeing other ways to cross the span. Quickly the company moved on, their brands wavering, many going out. The wind swirled around them like a tide, slowly subsiding as they went still deeper into the caverns. But as it softened, they heard fresh winds ahead, howling and complaining as though angered at the trespass of beings from the world outside.

Grimander danced up and down with a sudden excitement. "Light! Light!" he called, cackling.

"Have we come through at last?" said Ottemar.

But it was not so, for although they could make out the

promised light, they found themselves in a peculiar place. It was an opening in the cavern, a massive crack that soared upward further than the eye could follow, and it was sunlight that came down from above. The air was pure here, warmed by the fantastic depth they were at, and the light had somehow been magnified by the substance of the rocks. They were still alien to the Stonedelvers, but Brannog pulled up in sudden realization.

"I remember the workings of the Icewrought, when we dropped into a glacier they had opened. The light from far above us was transmitted in just such a way. Who could have made this place?"

Einnis pointed to the faces of the cliffs, which could now be seen a little more clearly. They had been carved into huge visages, of bearded, helmeted warriors. Their sheer size had contorted them, but it was obvious now that their mouths were like open caves. It was from these that the wind howled, as though the company was in the presence of giants, or even gods, trapped in stone, howling in anguish, imprisoned in a timeless realm. As they looked, Brannog and the others seemed to see the mouths twisting, writhing as the faces strove to impart some frightful message.

"Stonedelvers made these," said Einnis, though he was troubled by his own assertion. "I am sure of it. Though I do not recognize them from any lost mythology. I am sure that our ancestors had a hand in this."

"But what is their purpose?" said Wargallow above the din.

"A warning!" shouted Grimander. "The Wood Healers came here. These guardians howled at them as they do at us. Their words are the elemental words of the angry mountain. They speak of the Land of Anger, which is beyond us."

"How far is it?" said Wargallow.

"Days yet. Days and days!" Grimander cried.

"What else do these stone giants tell you?"

"They say very little," said the Woodweaver. "Go back. Deaths waits you otherwise. Anger will devour you. Crush you. They speak of grinding, of pulping, of closing up their walls of stone. They have been here as long as the mountains."

"You did not bring us here for this!" snapped Wargallow, pulling the Woodweaver almost off his feet. "There must be a way past them."

"Only a few of the Wood Healers got by."

"How do you know these things!" Wargallow yelled, above the wind, as though the furious voices of stone were trying to shout him down.

Grimander laughed, unmoved by Wargallow's annoyance. "Woodheart knows! Woodheart feels! He is crushed, maimed, the price for his scorn of these places, but he lives yet. They could not turn him back, not his power. The Wood Healers knew it also. There is a way. If you have the heart for it. If you can match the vision of Woodheart, his strength of purpose."

"Woodheart!" cried Einnis. "Here? In this stone hell?"

Grimander wrenched himself free and raced across the long floor of the open chamber. On either side of him the terrible faces glared down, mouths screaming as if in obscenity. Wargallow motioned for the company to follow.

"There is immense danger here," Einnis shouted to him. "We crave secrecy, Wargallow, but I beg of you, prepare to use the rod of power. If these walls move in on us as they promise, we are doomed."

Wargallow did not acknowledge him, bending into the wind as he marched on, Coldrieve close at his heels.

Grimander had reached the far end of the opening and he stood, defying the gale, pointing downward. There was yet another narrow cleft, descending into a new darkness. "Raise a torch and see!" called the Woodweaver.

Einnis brought one, ducking down to look. He could see a wider passage beyond, and insisted on being the first to go down. Grimander went with him, and after the company had successfully crossed the cavern, stumbling as they ran, they filed into the cleft as quickly as they dared. Once they had all come into the new cave system, torches were ignited. The chamber was neither high nor wide, but it was far less noisy than the tall fissure of the stone faces.

They moved onward, downward, for they seemed not to have come to the depths of the mountains. Many small fissures ran off this new tunnel, but Grimander insisted they were dead ends.

"I cannot believe you can read this stone," said Aumlac to him. "Nor can any of us."

"Woodheart knows, Woodheart feels," said Grimander, almost in a chant, but no one understood him.

They had gone beyond the range of sound of the awful winds, still in darkness, when they first felt the movement of the earth about them. Like the ripple of a huge worm, the tunnel moved. Some of the men fell, overbalancing. They were on their feet quickly, but shaken.

"Angry stone! Angry!" snapped Grimander.

"Be silent," warned Einnis. "The stone does not want to be prompted by more movement." But it moved again, and there were grim crackings in it; small clouds of dust hinted that there was further, subtle movement.

"We'll be crushed," someone yelled, racing back into the dark as if no longer able to contain his terror. He had not gone far when he let out an agonized shriek, as though something terrible had taken him.

"Are we still being followed?" said Ottemar.

"Always," said Grimander. "We are hunted. But save your fears for the stone. It will devour us if it can."

"Then what are we to do?" asked Einnis. "What would the Wood Healers have done?"

"They fled. Wisely. Woodheart tried to save them, but how could they hold on to their reason?" The ground shook again and ahead of the company there was a rumble like thunder as rocks fell somewhere.

Grimander had his back to a smooth wall and suddenly he turned to it. "Hear me, Woodheart! I feel your agony in this place. Wake in spite of it! Wake, I tell you. Let the girl help you." He drove his gnarled fingers into the stone as if it were sand, and as it crumbled, Wargallow gasped at what was beyond.

"I have seen the like of this," he began.

"Under Xennidhum!" cried Brannog. "The roots—"

"But there was *never* a root like this," said Sisipher.

Grimander laughed in defiance of everything they had been through. "Beyond! Woodheart is here. You see." The earth shook again, intent on crushing those who dared come to this sacred realm. But the expanse of root that Grimander had exposed was a mere fraction of what was there. Sisipher was right, for this root was unimaginably huge, and must be hundreds of feet across. For a moment they thought of the roots they had glimpsed above the Ravensring.

"Woodheart forced himself under the Edge," said Einnis. "As he has done under countless hundreds of miles of Omara. And this part of him, this *root* has opened a path to the Land of Anger."

"Yes, yes!" cackled Grimander. "Almost deadened by the weight, closed off from that part of him in the Deepwalks so far from us, his own heart. And the mountains spat out Gloomreach to poison him. They tried, but the stone could not do it. Cannot kill Woodheart. He lives, and he lives *here.*"

"But the passage ahead is too narrow. The roof is about to fall," said Einnis. "I can read that much. We are trapped here. Or can Woodheart force the walls aside?"

"Not strong enough, far too weak," said Grimander. "He is barely awake."

Einnis turned to Wargallow and Ottemar, shaking his head. Nothing the Stonedelvers could do would prevent the closing-in of the walls.

19
Sheercastle

ANOTHER LOUD crack sounded somewhere above the company, and more earth slithered from the rock ceiling. The ground shifted restlessly, as though an earthquake had begun. Wargallow was about to grasp the Woodweaver in exasperation once more, but Grimander had put both his hands upon the root surface and was muttering to himself, eyes closed as if in prayer. Instinct warned Wargallow not to interfere. The wall that buried the root was splitting, revealing even more of it, confirming its enormousness, and as it did so, a crack appeared in its horny surface as if it, too, were breaking up under the weight of the mountain. Fluid gushed from the split until it became a slow seep and the opening widened like a vertical mouth.

"Enter!" shouted Grimander, and for a while no one grasped his meaning, thinking he must finally have lost his reason. But he pointed to the split in the root. There were cries of anguish from the darkness as chunks of rock came toppling down on more of the company: Earthwrought and Stonedelver were no safer than the men.

Einnis stepped to the root and Grimander pushed him forward. "Go in, go in! Woodheart preserves us. Douse your brands!"

Einnis did as bidden, struggling through the wall of the root. To his amazement he found himself in a chamber beyond, for the root was partially hollow, easily large enough

266

for a Stonedelver to stand up in. He held up his staff and there was a faint light, as if the plant provided it.

Others followed him, while Aumlac and Bornac stood at the rear of the company, striving to work power against the pressure of falling stone. They could feel the determination of the mountains as they sought to crush the company. Gradually the effort of the company to get inside the root became easier, though Aumlac could see that a number had died, killed by the stone falls. When he at last ushered Bornac through the vent and followed him, they took stock of their numbers.

Kelloric's face was livid. "Over half my men are dead. And Earthwrought have died under this cursed mountain range. Earthwrought!"

"We have no powers here," said Graval helplessly. "We feel the agony of the stone. Something malign has entered into it."

"Aye," nodded Bornac, gulping for air. "We Stonedelvers could do much more if it were not for the poison in this place. It is astounding that Woodheart has survived."

Brannog put a gentle hand on Grimander's shoulder. "You are a creature of mystery yet, Woodweaver," he told him, though not in anger. "You spoke to Woodheart for us and he has answered. But you told him to let the girl help him. What did you mean?"

"His pain is great. He closed himself off from it. She has soothed it from her place beyond the Ravensring."

"Ruvanna?" said Brannog softly.

"She has great powers of healing. She is with us here, in Woodheart," grinned Grimander. "Easing his pain."

Brannog gazed into an invisible distance, as though he could see his wife above the stones of the moor. It was a power he understood.

They all studied the root walls, even now feeling the shock as the stone fell on their outside, the crack closing up. But this root had endured for countless years: it would endure yet. It ran away ahead of them, dipping inevitably down, its glistening corridor giving off a gentle glow, its shape twisting, in places smooth.

Graval let out a sudden cry, pointing to himself. "Our

body-light returns here!'' It was true, for the other Earth-wrought emitted the faint radiance that had deserted them in the caves outside. ''Woodheart has indeed blessed us.''

''How far will this root take us?'' Wargallow asked Grimander.

''I have tried to commune with Woodheart,'' replied the Woodweaver. ''But his thoughts are clouded by pain. But we can travel for many, many miles this way. Beyond the place where the rock walls close up.''

They paused only briefly to eat and drink, taking as little as they could, not knowing how much further, how many more days they must travel on. They felt less weary now, progressing down the strange, slick tunnel, and as they went, they talked softly of those who had perished. The company had been reduced by more than half since entering the mountain caverns.

The journey was not easy, for although they had light, the walls pressed in and the going underfoot was always wet, sometimes sticky with thick sap, and in places there were tough filaments that they had to push through. Coldrieve suggested that they be cut, but Grimander was adamant that they should do no harm to Woodheart.

They stopped to sleep, though fitfully, and the silence that crowded in was absolute, like the silence between worlds.

During one such rest, Wargallow sat beside Dennovia. The company was exhausted. No one listened to private conversations. Even Grimander had taken an opportunity to sleep, curled up like an animal.

''Perhaps,'' said Wargallow, his voice barely above a whisper, ''you wish you had not come on this venture.''

In spite of her own tiredness she smiled. ''It was your order—''

''Is that so?''

She looked away from his eyes. Had he spoken to Ottemar? Had he learned the truth of her deception? It seemed so long ago. ''Why should I wish to come on such a journey?''

''I've asked myself that question more than once. I've not asked you as I didn't expect the truth from you. But here, in this desperate region, perhaps you're ready to tell me.''

"Or I'll die, is that what you mean?" Her eyes flashed suddenly, filled with an anger that he had seen in her before.

"No," he smiled. "I owe you too much, Dennovia. I remember another enclosed place, deep inside Zoigon. Brannog pulled Ruvanna to safety before he gave me a thought. It was left to you to help me."

"You've repaid that debt."

"Some would say so. But Goldenisle did not satisfy you. Your position with the Empress wasn't enough. So why did you come?"

Again she looked away.

"I suspect," he added, his voice very soft, "that it was out of desire."

Her lips remained tightly pressed together.

"Your eyes answer for you. But you must understand that you can never have what you seek."

She stared hard at the wall of the root opposite her, though she did not see it.

"It is always watched, always guarded."

She turned to him with a scowl. "Guarded?"

Again he smiled. "Coldrieve and I will not relinquish it while either of us draws breath."

Before she could answer this, the fingers of his left hand closed very softly over her mouth. He did not hurt her, but she could not speak.

"You could never have stolen it," he said. "And even if it had been given to you, you would not have been able to control it."

He would not release her mouth, though her eyes sought to deny his accusation.

"I'll speak no more of this," he said. "But you must put all thought of the rod from your mind. If we survive, you will still have much to live for. And you'll have power."

He released her and she shook her head. "You're wrong," she began, about to launch into her own explanation, but there was a cry from down the tunnel. Grimander was on his feet, hopping about, ears catching at every hint of sound.

"We must leave at once!" he cried. "An attack, from without."

"More movement of the earth?" came Aumlac's call.

"Nay, the rocks are still. But there are creatures beyond the root. The are huge, blind things, but they hunger. They have smelled us out, and they will attack the root to get at us if we remain here. If we move onward, they'll lose our scent. Quickly. Rouse yourselves!"

It needed no repeating of the command, and moments later the entire company was moving quickly on down the root. Wargallow joined Coldrieve at the head of the column and Dennovia was left to travel beside Brannog, her chance to deny Wargallow's accusations for the moment lost. She saw Ottemar and Sisipher, stiffly trying to avoid each other and yet close to each other, but it was no time for any discussion. The journey had a feel of disaster, and Dennovia wondered if there was any real hope for this expedition.

As they moved on, they caught distorted glimpses of something beyond one side of the root walls, like huge fish swimming beyond one side of the root walls, probing at its walls with slack mouths, bumping against the root in an attempt to puncture it. They slipped away, but returned again and again, striking the root in an eerie silence. After two hours the shapes had gone, as if thwarted.

"We must keep moving," said Grimander and the others wondered where he found the energy to drive them. Aumlac suggested he must be sapping it from Woodheart and the Woodweaver chuckled as if not really concerned about their plight. He did, however, bring them to a halt. It was safe to rest once more, he announced, and the company slumped down, Stonedelvers included.

For a few hours the walls of the root echoed to the snores. Dennovia looked for Wargallow, but he was with Ottemar and Kelloric. He did not intend to speak to her alone again, it seemed. She, too, fell into the sleep of exhaustion.

When the company roused itself and took another frugal meal, Grimander pointed ahead. "The root plunges deep down beyond us. It is too dangerous for us to descend."

"Down?" said Ottemar, aghast. "Already we must be miles below the surface."

Grimander merely grinned. "We can take our leave of Woodheart here. We are beyond the place where the mountain would have crushed us. It will no doubt assume us dead."

There were nods of relief, but no cheers. Wargallow and the others watched as Grimander performed his odd ritual with the root, and after a time the Woodweaver had succeeded in opening another way to the outside. The company used it, emerging into a tall tunnel, the walls of which were dark and glassy smooth. To their relief, the Earthwrought found that their body glow was not reduced as it had been previously. There was no immediate need for firebrands.

"In a few more hours," Grimander told them, "we will be through."

This gave great heart to the company and it moved on now with renewed resolve. When it came to another wide cavern with its own dark lake, Grimander pronounced the water safe to drink. "Meltwater from the high snows," he said. "But do not swim in it," he cautioned, adding no more.

Ottemar grunted as he dipped his fingers in and quickly pulled them out. "Swim! It would freeze the blood of an Icewrought!"

There was some laughter at this, the first for many long days.

Beyond the cavern there were numerous tunnels, one of which wound upward. Grimander stood within its confines for some time, sniffing at it as a hound would have. "Ah," he grinned. "I smell better air. Cleaner, at least, than what we've been breathing down here."

Einnis stood with him. "I feel it, Grimander. But it is not pure. It has a strangeness to it. And something else." His voice trailed off. The Stonedelvers came to him, puzzled, almost bemused.

"Do I hear voices up there?" said Aumlac.

"Aye," nodded Bornac. "Whisperings from time. But not enemies—"

"Ghosts," said Einnis. "Talking of the past. The long ago." He wore a troubled expression, as if he could not quite close his hand on something.

"Is it safe to ascend?" said Wargallow. "I hear only the wind."

Grimander shrugged.

Einnis looked at them both anxiously. "I think it is not

dangerous, but I am wary. Do you know what the voices are, Grimander? There is a deep sorrow in them."

"Pain, maybe," muttered the Woodweaver. He touched his chest. "Here. But it is not evil."

Einnis looked to Aumlac, but both yet seemed unsure of themselves.

"We go up," said Wargallow.

The company prepared itself for an attack, though they were told it was not likely to come, and they moved up the incline. The whisperings that the Stonedelvers heard were no more than the hint of the wind to the rest of the company, and when a glimmer of light showed far away, like a rent in the fabric of a night sky, there were cheers. Although these were quickly silenced, the company sensed that at long last they were going to break free of the caves.

Long before they had reached the widening source of light, the air came in at them, with a renewed promise of freedom. It gusted about them, lifting the dust in clouds, but they laughed, weariness sloughed off. Only the Stonedelvers seemed unsure of what would be beyond.

Pillars of ice ran down the walls, forming columns that sparkled as if embedded with stars, frozen cataracts. The company passed through them and were at last outside. The fissure from which they had emerged opened on to a slope of rock debris, tumbling down to an area of jagged stone and huge boulders. These had formed a narrow valley, the sides of which were bare, devoid of plants or any growth, and higher up there were only the great gray boulders and not a single tree to break the monotony of stone. Ice gleamed, a thick crust of frost, while further up there were snow banks in the heights. The sky was gray, thick with unfriendly cloud, and the company could sense the immensity of the mountain range through which they had passed, rising up behind them as if still determined to fall upon them.

"Is this the promised Land of Anger?" said Wargallow.

"Not yet," said Grimander. "We must follow the valley."

"This is a desolate place," said Einnis, hugging his cloak to him. "The wind itself mourns this broken land."

Although the terrain was broken and treacherous underfoot, the company was pleased to be out of the dark. Their eyes streamed in the cold daylight, but they had soon traversed the valley and gone beyond the two narrow cliffs at its end. Behind them the upper mountains were obscured by dense white clouds, while ahead of them there was a thickening mist that shifted, obscuring the land beyond. Out of it poked two huge pillars, and at sight of these, Einnis pulled up short.

"I should know this place," he said. His Stonedelvers remained bemused, as though the elusive words of the wind came to them still.

Graval indicated the two pillars. "They are gates," he said. "Or once were. This is some ancient citadel."

Aumlac was the first to approach the two pillars and he put out a hand to one of them. He closed his eyes, listening. Bornac went to the other and, like twins, the two Stonedelvers waited.

"These stones are far older than the rocks of this region," said Aumlac.

"They have been brought here," nodded Bornac.

"By Stonedelvers," said Einnis.

"For what purpose?" said Wargallow.

"If I am right," replied Einnis, an expression of amazement on his face, "there is a city beyond these gates, and it overlooks the Land of Anger. It is a place of legend, of myth."

"Can it be Sheercastle?" said Aumlac. His fellow Stonedelvers gaped at the pillars as if expecting them to vanish into the mist.

"Can a dream have substance?" said Einnis. "Set here long ago to watch for the evils of the place beyond, the hole in the world." He looked beseechingly at the rest of the company. "You must forgive us. We did not expect this. I was a child when I heard the old ones telling stories about Sheercastle. How, in the earliest days of our people it was set in a far range of mountains to watch over an evil place, from which great peril might come to threaten Omara."

"The hole in the world?" said Wargallow. "What is that? Another gate caused by the working of the Hierarchs?"

"Perhaps. A parallel story. But Sheercastle was said to be a fabulous place, a place of rich stone, of gold, of precious metals and gems. A place such as legends are made of. But here there is a poverty of stone. And only the ghosts of a long dead realm.''

''We hear only the wind,'' said Kelloric bluntly. ''After the gales we faced under the mountains, this wind is tame.''

''Yet there is a terrible sadness in it,'' insisted Einnis.

They moved on between the twin pillars and beyond them there were the ruins of once vast structures, tall towers and large blocks that could once have formed walls. Dust had piled up irreverently against them, and drifted about what had once been streets. The mist seemed to creep in at the company from the far end of the citadel, a silent tide, obscuring what was beyond, but as they crossed a large open plaza, they were suddenly brought to a halt by a great fissure. It ran from one side of the square to the other, its far side invisible. But as the mist rolled back, the truth of the fissure's size became evident. It was not a fissure, but the crest of a cliff. The entire landscape beyond had slipped away, broken off, and the world opened up in a gulf, a fathomless abyss.

Einnis stood at its edge, stupefied by the revelation. ''Gone,'' he breathed. ''Almost the entire citadel. Fallen far below to whatever lands are there.'' It was as he said, for the cliff edge ran away on either side, curving around the mountain side, left and right, like the edge of the world itself. Einnis gazed back across the plaza to the stoneworks set in the mountain. They were no more than a fragment of what had been.

''Was Sheercastle a large place?'' said Ottemar, staring down into the emptiness ahead.

Einnis shook his head. ''Not vast. But a shell remains, no more.''

''There's fresh water to be had here,'' said Graval. ''And the earth under us is no longer cold and sterile.''

The company prepared fires for the first time in days. Sisipher wished that Kirrikree had been able to make the crossing, for he would have found them meat, although the mountain slopes looked barren and snow-locked. Einnis and his fellows went among the ruins, leaving the company for a while.

''This discovery has hurt them deeply,'' observed Brannog. "The journey was cruel to them, for the bitterness of the stone gave them much grief. But there are ghosts in this place. It is as though their hopes have been dashed."

Wargallow nodded, calling Grimander to him. "Well, Grimander? You have proved the most valuable asset of all. Your faith in Woodheart was well-founded."

"Aye!" grinned the Woodweaver. "You have trusted me where my own folk did not. But it's not done yet. You have reached the battlefield, that is all! You have not even glimpsed the spears of the enemy."

Wargallow frowned, the point well-taken. "What do you know of the Land of Anger? Is there a way down?"

Grimander shrugged in his infuriating way. "I know nothing, save that Woodheart is below us yet. He taught me much as we passed inside his roots."

"You'll share this knowledge, I hope," said Kelloric testily.

"Gladly." Grimander sat with them among the broken slabs: they were equals in this terrain, leveled by their exertions. "Woodheart knew this place, though he is far, far below it. It was made by the first of the Stonedelvers to dwell in Starkfell Edge, just as Einnis Amrodin thought. But Sheercastle died long ago."

"Why did you not tell him?" said Kelloric, looking about him for the Stonedelvers, but none were in sight.

"Too much pain in that. Woodheart would not distress them. Though they will learn its secrets."

"What happened here?" said Wargallow.

"For many years the Stonedelvers were able to watch the Land of Anger, though they knew it by another name. There were Ferr-Bolgan in the mountains, too. But they did not come here. Finally their numbers became too great, and many of the Stonedelvers had to go north, along forgotten paths, to journey around the high range and come to that part of the land that reaches north east toward the range of the Slaughterhorn.

"Those that remained found their powers sapped, their control of the stone weakened. Until at last Anger had its way and pulled down the very mountain. What you see is all that remains. The Ferr-Bolgan flooded in, their numbers too vast. The eyes of the west were closed in this place and the lights went out. Since then, no word has come through to the Deepwalks.

"Woodheart still reaches out from below, but at what a cost! It is no longer possible for him to bring back word of the west. He does not have the servants he once had, for the Wood Healers are dispersed, those that live. All he has is the pain, and it has paralyzed him, until we came. And Ruvanna helped him." Grimander began to mutter to himself, and the others again wondered if his own mind was becoming unhinged by the grim journey under Starkfell Edge.

"How are we to find our enemy?" Kelloric asked Wargallow.

Wargallow looked along the cliff edge. "We will have to go south from here. If the armies of Anakhizer go out from the Gates of Anger, they must enter the mountains from that way somewhere. There must be a citadel or fortress."

"And are we to storm it?" said Kelloric acidly.

"The journey has worn out your patience," said Wargallow quietly. "But if you have suggestions, we will be glad to hear them."

"Look at our company!" Kelloric retorted, though he kept his voice down. "How many have I lost? And Stonedelvers, Earthwrought. More than half of us are dead. The rest of us need rest. Not another march. And we'll need supplies, proper food. Where will it be found in this wilderness!"

No one answered for a moment, but Brannog straightened up. "All you say is true, of course. We all know that, Kelloric. But we have the weapon. The key. It must be that which unlocks the door to Anger."

Aumlac's voice boomed out from across the plaza, high up in the buildings, cutting short the discussion. "This way!" he yelled. "See what we have uncovered."

The remainder of the company went to him, climbing a huge but broken stair. They found Einnis and the Stonedelvers in what had once been a hall, though its roof had collapsed and one wall was buried under a long slope of debris. Einnis pointed with his staff to an area of wall that he had wiped clean of its dust. There were letters cut into it, though in a language the men did not recognize.

"It speaks of the Abyss, which we call Anger," said the Stonewise. "And in an almost forgotten language. It tells of the disintegration of the mountains, the colossal landslides and the alienation of the forces of the mountains, which are now turned on all life that approaches them. Anger, or the Abyss, it says, has no bottom, and is a sink into another realm, another world."

"Another Aspect?" said Wargallow. "Is that what it tells us?"

"I cannot say," said Einnis. "But the Abyss is like a great wound in Omara's flesh. It is open, like a window on the sky."

"Then how do the Ferr-Bolgan cross it?" said Wargallow. "Or are they spawned under the Edge, with the angarbreed?"

"The stone speaks of the vermin of the caves and of the evil lord who rules them. It says only that they dwell here, in abundance."

"Where is Anakhizer?" called Kelloric angrily. "Out there in the mists? Or hiding under the mountains? There has to be a way of knowing."

"There must be Ferr-Bolgan close at hand," said Wargallow. "And if so, we shall find them and question them."

Kelloric nodded slowly. "Very well. I'll organize units. We must search." He turned on his heel and stormed away, eager to be on with the task.

"He feels the loss of his men," said Einnis. "He needs to act, to slake his own anger."

"We all do," said Wargallow. "But we'll spend a night here, resting. Tomorrow we'll hunt the Ferr-Bolgan and any other agent of Anakhizer. There will be a path to his hold."

WHEN TWILIGHT turned to night, it brought a fresh terror. The sky, which had been overcast and thick with cloud, cleared, and at first it was pure darkness, starless and alien. But as the mist across Anger faded and the heavens cleared, the company saw for the first time the utter strangeness of the firmament above them.

Ottemar drew in his breath. "Sky? It looks more like the roof of some immense cavern."

Wargallow stared upward, no less mesmerized. "I swear it's the sky, but there is some illusion in this. As you say, it resembles a cavern—"

"I have seen something like this once before," said Brannog. "When I was far down under the earth in the east. In the Far Below. An immense underground working. With a stone ceiling that looked like amassed clouds."

"But that is the night sky!" said Ottemar. "Einnis! What do you read into these heavens?"

"The Abyss is a window, the stone told us. And—" He stopped, almost stumbling as further visions appeared in the heavens. It was as if a sudden storm came to life in one part of them, a whirlpool of stars and darkness, whirling rapidly to become a tunnel that curved far away into infinity like the inside of a tornado. Two other such awesome pools churned the heavens, spiral storms of light.

"It is like the sea!" cried Kelloric. "As if we are looking down upon an ocean instead of upward."

Sisipher had gone white, rigid as a rock. Ottemar swiftly put an arm about her. "Brannog!" he called. "Your daughter—"

Brannog rushed to her, holding her. "What is wrong?"

She shook her head, eyes opening, but on some deeper horror. "It is the sky, but not our sky, not Omaran sky." The sky was flecked with strange lines and curls of scarlet, and it resembled now the lining of some fantastic organ, pulsing with strange fires and life. The three orifices were like immense arteries, leading off into remote distances as if into the body of a being as large as a world.

"Through them," whispered Sisipher. "All Omaran life will be bled through them."

"The leeching of the world," said Einnis. "The sucking dry of all life on Omara."

Like the lid of an eye of the gods, the cloud layers drifted in, shutting out the visions of nightmare. As the cloud thickened, the watchers shook themselves, wondering if they could truly have seen the spectacle above.

There was no time to deliberate. Kelloric's guards were rushing across the plaza. Kelloric heard them and their wild shouts. He stood before the Emperor, bristling.

"The advice to rest may not have been good, sire. We are attacked."

"By whom?" said Wargallow as swords rang out from sheaths.

"Ferr-Bolgan, sire," came a cry. "And others."

"Gather the company," said Wargallow. "Kelloric, get your men in line."

Kelloric swore crudely, striding into the night, and within moments the company was preparing itself. The attack, it seemed, was coming from the southern side of the range, at the foot of the mountains. Nothing had followed the company from out of those dark passageways.

"How many?" was the call.

Wargallow caught the answers, all of which agreed. "Too many to number."

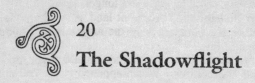

20
The Shadowflight

KIRRIKREE, SKYRAC and the eagles had watched over the Woodweavers as they had recrossed Gloomreach, threading along the edge of the mire to its northern boundary before working their way through the fallen trees to a place where they could ascend to the Deepwalks in relative safety. There were further attacks by the denizens of the mire, but few of the Woodweavers were lost; Gloomreach appeared to have spent its greatest efforts attacking the full company, and Kirrikree wondered if there was anything sinister in that. Could Anakhizer have spies in such a place? The owl knew that Wargallow was relying on surprise when he reached the Land of Anger, and if Anakhizer was waiting for him, the consequences would be dire.

The birds saw the Woodweavers safely up into the forest, and the last of them to disappear, Svoor, waved in thanks. No words were exchanged, but the gratitude of the wood people was evident. Within moments they had blended into the undergrowth, swallowed in silence.

"South," Kirrikree told Skyrac, wheeling. "We must find Rannovic and the Woodhurling."

The eagles winged away with the owl, deliberately skirting the edge of Gloomreach, for two crossings had made them wary of it, eager to be free of the depression it brought. They agreed to rest that night, for they were very tired, and they found a high perch among the colossal trees of the Deepwalks. Kirrikree took the first watch, and no sooner had he settled, looking sleepily out over the whispering forest ceiling, when a number of dark shapes swooped toward him.

"Kirrikree," they called in their hoarse voices. They were from the Ravensring. They no longer saw him as a threat, but they circled him and did not land.

"The company has entered the mountains," the owl told them.

"Woodheart understands," they croaked.

"What of Rannovic? What happened at the Fellwater?"

"We have not seen the Woodhurling. But there was a great conflict. Woodheart moved the land. Many Ferr-Bolgan and angarbreed have died, but more flock from the Gates of Anger."

"We fly with the dawn," said Kirrikree.

"There are other creatures abroad," the ravens told him. "Something dark hovers high over us yet, from the mountains."

Kirrikree swung his head to search the night skies, though he saw nothing. "What creatures do you speak of?"

"Shadowflight. They fly by night and are so dark it is not easy to see them. From Starkfell Edge. Huge things, though they keep away from the forest and fly over the Fellwater, unless they go very high, where we dare not follow."

Something turned in the sky to the south of them as they spoke and the owl opened his great wings. "There is movement!"

"It is Aark," said the raven. "A scout."

Moments later another raven winged toward them with great swiftness, alighting on a branch near the sleeping eagles, which had not stirred.

"The Shadowflight," came the hoarse voice of Aark. "I have heard them."

"You see!" said the first raven to Kirrikree.

"What did they say?"

"There are two. One has gone to seek news of the fighting at the Fellwater Gorge. The other is returning to the mountains. It has been searching for the company. Wargallow and his people were watched as they entered the Deepwalks from Sea Scarp. Since then the Shadowflight has not been able to find them."

"Is Anakhizer in the mountains?" Kirrikree asked.

"He is beyond them, in Anger."

"But how do these creatures reach him?" said Kirrikree.

The eagles were awake, stirring gently, listening to the conversation.

"We do not fly near Starkfell Edge," said Aark. "Our duty is to patrol the forest."

"Already we have had to stray further from the Ravensring than we would have liked," said the other. "We watch the Shadowflight when we dare. But even in force we would be no match for them."

Kirrikree turned to Aark. "Where is the creature you last saw?"

"It made for the high place in the cliffs. To rest, I think. It has been driven hard and there was exhaustion in its voice. Anakhizer has made them search relentlessly, though they have not been able to get low enough over the Deepwalks to find their goal."

"Exhausted?" repeated Kirrikree. "Then will it rest?"

"For a while, perhaps," said Aark.

Kirrikree stretched his wings once more. "Skyrac! Have you rested enough? We've another flight ahead of us this night."

"You would seek the Shadowflight?" said Aark.

"Yes. If they know of our masters, we must find out how much. If we can prevent them getting to Anakhizer—"

Skyrac's voice cut in, knife-like. "If they know a way, we find it."

The ravens watched in surprise as Kirrikree and the eagles took to the air, calling hoarse thanks before being blotted out by the night sky. Soon afterward the ravens had flown away north, back to the Ravensring.

Kirrikree spoke further on the things the ravens had told him, and the eagles fanned out wide of him, going as high as they could, knowing that the Shadowflight liked the upper air and secrecy. They flew quickly, tiredness slipping away from them as their new purpose gave them strength. Long before dawn they were close to the mountains, which loomed like a bank of jet-black cloud to the west of them.

Skyrac was about to ask where they should begin their

search, when they heard something below them, deep, croaking voices carried on the breeze. They were sounds made by no bird they had ever heard before. Dipping down, they searched the dark below them keenly, then circled gently, drifting on an eddy of air.

A great, dark shape soared below them, far larger than they would have expected, enormous wings rising and falling, propelling the thick trunk of the creature through the air laboriously. Its long neck stretched out before it, the head reptilian and beakless, the eyes like the eyes of a serpent. The creature was making for the east, following a line parallel to the Fellwater, though it seemed intent on journeying much further. To Goldenisle? Kirrikree asked himself.

Skyrac flew close by him. "It met another," came his blunt voice. "As large. You see it?"

"Aye, we must search for the westbound creature," agreed Kirrikree.

"There!" came the voice of another of the eagles, and as they looked far below, toward the towering cliffs of the Edge, they saw a faint movement against the black backdrop.

"Losing height," said Skyrac. "Nest?"

"Keep well above it until we reach the cliffs," said Kirrikree.

They said no more, winging quickly westward until they were closer to the rock face. They had lost sight of the Shadowflight, but as they began to spiral down, they heard its distant cries as if it spoke to others of its kind. But there was no response from below.

As they fell, they caught another glimpse of the immense creature, sailing on spread wings into an opening between two huge walls of rock, obscuring it. The birds dropped more quickly, careful to remain out of sight, so that when they reached the rock face they looked beyond it, uncertain of what they would find. The darkness made it difficult, for the rock itself seemed to emit an even greater dark.

"See!" called Skyrac. "Cliff not solid."

"A fissure," said Kirrikree, for he had seen the long crack. From a distance it was not noticeable, blending with the eroded strata around it, and even by daylight it would easily have been missed. But as they drew closer to it, its true scale became apparent. It was over fifty yards wide, quite capable of allowing the passage of a creature as large as the Shadowflight.

Kirrikree cautioned absolute silence, as he had no idea how many of the creatures there might be. He hovered near to the mouth of the fissure, knowing that the eagles were eager to go into it. They would not be easy to command in this venture, their temperaments very different to his own. A stream of cold air reached out for them like a hand, but they ignored it, flying forward. They were in the tunnel of darkness.

They could see very little, avoiding the sides of the rock by instinct. Ahead of them they could feel the passage of the Shadowflight, for it was not moving very quickly, perhaps tired as Aark had said. After a while there were hints of light, of movement, and they judged themselves to be several hundred yards behind them. It did not seem to have sensed them.

Kirrikree felt sure that this passage must lead through the mountains to the land beyond. Wargallow and the Emperor could not have climbed up to it, so he felt no annoyance at having discovered it now, but if the company could get under the Edge and through, the birds might yet find them.

It was a long flight and they began to draw closer to the Shadowflight. It did not look back, doubtless confident that nothing would dare pursue it. At last there came a lessening of the darkness as the fissure widened into a pass. High overhead there was a grayness on both sides that intimated snowy mountains, faces of ice, with a hint of dawn in them, reflected from the east.

They were coming through.

Skyrac swung over close to Kirrikree. "It must not go to its master," he called as quietly as he could.

"An attack?"

"Soon. It is tired."

As though the eagle had shouted, the Shadowflight swung its long neck about, and they saw properly its cold eyes, deep green, filled with an alien hostility. It had seen them and was in no mood to flee them. With a shriek of defiance that rang off the walls, it whirled about, far more maneuverable than the pursuit had anticipated. The eagles rose up as one, eager

for a confrontation: Kirrikree knew he could not prevent it.
He flew straight for the enemy.

It snarled like a beast as it came forward, and as Kirrikree
deftly flew aside, its mouth opened and a slick tongue like a
serpent's flashed. The eagles were above the creature, claws
extended; they dived as a unit, their talons raking one wing.
Shocked by the suddenness of this attack, the Shadowflight
dipped down toward the rock face nearest to it, barely veering in time to avoid striking it. Kirrikree followed up the
attack of the eagles with one of his own, his claws cutting
into the same wing that the eagles had struck. The creature
screamed hideously, ugly head darting at its enemy and the
owl barely swerved in time to avoid a lashing by the long
tongue. As he did so, the eagles shot down as one, raking
the other wing, finding the softest parts of it. Again the creature screamed, and as it turned in the air, it struck the rock
wall with a wing-tip, the wing immediately crumpling. The
creature was swung round to crash into the wall, using its
feet to brace itself, but it could not grip the slippery surface.
It fell, opening out both wings in desperation, though the
damage done to them made its flight clumsy and unstable.
Somehow it found a ledge below and clung to it, turning its
head to hiss at its assailants.

Kirrikree and the eagles flew past, keeping out of range.
They could hear the voice of the beast in their minds, like
the hiss of fire and steam. It warned them of death and pain.

Kirrikree turned his attention briefly to the land that had
opened up beyond the mountains. Mercifully there were no
more of the Shadowflight coming out of its thick mists.
Whatever the landscape beyond, it was cloaked in the grays
and blacks of that pervasive fog. Nothing protruded, no alp,
no hint of further mountain. But Anakhizer must be there, in
a fortress of some kind.

Kirrikree tired to question the wounded creature. "Where
is your master?"

The replies made little sense, as though it spat out insults,
mixed with its snarls of pain.

"Exhausted," said Skyrac. "Kill it."

"Wait," said the owl. He could feel the heat of the eagles'
killing need. They had their prey at their mercy and were

burning to destroy it. "There are things we need to learn from it. Shadowflight!" he called again.

But the beast reacted no differently.

"We bring you your death," Kerrikree told it, opening his talons.

A spark of fear showed itself in the mind of the creature. "Where is your master?"

Amongst the strange, alien sounds in the creature's mind, Kirrikree thought he detected an answer. Anakhizer was beyond, in Anger.

"Where?" the owl persisted.

Stranger images came to him, as though the Shadowflight was trying to depict for him a mental picture of the Land of Anger, but it was as shrouded and impenetrable as the fogs beyond the mountains.

"How do we come to your master?"

Kirrikree was able to learn little more, though it seemed that the only way to Anakhizer was by flight, perhaps to some rock stronghold above the dark land. He explained to Skyrac, who was unable to understand anything of the twisted sendings of the Shadowflight.

"Flight?" echoed the eagle. "What of Aumlac and the others?"

"We must find them," said Kirrikree.

"Kill this first."

Kirrikree tried once more to speak to the Shadowflight. "How far is Anakhizer's stronghold?" But the creature emitted another long scream, raising its claws as if it would attack in spite of its suffering. But it could not leave its ledge.

"We go there?" Skyrac asked the owl.

"First we must find our masters."

"Kill first," insisted the eagle, and Kirrikree could feel the weight of the others, their hunger.

No more was said; the Shadowflight had to be killed. Carefully they set about fresh attacks, and although it took an hour to wear down the defense of the grim creature, they did so at last, tearing at its wings before dragging it from the ledge. It tumbled into the pass below with a last, exhausted cry.

Themselves tired, Kirrikree and the eagles rested briefly

before going out into Anger. Daylight did little to enrich its gray hues, and it remained impossible to see any feature of it, as if it were no more than an ocean of mist. The birds turned northward, following the mountains' edge, knowing that somewhere ahead of them, miles away, Wargallow and the company would yet be under the Edge, possibly already trapped, or even dead. From time to time, Kirrikree risked calling to Sisipher, but his cries bounced back impotently from the dull stone and towering walls of ice and snow.

NIGHT STOOD watch over the snow-slopes. The company had been arranged with strict military precision: Kelloric was adept at strategy, knowing just how to deploy his men to the best advantage, and Wargallow could see how well he had done his job. It was a relief that the warrior was able to put himself and his men to good use, although the weight of the attack was daunting. Up in the jumble of rocks beyond the defenses, vast hordes of Ferr-Bolgan had materialized as if conjured from the air. They howled bestially, spurred on by the silent angarbreed.

Wargallow spoke to Brannog. "Are there Children of the Mound with them?"

He nodded. "There is one."

The attack was launched abruptly, and for the first time that the company could recall, the enemy used arrows. They had with them a number of angarbreed, dark-clad warriors in tight-fitting armor and helms that covered their faces entirely. These fought in a silence that hinted at far more intelligence than the Ferr-Bolgan. The angarbreed were more mobile and did not rely on weight of numbers as the Ferr-Bolgan did: they were far harder to kill.

Kelloric had effectively set up his defense so that the enemy was forced to funnel its attack through a miniature canyon formed by the fallen building. Although vastly outnumbered, the company was able to meet the opposition head on without being cut at from all sides. For a time the assault failed to break through to the plaza. The bodies of the dead heaped up appallingly, but few of them were defenders, who fell mainly to the arrows.

The Stonedelvers beat back the foe with stunning success,

but Einnis wore a look of grave concern. "I fear we cannot withstand this assault for long," he told Wargallow. "The numbers of the enemy are too great."

"Could we perhaps withdraw and fight a rearguard?" Wargallow asked him.

"It would be hopeless, I fear. We could skirt the mountains along the Edge, going south, but only if we broke through this attack. It covers the way we must go. And we yet have to find a way into Anger. If this battle goes on for too long, Anakhizer will know where we are. This, I am certain, is a chance attack. The mountains seeth with these creatures. They were not sent by Anakhizer, and stumbled on us. But unless we divert them, we may be lost."

"Divert them?"

Einnis' scowl deepened. "There is yet power in the stones of Sheercastle. I may be able to use it. But you must remove the company to the far end of the plaza. The Stonedelvers and I will keep the enemy at bay."

Wargallow was unsure what Einnis intended, but he had little choice. The company was slowly pulled back, Kelloric's troops covering the retreat while the Stonedelvers filled the gaps in the defensive wall.

"What does he intend?" Ottemar asked Wargallow, his eyes fixed on the white-bearded figure of Einnis.

Both Sisipher and Brannog looked to the Stonewise, a deep worry etched on their faces.

"He will use the stone," was all Wargallow could say.

Einnis stood behind his fighting giants, calling out to the stone, holding his staff over it. Aumlac and Bornac fought shoulder to shoulder, wielding huge stone clubs that they had fashioned from the rock bones of Sheercastle. They laughed as they fought and around them their warriors beat back the invaders with shuddering force. The dead choked the narrow streets and the archers could not pull back their bows. It became hand to hand, sword to war club. The Earthwrought had slipped back to join the company, waiting anxiously to see what Einnis would do.

Something in the ancient citadel reacted to whatever power Einnis was calling up, for abruptly there came a thunderous crack in the mountains above Sheercastle. A fissure danced across the rock walls, spreading downward until it crept like a miniature river delta across the plaza.

Brannog lurched forward, but Graval held him back. "The floor is breaking up!" Brannog shouted over the din. "Einnis cannot hope to hold it!"

"Stay, master," said Gravel. "He calls down death upon the mountain vermin."

The first of the boulders, loosened by the opening crack, tumbled from the mountainside, crashing down upon the Ferr-Bolgan masses, and within minutes a great shelf of rock slithered downward, brushing aside scores of them like ants. Aumlac and his warriors held their ground, chopping further into their foes and the floor suddenly opened up behind them, cutting them off from the rest of the company. Still Einnis called upon the power of the rock, but his voice was drowned out by the terrible din of breaking stone and landslide. Huge clumps of snow split from the heights and the threat of an avalanche hung over the land below, the roar and boom of breaking ground like underground thunder or the crashing of waves in a tempest.

"Call them back!" shouted Wargallow, realizing the danger to the Stonedelvers. Both Brannog and Ottemar shouted to the fighting warriors. But the fissure behind them had opened wide. Others split from it and scores more of the Ferr-Bolgan tumbled into them, the angarbreed also decimated. Dust rose up in a thick cloud: the far end of the plaza rippled like the body of a huge beast, buckling.

"Wargallow!" cried Kelloric, gripping his arm. "The rod! You must use it now. They'll be lost!"

A huge piece of the plaza fell away, a massive slab of rock ledge collapsing down into the gulf that was Anger. Beyond it another slice of the mountain ledge crumpled up and also shot away into the depths, taking with it the bulk of the enemy forces. As the dust cleared away, there was no sign of Einnis or the Stonedelvers.

There was no time to search for them, for a wedge of Ferr-Bolgan had found a way across to the plaza and they rushed forward eagerly, ignoring the terrible destruction. Wargallow's defenders met them and beat them back with ease, for their numbers were few.

Coldrieve, in the thick of the killing, called Wargallow to him, and there before him, trapped against a flat slab of rock, about to attempt the release of its own power, was a herder, a Broodmaster. Wargallow's eyes blazed with fury as he leapt forward and used his killing steel to chop into the arm and side of the being before anyone could react. It fell to its knees, eyes screwed up in pain as its blood flowed thickly from the frightful wound. Wargallow stood over it, his killing steel under its exposed throat.

When the eyes opened, they looked on Wargallow's face, which wore an expression akin to madness.

"Don't kill him yet," said Coldrieve softly, his own face devoid of his master's rage.

It took a long time for Wargallow to master his emotion, his thoughts on the loss of the Stonedelvers, but at last he withdrew his blade. Other weapons were directed at the throat of his enemy now, and the Broodmaster was powerless before them. Its angarbreed warriors had either perished or been dispersed, the last of the Ferr-Bolgan having fled into the darkness of the mountains, like a serpent with no head.

Wargallow sucked in a deep breath, calming himself. "Where is your master?" he said, his voice grating like steel.

The Broodmaster's eyes were slits under its hood, alive with agony. Any power it had been seared out of it by Wargallow's swift strike. When the being spoke, its voice was weak and fading.

"West," it said.

Sisipher came forward, gently putting an arm on Wargallow's. She could feel his fury, his anger at not being able to use the rod of power against this monster and its servants. He felt the loss of Einnis like a wound.

"Does your master have the rods of power?" Sisipher asked.

"He calls us all to him," growled the Broodmaster. "We are his generals. You cannot stop the war. We shall have the rods—"

Brannog gasped. "Children of the Mound, spawn of the Sorcerer-Kings," he said. "How the wheel has turned. They are to have again what they once held. But in Anakhizer's name!"

"What will you do with the rods?" Wargallow asked the Broodmaster coldly.

"Omara seeks to heal the chain of Aspects. Soon. The rods will combine, greater than the one that is missing."

"Are all the rods with Anakhizer?" said Coldrieve.

A rattle of laughter came from the tight lips of the dying creature. Its meaning was clear. The Broodmaster stiffened, eyes glazing, then collapsed. It was dead.

"We've learnt nothing!" spat Kelloric. "And the way to the south is closed to us. The mountain has been cloven in two."

Only now did the company go back to the edge of the plaza, gazing at the settling dust. They began to understand the true nature of the sacrifice to the Stonedelvers, for they had undoubtedly gone down with the landslide. Graval and the Earthwrought were on their knees before the huge fissure, their eyes filled with tears. Grimander, who had not taken part in the battle, was with them now, his own face full of sadness. Brannog and Sisipher also dropped to their knees, bowing their heads.

For a long time the company was silent, appalled by the weight of loss.

Eventually Graval rose and with him the company, one by one. He bowed before Ottemar, who felt more deeply moved by the death of the Stonewise and Aumlac, whom once he had saved from death, than he would have thought possible.

"Sire," said the Earthwrought, trying to hold his voice steady, "Sheercastle is a fitting grave for the Stonewise and his incomparable warriors. Though it was too soon." He bowed. "With your permission, sire, I will remain in this place and my people will work here. We will mark the passing of the Stonedelvers and we will make Sheercastle a gate once more, a watch over the Land of Anger. Einnis Amrodin has woken the stone and the earth lives on. We shall work it and give new life to it. Grant that we may do these things, sire."

Ottemar nodded sadly, Aumlac filling his inner vision. "Aye, Gravel. You shall do these things. And when you have secured Sheercastle, after we have won our cause, you shall bring your children here, and the children of those who have perished this day.''

Sisipher, who had been as silent as the Earthwrought, looked up sharply at the skies. They were clouded, lowering, as though they did not approve of the defeat of the Ferr-Bolgan. "Did you hear a cry?" she asked her father.

He shook his head.

"There!" She turned, facing south, over the gulf. "Can it be Kirrikree?"

"You imagine it," said Brannog patiently, but in a moment he, too, gazed southward with a new expectation. "And yet—"

Sisipher sent out a mental call, and moments later knew that the huge owl was indeed on this side of the mountains, impossible though it seemed. Grimander hopped to her side, unable to hold down his excitement.

The moments crawled by as they waited; it was almost an hour before Sisipher saw the flash of white. Then Kirrikree was drifting down, the eagles behind him, and there were shouts of jubilation from all the company.

Skyrac studied the faces of all those below him, but he saw not a single Stonedelver. Aumlac, his master, was disturbingly absent, nor was Einnis Amrodin here. Sisipher understood his surprise and distress at once, and she bowed her head as she whispered the news of their passing to the birds. The eagles soared upward, whirling out over the gulf, diving down into it as if they must go in search of those who had fallen.

"This is grave news," Kirrikree told Sisipher. "And though it is a joy to me to find you alive, I have further news that will not lighten your burden." He told them then of the Shadowflight and of the difficulty of traveling west. "We have searched for you for many, many days, and as we did so we looked out upon the mists of Anger. We have seen no way over it.''

Wargallow studied the owl in silence, but then turned to point to the darkness of the west. "Then if we cannot go over to our enemy, we must lure him out to us. We have what he desires most.''

"Too dangerous!" piped the voice of Grimander. "Invite

Anakhizer to you and he'll bring all his power down. No, no, keep to your first plan.''

"Kirrikree has told us we cannot cross," said Wargallow.

"Woodheart can cross. Woodheart can show you how."

The company looked baffled, but Grimander had surprised them all more than once before. The tiny Woodweaver walked to the very edge of the Abyss and spread out his hands in apparent supplication, calling to his strange forest god. He spoke garbled, alien words, chanting, seemingly cursing, then half singing, until at last, beaming back at the company like a child who has achieved that which he has been told he cannot achieve, he pointed.

"Woodheart hears. He is coming."

"Coming?" echoed Sisipher.

"Can you not feel him rise?"

As he spoke, the earth trembled. It seemed that the mountains themselves had shaken themselves awake from an eon-deep slumber.

PART FIVE

IN ANGER

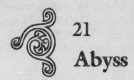

21
Abyss

As THE fresh clouds of dust settled across the plaza, the company saw movement beyond the cliff edge. They drew back, expecting another landslide, a continuation of the breaking up of the land begun by Einnis, but they saw instead something vast sluggishly moving up from the Abyss. Only Grimander stood his ground, flinging out his arms in a dramatic gesture in which there was no fear. It was adulation, they realized, for he began a strange new chant in which they recognized the name of Woodheart.

"Even here, Woodheart gathers strength from his own lands," Grimander called, looking back at the company. "And Ruvanna has put her own skills to work once more. She soothes his pain and gives him strength."

Brannog was the first to step forward, gasping at what he saw. He thought it must be some monstrous serpent, but another gigantic root had raised itself up from the deeps; it stretched out from the edge of the cliff like a twisting, looping bridge, disappearing into the mist ahead. It was fully fifty feet across, pale green and somehow pulsing with life, like the vein in a giant's arm.

"Have you summoned this?" Wargallow asked Grimander incredulously.

"Events here have done that. With a little help from my ailing gifts. It is Ruvanna who speaks to Woodheart for you."

There was further movement out on the great root, and as they watched, they saw shapes materializing in the mist, figures which drifted forward slowly like ghosts from a lost age. They were not unlike Woodweavers, though far more slender, with curious, trailing hands. Grimander looked stunned by them, quivering where he stood, transfixed. But Brannog could sense their thoughts, as he could sense the thoughts of the birds or his wolves. These figures, he knew, communicated in some similar way with Grimander, and a glance at Sisipher confirmed this.

"The lost Healers!" whispered the Woodweaver, their presence a complete shock to him.

"Are they spirits?" said Wargallow, for the figures did not seem to have the substance of a man, their skins being so pale as to be near-transparent. At times they became as pale as the mist, but then swam into focus more clearly.

"No, not spirits," said Grimander, still mesmerized. "But they have passed from our realm of existence to another. They are a part of Woodheart. They are—like his thoughts." There seemed to be tears in his eyes as he spoke.

Brannog put an arm about him, towering over him. "They address you?"

"I would have been one of them, but I was young, and not able enough—"

"Your love of the forest has rooted deep, Grimander," came the voices of the Wood Healers, soft as breezes, yet clear enough for Brannog and the others to hear. "You are lacking in nothing. And your time is now."

Grimander drew in his breath, unable to answer.

"Woodheart understands you. It is your care that has awoken us. But your work is not over. Yonder lies the path across the Land of Anger. To the place you seek."

"Will you guide us?" said Grimander.

"As you wish."

The Woodweaver nodded and stepped down on to the great root as though treading hallowed ground. The Healers drifted back, awaiting him; the company followed, called on by Brannog.

"Can it be safe?" growled Kelloric, the last of his warriors gathered about him uncertainly. Ottemar silenced him with an impatient glance, leading Sisipher by the hand after her father.

"There is goodness in the Healers," she told him quietly. "But I can feel their fear and the deeper fear of the root for what lies beyond us." She turned as she spoke, conscious of another voice in her mind. It was Kirrikree, who hovered over Sheercastle, the eagles with him once more.

"Mistress, I will wait here. Skyrac is not ready to fly with you, as he and his brothers mourn the Stonedelvers. I must watch over them—"

"Of course," she agreed, relaying the message to her father.

Beyond them, on the root, Coldrieve bowed briefly to Dennovia, who looked horrified by the prospect of following the root out into the emptiness. "Walk with me," he said.

She would have replied, but her mouth was dry. She remembered vividly the crossing of the Bay of Sorrows, but even that had been nothing to this new trek into oblivion.

As the company moved out along the root, Graval and his Earthwrought assembled behind them on the lip of the plaza, standing solemnly to attention like carved sentinels. They saluted in silence, the mist closing around them.

Kelloric's guard drew their weapons, watching the darkness on either side as if it would disgorge unimaginable horrors, though it gave no hint of movement and was as silent as a vacuum. Yet it seemed to belong to some other region than Omara, promising no warmth or salvation.

Brannog went ahead to walk with Grimander, followed by the two Deliverers and Dennovia, and although the Healers never disappeared, they kept their distance, as if contact would disperse them. Soon the company was surrounded by the night and the mist, their only link with the world the thick root beneath them, solid as stone. It had a faint glow to it, so there was no need of brands, although some had been brought in readiness.

"Is there *nothing* below us?" Brannog asked Grimander, whose eyes were fixed on the Healers as a child watches its heroes. "There must be a bottom to this Abyss."

"Their thoughts cannot penetrate it," replied the Woodweaver. "And Woodheart has not tried to fathom it. It may be a gate to another realm. No one knows."

The dawn began to break as they moved on, filtering

through the mist behind them, causing the thickest of it to disperse, but it hovered yet at the edge of vision, making it impossible to see any land on the horizons or an end to the Abyss. The dark sky above gradually turned grayer, and then pale, but it, too, suggested infinity. The company traveled on in a kind of daze, not exhausted, but moving with an automatic tread, almost as if hypnotized, their minds locked.

"We should rest," Sisipher said at length, though to no one in particular and Ottemar, who was again beside her, jerked as if she had slapped him.

"What? Of course! We are moving on like sheep. Wargallow! Call a halt. Let us rest here and eat. It seems as safe as anywhere, though I'll be glad to get off this bridge."

Wargallow nodded, recalling the Emperor's terror of heights. Ottemar had concealed it well on this crossing, though the root was wide.

"Yes, rest. Grimander! Do the Healers know how much further we must go along this path?" Wargallow asked.

"You will see the place of the enemy soon enough," was the reply. Grimander sat down, crosslegged, never taking his eyes from the Healers. They hovered some way ahead, shimmering, not moving from the place where they had halted. They were in no hurry.

Brannog sat with the Deliverers, joined by Ottemar, the two girls and Kelloric. "When we come to this place, said Brannog, "how are we to enter it? We took Mount Timeless by stealth, but you'll recall," he added, with a pointed glance at Wargallow, "that we had an army with us."

"As we did at Xennidhum," agreed Wargallow.

"You've seen my men fight," said Kelloric. "But look at them now! A score of them remain. We have no Stone-delvers, no Earthwrought—"

"If we had brought the combined armies of Xennidhum, Elberon and Ulthor Faithbreaker with us," said Wargallow, "we would have been leading them into the teeth of disaster. It is just what Anakhizer would have wished. He would merely have unleashed the power of the rods upon them all, and all that he desires would have been his."

"Yet you stormed Xennidhum and Mount Timeless!" persisted Kelloric. "The power of the armies carried the days then!"

"We had Korbillian at Xennidhum, and he bore the immense power of the Hierarchs," said Wargallow patiently. Brannog was nodding. "And the Sublime One did not use the rod against us. Mourndark had stolen it by then."

Kelloric did not look mollified. "But how can we hope to overcome Anakhizer? Will you not now reveal your plan? The men must have hope. For the moment they see darkness ahead of us. We have lost so many. We seem doomed. Show us that we are not."

Wargallow did not flinch, but he understood Kelloric's frustration. What he asked was not so unreasonable.

It was Dennovia who surprised them by answering, hotly, her eyes flashing with suppressed anger. "You've not seen the rod used as I have," she snapped to Kelloric. "I saw how it sucked the power out of the Sublime One's followers. How it would have drained the entire army if Mourndark had been given the chance to use it. Tell your men to have faith in the rod, Kelloric."

"And what of the rods in the fortress?"

"If Anakhizer discovers us," said Wargallow, "he will turn them on us."

"Then you insist on surprise?"

"From the day we first planned this journey," nodded Wargallow.

Dennovia glared at Kelloric. "Have you lost your stomach for the task?"

He looked at her as if he would have struck her. "How dare you speak of cowardice!"

"Enough of this!" said Ottemar. "Simon, we must have a clear strategy. I cannot believe you have nothing in mind. It's not been your way to blunder into things."

Wargallow managed a smile. "I hope not."

"Then what is it to be?"

"Like yourselves, I have not seen the fortress. But there must be a way into it. It was assumed to be unreachable, except by air, but Woodheart has shown that to be a fallacy. Anakhizer would never expect us to be able to cross the Abyss. Therefore we still carry the weapon of surprise."

"And if we get across?" prompted Kelloric.

"Assuming we get into the fortress, we search out Anak-hizer. I am certain he will have his mind on other things, believing himself secure. He may be watching the mountains, but Omara will interest him more. The attempt to make good the Aspects and the chain. That will preoccupy him."

"But his fortress will not be empty!" said Kelloric.

"No."

Sisipher cleared her throat in the brief silence. "Since you bear the rod of power, and since it must protect you from most things, would it not be wiser for you and you alone to go up into the fortress?"

For once Coldrieve showed some emotion, his eyes fixing her.

Dennovia turned to her in immediate protest. "No! You have no right to suggest such a thing!"

Wargallow put a restraining hand on her arm. "She has every right. And it is my rights that are in question. Correctly so."

"You have acted correctly throughout," said Ottemar.

"It is time to think about what we are doing," said Wargallow.

"This is no time for indecision," cut in Brannog. "We have crossed half of Omara to reach this fortress."

"Death waits for yet more of us up there," said Wargallow. "No one should be forced to go. It is true, I control the power of the rod, the limits of which are not known to me. But you must all speak for yourselves."

Kelloric turned to Ottemar. "Forgive me, sire, but I am compelled to say that you should go no further. We have won through to this place by some miracle. Let Wargallow finish what he has come to do. Let the men escort you back to Goldenisle."

"Goldenisle!" snorted Ottemar. "What we do, we do for *Omara*. For every land in it."

"Sire," Kelloric went on, lowering his voice. "Goldenisle is your responsibility, your Empire. Lately risen from years of civil war. Your duty is to secure her first." He looked angrily at Sisipher. "Whatever other motives seem right and proper to you—"

"What are you implying?" Ottemar snarled, leaping to his feet.

Kelloric rose slowly, controlling his own temper with great difficulty. "Not only do you have an Empire to maintain, sire, but you have a wife, and an heir in whom the Empire is invested."

Ottemar's fingers closed over his sword haft, but before he could draw it, Sisipher stepped between him and the burly warrior. "Think with your head, Kelloric," she said calmly. "Not with your emotions. If Ottemar had come here merely to follow me, whom you wrongly suppose to be his lover— yes! you need not deny your thoughts, I hear them as though you shout them—then we would have turned back to Golden- isle at the Horn Moot. And in safety, with as large an escort as we had wanted."

Kelloric could not meet her eyes. He turned instead to Dennovia, who was on her feet, as were all of them. "And this girl?"

"I've told you, I'm here because I'm a threat," she said. "I covet the rod of power and want it for myself. I mean to betray you all to Anakhizer, is that not so, Wargallow?" She faced the Deliverer, eyes full of challenge.

"Jest often covers truth," said Kelloric stiffly.

"Again you are ridiculous," Sisipher told him, fixing him with a withering glare. "Dennovia once had the rod in her possession. But for her, we would not possess it now."

"Then why," he said through his teeth, "is she here?" Behind him his men were standing uncomfortably, listening.

Wargallow broke into the sudden silence. "Tell me, Kel- loric, who do you serve?"

"I serve Goldenisle," was the terse reply.

"Laudable." Wargallow glanced at Ottemar. "Perhaps you would serve your Empire better, sire, by returning to it."

There was a moment when it seemed that Ottemar might snap, the weight of the past months finally overcoming him, but instead he drew in a breath and smiled. "I may be Em- peror, but it seems the world wishes to make my decisions for me. I will go on to the fortress. And if you consider yourself loyal to Goldenisle, Kelloric, you will follow, with your men."

"As you wish, sire," Kelloric bowed. He abruptly spun round and went to his men, but they greeted him with tight-lipped silence.

"I understand his concern," said Wargallow. "He's a military commander, and an excellent one. I'd rather he was with us."

"I have no desire to desert you," said Brannog. "Yet my heart cries out that I should return to Ruvanna and that my daughter should go back to safety. And Dennovia, too."

"But you don't make my decisions," Sisipher smiled, hugging her father's arm. "As you already know."

"Yes, indeed. But what of you, Dennovia? Are you here of your own volition? It is time we knew the truth of this matter." Brannog looked to Wargallow, for he had never understood why the girl had been brought this far. Wargallow had not declared his motive, and he must have one.

Dennovia straightened. "You are right to look to Wargallow for your answer. I am a prisoner."

Wargallow smiled, taking Brannog by surprise. "I should have had you locked up in Goldenisle," he told Dennovia. "But that hardly seemed fair, considering the debts I owe to you. But you're no prisoner, Dennovia. As with the others, you are not bound by our quest."

Ottemar was frowning, wondering himself why it was that the girl had wanted to come. She had worked hard to win his support, but clearly she had not come for the reasons she had given him, that she loved Fornoldur. "You came here for your own reasons," he said to her. "As I well know."

Wargallow smiled again. "Do you wish to leave us?"

Dennovia snorted, tossing back her dark mane. Even here, after all that the company had endured, her beauty was undiminished. "Alone? Wander back along the root to Sheercastle, and then cross the mountains? Or crawl under them?"

"Ah, then you'll come with us?" said Wargallow blandly. She turned away, gazing out at the Abyss.

"Then we go on as a unit," said Ottemar. "Unless your companion has had enough of us." He nodded to Coldrieve, but the latter's face was impassive.

"Harn is with us," said Wargallow bluntly and Coldrieve

made no attempt to argue, apparently ready to move on at once.

They did so shortly afterward, Brannog again joining Grimander as the Healers drifted on down the curling root, which yet led on into the distance. There was little conversation, as if the arguments had not cleared the air, but seeded it with resentment, bitterness. Ottemar walked beside Sisipher, but she moved closer to Dennovia, anxious not to get drawn into another whispered conversation with the Emperor. Her sharp words to Kelloric had not dispelled the commander's anger at the thought that Ottemar yet pursued her, she knew that.

When the Healers indicated at last that something was ahead of them, it came as a relief. The company quickly gathered about Grimander to study the mists, which were parting as if under instruction from the Healers. The thick root wound into a darkness from out of which rose an enormous mass. It was the promised fortress, though it was nothing like the company had previously seen, and not a construction wrought by men or their allies.

It seemed to be a gigantic chunk of earth, a fragment of the world, ripped from its bed and set free in the skies of this Abyss. From its base hung thick clusters of root, or tendril, or both. These looped downward into the gulf like innumerable cables, as if they anchored the fortress like the immense cables of a ship, or like the vast threads of some monstrous web. Woodheart's root wriggled between a host of them, shadowed by them and lost in their maze. High overhead, the fortress itself was motionless, a small moon, thick with alien vegetation that was rampant and spilling over its edges in chaotic profusion. Nothing else stirred in the skies, and the cables hung tightly, themselves draped with plants like weed clinging to the lines of a ship in port.

"It draws itself closer to the mountains, day by day," said Grimander.

"Is it *alive?*" asked Brannog, thinking of Naar-Iarnoc, the mutated Sorcerer-King, although he had been nothing like as large as this vast structure.

"Not as the earth is alive," said Grimander, passing on the thoughts of the Healers. "It is controlled by that which controls Anakhizer, the Primal. It is not of Omara."

"Then from where?"

"It is a parasite, and will cling to the stone of Omara, to begin the capture of the host. The feeding of the Primal."

"Can it sense us?" said Wargallow.

"No, for we are nothing to it. It is the talon of a world."

Brannog grunted. "Then if we enter it, it won't be aware of us. Is it guarded?"

"There are no Ferr-Bolgan, nor angarbreed, but Anakhizer's servants are there. As are the rods. Woodheart can feel their power. As soon as Omara begins her work, the Primal will begin its own, through Anakhizer. Even though Anakhizer does not have the full use of the rods, he will unleash their power." Grimander was saying this as if repeating things spoken silently to him. Brannog could sense that there was a deepening bond between Woodheart, the Healers and Grimander, as though they had all tapped in to whatever occurred high above, within the immensity of the fortress before them.

"Anakhizer's forces were rebuffed on the Fellwater, for Woodheart smote them, as he has done further south on his boundaries. But all over Omara, the forces of the dark prepare. The Shadowflight will be coming soon, and the Broodmasters and Broodmothers have gathered, ready to carry the rods. It will be as it was feared at the Horn Moot. A bloody war, long and universal, the life of Omara and all those that fall bled off to feed that which waits outside."

"This knowledge reaches Woodheart from all parts of Omara," Brannog told the company. "And through Grimander it comes to us. Woodheart has indeed come to life."

"Ruvanna!" laughed Dennovia. "She thought that her powers had deserted her. But her healing gifts have helped Woodheart to this end."

Brannog nodded proudly. "Yes."

"If Anakhizer unleashes war in this fashion," said Wargallow, "then it is an act of desperation. Fear, perhaps."

"The Primals know no fear," came the voice of Grimander.

"Nor patience," suggested Brannog. "Wargallow is right. To begin a war now, without waiting to claim the last of the rods—"

"Omara has brought this upon herself," said Grimander. "Though not wittingly. But the sealing has to begin. Omara must pour all her power into it. Woodheart can feel it happening. If you are to go up into Anakhizer's fortress, you must hasten. All Woodheart's power may have to aid Omara."

Wargallow nodded. "Very well."

They hurried on down the rootway, the elusive Healers still ahead of them. Sisipher pointed up at the towering masses of tendril, now a few miles beyond. "How are we to ascend?"

"The Healers will weave a way for us as soundly as any Woodweaver could," promised Grimander.

When they reached the place where their root went into the mass of the lower fortress, the roots were even more like wire cables, hanging down in festoons, crossing and criss-crossing, some wrapping themselves to Woodheart's root like mighty vines. Shadows swallowed the company, for in spite of the sun, it was as if they had entered yet another cavern, with countless tunnels leading off into the interior of the root mass. It was another world, alien, crawling with a hostile silence, the twisting roots thick with their own roots and suckers as if in the darkness they probed for something on which to latch, to drag at Omara and cling to it with a dreadful eagerness.

The Healers were lost to sight, having gone, said Grimander, upward, spinning a protective web like so many spiders.

"How high is this climb?" said Brannog.

But Grimander did not reply. He went upward, as agile as any fresh warrior. Coldrieve and Wargallow followed Brannog, keeping very close to one another. Brannog was certain that whatever Wargallow had planned involved Coldrieve. Perhaps its success depended on utter secrecy, and certainly it would not be something left merely to chance. That was not how Wargallow thought. He was far too meticulous for that. Brannog wondered if it would have been wiser to talk quietly to Kelloric, explaining how Wargallow worked, but it was too late for that now. Surprise was vital. And trust. Brannog, who had once thought only of destroying Wargallow, was now content to trust the Deliverer with his life. But this last venture, this ascent into the nameless fortress, was not necessarily going to be successful. The apartness of the place closed in, hot and uncomfortable, its smells unlike the smells of the earth, or of stone. The silence clogged the ears with its intensity, its promise of eternity. Light faded.

Brannog peered down to see Sisipher and Dennovia below him, though they both grinned in spite of their fears. Below them Ottemar gritted his teeth and gripped the woven strands of root fashioned by the Healers. Was it love that drove him? Brannog wondered. Would he follow Sisipher wherever the quest took them? His daughter had adroitly deflected Kelloric's accusations, but the fact remained that Ottemar loved her, even if he was not her lover. This was something that would have to be resolved, although how could it be in such a place, with the death of a world hanging over them?

The Healers had worked their way up what appeared to be a spiral in the root system, for it penetrated greater heights, its sides strung with tiny filaments of root and vine, easy to climb, but tiring. Brannog looked up to see Coldrieve pull something from his robe.

It is the rod! his mind cried. There was no mistaking its length, its pale blue glow. But *how?* How had Wargallow managed to give it to him? Brannog let the shock wash over him, hanging on tightly. It had been part of Wargallow, made for him by Zoigon. A dozen questions shook him.

Above, Wargallow had wedged himself across the chimney, and while Brannog gaped, the Deliverer stripped himself of his own robe, balling it up and thrusting it into a gap in the roots beside him. He tugged at his shirt sleeve and brought it free of his killing steel, revealing the latter and the twin sickles. Above him, Coldrieve tightened the stays of his own robe and lifted his hood, covering his face. Then he began the climb again, with the rod in full view at his belt.

Wargallow looked down and saw Brannog's expression. But he said nothing, turning to climb.

It struck Brannog suddenly what Wargallow had done. He had found a way to rid himself of the rod and had sent Coldrieve up in his place, disguised as himself. But *why?* How could he possibly think of allowing another, even one as loyal as Coldrieve, to take his place? And the rod!

But there was no time for further thought. Those below him were pushing at him, urging him on. The climb began anew, and went on for what seemed an age. Each time Brannog craned his neck to see upward, Coldrieve was further away, a distant spider. Of Grimander there was no sign.

"Wargallow!" Brannog called, the name whispering back from the tangled walls.

"Speak no names here," cautioned the Deliverer.

"Where are the others?"

"Grimander is far above us now. He has joined the Healers. They have spread out, searching this maze like weevils. They'll find us a way to our goal." Wargallow gestured for silence, climbing swiftly so that Brannog had to use all his energy to keep up. The two women were not far behind him, though they could not see what was happening overhead. The words were distorted here, just as time was.

Kelloric was close behind Ottemar. "What are they doing above us?" he said. "How can we be sure this passage is safe?"

"Grimander and the Healers won't lead us astray," Ottemar told him.

Wargallow had reached a winding opening that stretched like an artery across the chimney, and he reached down with his left arm to help Brannog up. He was exceptionally powerful, and Brannog marvelled at that strength, knowing it had not been that long ago when Wargallow had been on the point of death.

"Where's Coldrieve?" Brannog breathed.

Wargallow smiled. "Grimander says there are numerous ways to penetrate this place. It is like a sponge. Coldrieve has gone another way. But Grimander is with him. Trust us, Brannog."

"I don't know what it is you plan, but it seems to me to be a dangerous game."

"No game," said Wargallow as he bent to help the first of the girls, Dennovia, over the threshold. He lifted her easily and held her for a moment with his left arm. She eyed the killing steel of his right with a grimace, then glanced about her.

"Where's Coldrieve?" she said softly.

No one answered her.

"Which way?" said Sisipher as her father helped her up.

She studied the curious passageway. It was curved, its sides fashioned out of something that might have been soil, or flesh, even metal, or a combination. The total alienness of the place came home to them with a force that was brutal.

Wargallow listened, as if to unheard voices. He pointed.

They moved along the passageway, following the Deliverer, who they saw wore only simple clothing that did nothing to distinguish him from the rest of them. Apart from his killing steel, which he kept in shadow, he was not recognizable as a Deliverer.

Sisipher hung back a little and pulled at Brannog's sleeve. "You know him better than I, Father. Surely he has not betrayed us."

"He has given the rod to Coldrieve," Brannog said into her ear.

Her eyes widened. She was about to protest, but the appearance of Wargallow in front of them cut her off. But he had not heard their exchange. He was pointing ahead. Daylight awaited them. They were about to emerge into the heart of the citadel.

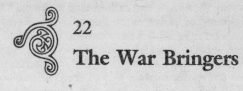

22
The War Bringers

GRAVAL AND his Earthwrought had concluded their brief ceremonies to mark the deaths of Einnis Amrodin and the Stonedelvers and all those who had perished during the battle with the Ferr-Bolgan and the angarbreed at Sheercastle. As they began work moving stone, testing the ground for further weakness and considering how best to make the citadel secure against the darkness in the west, Skyrac and his eagles circled restlessly, as though they expected to see the spirits of the dead rise again. Kirrikree perched on one of the higher rocks, watching silently, himself sharing the grief of his companions. The cost of this war was so high. Ternannoc, his home world, was little more than a cinder, and here in Omara, far too many had perished. The eagles were unlike him in many ways, more barbaric in nature, but their fierce loyalty to the Stonedelvers, for all its rawness, seemed a just part of the spirit that had forged the union between nations in the war. Kirrikree's own folk were depleted, most of them scattered across Omara, tired of conflict, seeking remote places where they could bring up their young in peace. If he had summoned them, they would have come, but Kirrikree could see no point in using up more lives. The key was with Wargallow and his companions now.

The white owl watched Graval's people for a while, toiling in the rubble, putting aside their grief in order to labor on. If Wargallow failed, this place would never stand.

Kirrikree shook himself, attempting to rid himself of the

gloom which threatened to engulf him. He looked up at the endless peaks of Starkfell Edge, white and jagged overhead. They were only mountains, but their malevolence was like a shout. Among the clouds that drifted high up there, Kirrikree caught a glimpse of movement, a flap of wings. Ravens? No, Woodheart's birds could not have crossed the range.

Kirrikree took to the air, keeping low to the surface of rock and ice, his shape absorbed by the snow terrain. As he flew closer and closer to what he had seen, he realized what it was. A cloud of large hawks, black-feathered and keen-eyed. They were hunting, and it was clear what they sought. Kirrikree turned and glided back swiftly to Sheercastle.

He called to Skyrac and Graval. "The enemy seeks us out."

"Where?" said Skyrac eagerly. A fierce desire to attack those who were responsible for the death of Einnis and the Stonedelvers blazed up in him and his eagles: Kirrikree felt it like a hot cloud.

He warned them to be careful. "There is a host of them. Hunting hawks. They are trying to find the place from which our masters emerged. It is best if we conceal ourselves."

Graval nodded, summoning his Earthwrought. They began doing as the owl had said, blending with the earth and stone so that no one would have known they had ever been in the ruins of Sheercastle.

Skyrac was not so easy to reason with. He wanted blood and his killing drive ran hotly in his veins. Kirrikree understood what this meant. He could not expect the eagles to wait idly by until the enemy had passed. It would not be in their nature.

"If we go out to do battle with them," he told the eagles, "they will kill us. There are scores of them. But we may be able to lead them away from here and cover the path of our masters."

Skyrac agreed at last, though with an effort.

They took to the skies together, leaving Sheercastle, flying at an angle to the land that would take them along the southern rim of the Abyss, knowing that they would be seen by the hawks. Skyrac felt the urge to wheel and attack the hawks like a command in his ears, but he allowed himself to be led by Kirrikree.

"They come," called one of the others, and as they looked, they saw the hawk cloud descending from the high peaks. Swiftly it made for them, but they angled further southward, away. The hawks would be faster, but over a short distance only. If Kirrikree and the eagles could keep from their grasp for long enough, the hunting birds would tire.

Kirrikree kept glancing upward, knowing that the hawks came on at great speed. Skyrac and the eagles hated fleeing, their every instinct urging them to swerve upward and attack. No doubt, thought the owl, they would have created chaos among the hawks, taking a heavy toll on them, but there were far too many. Kirrikree was thankful that the eagles kept with him. If they could keep on for a little longer—

But movements ahead of them, to the south, made him curse. Something else approached them, flapping up along the edge of the Abyss, great black wings shining in the sunlight. It was one of the Shadowflight. It, too, was seeking out its enemies. And it was coming directly toward Kirrikree and the eagles. Skyrac had seen it and he let out a fierce cry.

"We will tear it from the air!"

"The delay would be too dangerous," said Kirrikree. "Besides, the Shadowflight is not alone." He was right, for another cloud of hunting hawks came with it, vaster than the first. There was no way to avoid it, for to turn aside now would mean a clash with the hawks who closed in on them from the mountains.

"Blood in the air, Kirrikree," said Skyrac, his voice thick. "No more fleeing. Fight."

They flew onward, directly at the Shadowflight. "Then we'll attack the one ahead of us," agreed the owl. The eagles would not be controlled now. "We must not let word of our masters get back to Anakhizer. He must not learn where they are."

Skyrac let out a harsh shriek of agreement, hungry for the kill. He and the eagles flew on more quickly and the hawks that accompanied the Shadowflight flew ahead of the monster to meet the onrush of their enemies, filling the air with their hunting screams. They were sleek birds, their beaks curved and vicious, their talons sharpened like knives, and they moved with startling speed and skill in the air. But Skyrac drew first blood, ripping one of the hawks almost in two with his first pass. His fellows were also quick to wreak havoc amongst the smaller birds.

Kirrikree sailed up and over the first attacking cloud and found himself only a short distance from the Shadowflight. He could feel its hatred of him, its realization that here were the birds that had brought down one of its brotherhood. Kirrikree could feel, too, its evil search of his thoughts as it tried to drag from them the knowledge that is sought. But Kirrikree had powers of his own with which to blunt this probing, and he had no need to blanket the thoughts of the eagles, for they were drenched in the killing lust of their kind.

The Shadowflight kept its hawk guard from Kirrikree, letting them concentrate on the eagles. Kirrikree understood that the creature meant to corner him, the information he carried forced from him before they ripped him apart. Skyrac was under fierce attack, as were all his fellows, and soon the hawks from the peaks came to join the unequal battle, winging in with piercing shrieks. Kirrikree swerved under the outstretched talons of still more hawks, but he could see they were circling him, trying to drive him closer to the surface and the rocks. There were numerous cliff edges and steep scarps, and their intention seemed to be to box him into a canyon. The Shadowflight swung round ponderously, but Kirrikree read its patience. It had what it had come for, and it was sure of its prey.

The first of the eagles was torn from the sky, feathers shredded as the hawks crashed into it. As it tumbled, neck broken, its companions were smothered under fresh attacks. They had killed and maimed numerous hawks, but the sheer force of numbers inevitably overcame them. Only Skyrac survived that grim wave of assault, and he tried to win his way to Kirrikree's side. But he was prevented by a black cloud. He was being attacked on all sides, from above and below, beaks stabbing, claws tearing. His feathers were dragged out of him, his wings broken at last, until he fell, spinning like a stone, down toward the rocky terrain below. There was no last cry, no final word of defiance. Kirrikree lost sight of the fall. If it had been a ploy, it had failed, for a cloud of hawks flew down with him to be sure that their bloody work had been done thoroughly. A shriek of unified triumph told Kirrikree that the hawks had accomplished their designs. The eagles were no more.

Alone, Kirrikree swerved again, narrowly avoiding a rock ledge as the hawks still sought to steer him into a canyon. He let himself drop, too fast for most of them, flying far under the belly of the Shadowflight, but the pursuit was relentless.

Since he could not escape by way of the mountains, Kirrikree decided to see if the Abyss offered any possible sanctuary. Its depths were draped in darkness and he had no idea what they held. Instinct told him it would be extremely dangerous. But the upper air meant capture and eventually death. He plummeted, going down into hot air that was dark and forbidding. He could sense the hawk cloud coming after him, but in the mind of the Shadowflight there was a strange reluctance to go downward. Perhaps the flight into the dark would win the owl time.

Silence closed in like the sea, together with the clinging darkness, but Kirrikree found new strength, flashing past rocky shapes as he went outward, leaving the smooth sides of the Abyss wall as if going on under an ocean, an unfathomable reach of night. Still the hawks came on, not far behind him. The Shadowflight screamed at them to encircle him, to herd him back, but as some of them drew alongside, concentrating on him, they did not see the thick vine that reached up from below like a mooring rope. They crashed into it, a dozen of them, bursting with the power of their impact.

Kirrikree swerved quickly aside as another of the strange vines, or roots, he could not be sure which, crossed his flight path. There seemed to be many of them, invisible until very close, stretching this way and that like a jungle of colossal weeds on a sea bed. Some were thin, others were vast. The owl wondered what manner of life they could be, for there was that about them which hinted at the tortured.

His eyes were better suited to flight in darkness and he began to accustom himself to avoiding the many traps. Others were not so fortunate and more of the hawks crashed into the trailing vines. Some became enmeshed in the strands of a vast web of roots, struggling in vain to free themselves. This

world of shadows had, it seemed, no sympathy for any life
that dared it.

At last Kirrikree outdistanced the hawks, but he had no
idea where he was, or whether he had flown westward or to
the south. He looked back, but there was no immediate sign
of the hawks. But somewhere high overhead, he heard the
passing of the Shadowflight, like a huge ship of the sky. He
found a wide root and alighted on it, concealing himself. It
felt cold, alien, as though it could not belong on this world
and was somehow linked to another. There was a crawling
evil in it, a force that seemed to slide along it, and the owl
flew upward, unable to bear contact with it any longer. He
hovered, listening with his mind.

With evident desperation, the Shadowflight was trying to
probe below it for the owl. But it met only emptiness. Strange
images from its angered mind came to Kirrikree, a mental
raging that was an echo of the rage of its lord, Anakhizer.
Its anxiety at not finding Wargallow was filling it with fury,
crippling its efficiency.

Kirrikree waited until it had gone, though it passed back
and forth for an hour, and then he flew on into the maze of
the dark, not daring to go up. But he was lost and could find
no way back to the edge of the Abyss. Tiredness began to
assail him, and the threat of weariness was like another dark
cloud. Yet if he succumbed to even a brief sleep in this dismal
realm, he doubted that he would wake from it.

THE CURVED walls of the chamber pulsed, shot through with
reds and greens, veined like marble and flesh. There were
crackles of power and from somewhere a dull, monotonous
thump, like the ceaseless beating of a great organ. Roots and
tendrils trailed across the floor, disappearing into the walls.
They changed colors periodically, darkening to a rich scarlet
and then becoming pale pink. There was light, but generated
as much by the profusion of color as by external light. High
overhead there were openings on to the bizarre sky, from
which light spilled and flickered.

There was no furniture in this place, the chamber more like a
garden, though no earthly garden. Stone slabs had been set at
random, fashioned from a kind of rock with little thought of grace

or beauty, and they looked as if they did not belong here, as out of place as any of man's trappings would have been.

Into the alien place came a dozen figures. Robed in gray, heads covered as if in shame at being here, the figures moved like automata, their wills seemingly tied to threads which could not be seen, but which like the filaments of the chamber were absorbed by it, as if they moved at the whim of another, greater power. In silence they took their places, sitting on the stones, heads bowed, arms folded, hands hidden. Beyond them, at the end of the chamber, was an opening that showed a glimpse of the darkness between their citadel and the land far beyond it in the east, the ranges above Starkfell Edge.

Throughout the day these hooded beings had been arriving, carried by the Shadowflight, Anakhizer's huge messengers, which had been spawned and bred somewhere here in the complex of rock and steel that was his citadel. The hooded ones watched another of the Shadowflight closing with the fortress. It bore no rider but it was followed by a cloud of smaller birds, hunting hawks, which had also been bred here.

A single figure emerged on the edge of the balcony to stare out at the incoming Shadowflight, and the hooded ones heard it challenge the creature for news. There was an exchange, and one of anger, before the great creature turned away, out of vision, and later was seen winging its way back to the distant mountains. The figure on the balcony entered the chamber and at once the hooded ones stood up.

The lone figure did not reveal itself, though they knew it to be their own immediate commander, the one chosen by Anakhizer to be their warlord, the master of the armies. Like them all, he had once been a Child of the Mound in Xennidhum, and his forefathers had been the Sorcerer-Kings of Omara, those who had wielded more power here than any other before them. Now, corrupt and debased, they yet shared power, but its source came from elsewhere, meted out to them by Anakhizer and the power that ruled him; they were dependent on it, tied to it, empty without it. They craved it, and nothing was too evil for them to suffer to win power. They had been promised more, far more, when the Change was complete, the entering from beyond, and they knew they would be the only life form in all Omara to survive the Change. Their own transportation had already begun.

"Still he has not been found!" snapped their commander as he strode among them, his eyes ablaze with fury.

"He uses power to cover himself," said one of the Broodmasters.

The commander spat in disgust. "Then why can we not trace its use? If he has used as much as a spark of the rod's power, we would have felt it. Your own rods would have warned you. Not since the rod was used at sea has Wargallow been tempted by it."

"Then how could he avoid our servants? How could he have left Gloomreach without our knowing?" said another.

"Gloomreach!" snarled the commander. "He is not there. But he crossed it. He has many allies. Omara's disparate peoples flock to him yet. They use their own powers, the earth, the stone, the forest."

"Woodheart's power does not extend beyond the boundaries of the Deepwalks," said one of the Broodmothers, but again the commander stopped her short.

"You think not? You underestimate that monster. Woodheart has been trying to penetrate the Edge for centuries. The angarbreed have found much evidence of that. Gloomreach prevented it, but an ocean of poison would not kill that crawling being."

"If Wargallow has crossed Gloomreach, where is he now?"

"Starkfell Edge has been scoured in the east. Even the Stonedelvers would not attempt to climb it. Nor cross the range above it. But Wargallow went below it, with his allies. There have been reports of killings far under the mountains. Ferr-Bolgan and angarbreed have been sent in force to patrol this side of the range, led by one of your number. And the Shadowflight have been watching it. *And there is no word!*"

"Then Wargallow is trapped," suggested a Broodmaster. "Even his force could not come through the caverns below Starkfell Edge. Not without use of the rod."

"Perhaps he is dead," said another.

"But the rod is not found! The war is about to be launched. Anakhizer has called us all here to prepare us. Our armies are awaiting our leadership in all parts of Omara," retorted the commander.

"Then why do we delay further? Must we have the last of the rods—?"

"War is time-consuming. It may not be over in time. Omara is already concentrating her own power on the repair of the chain of Aspects. The war must be concluded before Omara achieves the Encirclement. If we had the last of the rods, our work could be done in a matter of *days!* Omara would be emptied of all life, all power, and the Change could be effected swiftly."

"And if the Encirclement is concluded before the war ends?"

"Anakhizer's cause may be lost. Even should we carry the war, the gates will be closed up. The destruction wrought by the Hierarchs of Ternannoc will be made good at last. The chain will be as it was, and there will be no power capable of breaking it again. Though we enslave the races of Omara, though we annihilate them, we will have failed Anakhizer."

"But he would rule!" protested a number of them.

"It will not be enough," said the commander darkly, and they all felt the stirring of terror that went among them, the knowledge that beyond their master a greater force prepared itself.

"When do we begin?" someone called at last.

The commander shook himself free of his own fears. "The Shadowflight are gathered below us. As are the rods of power. Each of us is to bear one for the ritual. But remember this, you are a servant of Anakhizer. If you think to use the rod for your own ends, it will go badly for you. Serve Anakhizer well and the rewards will be unimaginable."

They bowed. Not one of them doubted that they would better serve Anakhizer than themselves. Their greed overrode all other emotions, and if there had once been dignity in them and self-respect, it had long since been swallowed by the hunger put in them by their new master.

"We will wait no longer for news of Wargallow. We must assume he is either dead or trapped. I will summon Anakhizer."

"WE'RE LOST," whispered Ottemar to Sisipher, but she shook her head, pointing upward. The discovery of light had not brought them out of the maze.

"Do you feel nothing?"

He scowled. "Such as what?"

"This place is alive. And there is colossal power housed here. The rods—"

Brannog leaned toward her in the shadows. "You feel them, too?"

"I'm sure it is them, Father."

He nodded. "Far above us. If Ruvanna were here, she would know them. On Mount Timeless—"

"Can we not steal them?" said Kelloric softly behind them. They were in a slightly wider chamber, clogged with thick, root-like growths, the light again very faint. The warriors circled them, a fresh fear in them, a need to act.

"Perhaps," said Brannog. "But we must be guided by Wargallow. If he can somehow control the rods—"

"Then what?" said Kelloric. "What power will he have?"

"If that thought disturbs you," came a voice from the darkness ahead, "it concerns me also." Wargallow, who had been investigating another tunnel, came out of the shadows.

Kelloric frowned. "Is it wise for one man to expose himself to so much power?"

"No," said Wargallow. "But that is why we are here."

"Come," said Ottemar. "Keep moving. Find better light."

"Have you seen Grimander?" Sisipher asked.

Wargallow shook his head. "He's disappeared. As have the Healers. I think they find this part of the citadel too disturbing. It works a kind of madness, do you not think?"

"Aye," growled Kelloric. "I'm for moving on quickly."

"What of Coldrieve?" said Brannog.

"He's not far ahead of us," Wargallow confirmed, but would say no more.

They moved on again, coming out into what at first seemed to be a vast cavern, but which they saw after a while was an immense vent, a shaft that rose up from the bowels of the citadel to the very sky. They could not see the other side, for light shone down into it in a haze of color, but it was spanned by numerous strands of vine, or root, or whatever growths they were in this place, strung like tendons between walls of muscle. They climbed a spiral path, though it was merely a way upward and had not been devised as a path, moving for an age. The sound of the wind reached their ears, together with other sounds as alien as the ground they walked. The air was oppressive, thick as the atmosphere in a jungle, and they drew breath with an effort, their strength being sapped as though the citadel absorbed it from them.

Dennovia, close behind Sisipher, whispered to her. "This place is like a living organism, as Zoigon the Seraph was. How can we pass through it without being discovered? Does it not sense us?"

"I think not," said Sisipher. "It is too large. I think we would rouse it if we used power. Wargallow has resisted the use of the rod on our journey. The only time he used it, we were almost lost."

"But if we are discovered—"

"Just keep moving."

Their nerves were tightening, their skin tensing for an invisible touch, as though the citadel would suddenly grasp them, crushing them like insects. It was impossible to escape the feeling that a massive weight was about to collapse, or a dam burst its banks.

A brief flicker of light from a side passage made them close ranks, swords shimmering in the haze from the central shaft. Wargallow held the men in check. "It is Grimander."

The Woodweaver edged forward, his feet silent on the tangle of root and vein that comprised the floor. His face was screwed up as if he were either in great pain or concentrating fiercely. "Woodheart lets his power in, even here. Anakhizer does not realize. All his power is focused elsewhere. But Woodheart has found the rods. I can take you to them."

"Are they not guarded?" said Brannog.

"Oh, yes. The Broodmasters are gathered. One for each rod of power. And the Shadowflight are here also, ready to carry war out to the world."

"Take us to them—quickly!" said Wargallow. He looked back at Ottemar and Kelloric. "This time you will need your swords."

"Surely you don't mean an open attack," said Ottemar. "We'll be walking into fire."

"There'll be a precise moment at which to strike," said Wargallow.

"When?" said Brannog, as uncertain as the others.

"If Anakhizer is to share out these rods to his Broodmasters, their power will be equally dispersed. Any one of the rods is capable of controlling all the others, but Anakhizer must have abandoned that plan, not being in possession of them all."

"Why should the rod you carry be the one to control them?" said Kelloric.

"Because I will be the one in possession of the most powerful of them. Zoigon has given my rod vast power, and if you all put your own special powers into the rod, as will Woodheart—"

"You are sure of that?" said Ottemar.

"Grimander confirms it. For a short while, our rod will be a focus of great power, and if the other rods are within its range, it will draw their fire like a magnet."

Kelloric yet looked grim. "And what powers do my men and I have? The power of the sword?"

"We may need that. Brannog has power, as does Sisipher. Use whatever you have, your hatred of this evil place, your anger, your will."

"And Coldrieve?" said Brannog quietly.

Wargallow looked suddenly grave. "Harn is my shield." He would say no more, gesturing for Grimander to hurry on and show them where the rods could be found.

Sisipher touched her father's hand, and he felt her voice in his mind, as he had felt the minds of his wolves touch his. It made him tremble, but he masked his surprise.

"Father," she said, more subtly than if she were whispering, "I think Wargallow will be the shield. He knows Anakhizer will concentrate every effort upon himself. So he's somehow given the rod to Coldrieve! He has bought him the time to do what is necessary to control the rods."

"It's too late to interfere," Brannog replied, speaking only to her mind. "There is no other plan. No time. If it works—"

"He'll die," said Sisipher, and there was, for once, concern for the Deliverer in her voice.

He did not need to reply.

Their movements up inside the walls of the vast shaft went on, as though the shaft reached into another realm and went on endlessly, but Grimander assured them with an occasional whisper that they were not lost. It was as though he were abroad in his own Deepwalks, knowing every branch, every bough, though the growths in this place were like nothing in the forests.

The Woodweaver halted. He pointed to an opening framed in a gnarled, wood-like growth, like the bark of some forest giant. Beyond it there was further, garish light, and something else. Voices. The first they had heard in the citadel. Slowly they went up to the entrance, keeping in its shadow. A hint of movement in the corridor beyond made them flinch, but a hooded shape moved away up another tunnel, with something in its hands that seemed to reflect the light.

"Coldrieve," Sisipher said in Brannog's mind.

He nodded but said nothing. Instead they were trying to hear what was being said beyond the archway.

"Omara has begun her working!" came a deep voice, roaring across the chamber like a wind, the power in it evident but incalculable, and each of the listeners knew at once that it was Anakhizer himself. If once he had been flesh and blood, he was beyond that now, a demigod, a vessel for vaster things than simple mortality.

"I shall begin mine! You see the open heavens. You see what it is that comes through them. When we close with the mountains, we shall draw them to us, and the Transformation will be upon Omara."

Wargallow dropped to his haunches and crawled through the opening. He was on a ledge that projected into yet another vast shaft. The others followed him carefully. With infinite slowness they looked over the lip of the ledge, to gaze down on to a scene of terrible foreboding. They felt their hopes ground down by the magnitude of what faced them.

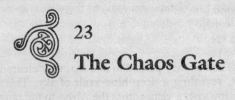

23

The Chaos Gate

THE BROODMASTERS and Broodmothers were spread out
in a semicircle, each facing the end of the huge chamber that
opened like a womb into the Abyss. Before each of them,
resting on a slab of black rock, was one of the rods of power.
They were deceptive things, for they looked no more than
dull gray lengths of metal; no light reflected from them. But
the watchers above knew well enough how dangerous they
were. Dennovia drew back at the sight of them and she imagined she could feel the touch of their steel, just as she had
first felt it when Mourndark had forced her to pick one up on
Mount Timeless, testing its power with her as his expendable
servant. The chamber itself shifted gently, its sides molded
from whatever alien substance formed the flesh of the citadel,
neither stone, metal, nor vegetation, but somehow a curious
mixture of all three. There were what appeared to be veins
in it, though they could equally have been roots, or wires,
for the organic and the inorganic laws that governed this life
form were not as they were in Omara. If this vast structure
had come from another Aspect, or the void between, it had
brought with it a form of life that confused the eye and the
mind. Too much contemplation of it, Brannog realized, would
lead a man away from his reason.

The hooded ones were motionless before their ruler, for at
the open end of the cavern a solitary figure stood with his
back to them, facing the huge wall of flickering light that was
the window on the Abyss. He was clothed in a single white

garment from which light seemed to stream, dazzling the eye, and his head was obscured by the fierce glow. His arms were outspread, drawing in light and power from the great openness beyond him as he spoke words unknown to the races of Omara, words of an outside realm which struck out into the light like spears, ringing back from the walls of the cavern.

Into the beyond, shapes moved, drifting across it like thunderheads, and as they passed to and fro, they cleared the mist and light, revealing a deep blue vault of sky. This was not, the company saw, a vista across the Abyss to the ranges above Starkfell Edge. It was a view of the far west, upward above the world. Each of the watchers recalled clearly the night sky they had lately seen and the three great orifices into it. They saw them again here, but it was as though they had been magnified, for they loomed beyond the portal, gaping like open arteries into some unimaginable realm. The watchers tried to convince themselves that what they saw was illusion, for no sky could open up like an organism.

Anakhizer turned his back on the heavens and faced the Broodmasters and Broodmothers. Again the watchers were shocked, for the visage of their enemy was not as the faces of other men. There were no external features, for the entire face was smooth, a sheen of skin, and under this were the suggestions of eyes, nose and mouth. The mouth did open moments later, a scarlet orifice; the voice rumbled from it like thunder, itself alien and unearthly as if speaking across a great distance, powered by something that was not human.

"Are the Shadowflight prepared?" he called.

The commander of his servants stepped forward with a low bow. "They are, Lord. We are ready to carry the war across Omara." He pointed to a flat surface of the cavern wall, which shimmered like a pool. Moments later it had become a picture, a view of a far landscape, and the watchers recognized Teru Manga and its numerous caves. Not only were the Ferr-Bolgan massing, but they had crude ships, and in the seas there were countless scores of issiquellen. And the angarbreed, the silent, black-clad beings from the mountains, were with them, controlling them, preparing them. The vision on the wall faded and was replaced by other scenes, each a part of Omara, each showing that the Ferr-Bolgan and the hosts of darkness were gathering.

Wargallow nudged Brannog, indicating that they must find a way down the coils of root and web at the end of the arch that would take them to the chamber below. He moved off and Brannog followed, both doubled over, conscious of the vivid light. The others followed, swords gripped tightly, hearts thundering as if they would betray them.

The Broodmasters were still studying the visions of Omara as Wargallow wound down among the curves of the inner wall to the floor of the chamber. He was motionless, eyes searching every part of the vast area opposite him, following the curved line of its wall. At length he saw what he was looking for. It was Grimander, blended with the lining of the chamber so that if he had not been looked for, he would have been invisible. Anakhizer and his servants would never dream that their enemies would dare approach them like this, Wargallow was certain.

Grimander saw Wargallow and with the gentlest of movements indicated another figure. It was Coldrieve, and in his hand was the rod. It pulsed faintly blue. Wargallow nodded grimly. They must begin.

Brannog also saw the rod and opened his mouth to speak, but closed it. This was a perilous ploy: surely the rod must attract the attention of the Hierarch!

Wargallow glanced back behind him. Kelloric's warriors were as taut as wire, expecting discovery at any moment. Kelloric's eyes begged that his men be allowed to act soon, to use their weapons before the enemy could react. But Wargallow slowly shook his head. They must wait.

The silence of the chamber was broken as some of the Broodmasters murmured at the visions they had been shown. Anakhizer raised a hand for silence and was about to address them, when he stopped, his frightful visage aimed at the far end of the chamber, beyond the semicircle of hooded servants.

Coldrieve had stepped out into the chamber, his rod held before him like a blade, its point aimed at the gathered servants.

''Who dares to intrude?'' came the voice of Anakhizer.

Coldrieve spoke sharply, clearly. "You've sought me and what I carry for many a long month, Anakhizer," he called, and the Broodmasters and Broodmothers gaped. The name of Wargallow was on many lips.

Anakhizer was temporarily silent, but then a gale of laughter struck the chamber, echoing from the ceiling far overhead. "You dare to confront us *here!* Before *these?*" And he pointed back to the yawning orifices in the sky. "One rod against so many?"

None of his servants had moved, though they turned to stare, their eyes like coals, fixed on Coldrieve's rod.

"If any of you touch your rods, I will destroy you," Coldrieve promised them, his voice icy. No one doubted his purpose, his lack of terror.

Anakhizer laughed again, his blind eyes gazing, fixing Coldrieve with malice as though they could direct a bolt at him. "How did you reach us, Simon Wargallow? How did you find your way into my citadel?"

"You considered yourself secure, but Omara sought you out," said Coldrieve, stepping forward slowly. The Broodmasters and Broodmothers inched back, but none of them attempted to pick up a rod.

Brannog was watching Wargallow. The Deliverer had pulled back his shirt sleeve to reveal his killing steel, and as he did so, Brannog felt a haze before his eyes, a sudden rising of tremendous heat. He closed his eyes for a moment, and when he looked again, he saw that the killing steel was gone. It had been an illusion. In its place there was now a hand, perfectly formed. And as Brannog gazed at it, it began to glow, a pale blue. The light in his hand grew in intensity.

Brannog swallowed down his shock. *This* was the true rod! Wargallow had never relinquished it. But what was it that Coldrieve carried? A replica? For an instant Brannog's mind swung back to Goldenisle, the amount of time that Wargallow and Coldrieve had spent in secret, working together: did someone suggest they had worked with a metalsmith?

Wargallow had seen Brannog's expression but ignored it. He did not look at Coldrieve, who was rigidly holding his position, just as told to. Wargallow lifted his hand, extending the fingers, spreading them and pointing them at Anakhizer's servants, who had still not seen him. The hand grew very bright, so that Brannog had to turn away from it. Sisipher was trying to see, but he shook his head. The others kept deathly still, though they had glimpsed Wargallow's hand.

Anakhizer let out an abrupt roar. "You think you can control the rods! You are ridiculous to come here to attempt such a thing," he told Coldrieve.

The rods had all sparked into life, each of them burning with a pale blue radiance; they hummed faintly in response to the hand that had awakened them. Brannog was staggered by Wargallow's discipline, his nerve. To do this here, before the portals of Anakhizer's master—

Even now the Broodmasters dared not touch the rods, their eyes fixed on that of Coldrieve. It glowed very faintly, but there was no intensity in it. Yet the deceit held them.

Anakhizer called something and there was an abrupt explosion of light. A ball of pure white heat flew across the chamber, crackling like lightning and the rods glowed fiercely as if molten. The hooded ones were sent tumbling by the shock. Coldrieve stumbled to his knees. But he got to his feet again, holding his rod as if it would spew fire. He could no longer see clearly, his eyes smarting under that explosion of light.

Some of the Broodmasters saw him waver and they snatched at their rods, aiming them at Coldrieve, though still not using them to unleash power. Coldrieve remained still, maintaining his illusion.

"Take your rods!" snarled Anakhizer. "He cannot prevent you!"

Spurred by fresh terrors, his servants did as he commanded until all of them held their rods. They faced Coldrieve, each rod pointing at him, blazing with blue fire, ready to stream at him if directed. They could feel the power of the rods being slowly drawn from them, their own control being sapped, little by little.

Wargallow had gone white, his face a sheen of perspiration as he used his hand to pull at the rods, exerting every fiber of his will to bring them under his control. As long as Coldrieve held their attention, held the deceit, success was possible.

Anakhizer roared his fury anew, and another bolt of white light crashed outward and smashed into a wall, bursting in countless stars. This time Coldrieve felt his vision going, for there was a blank white wall of fire before him. His head rang and he began to sway, but he gripped his rod more fiercely. He was forced to one knee, his free hand on the floor to steady himself.

"He cannot maintain his attack," Anakhizer shouted. "Hold your own powers fast!" All the other rods were aimed at Coldrieve's now, as if locked on to a magnet.

Wargallow glanced once at his friend, knowing that he could not go on for long, that he was doomed. But already Coldrieve had opened the way to triumph, for Wargallow could feel his rod beginning to master the others, just as Zoigon had promised him it could. They had offered no resistance to him, and thus he had been able to begin the ritual of control. He rose up and moved so swiftly across the chamber that the Broodmasters had not realized until he stood in front of Coldrieve, shielding him. He held out his hand, a livid blue fire streaming from it, and the servants of Anakhizer stepped back, their own rods wavering before it.

Coldrieve collapsed, his rod falling from nerveless fingers, rolling a few inches before lying still, returned to its former dull grayness.

Anakhizer had gone rigid, watching this new figure from an empty face, the mouth open, fist raised to hurl more fire. But he did not.

Wargallow concentrated on his task, saying nothing. Behind him his companions broke their formation, and Brannog led Ottemar, Kelloric and the warriors into the chamber. They were confused, wondering if they should use their swords on the Broodmasters, or indeed, on Anakhizer himself. But the shimmering power about them held them back.

The faceless creature at the portal turned to them with another derisive laugh. "Your creatures of power?" he cried. "Is this all? Is this your Omaran host?"

Wargallow would not speak, break concentration. He shut his mind to the fact that the others had moved, should not have. Before him the Broodmasters were locked in the contest, themselves not wavering as they fought to halt the slow drip of power from their rods into the hand of the intruder.

"No one rod is greater than another," said Anakhizer calmly. "This is a deadlock. You cannot hope to defeat us."

Sisipher and Dennovia had emerged behind the line of warriors, but Sisipher pushed through them. She spoke softly to her father's mind. "I will add my powers to those of the rod, Father. Use what powers you have been given by Omara to do the same. Strengthen Wargallow. Grimander and the Healers will do so also. And if Woodheart still has presence below us, he will also do so."

Brannog nodded, concentrating ferociously. He and Sisipher went rigid, throwing their own powers into the struggle. They drew not only upon themselves, but upon that part of themselves that stretched far back into their line, to other Aspects, fueling it with an all-consuming passion for survival.

Anakhizer lurched back, realizing what was happening. He felt the sudden surge of power enter the arena as Woodheart assisted his enemies. The hand of the Deliverer was white now, and lines of light were radiating across the chamber from all the other rods, power being drawn irresistibly into the one disguised rod. Anakhizer knew that he must reverse this swiftly, or the rods would come under its absolute control. He cast his mind out like a net, desperately seeking power to use to assist his servants.

He could not disrupt Wargallow's concentration, for it was locked into his rod, as was that of Brannog and his daughter. Anakhizer searched the minds of Kelloric, Ottemar and the warriors, but they were men and had no power, save the power of their arms, and that meant nothing here. There was the other girl, who stood to one side, shivering with terror. Terror! That was as fine a weapon as any. The casting of madness had been a useful weapon in the past.

Anakhizer seized on Dennovia's thoughts, entering her mind like a claw and grasping her will effortlessly. He read her hatred of the rods, and in his brief study of her he fed on what he needed. He saw her fear of power, but something else. Her fascination for it. How such fascination had brought many of his enemies to their fall! It would do so again.

Dennovia stumbled out into the chamber, her eyes wide.

For an instant Wargallow felt his concentration ripple, but he forced himself not to look at Dennovia.

Anakhizer's voice came to her across a great distance, alluring, coaxing. In its strength she understood power far beyond that of her former master, Mourndark, who was a child compared to this monstrous force.

"You seek power, Dennovia? You shall have it. That which you desire most shall be yours. When the Transformation comes, you will be with us, and you shall possess the rod you have lusted for, the extreme focus of power that will be everything to you. Help me now, Dennovia. Use your will with mine, against him."

There was a power in the girl, Anakhizer read it, the pure elemental power of anger, of desire, of hate and fear. Fashioned into a spear, it could yet rob Wargallow of control.

Sisipher felt her own mind diverted by what was happening. "Dennovia!" she cried aloud. Was this why she had come? To win power? To take her revenge on them all for the life she had led?

Dennovia's face suddenly changed. She was no longer wide-eyed and bewildered. Instead she smiled, but in a disturbing way, as if the secrets of the remotest part of the world were hers. She turned to Anakhizer with a look of satisfaction.

Wargallow again felt himself shaken, the flow of power momentarily held in check.

Dennovia turned away from Anakhizer and walked deliberately to Wargallow. No one else moved. Neither Ottemar nor Kelloric understood what was happening and made no move to prevent her. When Dennovia took Wargallow's left hand in hers, they assumed she was giving him support in the only way she knew how. But Anakhizer laughed mockingly, waiting for Dennovia's power to shatter Wargallow's hold on his servants. His own power burned, seeking out Dennovia's emotions, strengthening them, adding fire to them, focusing his own fury and hatred as he had done so often in the past. And the girl welcomed the power, fashioned it like a smith, taking raw energy and beating it into a weapon of livid purpose.

Wargallow felt the grip of her fingers, the sudden intense heat, knowing that power was flowing into him through her. Was this why she had come? To win power for herself at any cost? How could she ward off the urgings that Anakhizer was using, escalating? Wargallow could not release her hand, could not spare a flicker of power: his own task demanded everything he could give to it.

Dennovia sensed the flow of power through her, pulling at her and the feelings within her like a lover confident of seduction. She seemed to be shrouded in blazing light, but there was a darkness at its edge, a coiling mass that probed at her, thick with evil. Corruption and lust throbbed like great denizens of that dark sea, seeking to draw her to them, as though all that she could wish for was there, with them in that place.

She resisted. Mentally she forged the light into something that could bludgeon back that dark and drive the shapes further from her into their own vile realm.

Anakhizer staggered as if he had been struck. His power had been bent back on itself, as though it had glanced off a solid surface. Again he thrust with his mind, but he could not find his target. This time his power was drawn from him, reluctantly, and used. But it was not used as he had intended it to be.

Wargallow felt a sudden jolt of power. Dennovia was not weakening him, she was aiding him, somehow giving him additional power. But from where? She was not a creature of power, such as Ruvanna or Sisipher. Yet the power came again, strongly. The Broodmasters held their positions with difficulty, some of them already on their knees. There was a piercing shriek, and the watchers gasped as one of them burst into flames, the rod falling to the ground, a bar of light. Then others had become columns of fire, their rods dropping. The power spreading from the rod of Wargallow was taking control of them all. Dennovia had given him the power that had swung the balance.

Anakhizer fell back, clutching for support, unable to understand why such an infallible ploy had gone awry. Power danced about him, further confusing him, but he saw enough to know that soon Wargallow would be in total command of the rods, and when he was, nothing on or beyond Omara could withstand them. Anakhizer turned and melted away through an opening in the chamber wall.

Dennovia's fingers tightened around Wargallow's left hand and she pressed herself close to his side. The blinding light about her had subsided, for she had found a way to control it, now that she understood it. And she gave it to Wargallow. He used it swiftly to destroy more of the hooded ones. One by one they died, in flames, their rods before them. As if pulled by magnetic force, they rolled across the chamber, lined up before the Deliverer, his prize.

He watched the death agonies of the Broodmasters and Broodmothers, lowering his terrible hand of power only when the flames were low. Dennovia put both arms about him and held him tightly, and he put an arm about her shoulders.

"Perhaps now you understand why I came," she said softly.

His eyes never left his dead enemies, but he smiled. The intensity of Dennovia's power had stunned him, almost thrown him from his task. "You could have had all the power you ever wanted," he whispered to her.

She shook her head. "You made the same mistake that Anakhizer made. He thought I had followed you halfway across the world out of greed. Perhaps he saw a reflection in me of my past, or of Mourndark and the ways he imposed upon me. He did not think of the obvious, and neither did you."

He did turn to her, oblivious of the other watchers. "Had you not done this, we would have been locked, eventually defeated."

She looked away, and in so doing saw the fallen Coldrieve. She knelt by him at once, and Wargallow was beside her. "Is he alive?" he said so that she barely heard him.

"I think so. But he is drained."

"Harn—"

Dennovia examined the Deliverer, loosening the cloak, Wargallow's cloak. An exclamation behind her made her turn. Wargallow also looked startled. The others were rushing across the chamber.

Sisipher looked ashen, and Brannog was holding her back,

as though she sought to rush from the chamber. There was
no sign of Ottemar or Kelloric, and the last of the warriors
were at the far end of the chamber, where Anakhizer had
disappeared.

"What is wrong?" called Wargallow.

"Anakhizer," said Brannog. "He fled. Ottemar and Kelloric have followed him."

"Then they are fools!" said Wargallow. "They should have
more sense. He is still a dangerous adversary." He studied
Coldrieve once more. "Dennovia, can you help him?"

She smiled, nodding. "I'll do what I can." For a moment
he stared at her, his hand reaching out to touch her hair, but
then he was up and racing after the warriors.

When Anakhizer had quit the chambers, Ottemar had been
the first to react. A sudden fury had burst within the Emperor
and he raced after the white-robed figure, his sword drawn.
Sisipher shouted something, but he was deaf to it. The
Broodmasters and Broodmothers were being destroyed as
Wargallow used whatever immense power he had tapped to
finish them.

Kelloric went after the Emperor at once, calling his men
to him, and they were relieved to have a part to play at last.
Beyond the opening that Anakhizer had taken, they found
themselves in a fresh series of artery-like tunnels, their sides
an interwoven mass of roots, fibers and luminescent growths.
Kelloric divided his men up. There were four main corridors
here, and he sent groups of his men down each of them. He
himself led some of them down the branch that he thought
Ottemar had taken, though he could not be sure. The Emperor had moved unexpectedly quickly and without warning.

Ottemar was already some distance ahead of his warriors.
He could see the light from Anakhizer not far ahead of him
as he wound his way up and around a spiraling corridor,
stumbling now and then over the protrusions of its floor. Fury
spurred him on, fury that this madman had brought such
misery to Omara and would have brought its utter destruction
upon it if he had had his way. Already he had sacrificed
countless numbers in his black cause.

When Ottemar emerged from the tunnels, he was in another chamber, though narrower and lower than the ones be-

low had been. It had its opening, its eye on the western heavens, and as the Emperor stepped into the chamber, he looked up at those frightful, whirling orifices that seemed to be about to suck in Omara itself. A crude stair led up to this opening and at the top of it was a dais. Anakhizer stood upon this, his arms flung out as though he was appealing to the skies for power.

"Anakhizer!" Ottemar screamed, rushing forward and bounding up the stair, all thought of exhaustion gone.

The white-robed figure turned, its terrible featureless face looking down. The red mouth opened in a snarl, like that of a beast, and Ottemar stopped, a few stairs below, wary of the hands, which were like the claws of a jungle predator.

But the voice was gentle, mocking. "The mad Emperor," it said.

"Madness is something you understand very well," said Ottemar coldly. "You have used it on us liberally. But no more, Hierarch."

"Omara is weak," said Anakhizer. "Her strength is sapped by what she is trying to do. It is a pitiful waste of effort. Do you think Wargallow can prevent the Transformation that is coming?"

Ottemar moved forward slowly. As he did so, his mind raced, much of the past two years flooding his thoughts. He saw again the moments when his own fear, his own weaknesses had almost undone him and had undone others. And he saw how his indecision had at times compromised the Empire. Even on this journey his men questioned his motives: he had felt their eyes on him. Then let there be an answer to them all, a reckoning. He held his sword; he had never enjoyed using one, and it had never been a natural skill to him, but today he would not hesitate. Anakhizer could read that surge of will in him. He held out his talons, but there was no flaring of power, no bolt of light. Ottemar jabbed with the point of the short sword, and the Hierarch moved back. Ottemar stood just below the dais and he swung his blade in a chopping blow that almost struck the foot of his enemy. Anakhizer moved further back, to the far edge of the dais, standing on the brink of the Abyss itself, for the drop beyond was sheer. But under the skin of his face was a crawling fury, and no fear. He lunged at Ottemar as he climbed on to the dais, and a claw almost took hold of the Emperor's shirt.

Ottemar thrust again at the tall figure and the latter struck downward with his hand, deflecting the blade. Ottemar felt a blast of heat: he must end this swiftly. Before he could drive ahead with another attack, Anakhizer grabbed his blade and tried to drag it from him. Light flared and the blade grew hot. Ottemar gasped as the heat seared his hands. He tried to push the point of the weapon into his enemy, but the Hierarch had awesome strength. He was resisting easily, and he began to laugh.

Something blurred the light beyond them, rushing up from the drop below. Ottemar wanted to cry out with pain, his eyes stinging. This was his death gloating down upon him.

Anakhizer's head went back and he let out a howl, hands releasing the blade. The heat in it began to die at once and Ottemar did not let it go, trying to understand what had happened. But he heard the flurry of wings and as he gasped, he saw the white owl, Kirrikree, talons locked in the shoulders of Anakhizer, dragging him back toward the lip of the Abyss.

Even now Anakhizer resisted, his claws trying to beat back at Kirrikree, whose own claws had drawn blood, fixed deep. Scarlet stained the white cloth of the robe as the Hierarch staggered; Kirrikree beat at the air with his powerful wings.

"Strike now!" the owl cried in Ottemar's mind, and the Emperor was jolted into reaction. He ran the blade with as much strength as he could muster straight into the open mouth of his enemy. Light seemed to flood from it, washing the blade. Ottemar howled louder than his victim, for the blade had again become searingly hot. The light became a white sun before him, but he could not turn from it, nor shield his eyes from it, hands locked on the sword haft.

Kelloric burst into the chamber and saw the strange fusion of figures above him. He shouted, but could do nothing to help the Emperor. As he ran forward, Ottemar at last fell back, tumbling from the dais to the stair. Kirrikree gave a last heave before releasing the shoulders of Anakhizer, and the Hierarch toppled from the dais and out into the endless deeps of the Abyss before the open maws of his god.

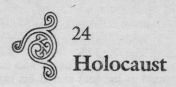

24

Holocaust

KELLORIC RACED up the stairs, his sword clattering behind him as he went to the aid of the Emperor. Ottemar sprawled, groaning as he fell, and Kelloric was beside him in a moment. He helped him to his knees, feeling for a wound or for a sign that Anakhizer had used power on him before going to his doom. There was no blood, but Ottemar's hands were curled up as if they knotted themselves on agony. The Emperor could barely stand.

"The light," he gasped, hands trying to shield his streaming eyes. "What is it?"

Kelloric glanced up to where the huge white owl hovered, its own claws dripping blood; behind it the heavens had split to reveal the yawning darkness of the void between worlds.

"I cannot see." Ottemar said it again and again, as though it drove thought of all else from his mind. Kelloric made him sit on the stairs, his head in his hands.

"Sit quietly, sire. You have sent Anakhizer to his death."

"Kirrikree!" said Ottemar suddenly. "Did I imagine the owl?"

"No, sire. He's here, above us."

Kirrikree was silent, his mind still filled with the shock of finding Anakhizer up here, with Ottemar attempting to kill him. The immensity of that act had been something that the owl could not have foreseen, not from the Emperor.

There were voices below them, and in a moment the warriors burst into the chamber, staring up in amazement at the sky beyond the portal. In a moment Wargallow entered the chamber, going at once to the stricken Emperor.

"Ottemar," he said softly, sitting with him. "Why didn't you wait?"

The Emperor grinned, though his eyes were still closed, filled with tears of pain. "Ah, but I've killed him, Simon. Men will remember that. And I had the help of Kirrikree—"

Wargallow looked up at the hovering bird.

"It's true," said Kirrikree to his mind. "Anakhizer has fallen into the Abyss. He will not survive the fall. He is of no use to the powers beyond us."

"What happened to Ottemar?" Wargallow asked silently.

"Anakhizer's failing power drained into the blade. Into Ottemar."

"I see the burns. Is he otherwise wounded?"

"I fear he may be blinded."

A cry echoed across the chamber as the owl told Wargallow this and they both looked down. Sisipher was coming forward, her father behind her. They had both heard Kirrikree's mental words. Sisipher came to Ottemar as quickly as she could and knelt in front of him. Kelloric, unsure of what to do, stood back.

"Ottemar!" Sisipher cried, taking his damaged hands in hers. Her touch did not harm him. She examined his eyes and put a hand over them.

"The light," he murmured. "It was the light."

"He's otherwise unhurt," said Kelloric uncomfortably.

Sisipher turned to face her father, who remained at the foot of the stair, a deep frown on his face. Although the girl did not speak, it was plain to the others what she was implying by her glance at her father. Brannog nodded.

"Ruvanna can help him, can't she?" Sisipher spoke into her father's mind. "She can restore him?"

Brannog nodded slowly. "I expect so."

Ottemar's hands tightened on those of the girl. "Stay with me for a while," he said quietly. "I cannot see."

"Yes, of course."

Wargallow had climbed the stairs to face the things that gathered in the skies beyond. Whatever Anakhizer and his masters had begun was far from over and the heavens gathered themselves as if about to unleash every vestige of power within them.

Brannog tore his gaze from the stricken Emperor and looked about him as if he had felt a sudden movement in the massive structure of the fortress. "Wargallow!" he yelled and at once the Deliverer spun round. "The danger to Omara is not yet over. This place is moving, dragging itself toward the land of the mountains. It is too powerful to resist."

"Do you understand what it intends?" said Wargallow.

"A little. It will attach itself to the land and become a portal, not to another Aspect, but to the void. Through this vent the Primal will come, if it can. Even without the power of the rods to give it the power of the sacrifices, it will try. Omara is weak. The chain of Aspects will be sealed, but there is a danger that the Primal will be sealed *in.*"

Wargallow scowled, deep in thought. He had control of the rods, but how must he use that power?

"Woodheart is already at war with the place," Brannog went on. "He is below us, many of his roots caught up in the conflict with what lies beneath this fortress. It has fastened on to Woodheart and is using him as a means of dragging itself to the land. Each moment, its strength increases."

Wargallow nodded, gesturing for them all to go below. He helped Ottemar to his feet, and Sisipher and Kelloric guided the Emperor's steps. Wargallow and Brannog led the return to the larger chamber, Kirrikree winging after them.

The Broodmasters and Broodmothers were destroyed, all of them. Nothing but their smoldering remains littered the chamber, but no one spared a thought for them now. Wargallow went over to Dennovia. She was still sitting with Coldrieve, but he was stretched out on the floor, his eyes closed.

Dennovia gazed up at the portal where the heavens churned sluggishly.

"Dennovia?" said Wargallow softly, touching her arm.

She smiled, but her eyes never left the awful vision above.

"What is wrong with her?" said Brannog.

Wargallow grimaced. For once his calmness wavered. "I— I cannot say."

"Is Coldrieve alive?"

Wargallow touched him as though a fallen brother lay before him. He did not answer Brannog's question.

"He deceived Anakhizer," said Sisipher. "Long enough for you to take control of the rods. Just as you planned from the beginning."

Wargallow nodded. "Yes. Harn knew what it would mean."

Kelloric gestured with his sword at the skies. "And what of that?"

"I will deal with that," Wargallow said bitterly.

Sisipher was looking at the motionless Dennovia. "What is wrong with her?" Dennovia's vacant gaze disturbed her.

"She aided us and is not recovered yet," said Wargallow.

"Did you *know* she would help you?" Brannog asked him. "Is that why you brought her?"

Wargallow shook his head. "I thought she had come for the same reason that Anakhizer thought she had come. We were both mistaken."

"She desired power?" said Brannog, confused.

"I have always assumed that it was her goal. It was the only way of life she had known, like a disease given to her by the Steelmaster."

"Then you did not use her—"

"Use her?" said Wargallow angrily, his eyes flashing. But he subsided. "You mean as I've used others?"

"Aye," nodded Brannog.

"As I used poor Harn. Though he was a party to this plan. We could not risk failure, whether we survived or not. But I did not use Dennovia. I had no intention of drawing her into this final contest of wills. That was her choice." Wargallow could see that they did not understand. "You remember Zoigon," he said to Brannog. "He gave me the power of the last rod. I wondered for a time, on that strange voyage back to Elberon, why he should have put his trust in me. But it was because he knew I would be single-minded enough, cold enough, to use it for Omara, no matter what the cost in lives."

Brannog felt a stab of pity for the Deliverer, who could never have said this until now. "And Dennovia loved you! Even Anakhizer did not realize—"

"If he had done, we would have lost. He would have used that to destroy us all."

"Why did you bring her?" said Kelloric.

"For no other reason than I thought her dangerous. It is better to have an enemy where you can see him. I thought Dennovia my enemy."

"I think it goes deeper than that," said Brannog.

Wargallow could have answered him, but the chamber gave an abrupt shudder, as though something vast had struck it.

"Woodheart!" cried Brannog. "He resists the coming of the fortress, but he must have help."

"Very well," said Wargallow. He turned to the others. Sisipher supported Ottemar, who yet seemed dazed. "It's time to leave." He glanced about him at the scattered rods. They were like dull lengths of metal, burnt out and useless.

"What must we do?" said Kelloric.

"You must get away from this place as quickly as you can," Wargallow told him. "Brannog, you must get Woodheart to aid you. Where is Grimander? You must go back the way you came."

"You speak as though you do not include yourself."

"My work here is only now beginning."

"Woodheart will help us," said Brannog.

"Then go at once. All of you. Kelloric!" Wargallow called, turning to the warrior, who came to him swiftly, full of respect for him now that he had seen his staggering conflict with the servants of Anakhizer.

"Sire?"

"Get back to the land as quickly as you can. Go down the way you came up. And look after the Emperor."

"My life on that," nodded Kelloric.

Grimander had appeared like a shadow from a corner of the chamber. He came to Dennovia's side and helped her to her feet, but she still had a distant look on her face, as if somehow a part of her mind had been damaged in the mental turmoil of earlier.

"The Healers and I will remain with you," Grimander told Wargallow.

But the Deliverer shook his head. "No. You must guide the company back. Protect the Emperor with your lives."

"What ails him?" said Grimander, suddenly realizing that Ottemar needed help to stand.

"He is blind," said Brannog.

"I will be his eyes," said Sisipher.

"As will I," came a voice, and Kirrikree hovered above them.

"Hurry!" said Wargallow. "I must collect these rods."

"What will you do?" Kelloric asked him.

"I will turn them against those who sought them."

Brannog lowered his voice. "And Dennovia?"

Wargallow drew in a deep breath. Dennovia still seemed oblivious to the conversation. "She will be safest if she goes back with you."

He had not seen Sisipher come to his side. "If you asked her and she could answer, she would remain."

"Do you know what is wrong with her?" Wargallow asked her.

"I've tried to reach her. But it's like looking for someone in the dark."

The fortress again shuddered. Kelloric called his men together. "Come on! We leave at once. Help the Emperor."

Sisipher ran back to Ottemar, holding him as he walked, and Brannog led the company to the stair that would take them back down into the heart of the citadel and the way that Woodheart kept open for them. Wargallow watched them go, Brannog the last.

"Good luck, Simon Wargallow."

"And to you. Take care of my friend Lawbrand when you get back to him."

"Does it end here?"

"I think perhaps it does. Now hurry!"

Brannog nodded and was gone, leaving the chamber empty, save for Dennovia. Wargallow went to her and put his arm about her. He longed to speak to her, but for the moment he could find no words. Instead he guided her to one of the dark slabs and sat her down. She continued to gaze up at the open sky.

He collected the rods. They tingled as he touched them, flaring slightly and his own right arm throbbed with faint light. When he had put all the rods in the center of the chamber, he was aware of the great white owl above him, swooping down. The huge eyes were fixed on him.

"What will you do now?" came his voice.

Wargallow grinned. "I shall close up that pit—"

Kirrikree blinked. "No doubt you will. You have a way of gaining your goals. You were right about the Seraph. But nothing is achieved without suffering and loss. My race is not, as you know, a sentimental one, though I understand such things. Your race has shown me this. You, I think, have sacrificed more than any other."

"Perhaps. But you had better go, Kirrikree. I've not forgotten the debt I owe you."

Kirrikree stretched his wings majestically and rose up. "Close that eye of chaos and consider it paid!" he cried, and soon afterward he had flown through the portal and was gone.

Wargallow took Dennovia by the arm. She went with him without resistance. Searching the upper halls of the citadel, Wargallow at last found the place he was looking for. It was another giant chamber, and it housed the Shadowflight. They were shrieking and calling out in their fear, for the structure rocked now as it moved more quickly across the Abyss toward the land.

There was a sudden rush of movement and Wargallow found himself confronted by a score of the black-clad angarbreed like those he had fought on the slopes of Sheercastle. They were seeking leadership, but on seeing Wargallow they leapt forward, ready to attack. He raised his hand and unleashed a bolt that struck them like a wave. A blaze of fire tore into them and Wargallow was staggered at the destruction he had so easily wrought. None of the warriors had survived and a number of the Shadowflight took to the skies beyond the portal. Others screamed in fresh terror, some of them chained, others about to take flight. Dennovia did not react. She merely followed Wargallow across the chamber woodenly.

He set each of the creatures free and commanded them all to go out into the skies. Riderless, without fresh commands, they made for the highest range they could find, most of them flapping far away to the south, where they knew there would be few people. If they were able to begin a new life there, and not trouble the people of Omara, Wargallow was content. He did not have the stomach to turn them to ashes as they fled.

Instead he went to the very edge of the portal. Below him he could see the mists of the Abyss and in the distance, the peaks above Starkfell Edge.

"Brannog!" he called, his voice lost in the distances below.

Something came to him, a brief hint of a reply. Were they crossing?

Wargallow held his hand of power before him. It had been perfectly fashioned, though he had used a little of its power once to give it the disguise of the killing steel, which had deceived his closest allies. As he looked at it now, it glowed. So much power was in it. The very thought of it was terrifying. I stand here like a god, he thought. But he did not relish the idea. Once he would have done.

He pointed with the hand at the Abyss, trying to use power to contact Woodheart, wondering if it would be possible.

There was no answering voice, but there was a contact of some kind. He could read the strange thoughts of the immense being. Brannog and the company would get across in safety, but the remainder of the Abyss was in turmoil. Woodheart could not exert enough power of his own to prevent the intruder from pulling itself to the land.

"Then I shall do it," Wargallow said aloud. "Show me what lies below."

His hand lit up like an azure torch, and as light streamed from it, the mist in the Abyss evaporated swiftly, seared like webbing. The landscape that was revealed stunned Wargallow for a moment, but he held firm to his reason. He could see an enormous mass of vegetation, a vast tanglement that stretched from the base of the citadel out across the Abyss. Deprived of light, it was pale and splotched, like the limbs of a leeched corpse. Thick roots from under Starkfell Edge had been gripped by the vine-like growths from the fortress and the two had intertwined. In silence the struggle for supremacy went on, and although little movement could be detected, the impression was one of exhausting combat, of locked powers, thrashing and heaving.

Wargallow singled out a thick tendril of alien growth and pointed at it, releasing a shaft of blue light that ripped into it, scorching it and convulsing it. Wargallow felt Woodheart's agony as part of the power struck his own roots, but the great plant encouraged Wargallow to go on. He had to sever the tendrils that dragged the citadel to the land. Again and again he struck down, sending out great bolts of energy, the blue light crackling and sizzling as though a dozen thunderstorms collided with one another and released their full blasts upon the world.

Root after root burst into flame, the citadel shuddering like a huge beast as its supports were rocked by the blasts. The light grew in intensity as though Wargallow had placed a sun in the Abyss, its molten fury pouring along the cable-like tendrils of the citadel. It tore upward, scores of thick roots dangling like maimed limbs, fire spreading, eager to lick at the base of the citadel.

Wargallow cut off the flow and looked to see what harm had been done. Woodheart had lost many roots, but had been more than willing to sacrifice them if it meant being free of the terrible grasp of the citadel. Again there was a shudder as a vast tap-root broke in half, its end trailing fire. The citadel was hanging on by no more than a few threads. Wargallow turned to each in turn and sent fire into them, cleaving them in two as if he were simply severing the strands of a spider's web. With a final lurch, the citadel sprang free, floating upward like some enormous seed released into the wind.

Gripping Dennovia with his left hand, Wargallow pulled her from the chamber, crossing the rocking citadel to its far side, so that he could see what transpired in the western skies. It was a difficult crossing to make, for the citadel trembled like a leviathan in agony, the fires below it having taken a dreadful hold on it. The floor heaved, roots writhing like serpents. But they reached the chamber of rods. Each of them glowed in empathy with the hand of Wargallow.

He left Dennovia in the center of the chamber and stood facing the churning maw of the heavens, which seemed to reach out for the very sill of the portal. Sucked up by the whirling powers, the citadel was returning to the void from which it had come, powerless to drag itself back to the Omaran terrain below it. From within the orifices a fresh darkness had arisen like bile, and it seemed that it must surely gush forth and pour into Omara, for all the power set against it.

BRANNOG LED the company on to the great root of Woodheart that yet reached under the citadel, though already it quivered and shook as though it must surely fall deeper down into the darkness below it. Somewhere high above there were cries, strange sounds of despair and fear. When the company looked up, they saw a flock of the great black shapes that were the Shadowflight. The huge creatures circled briefly, apparently milling in consternation and not in an attack formation, before they began to swerve away to the south.

"Wargallow has released them," said Sisipher.

"There's no time for delay," Grimander told them. "We must hurry." His voice echoed the pain that Woodheart must feel.

Again the root shook and the company were aware that other huge roots and growths heaved alongside them, as if beasts were beginning a great battle there.

Sisipher had an arm about Ottemar, who seemed utterly spent. "Is it any easier for you?" she asked him. Kirrikree was not far away, circling, watching out for the slightest sign of danger from either side.

"The light has gone," said Ottemar. "But I fear the dark more. Will I see again, Sisipher?"

"In time."

They moved on, the warriors guarding their backs, though mercifully there were none of Anakhizer's forces to harry them. Brannog could feel the anguish of Woodheart, sensing the vast effort it was taking to keep this root in place so that they could cross it. The Healers had disappeared, lending their skills to the battle elsewhere, though Grimander seemed even now to speak to them.

Kelloric pointed ahead of them. Something titanic raised itself up in the mist, a massive cable that reached far back into the sky to where the citadel seemed to hang. Wrapped around the cable were countless roots and vines, and if they were part of the citadel or part of Woodheart, it was not possible to guess which.

"Woodheart will not be able to free himself of this para-site!" shouted Brannog angrily. "I feel Ruvanna's despair."

On either side of them the huge roots looped up as if torn from their beds by the efforts of the alien citadel. Woodheart's root dipped and the company fell as one to their bellies, clinging on. As they did so, they felt a blaze of heat to their right. Blue light burst there and the mist evaporated. A sear-ing bolt tore into the tangle of roots, setting fire to them, and almost at once another white bolt of fire tore into the vege-tation on the other side of the root bridge.

"Wargallow is trying to rip the citadel free," said Bran-nog. "He's using the power of the rods to break the grip of the citadel on Woodheart." But at what a cost! his mind exclaimed. Woodheart encourages him in this, but the pain it is causing him! Surely Wargallow cannot realize.

It came to Brannog then that perhaps Ruvanna would also be hurt by this holocaust, but he could not know, could not contact her.

They had to move on, up and running once more, and although they tumbled again and again, they at last saw the edge of the Abyss ahead of them and the stone ridge that meant the broken plaza of Sheercastle. They could see the Earthwrought waiting for them, and when the earth people saw them, they jumped down and ran to help them, helping them across the last of the span. No sooner had they got back to the stone, than the root fell away into the Abyss, and a deep silence followed its passing.

It was broken by yet another rain of blue fire as power from the citadel beyond wrought further havoc among the roots. There seemed to be a number of conflagrations in the Abyss, the lower reaches of which were a mass of writhing tendrils. But at last the citadel was breaking free of them, rising up like some impossible ship, trailing thick clouds of smoke and blazing fire.

"Woodheart is free of this curse!" said Grimander, sud-denly diminutive on the stone, as if contact with the root was everything to him.

"He will survive this destruction. And the Healers?"

"They will pass on," said Grimander.

Graval was the first of the Earthwrought to come to him.

"What has happened? Have you found the lair of Anak-hizer?"

As the company sagged down where they stood to watch the huge citadel moving slowly upward, away from the raging fires below, Brannog told the earth people what had occurred.

Kirrikree alighted on a rock near to Sisipher and Ottemar, and in a moment the Emperor drew in his breath sharply, his white eyes looking up. "I see it," he whispered. "The citadel—"

"Kirrikree and I show you this," Sisipher told him softly.

Kelloric was staggered. It was evident that the Emperor's eyes had been seriously damaged in his fight with Anakhizer, and yet he could see! Through the girl? Did she have such marvelous power?

After a moment, Kirrikree spoke in Sisipher's mind. "If he is to rule his Empire as he should, he will need his sight."

Sispher understood what he meant and nodded. "It will be a demanding role. And you will remain with him?"

"I will, mistress. It will take us both to do this for him."

Sisipher noticed Kelloric gazing at her. This matter must be settled now. The uncertainty and distrust must end, one way or the other. But before she could speak, the big warrior came and bowed to her.

"My lady, what you are able to do is beyond me. My wish is to serve the Emperor in everything." In his mind he would always see Ottemar locked in combat with Anakhizer on the brink of chaos. "My sword is yours, as it is his. My men also."

She nodded, looking out at the troubled skies.

"I cannot believe," said Ottemar, his grave face turned to the citadel as it began to dwindle against the turmoil beyond it, "that he is not with us. Can we have lost him?"

Grimander stiffened, not understanding. "He is hurt, sire, but though a part of him dies, Woodheart abides."

Sisipher squeezed Ottemar's hand before he could reply, and the Emperor shook his head, staring for as long as he was permitted at the receding citadel, thinking of the man within it.

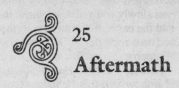

25

Aftermath

WARGALLOW WATCHED as the darkness from the orifices above him began to coalesce. It was seeking to take shape in such a way that his mind would be unseated, lost, just as Dennovia's mind had been stolen. He glanced back at her. She stood without moving, her face expressionless, as if waiting for a signal that would reanimate her.

He lifted his hand of power. Here, in this hand, he thought, there is immeasurable power! I could surely restore her.

The roar of sound beyond and above him made him turn about, raising his hand instinctively. The sky had darkened, the orifices sucking in the light. Wargallow could sense the other power gathering about the citadel, the power of Omara, trying to bend itself to the purpose of healing up the wounds that had been made so long ago by the Hierarchs. Korbillian had sealed the Aspects, but Omara needed to remake the Chain, restoring the balance that had been so crippled by that one great working in Ternannoc.

You will need all your power, said something to Wargallow, the ghost of Korbillian, perhaps. Everything that is in the rod, the last of the Sorcerer-Kings' strength, the essence of Omara.

He wavered. All the power? Every vestige of it? He could not look back at Dennovia. Without help she would remain as she was.

He saw Korbillian's anguished face before him, understanding the terrible burden he had carried better. Lifting his right hand, he spread the fingers outward at the gathering madness beyond the portal. But again he lowered the hand.

Somewhere he felt a groan, as if Omara herself had cried out in pain, for aid. Wargallow dashed back to the girl and took her by the hand. He led her with him to the brink of the portal. She did not resist. He put his left arm about her waist.

"There will be an end to sacrifice," he said, though the words did not reach her. "The power I wield is not mine. Everything I have done, I have done for a cause.

"Hear me, Omara!" He raised the hand of power, balled like a fist. It glowed vividly, blue and brilliant. "I will not desert you now! But remember what you have taken from me and your children. Think of those who have put their blood into you."

He kissed Dennovia's cheek, pressing himself to her. "I cannot save you, but we will destroy this evil together."

She did not move, rigid as a statue, eyes fixed on emptiness.

With a howl of anger, disgust and despair, Wargallow raised his arm and released the colossal power that was stored in the rod. A thick stream of light poured from it as if being drawn off from an immense reservoir somewhere deep within the world. It arced out over the vault until it seemed to be curving down into the great maw. Tongues of light fled from it, spearing out on either side, and there was a roar of sound, a deafening peal of thunder as though worlds had hammered into one another.

Wargallow shook, his every fiber of being seeming to scream either in protest or joy at the release, but he clung to Dennovia, still wanting to divert something from that torrent of power for her. But it was impossible. Now that he had begun the working, he could do nothing but let it course outward, filling the heavens with a dazzling shower of light and sound. He was no more than a vessel, a lens as Anakhizer had been for greater things. Omara herself seemed to have shaped something from the heart of the earth and plunged it into the river of blue fire that soared across the vault.

Overhead the whirling darkness scattered, a dozen storms blasted from it, and it became a formless mass, the huge tunnels into the sky to the left and right collapsing in on themselves like mouths, the sky racing in to the gap. There remained only the central orifice, but it was bathed in light, forked shafts of it zigzagging across it like some monstrous web.

Even now Dennovia's face remained blank, as if she did not see the tumultuous scenes before her. Wargallow held her as tightly as he could, knowing that the power was being drawn from him at incredible speed. Although it had taken no more than moments for the release, it seemed to him to have been hours. He felt himself weakening as the power roared on: would it drain him utterly? Perhaps it would. Part of his mind fought this, seeking a way of getting back to the land, though he knew that must now be impossible.

Then it was over.

The blue stream shut off abruptly, and with it the roaring died. Wargallow watched the last of the light soar out across the void and up into the maw of crimson light, which had become a huge ball, a sun overhead, though he did not shield his eyes from it. He could see nothing but the light. His hand fell, empty of power.

Gradually the sounds died away to the remote distance, where he could hear the storms that yet raged, though they seemed to be coming from very far away. He looked at his hand. It had quickly cooled, a dull metallic color, perfect in every detail. But there was no power there. As promised, it had been utterly spent. He had been allowed nothing for his service.

He stroked Dennovia's hair gently as if she were a child. "The others should be safely away by now." He imagined that she replied, and he spoke to her as though she could hear him. He told her many things, of how he had always been unsure of her, thinking that perhaps she did seek power for its own end, as he once had.

I used that as an excuse to bring you on this journey, though none of the others would have guessed such a thing. It was a secret I kept from myself, a weakness as I thought, that would put a weapon in the hands of the many who would have seen me brought down. Yet at the end, you were my strength. Omara's strength.

He searched her face for a glimmer of response, but there was none. He was to be denied even the chance to tell her the truth, to let her see his tears. Slowly he edged her forward, preparing to take the final step that would plunge them both into the waiting Abyss.

It was the sound behind him that checked him. He looked back, expecting to see no more than the remains of his slaughtered enemies. But a figure was crawling brokenly up the steps toward him.

Wargallow cried out, pulling Dennovia to safety. He went to the figure in horror. It was Coldrieve. Not dead, but able to move like some maimed insect across the floor.

"Harn!"

Coldrieve's face was white, a window on the agony he was suffering. He reached up, trying to speak, but could not. In his hand was clutched one of the rods.

Wargallow felt a sudden shock of recognition. It was the false rod that he and Coldrieve had devised, the one they had had cast by the smith of Goldenisle.

As Wargallow took it, Coldrieve collapsed. "Harn!" Wargallow cried again.

Coldrieve's lips moved, but he could sound no words. His eyes closed.

Wargallow felt something in the rod, warmth, a stir of power. It came to him then what Coldrieve had done. Wargallow had deliberately put a little of his own rod's power into the false one in order to make the deception complete. And it was there yet, unused.

Dennovia stood close to the brink of eternity, motionless. Wargallow dragged her away and opened her hand. He put the rod into it and closed her fingers upon it.

"Dennovia!" he said, repeating the name as if it were an incantation.

Like something alive, the rod pulsed. Wargallow tried to focus his shattered strength upon it, using it as a surgeon uses his skill on a patient.

The minutes seeped away; Dennovia exhaled a heavy sigh, her hand going to her head. Before she could fall, Wargallow caught her. She moaned, the first sound she had made since the working with the rods. But her arms clung to him. Gently he guided her to one of the stone slabs and sat her down. The rod dropped to the floor and rolled, forgotten now as the girl rubbed at her eyes.

Wargallow turned to Coldrieve, bending to him and feeling for his heart. But it was still, and Coldrieve was very cold, as if he had been dead for an hour. Then *how* had he crawled here?

But there were no voices to answer him.

"Simon?"

He looked up, amazed. Dennovia was staring at him, puzzled by his tears. But she saw the body of Coldrieve.

"Is he dead?" she asked.

He forgot his exhaustion and rose, walking very slowly to her. The rod had done its work. It had restored her. He put out his hands and she took them, herself standing uncertainly.

"Yes, he is dead."

And as the light beyond them blazed in its final fury, they held each other and kissed and said the many things they had waited to say for so long.

GRAVAL AND the Earthwrought were watching the chaotic storms in the western skies. A premature night had fallen, all light being sucked into the upheaval, and an incessant rolling of thunder filled the heavens. Behind the watchers, Brannog and the company had collapsed, most of them sleeping the sleep of absolute exhaustion, and even the great owl was asleep up among the higher boulders.

"See, that patch of gray against the light," said Grimander, pointing.

Graval was amazed that the old Woodweaver could see so well, screwing up his own eyes to search. "Aye! Is that the citadel?"

"It floats upward yet, drawn into the light."

"It is not part of Omara," affirmed Graval. "It will be cast out, if this great working succeeds."

"That is so," nodded Grimander.

Graval grunted. "Although Woodheart has been sorely hurt by the release of the power Wargallow held, it will lead to

Omara's hour of triumph. Can you not feel something in the earth?''

Others agreed. It was not something they could describe to each other, but a slow gathering of power seemed to be seeping into the earth, for all its hurts.

When Brannog and Sisipher woke, they felt it too, speaking of it. They studied the western skies, but could see nothing other than a ribbon of light.

''He has closed that vent,'' said Brannog. ''The restoration of the Chain of Aspects is complete. The Encirclement.''

There were no cheers from the waking men, but they nodded, relieved, their own energies spent. Kelloric, himself so tired he could hardly bring himself to stand, pointed to the mountains behind them. ''And do we go back through those caves?'' The thought did nothing to raise morale.

Brannog shook his head. ''No. It will be a long time before the mountains are free of Ferr-Bolgan and angarbreed. I doubt if they will ever be fully clear of them. And Woodheart has been badly wounded. He would not be able to guide us back, though we must return to the Deepwalks. I think we must bear north, and hope that we will not be discovered. There will be much confusion among our enemies. The Broodmasters and Broodmothers are destroyed, but the angarbreed have intelligence enough to organize themselves. They may yet attempt to make war.''

''It will be a long journey around the mountains,'' said Sisipher. ''But I agree it will be the least dangerous.''

As the preparations began, Graval spoke privately to Brannog. ''My people and I have sworn we will rebuild Sheercastle and guard against the west. But if you wish me to provide guides, sire—''

''No, Graval. Your work is here, as you rightly say. The land heals slowly. We will find our way around the mountains and back to the forest. And when we come there, we shall send others to you. The women and children. We will open up a new road through Starkfell Edge and drain away the poison there. Then we shall put the Ferr-Bolgan to flight.''

Graval beamed, the vision already in his eyes.

Soon afterward the journey began, and it was to be a long and demanding one. Kirrikree scouted the ledges and the passes, and although a few of the enemy were seen, there were no skirmishes. Food was scarce, the hunting not good, but the company had enough to sustain them, their hopes of returning to their allies always before them. No journey could be as terrible as the one they had already undergone. They all watched the western skies, but darkness had gone from them, and where the orifices had been there was nothing now but cloud and open sky, and at night the stars that belonged there. Whatever rent had existed in the fabric of Omara had indeed been sealed. In the Abyss, the silence and shadows had moved in, a shroud over what had been there.

If they thought of Wargallow and Dennovia, they did not speak of them, saddened by their loss, knowing that they could not have survived the release of power and the conflict that followed it.

At last they reached the passes that led around the far north of Starkfell Edge, and though these were deeply lined with snow, they made their way carefully along them until they were once more in the mountains north of the Deepwalks. They found numerous signs that the Ferr-Bolgan had been here, and as they trekked southward through the mountains, they were certain that their movements were watched by hostile eyes, but they were still not attacked.

It had taken many weeks to reach the upper borders of the Deepwalks, but when they came there, they were met by a great party of Woodweavers, all of whom leapt and capered in a way that had never been seen before in their kind. It brought tears of gladness to Brannog and Sisipher, and even the stout warriors of Kelloric were moved by such a reception. The Woodweavers were appalled by Ottemar's affliction, but Sisipher cheered them by explaining how she and Kirrikree were able to take care of the Emperor. Already his hands had healed, for Grimander's gifts had not deserted him, and he was treated now with a new reverence: his chest swelled more than once as he heard the name Wood Healer applied to him by his people.

"I see better than ever!" laughed Ottemar, though no one could mistake the burden of anxiety he yet carried.

A vast cloud of ravens darkened the sky as the black birds came from the heart of the forest to meet the company, in particular Kirrikree, who was to them as much a hero as Grimander was to the Woodweavers. They demanded news from him, tales of how he had flown beyond the Edge and what he had done there. He obliged them hesitantly, unused to this adulation.

"There is a new home for the owl here in the Deepwalks," said the Woodweavers. "Why, he could be an Emperor himself, for the ravens would gladly make him their ruler!"

Sisipher smiled, though she said nothing to Ottemar.

"You honor me too much," said Kirrikree to the Woodweavers. "But I have another calling now. And although I would be content to live here, there is work elsewhere, for a time at least."

"Wars?"

"Undoubtedly," the owl agreed. "Though the defense of the Empire and of the east will not be so difficult now that Anakhizer and his masters have been thwarted."

"We will carry the war to the enemy," said Ottemar.

"You won't be going anywhere," Sisipher told him. "You can direct things from Goldenisle. Aren't you tired of travel?"

He laughed softly. "Yes, I suppose I am."

The mood of them all had lightened, and as they passed deeper into the forest toward Woodheart, they felt their sorrows of the past being greatly eased, and the shadows that had draped their lives for so long were lifted. They reached the Ravensring, where another vast throng of Woodweavers had gathered to meet them, and there were more celebrations. Then, as evening drew over them, Ruvanna came from the mists at the heart of the moor, escorted by the envoys.

Brannog swept her from her feet and they embraced for long moments while the entire company cheered. Ruvanna's weariness disappeared as her huge husband carried her, ignoring her protests, to Ottemar and his daughter.

"Woodheart recovers," she told them. "His wounds heal."

Brannog took the Emperor to one side. "Ottemar, we have been through a good deal together. The worst of it is past, though there's more work ahead of us."

"Where will you go?"

"Soon I will journey back to the east. I must see Ulthor

Faithbreaker, who has probably still not forgiven me for not permitting him to come with us on our journey to the west. And Carac and many old friends there. But before I go,'' he added, nodding at the silent figures of the envoys, ''I am to go into the heart of the forest.''

Ruvanna appeared beside him. ''Woodheart has honored me,'' she smiled, and it seemed to the Emperor that a new radiance shone from her, a new power. ''And now he would honor my husband.''

''Of course!'' said Ottemar. ''And I have work. Kelloric! We must get to the sea and build ourselves a ship!''

''That won't be necessary,'' said Ruvanna.

Kelloric and his men gathered around, puzzled by her words.

''The Woodweavers will take you to the Fellwater. You need have no fear of that place now. The angarbreed and the Ferr-Bolgan shun it since their defeat. When you reach the gorge, you will find a gift. Woodheart shaped it for you.'' She would say no more.

They sat that night and told many tales of what they had done in the west and of what had transpired here in the forest since they had been gone, and many of them did not sleep. Dawn found many of them still talking quietly.

Brannog and Ruvanna said their farewells to the company, promising to visit Medallion when they could, and Sisipher watched her father through her tears, arm about his tiny wife, as they followed the envoys back up the moor to the mists that obscured the giant sentinels of Woodheart. Ottemar comforted her unashamedly, his arm about her, and neither Kelloric nor his warriors made comment or hinted in any way that they did not approve.

The company followed the circle of moor that ringed Woodheart until they came to the southern flanks where the circle of stones stood. This was patrolled by a small company of Woodweavers, who jumped to attention as Ottemar's company arrived. Sisipher recognized the Woodweavers as those who had gone on the Woodhurling with Rannovic to the battle in the south.

While the company rested, Sisipher went to one of the tall standing stones. She put her hand upon it and looked out over the forest at the distance, where the Fellwater awaited them. Below the standing stone on the moor there was another stone, a round slab, which she had not noticed on her earlier visit. As she looked at it, puzzled, one of the Woodweavers came to her. It was Raal.

"We brought him here, mistress," he said. "Though he was sorely wounded."

"Rannovic?"

"Aye, mistress. He insisted on coming to this very stone. Though he was dying, he put his hand upon the stone, near to where your hand rests now."

Sisipher caught her breath, remembering Rannovic's promise that he would meet her there. "Did—did he say anything?"

"Aye, mistress. Curious words. He said that there was yet warmth in the stone. And that it would always sustain him."

She turned away to hide her tears, realizing now what the other stone must be. She went to it, gently touching it. Underneath it, Rannovic would be at rest.

Later, Kelloric and his warriors saluted their fallen Hammavar comrades, none of whom had survived the Woodhurling. Then the journey to the south began. There was a sadness about the company, for not only did they think of Rannovic and his company, but they thought of all those who had fallen during this campaign. When they came at last to the Fellwater, their spirits were low.

A number of Woodweavers met them, materializing out of the forest as if the trees had come to life. They led the company to the river before the gorge and all of them were amazed by what they found waiting for them.

"It is a gift from Woodheart. Only the best wood was chosen, and we trust that the craftsmanship is to your liking," said the Woodweavers.

Kelloric was astounded by the ship. It was superbly made, sleek yet strong, her lines perfect. Even in Goldenisle there were no ships like this. It had been made in such a way that it seemed to be caressed by the water, its lover. And the Woodweavers had made it on Woodheart's instructions, a gift beyond compare. The company gave thanks and they heard the forest stir as if sighing its satisfaction at their pleasure.

When they at last set sail, wishing the Woodweavers and the forest a last farewell, they found the ship wonderful to crew. She responded to every whim of her pilot, and Kelloric spent long hours at the helm, entranced; his warriors were content to tend the ropes and sails as the craft sped across the open seas beyond the Claws. Kirrikree sat at the masthead, silent and for once content to be at sea.

Long before they reached the waters of the Crannoch Isles, west of the Chain, they were met by a small patrol fleet, part of the navy that had been readied for the war. The ships escorted Ottemar to Medallion, some of them speeding on ahead to relay word of the Emperor's return.

The quayside was thronged with soldiery, merchants, and citizens, the noise deafening as they cheered the Emperor ashore. Kelloric was hardly able to mask his delight at such a reception, but he ordered his warriors to clear a path so that horses could be brought to convey the Emperor up to the palace as quickly as possible.

Ottemar mounted his horse and called to Kelloric. "Prepare a Council of War as soon as possible."

At the palace gates the throngs moved aside to allow him and Sisipher to ride, side by side, into the courtyard. "Don't fail me now," he told her. "Don't let me stumble before Tennebriel."

Otarus and the Law Givers were waiting in the palace and they greeted Ottemar joyfully; with them was Eirron Lawbrand, now the ruler of the Deliverers. Word of what had happened in the Land of Anger had already arrived here ahead of the company and Lawbrand knew the fate of Wargallow, though he did not choose to speak of it here. Ottemar insisted again that they must have a council as soon as possible, and although there was great concern for his health, he waved it aside. Physically he felt as well as he ever had.

"Do not be deceived by my eyes," he told them. Sisipher had suggested on the voyage that he cover them, but he had stubbornly refused to do so. "Let them all know that by rights I ought to be blind," he told her. "And then they will understand why you and Kirrikree are so necessary to me." She did not argue, sensing the guilt that he felt, sharing it but prepared to pay the price before his subjects.

The war council met and was brief, an affirmation that the armies and navies would no longer adopt a defensive attitude but would instead take the war to the servants of Anakhizer wherever they might be. Ottemar was brusque but decisive, and those who had not been with him on the quest in the western lands noticed in him a new hardness, a bitterness almost. His position, his instructions, were not to be questioned.

Afterward, in the relative sanctuary of his own chambers, he was visited by Otarus. Ottemar was restless, as if already anxious to be away to the wars. The Law Giver looked up at the thick rafters of the hall, where the huge white owl sat: apparently the bird would live in the palace now, as would the girl with the strange gifts, Sisipher. She smiled at the old man, understanding his concern.

"I hope you will not think of me as an intruder," she said to him.

"She is my eyes," Ottemar said, turning sharply to face Otarus, his white orbs challenging him to argue. "I trust no one will dispute that."

"Softly, Ottemar," said the girl, taking his arm.

Otarus bowed. "I have heard of many wonders, sire," he said. "I am not here to dispute any of them. Nor will your people. They clamor for you. You and all the glorious company. Already the tales of your voyage and journey multiply about the city. Will you come to the city and the people?" Otarus spoke with such respect that Ottemar grinned at him, more like the man than the Law Giver had known.

"Of course! But first, it is time you took me to my wife. She has not come to greet me."

"I am surprised she has not done so, sire. Will you see your son?"

"Solimar? Certainly. I've already heard how he glows with health."

Otarus went to one of the doors in the hall and opened it. He spoke quietly and in a moment a handmaiden entered, carrying the child. Solimar was sound asleep, face screwed up as if in concentration at some dream.

Sisipher felt herself tensing, trying not to let the thought that this was another woman's child blur her control of Ot-

---

temar's vision of it. She watched him go to the baby and gaze upon it. Ottemar smiled, as if pleased, nodding at the hand-maiden, who went away again.

"He's twice as large as I remember. You'll be putting a sword in his hand soon, Otarus."

"I hope that by the time he is old enough, sire, there'll no longer be a need for that."

"He'll be the Emperor. There'll always be a need."

The Law Giver smiled politely.

"And Tennebriel?"

"I have sent word to her, sire."

"Where is she? I will go to her."

"My apologies, sire, but for the moment we have not found her—"

Ottemar frowned. "You've lost the Empress?"

"No, sire. But she has the freedom of the castle, naturally. And she has no liking for escorts. You know how she was once a prisoner and hence enjoys the freedom of the palace. Often she visits the old parts for solitude—"

"The ruins?"

"Aye, sire. She may be there."

Ottemar's scowl deepened. "Is anything wrong with her?"

"I think not, sire, though she is a melancholy child, if you will forgive me for saying so."

Otarus had been looking at the Emperor throughout the conversation, almost ignoring Sisipher, as though by so doing he had pointed a finger at her. But Ottemar chose not to acknowledge any possible accusations.

"The old palace," he said to himself. "Very well, Otarus, I'll go there. Without an escort. I wish to see my wife in private. Is that understood?"

Otarus glanced at Sisipher, but he could not read her expression. "Of course, sire." He bowed. "I will see that you are not disturbed."

After he had gone, Sisipher went to Ottemar, who put his arms about her. "Will they all see me as he did?" she asked him. "It is not fair to you—"

"Nonsense. You imagine that Otarus disapproves. He is in awe of you. Wait until we are able to speak of our journey in full, and when Brannog is here with Ruvanna. In the meantime I will rule here as I must. Now, come and help me find Tennebriel.''

They went out into the older parts of the palace, the lower reaches of which had been badly damaged in the chaos of the Inundation, Kirrikree flying like a white ghost between the crumbling towers. It was the owl who found the girl.

"She is below me," he called. "In an old courtyard."

Sisipher and Ottemar picked their way through what had once been corridors, though their roofs had fallen in and not been repaired. This part of the palace had been neglected and left to rot and it was a while before Ottemar realized why.

"Eukor Epta used these buildings. I have a feeling he kept some of his prisoners here, those who he thought would be a danger to his own cause."

They reached a breach in one of the walls and saw beyond a tower and what had once been a square courtyard. Sisipher shuddered as if a cold wind had gusted through the gap in the masonry. "There's blood in these stones," she murmured. "And it's as though the past whispers a name to me."

They stepped through the breach, the sun overhead throwing half of the courtyard into bright light, the other into shadow, for all four walls were high, strangely preserved.

"A name?" said Ottemar. "Whose?"

"No, the name of this place. Was there a Court of Tears in the old palace?"

Ottemar turned to her, seeing through her eyes her own sudden fear. "Yes. Is this the same?"

She didn't answer. Instead she stared into the shadows of the court. The girl was there, kneeling and facing the tall expanse of brickwork opposite her. Sisipher's instinct was to shield Ottemar's view of the girl, but he had already seen Sisipher's change of expression. He turned around and walked into the courtyard.

"Tennebriel?" he said.

The kneeling girl did not move. Kirrikree winged down, alighting on a fallen chunk of masonry, his claws struggling for a grip. Sisipher tried to say something secretly to the owl, but for once he had closed his mind to her utterly. Silence made a vacuum of the courtyard. Sisipher went quickly to

Ottemar, and then on to Tennebriel before he reached her. The Empress seemed to be praying, her eyes closed, her mouth slightly open. Before her, set in a broken slab were two rusted rings. In her mind, Sisipher saw the chains that had once been linked to them. She looked down and noticed a small piece of parchment clutched in the fingers of the Empress and she removed it before Ottemar saw.

As she looked up, she saw a naked warrior who had once been brought here, as clearly as if he had stepped from the chains of the past. There was a flash of steel, a cry. Sisipher screamed, staggering back, and behind her Ottemar gasped, reeling.

"What happened?" he cried. Sisipher was in his arms, shaking, holding him tightly. Darkness closed in on him, but for the moment he welcomed his blindness.

"I saw him," he said after a long pause. "Your vision of the past."

"Who was he?" she whispered.

"His name was Cromalech."

Tennebriel had not stirred, still rigidly kneeling before the two rings as if she, too, was chained to them. Sisipher unfurled the scrap of parchment and together they read the single sentence. Ottemar recognized his wife's perfect handwriting.

"Look after my son."

A long time afterward, Ottemar heard the gentle voice of the owl in his mind. "They are searching, sire. They will find us soon."

Ottemar nodded and coaxed Sisipher away from the courtyard, and he did not look back. "When we are gone," he said to Kirrikree, "lead them to the Empress."

Kirrikree did not answer, but he flew up to wait patiently on the tower, his eyes unblinking, his thoughts and emotions veiled. Around him the city stirred itself for war.

Epilogue

THE PERIOD of Omaran history that historians have come to name the Angarbreed Wars lasted for approximately fifty years. After the death of Anakhizer in 3589, there was disorder among the scattered armies he had been assembling at various places across Omara, as few of their commanders were able to agree on a unified strategy. Consequently those of them who favored unification of the armies and a direct war on the Empire of Goldenisle were unable to muster an invasion force to match the potential at their disposal. A significant number of the commanders, lacking the vision of the Broodmasters and Broodmothers that were intended to lead the armies before their destruction in the Land of Anger, preferred to go their own way and make war locally in attempts to secure for themselves parts of Omara that they could exploit for selfish reasons, with little regard for any overall war. There were other commanders who saw no benefits to be gained in an offensive of any kind and who took their forces to ground, usually in isolated regions, remote from men and their allies, where they could have a degree of sanctuary from the forces that the Empire was gathering together.

Goldenisle, in complete contrast, marshaled its own forces quickly and efficiently, so that not only was a vast fleet assembled in the Chain, but there were powerful armies in the east, under Ruan Dubhnor and Ulthor Faithbreaker.

On his return from the lands of the far west, Ottemar Remoon wasted very little time in preparing his offensives. He was also served by an excellent network of spies, so that there were few places where the angarbreed were active that he was not aware of, and certainly none of any significance.

When the angarbreed launched their first major offensive, Ottemar was fully prepared for it. The angarbreed had been readying themselves for a thrust at Goldenisle itself for some time, to be launched from Teru Manga. This was the central army of the enemy, and it comprised angarbreed, Ferr-Bolgan and vast numbers of issiquellen. They had constructed a fleet, though the craft were of inferior quality, and it was obvious to the Empire that Anakhizer had originally intended to send out two war fleets simultaneously, one from Teru Manga and one from the Fellwater river. Although the latter force had been smashed by Woodheart, the commanders of the northern force went ahead with their own invasion attempt, a matter of months after Ottemar's return to the Chain, in the spring of 3590.

Kelloric led the navy against this force from Teru Manga, and in a fierce sea battle, North Race, smashed the angarbreed forces utterly with remarkably few losses to the Empire. Those ships that fled from the encounter were hunted down ruthlessly under strict instruction from the Emperor, and Kelloric himself took a small fleet north around the Cape of Seals, dangerous waters where few men had ventured before. Shortly after the battle of North Race, the Emperor's ships went to Teru Manga itself. Although it was impractical to carry the war into the warrens of the peninsular, two citadels were established and during the course of the next few years these grew in size and a chain of forts was also set up, linking with the fishing village of Westersund. This in time became a prosperous garrison and market town.

The angarbreed and Ferr-Bolgan retreated from Teru Manga and the lands beyond the Slaughterhorn range, which itself became the north western border of Empire. The issiquellen, which had long occupied western waters, fled the massacre at North Race and for a while dwelt south west of the Chain around the large island of Monator. A number of offensives by Empire warships eventually harried them out, and, numbers dwindling, they fled further south, beyond the Cape of Gulls and further west, where they were to be of little concern to the Empire again. Monator became a valuable harbor for Kelloric's war fleet, and although the island was to support a number of large military bases, it was not to have a civilian population until the latter stages of the Angarbreed Wars.

The second major offensive of the angarbreed was launched from the land of Kotumec in the east, a rugged land that had never been colonized by men to any great extent and in which few of Ulthor's people dwelt. The principal line of march of the angarbreed forces took them down the Trannadens River to its flood plain, the target Elberon. This army was met by the combined forces of Ruan Dubhnor and his Alliance with Strangarth of the north and Hanool of the south, two fierce fighting tribes, and during the engagements, which lasted a number of weeks, the forces of Ulthor Faithbreaker swept from the east to relieve Ruan's army. Major battles took place in this land for two years, until 3593, the angarbreed host was finally broken. This was undoubtedly the largest and bloodiest battle of the Angarbreed Wars, and it proved to be the axis on which they turned. The angarbreed were beaten back, though they were able to regroup under their better commanders; even so, the combined strength of Ottemar's allies was overwhelming. They drove the enemy southward, into the mountains of Onathac and beyond.

This was to be the last serious invasion by the angarbreed. Their main forces had been humbled, their numbers decimated. There were other attempts to gain footholds in Empire lands, notably north of the lands of Strangarth, but after the victories south of Elberon, Ruan was able to divert his forces and inflict further crushing defeats on the enemy, the heaviest of which was in 3595. The inability of the angarbreed to synchronize their various invasions undoubtedly led to their undoing. Their assaults were not well planned, and their forces relied on weight of number and simple tactics that collapsed in the face of the calculated strategies of Ruan, Brannog and Ulthor.

The Empire established a number of small cities on its eastern borders, and these were soon populated by men and Earthwrought alike. Excellent lines of communication were established between Goldenisle and all its satellites and the angarbreed and their allies withdrew further and further into the wilderness, their numbers dwindling. Without the power they would have had under their Broodmasters and Broodmothers, linked to Anakhizer and the power that fed him, they were little better than a rabble, whereas the forces of the Empire were unquestionably the finest Omara had known at that time.

There remained one single thorn in the side of the Empire: the south-western subcontinent of Athahara and its principal city of Thuvis. This had, prior to the coming of Anakhizer and the Wars, been an outpost of Empire, little more than a toe-hold in Athahara, for the land here was a barren desert, lacking in mineral wealth. It had been used as a detention city for some of the Empire's criminals, and did not enjoy a favorable reputation. Freebooters used the port without fear of harassment, though not as openly as the Hammavars had used Teru Manga in their freebooting past.

When Ascanar had been permitted to leave the island of Tannacrag with the last of Eukor Epta's Administrators, he was taken to the lands south of Thuvis, which for one of his nature, were an ideal haven. It was inevitable that he should seek eventual sanctuary in the city, which he did. When he discovered that there were angarbreed collaborators and agents in the city, he was quick to offer his own services to them and had become an agent of Anakhizer's forces himself. While the Emperor's war fleets were engaged in battle at sea, Ascanar assisted the angarbreed in bringing about the fall of Thuvis, and when the angarbreed force occupied the city, the servants of the Empire were for the most part slain. Ascanar was made Warden of the city, and when it was clear that the Broodmasters and Broodmothers had been destroyed, Ascanar took the initiative of setting himself up as an angarbreed commander. He became far the most powerful of them, and set about securing Thuvis against reprisals from the Empire. He made the city a stronghold and convinced his forces that any invasion of Goldenisle or even Monator would be futile.

Ottemar Remoon did not turn his attention upon Thuvis for some years. Kelloric's navy had made a number of preliminary attacks on the city, but had been repulsed with minor losses. While major conflicts still went on elsewhere in the Empire, Ottemar did not consider it necessary to waste men and ships on a remote city that seemed to have no more ambition than self-preservation. It is likely that, without Ascanar ruling the city, it would have degenerated, leaving itself vulnerable either to an attack by marauding Empire craft or to internal quarrels, whereas instead it became independent, extending its influence south and west into the lands about which little was known. Ascanar insisted that no attempt was made to draw the attack of the Empire, and it is thought that he may have planned an alliance, seeing in it a better lifeline for his city. Although no official alliance was ever sealed, Ottemar evidently grew more tolerant toward the city, although there were those at court who pressed for its annexation.

Ottemar Remoon and the Consort Elect, Sisipher, lived on Medallion until the Emperor's son, Solimar, came of age. Solimar had already proved himself to be a particularly capable general, and had won a name for himself among the armies and navy at a number of battles with angarbreed units on the Empire's borders, for the latter periodically mounted assaults, none of which enjoyed any success of note. Ottemar decided that the only way he could prevent his son from getting himself killed on some remote island or in the northern mountains was to stand down as Emperor and let him take the throne, and in 3610, on Solimar's twenty-first birthday, he did so. The Empire saluted Ottemar's decision, although there was great concern that Ottemar and Sisipher decided to quit Medallion and go to the east. They went to the lands of Elderhold, where King Brannog and Ruvanna and their children had their home; they never returned to the isles of the west again.

Solimar, who was later to be given the exalted title of Solimar the Great, consolidated the strengths of the Empire and drove back the last real angarbreed threat. Under his rule, the Empire flourished even more than it had under his father, for Solimar had the ability to pick his advisers well, and his military commanders were equally as astute. Solimar was also more ruthless than his father, and where his enemies were concerned he was as single-minded and efficient as the legendary Simon Wargallow.

Solimar turned his attention upon Thuvis, demanding that tributes be sent to the Empire and that the city not only accept absolute sovereignty of the Empire, but that Empire troops be garrisoned there, with a resident Governor to be appointed by Solimar himself.

Ascanar knew that to have submitted to this would have meant the loss of independence, as well as the end of any dreams he might have had of restoring those of the Blood to power. He knew also that Solimar meant to take Thuvis if it did not submit: nevertheless he gathered his strength about him, summoned as many of the disparate angarbreed forces that he could, and prepared to receive the wrath of Empire.

It was a long and bloody affair, but Solimar would have no compromise. When Ascanar refused his demands, he sent in a huge fleet from Monator and began the siege. Solimar himself went south to conduct the campaign personally, in spite of some protestations at court, but he would not be turned aside from his intentions.

When the city fell at last in 3616, two years after the initial attack, Solimar rode into the city and put it to the torch. His forces had by now ringed it, so that very few of its defenders escaped alive. A number of the pirate fleets that had become part of the Thuvian Brotherhood as it was known, had accepted pardons in exchange for taking no part in the battle, and most of them sailed further south, into unknown waters. Many of the angarbreed were killed. Ascanar and his principal supporters, some of them Administrators from the days of Eukor Epta, were taken back to Medallion, where they were publicly executed at Solimar's insistence. It was said to be the only time that Ottemar sent a written rebuke to his son, an act which took Solimar, for the first and only time, to Elderhold. He may have attempted to persuade his father to return with him to Medallion, but if he did, was unsuccessful, though Ottemar praised his son's achievements before the gathered Earthwise of the Earthwrought race.

Thuvis was razed to the ground and later completely rebuilt by one of Solimar's three sons, though as a garrison city, housing troops from Monator, now a prosperous island that rivaled Medalion itself in splendor.

The Empire of Goldenisle thrived, gradually extending, until by the death of Solimar in 3661, it covered some two thirds of Omara. There were shrines built at the sites of Rockfast and Sheercastle, both easily reached by the new roads and passes that the Stonedelvers made, and new cities where Earthwrought and men dwelt in harmony and where the descendants of the once-feared Deliverers raised their own children in peace. Such of the angarbreed, Ferr-Bolgan and other evils as remained, had long since hidden themselves from the eyes of men, and power became once more a thing of mystery, those who had wielded it figures of legend.

 **Author's Note**

THE OMARAN SAGA

has taken me about four years to write and I could not let this opportunity pass without recording my heartfelt thanks to all those who have helped and encouraged me in one way or another in my endeavors. I am especially indebted to Dave Holmes and to Steve Jones, and also to Darrell Schweitzer for many a kind word along the way. I'd also like to thank Chris Baker for his stunning visual realizations and my particular thanks to Jane Johnson for her support and patience. Lastly, but most of all, thanks to my wife, Judy, and the children, to whom the Saga is dedicated with all my love.

Avon Books Presents

THE PENDRAGON CYCLE

by Award-Winning Author

Stephen R. Lawhead

TALIESIN

70613-X/$4.95 US/$5.95 Can

A remarkable epic tale of the twilight of Atlantis—and
of the brilliant dawning of the Arthurian Era!

MERLIN

70889-2/$4.95 US/$5.95 Can

Seer, Bard, Sage, Warrior... His wisdom was legend, his
courage spawned greatness!

ARTHUR

70890-6/$4.95 US/$5.95 Can

He was the glorious King of Summer—His legend—the
stuff of dreams.